Deception

by

Alex Meikle

Copyright © 2016 Alex Meikle

All rights reserved, including the right to reproduce this book, or portions thereof in any form. No part of this text may be reproduced, transmitted, downloaded, decompiled, reverse engineered, or stored, in any form or introduced into any information storage and retrieval system, in any form or by any means, whether electronic or mechanical without the express written permission of the author.

This is a work of fiction. Names and characters are the product of the author's imagination and any resemblance to actual persons, living or dead, is entirely coincidental.

ISBN: 978-1-326-62628-0

PublishNation
www.publishnation.co.uk

1: GEORGE SQUARE

Deceiving other people is easy. Deceiving yourself is even easier. My initial awareness of this and my first milestone on the deception road came as I heard what sounded like a crack of thunder followed almost immediately by a shock wave passing over and through me. The whole building I was in jolted and vibrated. I looked at the timer on one of the bank of CCTV screens covering the railway station.

It was 2.26 p.m.

I was on the second floor of an office block two streets away from George Square in the heart of Glasgow. The explosion and blast wave was followed by a dense silence. In that silence I recovered and shouted into my radio mike, breaking all security procedures.

"Tony, Tony, can you hear me? What happened? Are you there? Tony? Tony?" Silence gave way to sirens, and a scream or screams. I tried several more times to contact Tony, but nothing, not even static. I tried Tres on the other radio mike, but there was still nothing.

My mobile rang with its bland ringtone, almost mocking in its normality. It was the clipped tones of Mulrooney.

"Macintyre, what happened? It sounded like an explosion, a bomb!" Then a touch gentler, "Are you all right? We're getting nothing from Boyd."

Somehow I found a voice through my shock and growing despair, "I don't know, yes it sounded like an explosion and I can't get Boyd either. I'm still in the first CP, I'm going outside to look, I can hear sirens."

"McKay?"

"Oh yes, I'll try and get him. I'll call back as soon as."

"Ok, take care," and he rang off.

I walked out of the office, into the corridor. As I descended the stairs to the exit my mobile rang again. It was Mackay.

"Sir, you still in the first CP?"

"I'm just leaving now. What the hell's happened?"

"Dunno, Sir, I was hoping you could tell me!" Mackay was in the second command post or CP in a hired office across from Central

Station situated a quarter of a mile away. He told me that he'd only heard a dull thud and then the sirens. I told him to stay put and do nothing till I rang him.

I left the building and made my way to George Square. The streets around the square and all the roads feeding into it were one-way in a clockwise direction. Traffic, mostly buses and taxis, had predictably ground to a halt, their passengers milling around. There was no discernible sign of panic, just a general air of curiosity and confusion.

Most people were looking up at an enormous cloud of smoke and dust rising in a classic mushroom form above the square. There was no doubt in my mind that this was a bomb. As I walked up the road people were rushing past me dazed and stunned, their faces ashen white, some had streaks of blood and dust on them.

As I drew level with the entrance to the railway station, I could see its huge glass frontage had been shattered. This was Glasgow's Queen Street Station the third busiest railway station in Scotland, constantly ferrying people to Edinburgh, Aberdeen and the Highlands. At about two-thirty on a Wednesday afternoon scores of passengers had been entering and leaving the station when the explosion happened. The result was utter carnage.

People were lying about everywhere at the station entrance with lacerations where glass and rubble had penetrated clothes and of course skin, with terrible results. There was a bar at the station entrance with an open-air section where people could drink and smoke. Glass from the station and other parts had fallen into the open-air section and people who had been sitting at tables had been blown inwards. Bodies were lying about here covered from head to toe in shards of glass; one woman who looked to be in her early thirties had a large piece of jagged glass protruding from her neck, her body lifeless.

More sirens wailed as police cars and ambulances piled into the Square. I'd walked or driven through the Square countless times as man and boy. A former drained pond it was right in the epicentre of the city, home to a collection of statues honouring an assemblage of eminent dignitaries, including a former Prime Minister (Gladstone), Scotland's bard Rabbie Burns and a few others and a white marble cenotaph. It was also the setting for major civic occasions. Above all, it was where Glaswegians sat in good weather on the benches and grass patches dotted around it and took a break from the stresses of the city. Now it looked alien and horrific.

The black bronzed statues on the west side of the square had been split apart with only jagged stumps and plinths bearing witness that they had ever been there. Several buses had their windows shattered and one, a cream liveried double-decker, had had its entire roof blown off into the square. People seemed to be lying about everywhere in varying stages of distress; the walking wounded helped each other or were being helped by someone who had miraculously escaped unscathed.

The building on the west side appeared to have borne the worst of the blast as almost all of its façade and stonework had been ripped off revealing open spaces and offices as if a giant hand had cracked it open; on the third floor a large table yawed precariously over a ledge.

And the reason why this building had taken the full force of the explosion was evident on the street below. Halfway along the building where there was a Greek restaurant and beside a glass and steel bus stop which had disappeared, was a crater, perhaps twenty feet deep from which shards of dust were still rising. The mushroom dust cloud was now beginning to disappear allowing the crater and its debris to become starkly visible. A light breeze blew scattering more dust and in doing so stirred something on the edge of the square next to the crater.

Any lingering hope I had that this apocalypse which had befallen George Square had nothing to do with us, that it was just a horrible coincidence, was eliminated forever by the object the breeze had moved slightly. It was a piece of light blue plastic which had until a few minutes ago been part of the roof of a van, Sadeq's van to be precise. And the rest of the van had been incinerated or mangled to pieces in the crater along no doubt with Sadeq.

The conclusion was obvious. The source of the explosion was Sadeq's van. Tony Boyd, who I had fruitlessly tried to contact on my radio, was to have rendezvoused with the van at the bus stop on the west side of George Square next to the Greek restaurant: the precise spot where the crater was now. The van was being tailed by two cars, one ours' that is the Security Service, more popularly known as MI5, the other a police Counter-Terrorism Command or CTC car. Then there was Mackay and me in the two nearby command posts.

Sadeq was driving two young Glaswegian Muslims recently radicalised, groomed and trained, on a reconnaissance mission. One week from now they were going to set off two backpack bombs at the height of rush hour on the concourses of Glasgow's two main railway terminals: Queen Street and Glasgow Central. They were aiming to cause as much devastating impact and harm as they could while martyring themselves in an act of jihad and holy war.

Today they were meant to be going on a dummy run: one getting out here in George Square to reconnoitre Queen Street, the other to do a similar rehearsal in Central Station. They were accompanied on the drive to the city centre by the man who had recruited and groomed them and sent them for training: a top al-Qaeda-linked operative.

Sadeq was in fact our informer and we'd had this developing terrorist cell under detailed surveillance, including audio and visual monitoring, since its inception. No bomb-making equipment had been acquired yet and as soon as it had we would move in and arrest them. The van had been checked by me personally the night before and had been under close watch for the last two days and nights. So, apart from our listening devices, the van and its passengers was supposed to be clean: certainly no explosives.

And yet...the crater and the carnage in the square dramatically contradicted that idea. *How and where the fuck did they put the explosives in?* Did Sadeq know? Was he in on it? Or did the al-Qaeda man somehow under our noses plant a bomb in the van? Above all, how did we manage to let a van laden with explosives, under surveillance and tailed by us and CTC into the heart of Glasgow and blow George Square apart with Christ knows how many lives lost?

Police cars and ambulances were now piling into the square, their sirens blending into one cacophonous wail. The first tentative signs of order were being established as the 1st responders who had concentrated on helping the injured were now followed by senior officers who focused on clearing the square and treating the area as a crime scene. Which meant that any non-injured people such as myself would very soon be asked to move or come under suspicion as more than a gawking rubbernecker. I moved swiftly away from the square.

Retrieving my mobile from my pocket I saw there were a-half-dozen messages left; the noise in the square had drowned out the ringtones. I phoned Mackay.

"Abandon your CP NOW! Get to the Shields. It's a..." I had to be careful on the phone, in spite of our own rigorous counter-intelligence and counter-surveillance techniques mobile phones were intrinsically untrustworthy and anything said could be recorded and used against you. "...an explosion, almost certainly caused by a bomb, on the square next to the spot where Boyd was. Looks like a van was involved." I could hear an audible gasp from Mackay as he took in the significance of that. "Ok, out." The messages were all from Mulrooney. Was it a bomb? Where was Boyd? And so on. I replied:

Looks like a bomb van involved on way to Shields

This would have the same impact on Mulrooney as it had on Mackay and me: sheer absolute sickening dread at one massive fuck-up with all that was to follow.

2: THE SHIELDS

The 'Shields' was a large red sandstone villa in the Pollokshields district of Glasgow. Formerly in the possession of a businessman and his family who owned a drapery company, MI5 had bought it in the early 90s when the businessman had passed away and none of his family showed any interest in carrying on the business. This was a time when MI5 had just been put on a legal and official footing after decades of a semi-legal twilight existence, and terrorism and drugs had been added to its portfolio of counter-intelligence and counter-subversion. Glasgow had suffered a massive epidemic of heroin use all through the 80s and it was reckoned that the potential harm to society and the economy posed by widespread heroin use was in itself subversive. Allied to the possible links between dealers, criminals and terrorists, the drugs trade was now viewed as such a sufficient threat to liberal-democracy as to provide justification for an outfit like MI5 to get involved, and Glasgow was a prime location, not forgetting the city's historical and cultural links to the conflict still then being waged across the Irish Sea in Northern Ireland.

So to add to a series of safe houses dotted across the city and ad hoc offices used for operations primarily linked to monitoring, infiltrating and interdicting 'subversives' and terrorists and their various supporters, the Service had bought the villa in a discreet suburban location that combined offices and meeting spaces in one spot and afforded a more permanent presence in the city.

I'd done well from MI5's move into drugs. I'd been put in charge of my own section and started running operations in that netherworld between drugs and terrorism, but it wasn't the good memories of those days that came to the fore now. As I concentrated and tried to recall every aspect of the last two days and how Sadeq's van could have been infiltrated with explosives when we were supposed to have the whole project under control, the dark memories of another blowback took centre stage.

Seven dead heroin users, six men, one woman, one of them on our payroll, all overdosed on a pure batch of heroin lying amidst the squalor of a flat turned shooting gallery in Possil, a district of Glasgow that had become the centre of heroin distribution and use. Seven corpses, one a girl of only eighteen, all chalk white and lying scattered on the filthy floor with a TV in the corner broadcasting an episode of *Columbo*. To us it became known as the 'Possil Disaster' and was a direct consequence of our interference in the drug market. There was no big fallout, though, just seven junkies and some hard lessons to be learned. My section and I had walked away unscathed. No resignations, no career stoppers. George Square would be different, unless the governors could pull a miracle we were in some serious shit.

I walked up to the second floor of the Shields and entered the conference room where Danny Mackay was sitting at the long table. He looked how I felt, shocked, ashen-faced, eyes wide. I gave him a nod and said "Obviously no hassle getting away?"

"No, none," his head shook longer than the reply merited. I touched his arm as a gesture of support and he half-heartedly attempted a smile in return. I sat beside him. Across the table was Fiona, a woman in her fifties who was effectively admin support for the Glasgow section, notepad in front of her, pen poised in her right hand. She stared straight at me saying in her Fife accent, "A terrible day, they're talking about 100 dead, women, children!" she shook her head.

I felt like saying "Thanks a bunch, Fiona, that's all Danny and me need even before Mulrooney gets here," but instead I just replied, "Yes, bloody awful, Fiona, absolutely awful."

She continued staring at me, almost accusingly, as she would be privy to at least some of the details of the operation, but I didn't respond. There was just the three of us in the room and a tense silence hung in the air for a few moments broken only when the door opened and Tres Martindale and Wattie Craig walked in. These two had been in the MI5 surveillance car tailing Sadeq's van from the south side of Glasgow and, together with Danny Mackay and Tony Boyd, who had almost certainly perished amidst the carnage of George Square, made up the latest incarnation of my own team.

We'd been together mostly for the last five years, with Tony being the youngest and latest recruit. Tres had been a nurse, who became disillusioned with nursing and applied for a job with the Civil Service. She excelled at the exams and was fast tracked into procurement at the MOD where she was talent-spotted and sent to us. Tres wasn't what you would call overtly beautiful, but she wasn't supposed to be. Forget whatever you've read about glamorous spies or Bond girls on the big screen. Intelligence people who are field operatives, male and female, have to fit into the background and cannot attract attention which means they must be plain Janes or Jameses absent any striking features. So none of the guys in the room would have given Brad Pitt a run for his money and Tres wouldn't have worried Claudia Schiffer, but there was a presence about her which belied her plain appearance. Her eyes were what held you, deep, green and sensuous with a wicked smile.

Of course there was no smile on her face tonight as she acknowledged me and sat at the opposite end of the table while big Wattie Craig walked straight up to me and said

"Chief, what a fucking day!" and laid his big paw affectionately on my arm.

Wattie was all muscle and had come straight into the service from the army: the SAS and Afghanistan to be specific. The army was one of four main routes into MI5, the others being the Civil Service – as with Tres, the police usually CTC (Danny Mackay), talent-spotted at university (Tony Boyd) or informer turned agent recruit (me). I really appreciated Wattie's openness, informality and sincere expression on his well-worn features.

"Aye, Wattie." I replied wearily, "it's not been the best day." Wattie sat beside Tres.

The team were all here except Tony, the 'wean' as Wattie sometimes called him, and his absence and certain death in the field shrouded the air. I stayed silent for another minute or so and was about to start talking, to attempt a response to a million questions that the team would be likely to fire at me when the conference room door opened again to reveal the dapper, urbane figure of Colin Mulrooney, Scotland National Co-ordinator of MI5, my boss: charcoal grey suit, receding brown hair and sharp but twinkling hazel eyes. His demeanour and accent reminded you of Gordon Jackson in the 80s TV series *The Professionals*.

The team and Fiona all uttered "Sir" in various registers at his entrance. Standing next to Fiona he said calmly but commandingly:

"I know all of you are going through a lot of emotions just now, not least because one of your colleagues, young Boyd, is missing. What's happened is absolutely incredible," he was looking around all of us, his twinkling eyes apprising each of us swiftly. "You won't need me to tell you the press, the police, our lords and masters and not least our beloved friends who live in the big house across the river," (this was a sardonic reference to our erstwhile 'colleagues' in SIS or MI6 as it was more popularly known, whose London HQ was situated across the river Thames from MI5's head office) "will all be asking some searching questions," another swift but hard look at each of us. "So if I'm to do my job, which is to find out what happened on this operation and, and I'm going to be frank here, if there's the slightest chance of extricating any or all of us out of this mess, then I need honesty and for you to be upfront with me. Ok?" Terse nods of agreement from all except Tres and Fiona.

I looked at him. "Sir, has anything come out from our side about any," I paused and then said slowly, "any operation going on in Glasgow?"

Mulrooney looked at his watch before replying. "The bomb and I think we can safely assume that that is what it was, happened at 2.26pm. It's now 5.35pm. At 3.50 I and Superintendent McAllister of CTC were asked separately by the Chief Constable of Police Scotland what the alert status was around terrorist activity in Glasgow and did either agency know of anything that had alerted our suspicions. The Superintendent and I both replied that the alert status was 'black' and that we would make rigorous inquiries of our agencies about what they knew, if anything. Needless to say both the Chief Constable and the Criminal Justice Minister wants a complete list of all terrorist suspects –Irish, Islamic, anything-- updated ready for the Branch, us and the police to break doors down should a) George Square be confirmed as resulting from a deliberate explosion and b) the slightest link unearthed to a terrorist cause and associated group. So, to answer your question Eddie, it's been just under two hours since I was asked that question and they were looking for an answer ten minutes before they asked it. I expect I can hold off answering *truthfully* for another hour at the most. We can safely expect all hell to break loose once we do tell them that there *was* an operation going on and.... Well I don't need to say anything more.

"What I need from you is everything you can give me on this, everything," his voice trailed into silence.

I spoke first. "Sir, I have had no chance to debrief the team. You'll appreciate Martindale and Craig were in the Service surveillance car, Boyd was on foot in the Square and is missing and Mackay was in the second CP. This is the first time since the explosion that we've assembled."

"That's understood, Eddie, so let's get this debriefing underway, now," he commanded.

Outside, through the triple glazing, some male voices could be heard amid the vague, muffled sound of a car door opening and closing. MI5 rented, under cover of course, the upper floor of the villa. The ground floor was taken up by an ex-serviceman's club which was perfect cover for white middle-aged males to come and go to the villa without attracting undue attention from the neighbours in the quiet, leafy residential streets.

Most likely, the men I'd heard outside were a couple of ex-servicemen enjoying a long liquid lunch extending into the afternoon and now making their merry way home courtesy of a taxi.

I was about to speak when the door opened and in walked Dougie Anderson from Counter-Terrorist Command (CTC), or Detective Inspector Anderson to give him his proper title. Tall, ramrod straight, with straight grey hair and a crumpled brown suit which stood in such sharp contrast to Mulrooney's whose suits always looked as if they had been made bespoke that day. He acknowledged Mulrooney and gave a quick glance to the rest of us and then, with his arms in the air like he was semaphoring to someone in the distance, said excitedly:

"I've been trying to avoid Mr McAllister all afternoon. You," looking straight at me "and your squad told us we were tailing an empty van with al-Qaeda suspects on observation. We and your people tailed that van into the city-centre, more or less gave it a fucking escort, and it explodes right in the middle of George Square! Christ, my wife was in the town today, she could have been blown to pieces! I've got a five-year old boy, what do you expect me to tell him in years to come? Aye son it was your dad that escorted the George Square bombers into town!"

Not for nothing was Dougie Anderson known as 'Hammy Andy'. In court giving evidence, at the bar dispensing drinks, stories and wisdom or giving briefings to his team, Hammy Andy was always prone to histrionics: subtlety and diplomacy were never his strongpoints.

Mulrooney was about to tell him to calm down, but I got in first:

"Dougie, I, none of us, knew that that van had explosives in it. We lost one of our own there: we certainly don't go in for getting our own people killed."

"So al-Qaeda is supernatural now, able to place explosives out of thin air? You told us, you *assured* us the van was bugged, audio and video, it hadn't been out of your sight in twenty-four hours and was only being used for reconnaissance and now's there a hundred dead in George Square, what the fuck happened?"

Mulrooney stepped in. "All right, Dougie, we're all a bit overwrought. Let Eddie speak, he was just about to give us a debriefing. Eddie?"

I tried to concentrate, tried to focus the multitude of conflicting thoughts reeling through my head. In truth I'd no idea how to answer Anderson or account to Mulrooney. But I had to rally my team, stay composed. We were all in deep shit, me in particular. When word got out, as it inevitably would in the next days or hours that MI5 had set up an operation to surveil and bust an al-Qaeda mission which had ended so catastrophically, the shit would hit the fan in spectacular style. Conspiracy theorists would have a field day while cynics, opportunists, the Service's rivals and, not least the media, would round on the sheer criminal incompetence of all involved. So focus, tell a linear narrative, recount the facts as you know them.

"Ok," I started voice calm and controlled as best I could, "let's go back to the beginning. Abdul Sadeq Hamid, who we always refer to as Sadeq, has been a long-standing informer/agent for us since the early 90s. Twelve months ago, during a routine catch-up meeting, he informed me that a radical preacher at Sadeq's mosque, that we, through Sadeq, had been keeping an eye on, had brought a contact up from London. This contact, with the assistance of the preacher, was holding meetings in the mosque. The preacher would invite a select few people, invariably young in their late teens and twenties, to attend the meetings. There, the contact, much more overtly than the preacher during his sermons, would talk of jihad and holy war, of the corruption of decadent western society, of how that society was doomed."

"Christ, were you at these meetings yourself?" Anderson asked sarcastically.

"Aye, Dougie, a white, bald, middle-aged man amidst a crowd of disaffected south Asian young men listening to a radical Islamic orator in a mosque, I don't think so, do you?" Wattie chuckled, while Tres allowed a fleeting smile. Anderson retorted, "Only kidding!"

Mulrooney urged, "Go on, Eddie."

"The point Sadeq was making was that the contact was a good, powerful speaker. His exact words were 'an excellent orator, Mr Macintyre.' He was getting the young crowd worked up and painting a vivid picture of the struggle and paradise to come. By the third or fourth meeting he was on about martyrdom and openly talking about the 'martyred sheik' killed by the corrupt cowardly infidels from the Great Satan, referring of course to Bin Laden. When his name was mentioned the group of about twenty or so would applaud and chant 'Praise be to Allah'."

"Remind me, was Sadeq at these meetings?" Mulrooney asked.

"Yes, he was a staple of the mosque, well known to everybody, including the young group at the meetings. He had the confidence of the preacher and was introduced to the contact soon after he arrived in Glasgow. As you know Sadeq's qualities were the ability to blend into the background and to appeal to everyone. He had that ability of never actually openly committing to your views or position but to appear to somehow empathise with or endorse them so that people thought he was on their side. That young team would naturally have thought that 'old Sadeq' who was part of the furniture at the mosque and a friend of the preachers' was ok and was on their side. That was what made Sadeq such a great informer and agent."

"So the preacher thought Sadeq was sympathetic to radical Islam, could even possibly support terrorist activity and thereby introduced Sadeq to the contact?" Mulrooney enquired.

"Yes."

"Before the meetings started with the group?"

"Yes again. The preacher approached Sadeq and said 'you need to meet this man, he's a good Muslim, but a man of action', so Sadeq met him at the preacher's house not far from the mosque."

As I spoke I cast my mind back to an April afternoon a year earlier when I met with Sadeq at one of our regular meeting places in the small west coast Scottish seaside town of Largs where he updated me on a crucial development that would culminate in the devastating events at George Square.

3: LARGS

The town was a popular destination for mainly elderly Glaswegian day trippers or families. The centre of the place was a garish ensemble of amusement arcades, fast food outlets and tacky souvenir shops, at the heart of which was a pier terminal for the distinctive white painted *Cal Mac* ferries plying the short journey to and from the nearby island of Cumbrae. Either side of the terminal the town became more bourgeois with a collection of large villas, well-attended churches and a clutch of retirement homes.

We would meet on a bench on the northern esplanade. In April it was still quite cool but mild enough for two middle-aged be-suited gentlemen, one bald and white, and the other with receding grey hair, Asian and bearded to sit on one of the dark iron seaside benches without attracting undue notice. Our only company were elderly couples walking along the esplanade arm-in-arm, dog-walkers and the occasional jogger. The sky was slate-grey. A ferry was just disembarking from the pier terminal. Across the bay was the green, but otherwise rather barren northern end of Cumbrae.

I was always impressed at how Sadeq was able to blend perfectly into his surroundings. His dark brown suit, pink tie and white shirt on a portly frame indicated a respectable middle-aged businessman ideal for Largs on a spring afternoon. How different he looked when he wore his white skullcap and long, flowing grey robe redolent of a good Muslim and making him indistinguishable from other males at his mosque. Indeed the cap and robe seemed not only to make him appear slimmer but also to accentuate his beard and large brown eyes, almost to radicalise him, or was that my own cultural stereotypes and prejudices coming to the fore? I had also seen Sadeq in a casino or nightclub dressed in expensive casual designer clothes, beard neatly trimmed or shaven off, and ten years off him.

The variability of his apparel reflected Sadeq's different roles. He had a string of businesses ranging from newsagents, a couple of Indian restaurants, an interest in an import-export company, a share in a taxi firm as well as numerous other interests. A hard-working man he would take a turn behind the counter of one of his newsagents, or get behind the wheel of one of his taxis, or be a combined mine host- come-waiter chatting up the customers and taking their orders at one of his restaurants. It was not unusual for him to put in an eighteen hour day. This prodigious output did not stop him attending the mosque at least several hours over several days two or three times a week and becoming one of its mainstays, allowing him to have the run of the place and the confidence of its many and varied worshipers.

Then there was the family man Sadeq, at the centre of a large and extensive network, presiding over family gatherings and ceremonials: he had three married sons and two daughters, one still to be married. And then there was the Sadeq who dealt in shady goods including knocked off-fabrics, was involved in false VAT returns and occasionally played a part in trafficking people. Finally, there was playboy Sadeq at the casino or in the south of France or Dubai, a girl half his age by his side. In each role: businessman, faithful Muslim, family man, crook and playboy (and some of them shaded into each other), Sadeq put in the same amount of effort. Both agents and informers must have at least one of three good qualities: the ability to blend in, empathy with everybody they come into contact with and sheer hard work. Sadeq was adept at all three. Which made him one of the best agents I'd ever had and he'd never let me down in the time I'd worked with him.

Sadeq was debriefing me on the latest developments at the mosque with the radical Islamist contact, whose name was Qatib or Dr Qatib to give him his proper title.

"So, Mr Lomax," the name Sadeq knew me as and had always known me as, "I think the doctor is getting ready to recruit, to move on to a new stage."

"And what makes you think that, Sadeq?"

He paused before replying. Some seagulls cackled overhead just as the mild April sun briefly broke through the cloud. I cast a quick glance around. The seashore at Largs was perfect for a meeting like this: a spy meeting his Joe. The long pathways astride the beach, very few people about and all with a purpose, no stationery traffic on the otherwise busy main road some twenty yards behind us, all of it made life very difficult for a surveillance crew and my expert eye told me there was none here.

He resumed, "The doctor is going on more and more about the Sheikh and martyrdom and the example of the deed. Two nights ago at the mosque he said that we can all talk, but what we really need is action to avenge our brothers and sisters in Afghanistan, Palestine, Iraq, Syria and wherever the holy warriors are fighting. That is what he is telling them."

"Telling who?"

"The young men at the mosque. He is telling them that there are the active fighters at the front engaging in the armed struggle against the infidel. He is talking of the victories of the Mujahedeen Holy Warriors! Britain and America pulled out of Afghanistan; the Islamic State's Caliphate running rampant in Iraq. The corrupt dictator Gaddafi ousted in Libya and his counterpart Assad humbled in Syria. Everywhere in the former lands of the caliph, from Egypt to Yemen, the streets are ablaze with rebellion! He tells them the days of Western colonial powers and their decadent Arab servants are over.

"He cautioned the crowd that he had to be careful about what he says; that other speakers like himself at mosques have been picked up by the British authorities for saying the truth. Of course the crowd call back to him that he's among friends.

"Apparently reassured, he went on to make a distinction between the active front where the mujahedeen holy warriors are directly taking on the Crusaders, the Zionists, the Great Satan's and their lackeys and, he goes on, in the space of five years they have turned the occupied lands of the caliph into burial pits for the imperialist forces.

"But, he pointed out, there was another front. Not only, he says do the imperialists face a bloodbath in the lands of the caliphate, but they have to face attacks right in the heart of their corrupt homelands. Just as the Crusaders bring destruction and death to the people of the caliphate, just as they maim and burn the women and children of Gaza, so they can never rest, never know when their own precious towns and cities can also be bathed in blood. The crowd were now on their feet.

"The doctor emphasised that every time there is an attack here in the West it inspires the mujahedeen fighters and martyrs to go on with their struggle to victory. But more importantly the infidel's hearts sink and their will to fight to resist the onwards March of Allah and his will and his law is weakened. He told the crowd that the infidel are really corrupt, decadent, effeminate and above all weak. He concluded by saying that an action in the West is as important and as vital as the fighting on the frontline. A gun in Gaza, a bomb in Glasgow, he claimed is all part of the one world-wide struggle to bring justice, restitution and universal brotherhood. He sat down and the crowd rose to their feet chanting 'Praise be to Allah'."

"What happened after the meeting, Sadeq?"

"The doctor moved among the crowd chatting to people, oh, for about a good hour after. Then the preacher, the doctor and I moved into a small office the preacher has."

I asked sharply, "Neither the preacher or the doctor had any difficulty with asking you back to that office after the meeting, in other words, they were comfortable with you being with them?"

Sadeq laughed dismissively at this, "Oh yes, Mr Lomax, in fact it was quite the opposite."

I was confused, "What do you mean?"

"Well, we went into the office and spoke about how the meeting had gone. The doctor was pleased with it. He was looking at us very carefully, saying how it was so difficult and sensitive to bring up subjects like 9/11 even with an audience like that. He said it was so important to emphasise that attacks in the Western heartlands were a vital tool in the struggle for jihad. The preacher and I were nodding in agreement. Then he said to the preacher that he wanted a few minutes with me on my own, which the preacher agreed to."

"The preacher wasn't put out by being asked to leave?"

"No, he just said, 'of course doctor' and left. The doctor turned to me and asked what I thought of the meeting and all the talks he'd given so far. I replied they were inspiring and motivating and served to remind us of what jihad was about and what the mujahedeen were fighting for. Then he asked about the actions in the West which was code for 9/11 and the rest. I stared straight back at him and said, you spoke of it firmly tonight, doctor: they are as much a part of the struggle as the frontline is.

"Over some tea the preacher had made us, he looked straight at me again, his dark eyes fixed on me. He reminded me that he had begun his talk tonight by saying we can all talk but action is what is required. He said of the twenty young men who were in the crowd in the hall, how many would take up the armed struggle? He answered his own question by saying only one or two at the most. He said they always would comprise the small vanguard that will lead the rest.

"He told me he'd asked old Siddique the preacher to leave because, in Qatib's words 'he is a talker not a doer'. The doctor went on to say that there are hundreds, no thousands of men like Siddique in Britain and across the West. They speak radical if the mosque authorities or the police don't interfere. But, he said scornfully, 'They're all talk. They have a comfortable life and Siddique and his type are not men of action.' He explained that the most they can do is prepare the way by their sermons for people who are prepared to go forward. Qatib asked me if I understood."

Sadeq looked directly at me, another white Cal Mac ferry was coming in to the pier terminal; a white-haired man in his sixties was on the beach throwing sticks for his two Yorkshire terriers to fetch.

"Mr Lomax, his eyes were penetrating."

"How did you reply?"

"I nodded and told him I understood him. At last he looked away from me.

"He then said there were two men in the audience who he would like to have some further private talks with. I asked him gently who they were and if he had been able to catch their names. He had. One, he believed was called Khalid and the other Mohammed. He asked me if I knew them.

"I replied yes I did. Khalid was until recently what we would call here in Scotland a tearaway. He has been in trouble with the police a few times: hanging about in gangs, getting involved in fights, engaged in some acts of vandalism. He is typical of a lot of third generation Asian youths, the despair of his mother and out of the control of the father. Needless to say the family are very hard working, his father runs a halal butchers. We never saw Khalid at the mosque until recently. The real attraction seems to be Siddique's sermons at Friday payers and in the evenings, and I said that to the doctor.

"Mohammed by contrast is a much quieter boy, a bit older as well, twenty-one to Khaled's eighteen. He was doing well at school, kept himself to himself, helped out at his dad's newsagents. He moved up to university, but to his family's anguish he dropped out halfway during his second year. He started to read the *Koran* avidly, memorising entire sections and to hanging around the mosque. He still helps in his father's shop, but most of his time is spent at the mosque and he and Khalid have started gravitating towards each other.

"After hearing me talk about the boys the doctor said he was going to deliver one more talk to the crowd he'd spoken to that evening and he requested that I arrange for Khalid and Mohamed to meet with him privately after the meeting was over and the crowd had dispersed. No others were to be present and that included Siddique. I replied that I could arrange that and we parted shortly after."

The sun had managed to pierce through one of the slate grey clouds again as I asked Sadeq:

"Has the next meeting been arranged?"

"Yes, for tomorrow night."

"And Khalid and Mohammed?"

"I've already approached them at the mosque. They're eager to meet with the doctor privately. I've told them no boasting about that to the others who attend the group meetings or the doctor would never want to deal with them. I think that will be sufficient to get them to hold their tongues."

"And have you got a place for that meeting?"

"Mr Lomax, I have a furnished flat to let in the Battlefield area that is currently unoccupied. I have arranged to have the doctor meet the two boys there."

"Has the doctor asked you to be there?"

"Yes, he has."

That was truly significant and Sadeq and I both knew it, indicated by the hard glances we exchanged. I was excited, more excited than I had been for a long time. But I wanted to remain calm in front of Sadeq. Always remain calm and reflective with your agent, remain in control. You're asking them to do very risky work, the consequences for which if they were found out was at the very least loss of friendship, dismissal from a club, society or workplace, outed as a spy, an informer, a snitch, untrustworthy and, at worst, loss of life and a horrible way to lose that life as lurid and terrible means are employed to extract from you what it is you know.

"Sadeq, it's clear that Dr Qatib is recruiting. He's looking for two 'cleanskins' and he's on the money with Khalid and Mohammed. They're both disaffected and looking for a cause. More conventional imams or preachers would, frankly, have bored them rigid. Straight Islam would have had no impact. But Siddique with his radical firebrand sermons plants the seeds; sets the cannon up as it were. Then the good doctor comes along and provides the basis, the rationale, and the justification for going forward to…Where?"

Sadeq, who had been looking onto the bay and Cumbrae as I spoke, confirmed almost in a weary voice, "It would appear so, but yes, where?"

"Look at me, Sadeq," I spoke softly but firmly. "Qatib's recruiting for al-Qaeda or an al-Qaeda offshoot, it doesn't really matter which. The point is he's recruiting to get these guys ready to carry out a terrorist act, probably suicidal that will cause mass loss of life. Where and when is unknown but it's probably Scotland, most likely Glasgow." Sadeq nodded in agreement. "But the thing is, Sadeq," he turned to face me seemingly impassive, but I could tell there was lots of emotion coursing through him as there was behind my façade: "The thing is," I repeated, "Qatib trusts you, Siddique's role is over, after tomorrow's meeting, the imperative will be to isolate Khalid and Mohammed from their peers at the mosque, thus the meeting in a private flat. The next move will almost certainly be further indoctrination and that means training, not just in texts and lectures and videos, but physical training and that will mean guns, rockets, ammo and explosives. It means a camp and that will mean Pakistan, usually the remote frontier lands of Waziristan or the North West provinces.

"But I'm running ahead of myself. The crucial point is, Sadeq, Dr Qatib trusts you. He's asked you back after the meetings. He's pointed out to you two guys in the crowd who he wants to deal with apart from the rest and, most importantly, he wants you to be present when they have that meeting. From now on its' Qatib, Khalid, Mohammed and you. Sadeq you're in at the start of recruiting an al-Qaeda terrorist cell. Unknown and left alone, those guys would get trained and go on to commit a terrible atrocity possibly in Glasgow. They'll believe themselves to be martyrs striking a major blow for jihad and blessed by the Prophet with the key to heaven and living in paradise for eternity. Meanwhile back on planet Earth there's shattered dead bodies of men, women and children, Christian and Muslim, Jewish or Buddhist, it doesn't matter to these guys, because it's all predetermined and they're only fulfilling the command of Allah and when you sincerely believe that you can do anything because it's all justified.

"But Sadeq, you have the ability to prevent all that, all the suffering, the terror and the misery this could lead to."

Sadeq stared back at me, his face a picture of concern and deep sadness. He said "Mr Lomax, I despise people like Qatib, I really do. They take these young men and turn them into monsters. This is not typical of my people, this is not my God! For every sentence in the Koran you show me of war and vengeance and jihad I can show you whole screeds of the holy book that speaks of love, forgiveness, mercy and pity. That is my God, my Islam."

I replied gently, "I know, Sadeq. Qatib stands in the same relationship to most Muslims that fanatical protestant or catholic paramilitaries in Northern Ireland do to ordinary Christians. But because of al-Qaeda and all that's happened through them and their associates, a significant amount of people in the West, including here in Scotland, think that's all that Islam is about: fanatical terrorists blowing up people with weapons of mass destruction.

"And suppose that Khalid and Mohammed did go on to become suicide bombers. Suppose that they did carry out a terrorist action say in Glasgow, apart from the horror of that action in itself, think of the impact that would have on ordinary Muslims in the city, completely innocent people now targeted as terrorist supporters, open to abuse and attack. It wouldn't just stop at Muslims; anyone with brown or black skin would be fair game.

"But, I repeat, Sadeq, you have the chance to stop this, to prevent this calamity happening."

There was a long silence as he stared straight ahead. The wind blew a sudden gust as some schoolchildren walked noisily by on the promenade behind us. Finally, still staring ahead, he asked almost rhetorically:

"You want me to stay with Qatib? Report on him and on Khalid and Mohammed and there, ah, progress?"

"Yes. You'll be backed up by us, with a full surveillance team. I'll be overseeing the team and working with you constantly. I'll be with you every step of the way. Remember, follow MosBerBel Rules and discard SIM cards every time you arrange a meeting with me. We'll start with the Battlefield flat. Give me the address and a set of keys before the meeting and we'll have a bug put in. I'll also need Khalid and Mohammed's addresses and telephone numbers, if possible; you'll need to phone them to arrange the meeting at the flat."

I went on listing arrangements for routine contacts and 'crash' or emergency meetings and the safe houses to hold them. I also went over again the standard counter-surveillance procedures for Sadeq to assess whether he was being watched (besides my own team, of course) and to shake off tails. These were known as 'MosBerBel Rules".

Art imitates life which, in turn, imitates art. During the 1960s and 70s the espionage thriller writer John le Carre (himself a former SIS Officer, though of very brief duration) wrote a series of bestsellers around the fictional character of senior SIS man George Smiley. Deception, treachery, bluff and counter-bluff were the hallmarks of Smiley's world and to be able to navigate through this 'hall of mirrors' where nothing is ever what it appears and friend and foe can alternate instantly or blend into each other, le Carre has Smiley conjure the phrase 'Moscow Rules'. These, simply put, are rules of conduct and behaviour to live by when undercover in enemy territory, which Moscow was during the Cold War.

Le Carre's books shaped a lot of people's perception of the intelligence services and had an impact on people working within those services too, such that when I was first recruited by MI-5 in a position similar to that of Sadeq in the late 70s' part of my training for undercover work included learning to adopt and live by the MosBerBel Rules. Basically this was an adaptation of le Carre's phrase. 'Mos' stood for Moscow. 'Ber' stood for Berlin and referred both to the German capital under the Nazis during the Second World War as well as the spy zone both West and East Berlin became through the Cold War. 'Bel' was Belfast resonant of the hazards faced by MI-5 agents and informers watching and infiltrating IRA and other republican paramilitaries or, occasionally, UDA or equivalent protestant groups during the troubles. In effect the MosBerBel Rules were the condensed, collective wisdom of operating in three hostile, life threatening settings adapted to any undercover operation anywhere. They were in short rules for survival in a hostile world. All of us in the secret world quickly lived by the MosBerBel Rules 24/7. Even the most mundane, routine tasks: buying a newspaper, ordering a pint in a bar, going out for a meal, were lived by them. And now I was just reinforcing them to Sadeq, who interjected during my flow of reminders and instructions:

"Yes, Mr Lomax, I always do MosBerBel," he said wearily but firmly.

"Sorry, Sadeq, forgive me, of course you do."

I was in chivvying mode with Sadeq now. Moving and urging him on with the tasks in front of us, getting him to focus on the operation and not be too contemplative I ended by reminding him:

"Sadeq I've worked with you for twenty-three years, stood beside you, never let you down. I won't let you down now. And you'll have prevented a catastrophe occurring."

It was true that I'd always stood by and supported Sadeq. I'd, diverted him from the wrath of Scottish law enforcement on several occasions, including the fall-out from the Possil Disaster which Sadeq had been party to. But the truth was, infiltrating, reporting on and ultimately being responsible for the roll-up of an al-Qaeda cell and preventing an act of mass terror on the streets of a major city, were a long way from reporting on drug gangs, smugglers and money launderers. And this in spite of the fact that one of the initial reasons for our contact with Sadeq back in the early 90s was the connections between drug smugglers and Irish paramilitaries before the Good Friday Agreement capped the guns of the main IRA and UDA protagonists to the conflict. But that was a different type of terrorist and Sadeq was too long in the tooth not to know the difference.

"Mr Lomax, these people are fanatics, they blow themselves up; they fly planes into tall buildings! If Qatib or those behind him find out it was me who grassed on them and broke up their operation, I'm a dead man, and there's my family. What would happen to them?"

I tried to allay his concerns. "I promise you, Sadeq, your family will be looked after. If need be we'll move you all to a safe place, give you and your family new identities, no expense spared. You'll be compensated handsomely for services rendered to the country." In truth I was going out on a limb here as I couldn't one-hundred percent guarantee this, but I was sure our side would stand well by him and his family.

I continued, "But I don't think it'll come to that. Not only will we protect your identity and never reveal it in court or to the media or anyone else for that matter, but you said yourself the vast majority of Muslims have no support or sympathy for al-Qaeda, except for vulnerable, easily led young guys like Khalid and Mohammed, whose own families will be in despair when they become aware of what their sons have got themselves involved with.

"The fact is this is not the IRA or UDA or any offshoot thereof with deep connections, family, political and religious, with people in Glasgow with long memories looking out to get back at you for eternity. It's not even your run of the mill drug smuggler or money laundering gang who can hire people locally to come looking for you.

"Al-Qaeda invariably operates in isolation, recruiting isolated cells like Qatib's doing with Khalid and Mohammed with no substantial connection to any community. You'll be safe Sadeq I assure you. Just keep track of developments, give them access to flats or drive them around and help us out with the surveillance and monitoring when we need it. When we know the time is right, long before they can do any damage, we'll intervene, close down the operation and get you out of it with no one else any the wiser. Only you have the satisfaction of knowing you saved your fellow Glaswegians from a horror zone and the right people will know it was you and reward you commensurately."

Those words of mine seem like some grotesque black comedy now, given what's happened at George Square, but at the time I really believed them. And so it appeared did Sadeq.

"All right, Mr Lomax," he allowed a fleeting smile to come over his face, "I'll go through with it; I'll work with you on this."

I responded, "When all this is finished I'll never ask you to do another thing for us, you'll have the Service's undying gratitude."

We shook hands, his gentle while mine was firm. After the handshake I adopted a serious profile again.

"Two final things: first, keep acting as though you believe it. Do the usual Sadeq act and let Qatib and the other two and anyone else who gets involved know that you're completely committed to the operation.

"But," I paused, "secondly, at the same time don't initiate anything with Qatib, Khaled or Mohammed. This is vitally important, Sadeq, just respond to requests or instructions; make yourself useful to them and, of course, keep us fully informed. Just don't cross a line, don't suggest anything or make a first move. I don't want some fucking well-paid defence QC suggesting to a jury that these two hapless young men were set up by an agent provocateur or entrapped by you and us!"

"I understand, Mr Lomax. You don't have to worry. I have no desire to begin anything with them, but you can be sure I'll keep up the appearance as I've always done for you."

And with that, as a slight drizzle began to fall, we parted. I watched Sadeq's back from the bench as he walked to the main road, crossed it and made his way to the back of a church located a couple of hundred yards up the road at the rear of which he'd parked his car.

I sat for a further ten minutes perusing the beachfront and the promenade, but there was nothing untoward or suspicious. I then made my way into the town centre and retrieved my car parked beside the railway station, driving south along the coast with the Isle of Cumbrae and the deep water port of Hunterston on my right and then through the villages of Fairlie and West Kilbride before making a sharp turn and driving north, retracing my route back through Largs. The road north after Largs was scenic, narrow and winding affording plenty of opportunity to spot a tail. There was nothing. Just before I reached Glasgow I received a text:

Back from mosque, family all here. It was Sadeq to say he was home and, as far as he was aware, had not been followed.

I parked the car in a city centre car park where it would be picked up by an operative and returned to the car hire firm it was rented from. There would be nothing to trace the car to MI-5. I got the subway to my west-end flat and after performing routine MosBerBel precautions, which I did virtually on auto-pilot. I sat down, put on some nice chilled-out ambient jazz and relaxed.

I was elated and excited. I and my team were in at the start of something big and, if we played it right, which I had every confidence that we would, with Sadeq's help we would see this through and bag ourselves an al-Qaeda terrorist cell before it did any harm and then reap the kudos. I might even decide to retire from the service on a high and go into the lucrative world of 'security consultancy' with a fraction of the stress or the politics of MI-5, which in spite of the glamour and mystique associated with its name, was, at the end of the day just another government bureaucracy.

The truth was I was bored. By the mid-teens of the 21st century, at least as far as terrorism and even subversion was concerned, Scotland was a very safe country. Politics was non-violent, constitutional and democratic with support for the extreme left and right marginal and their influence non-existent, even during the referendum campaign of 2014 and subsequent campaigns for independence.

The drugs wars of the early 90s in Glasgow had settled down and we'd managed to break up links between the drug gangs and paramilitaries like the IRA. Sadeq had been invaluable; we'd recruited him at the height of the wars as his taxi firm was being used to courier drugs in and out of Possil. We'd detained him and made him an offer he couldn't refuse and he started informing for us.

Sadeq had been a star. He came through the drugs wars and their IRA connections intact and without suspicion from any quarter.

As another laidback jazz track came on the audio system I felt wrapped in a buzz of anticipation and excitement. This is what justified our existence. This is what the taxpayer expected an internal security service to do: stop and catch terrorists, put them away for good and deter others. Game on. I couldn't wait to start.

4: GRAND MINARET

Wattie Craig inadvertently came up with Grand Minaret as the name for the operation to monitor and stop our putative al-Qaeda Glasgow mass suicide bombings. Two days after meeting Sadeq in Largs, I assembled the team in the Shields: Wattie, Tres, Tony Boyd and Danny Mackay. I'd given each of them a brief summary of what was coming up and they were all as excited and motivated as I was; "Well up for it boss," as Wattie enthusiastically proclaimed. Like me, they were bored with years of routine, monotonous surveillance work, which either led nowhere or where other sections of MI-5 or another agency (usually CTC) received all the glory and acclamation. This was ours from the get-go and any other agency would only have a walk-on part.

I walked in with some briefing papers to a hubbub of animated chatter. Tres was talking to Danny about a movie she'd seen the previous evening while Wattie was talking to Tony about his time as an undercover SAS officer in southern Iraq after the invasion in 2003. This was unusual for Wattie as he wasn't the type to boast about his military exploits. What had brought this on was a report in the previous day's papers accusing British troops in Iraq back then of heavy-handedness against locals detained in British military custody. He was fervently defending the honour of his army comrades but had side-tracked himself into describing an undercover and very risky patrol he was on in the Shia holy city of Karbala, by-passing the shrine which was the third holiest place on earth for a Shia. "You should have seen this shrine, Tony, it was amazing with some grand minarets," he enthused. I pricked up my ears, put down my papers and interrupted everybody's chatter.

"Folks, Wattie has just given us the name for our exclusive, home-grown Glasgow operation." They all stared at me quizzically, especially Wattie. "Wattie has just described the holy shrine at Karbala as being possessed of some 'grand minarets' and I think that's a neat name for our operation, certainly better than some of the names our betters have given other operations recently. So, colleagues welcome to the start and hopefully successful conclusion of operation Grand Minaret!" I had a glass of water on the table and raised it in the air. All four of them did the same, even though two glasses were empty.

"Grand Minaret," they all replied followed by Wattie saying: "Aye, gaffer, and I hope to fuck it'll be something a lot stronger than water we'll be toasting the end of Grand Minaret with!" Over their laughter at Wattie I responded firmly:

"Rest assured, Wattie, it'll be a lot stronger than water and it'll not be in the Shields either!"

"And on the firm?" he asked, for the Scottish pound always spoke loudly through Wattie. I shook my head ruefully:

"Aye Wattie, on the firm." And I commenced the first briefing of Grand Minaret.

Ok it wasn't the most sensitive of names and there was opposition from London to the title for the association with Islam (they would have been even more incredulous if they knew it was inspired by Wattie's description of the Shia Karbala shrine as al-Qaeda were fundamentalist Sunnis and abominated anything to do with the Shias), but Mulrooney supported us and it became the official title.

I commenced the briefing with a transcript of the previous night's final talk at the mosque delivered by Dr Qatib provided by a bug placed in the mosque's lecture room by Sadeq. As predicted during the talk Qatib dwelt at length on the topic of martyrdom. With his usual soaring rhetoric, he spoke of how martyrdom and jihad were intimately related. Jihad, holy war, needed martyrs to advance Islam and re-establish the Caliphate. As such, martyrs dying while advancing jihad were holy warriors and guaranteed entry into the kingdom of heaven where they would reside in paradise for eternity. For that, Qatib declaimed, dying was a worthwhile sacrifice, indeed almost a sacramental duty for a holy warrior. After all, what was this life here on earth but a pale shadow, "a waiting room for the heavenly paradise that awaits the faithful, the true followers of Allah."

What was interesting was how Qatib dealt with a question from the floor about suicide bombings taking out civilians, women and children; "they could even be your own family members!" the questioner pointed out.

"Allah knows what you're doing," Qatib responded, "Because Allah knows everything and everything is his will. But Allah is also merciful and kind. But a necessary, no an *essential* tool of jihad is to hit the infidel in their commercial and residential heartlands, so they are never safe, never secure, and if through jihad their will to prevail in the lands of the future caliph withers, then the deaths of innocents, even of our Muslim brothers and sisters by an act of jihad is explained. Allah knows his own; the infidels will be banished to Hell, to eternal torment, and the believers and the innocent like the holy warriors, will enter into paradise. You see, the brothers and sisters and the mothers and the fathers, if they die through jihad, this is part of God's will, in the fight against corruption, evil, decadence and filth. They are also *martyrs*, unknowing but righteous warriors in Allah's cosmic plan.

"But let me ask you why do our warriors have to do these activities? It is not just revenge for the drone attacks and massacres of our old people, women and children. Where are the commentators and moral crusaders when a wedding party is blown to pieces from 5,000 feet by a drone in Afghanistan or Yemen? Where are they when the skin of our children is burned and peeling off while they scream in hideous pain when the Zionists drop cluster bombs in Gaza? Nowhere my friends, *nowhere*, their silence is deafening.

"But my friends it is not vengeance that motivates jihad attacks in the towns and cities of the west. Satan has equipped the colonialists, the Zionists, the crusaders (they are the same thing) with the real weapons of mass destruction, the tanks, the drones, the jets and bombers and, of course, nuclear weapons. Our weapons are stealth, courage, the willingness to embrace death through martyrdom and the ability to strike fear and terror in their people. For their people regard the transient moments that is our time here on earth as *everything* and they fear death. Therefore they will agitate for their politicians to quit: to stop supporting their puppets in the holy lands. And because these puppets have ultimately no other basis of support, they will fall. And then we will prevail, and the caliph will be restored, the rest of the world will abandon false Gods and idols and embrace Islam. Then earth will mirror heaven and the lives of future generations to come will be in a world of harmony and equality with proper morals and the law of God will rule supreme. And when that happens, the waiting room that is life here preparing us for eternal paradise will be bliss.

"My friends, jihad and martyrdom are not acts of vengeance or terror. They are necessary, but they are also acts of love because they are willed by Allah and Allah is *Love*! Praise be to Allah!"

Qatib sat down while the crowd rose to their feet, chanting "Praise be to Allah" in response and gave him thunderous applause. Qatib, through a clever combination of rhetoric, twisted logic and demagoguery, had just given his audience of disaffected, impressionable young men the ideological and quasi-moral sanction and legitimacy, in their own heads, to commit mass murder and blow people up. And, if truth be told, he followed in a tradition of demagogues like him in every religion and in every political ideology since history began.

Sadeq had also managed to place a bug in the same ante-room as before and the transcript also confirmed both that Khalid and Mohammed went back there with Sadeq after the meeting, but also, fired up by Qatib's rhetoric, they were eager to meet with him at the currently empty flat in Battlefield that Sadeq was the landlord of.

"All right," I spoke to the team after we'd all gone through the transcript, "Qatib has arranged to meet Khaled and Mohammed tomorrow night. Wattie, you and Tres will meet with Sadeq tonight to wire up the flat they're meeting in. Depending on the outcome of that get together I'll request Mr Mulrooney for surveillance on each of the boy's flats and we'll take it from there. Any questions?"

Tres asked, "Khaled lives in the middle of Govanhill surrounded by a large extensive family and Mohammed lives with his family in a leafy villa here in Pollokshields, are we getting support to tail them?"

She was referring to the fact that the five of us being white, soberly dressed and, with the exception of Tony Boyd the wrong side of 30, would stand out a mile in both these areas trying to plant a bug. Govanhill was a multi-ethnic, largely rundown area that had become a hotchpotch of different ethnic groups, asylum seekers and refugees while Pollokshields was a wealthy suburb where a lot of prosperous Glaswegian Asians had settled in Tres's leafy villas. In either case both men lived with their families and it would be difficult for us to gain access.

I replied to her, "Again, Tres, that'll be dependent on how Qatib's meeting with the two boys goes. But if the signs are go for an active terrorist cell in the making through Mr Mulrooney we'll get 'A' Branch assistance."

"We'll need it," she replied.

"I know," I said.

'A' Branch, among its many activities, specialised in getting access to premises to place bugs, sometimes through burglary and other times through a variety of deceptions. Since 9/11 and 7/7 'A' Branch had recruited extensively among Britain's ethnic communities. They would provide us with MI5 Asian and Islamic people who would be of assistance to us when required.

Danny Mackay asked, "Have we alerted CTC yet?" Danny was referring to the fact that if the operation was to proceed and we were able to catch the group about to commit a terrorist act be successful CTC, who were a combination of the former police Special Branch and anti-terrorism units, would actually make the arrests. He was ex CTC himself so it was natural he would ask that question.

"Too early yet, Danny, we've nothing to show at this stage. They'd either dismiss us out of hand or jump in and be all over it like a rash and move in too quick. We'd lose control. Sorry, Danny," I looked warily at him, "I know they're your ex-colleagues, but Hammy Andy never won any prizes at school for subtlety. The key with CTC is to judge when's the best time to bring them in and always make sure you're in charge of them. We're a wee bit away from that yet."

Danny raised a hand and said, "Totally understood boss," adding with a knowing grin "don't forget I worked under Hammy, sorry, Detective Inspector Anderson."

There were no further questions and after a final run-through of the operational details for the next few days and a brief pep talk from me about the momentous opportunity we had both to forestall an atrocity here in Glasgow and earn ourselves some rightfully deserved accolades and no doubt boosts to all our careers, we broke up enthused about the mission ahead.

*

It took longer to get Mulrooney's approval for Grand Minaret and with it 'A' Branch assistance than I'd originally thought. Dr Qatib was the reason for this. With Sadeq on the inside track Wattie and Tres had no problem placing three bugs in the rented flat in the district of Battlefield prior to his meeting with Khaled and Mohammed. In spite of its martial sounding name Battlefield (the name derived from the site of the battle of Langside in 1568 where Mary, Queen of Scots was defeated by the Regent Moray) was a residential suburb on Glasgow's south side. It mainly consisted of well-preserved red sandstone tenements in the well of a valley and rising up a stretched-out hill known as a drumlin carved out by retreating glaciers at the end of the last ice age; these were a typical feature of Glasgow's landscape.

The tenements were home to a mainly transient population of first-time owner-occupiers or renters, most of whom were working and out most of the day and hardly knew their often temporary neighbours and were used to lots of different people coming and going on a regular basis, which meant Battlefield was ideal territory for an intelligence service maintaining safe houses (as we had often in the area). Equally, it was perfect to host a meeting place-cum-base for a terrorist organisation.

The meeting went ahead with the two young men as planned, but Qatib was subtle, not to say downright cagey. Gone was the vibrant, soaring rhetoric about jihad and martyrdom. Instead Qatib concentrated on the boys' own lives. From Sadeq he'd learned of Khaled's troubled background and with him he focused on the importance of family in Islam and the need for families to stay together and for young men to respect their families. Khaled sheepishly replied that he had been recently staying out of trouble and trying to reconcile with his family, to which Qatib replied mundanely, "That's good". With Mohammed he concentrated on his studies and why he'd dropped out of university to which Mohammed responded adamantly that he wanted to devote his life to Allah.

"But Allah also wants you to love your family and by leaving university you broke your parents' heart and all their hopes and ambitions for you!" Qatib said to him almost as a rebuke. Mohammed didn't reply and appeared ashamed according to Sadeq who was present throughout the meeting and all the subsequent meetings. Qatib went on about the importance of devotion and loyalty to family and then abruptly ended the meeting but asked they get together again, same time, same place a week later. Somewhat confused and with dampened enthusiasm, they agreed.

The 'take' from the meeting was dreadful in terms of evidence needed to initiate a full blown anti-terrorist operation with the possible resources required. Qatib had come over as a cautious counsellor specialising in reconciling wayward young men with their families: a veritable pillar of the community; in the laconic words of Wattie Craig: "Fuck all there!"

The second meeting was even worse with Qatib going on about the importance of work and career for a good Muslim: Qatib the family counsellor had now become a virtual career advisor. Sadeq reported the two boys left in silence; it was clear this was not what they'd expected after the dynamism of Qatib's talks at the mosque.

Meeting number three heralded the beginnings of a different tack. Yes, family and career were important for a good Muslim; Qatib said he was the first to affirm that. But was there anything else that was equally as important, no, more important, he asked them? He had a copy of the *Koran* on a coffee table in front of them, the first time he'd produced the holy book in the flat.

"Devotion to Allah," Khaled said eagerly.

"Love of Allah!" Mohammed added equally as robustly.

"Yes, yes," Qatib replied nodding his head encouragingly, "but were devotion to and love of Allah more important than family and work?" he asked.

There was a moment's silence. The boys looked at each other not sure how to respond. Eventually Mohammed said haltingly, "Yes," echoed by Khaled with more conviction, "Allah is far more important."

"Wrong!" Qatib nearly shouted at them, before lowering his voice, "there is no either or here, no fork in the road between family and work on one side and Allah on the other. They are the same thing because when you devote your life to Allah you support your family and your work because only by devoting your life to Allah can you really love family and work and advance them. Your families are hard-working good people, but they live in a corrupt, decadent society. So when you work for that society you don't help your family, you work for Satan. But when you work for Allah you do.

"Remember also Satan and his accomplices, the infidels, have many ways of fooling honest, hard-working Muslims to work for them and unwittingly do their bidding. So, for instance Mohammed, you don't want to spend your time studying law or engineering or medicine for the infidel, do you?"

Mohammed shook his head with conviction, "No I don't!"

"No, you would rather work for Allah to further the cause for jihad and then, Allah permitting, study to help build a world of brotherhood and peace where Allah's laws, the moral laws for right conduct prevails, yes?"

"Yes, of course, totally," he responded enthusiastically.

"But of course your family, having been bombarded by Western propaganda that money, wealth and career are noble and a good education is the only way to achieve that, are naturally upset when their son turns his back on materialism. They don't see that their son, you Mohammed, have seen through the lies and illusions of infidel society; that you would only be helping the oppressors of true Islam by continuing your so-called studies.

"Gentlemen, you have both seen through the deception, you both know who the oppressors of our people are, who the enemy of Allah is. But, sadly often throughout history and especially the history of our faith, people like you, like *us* and I include our friend Sadeq here, are well in advance of the rest of our people and, with the help of the infidel's machinery of propaganda, they can resent us and be turned against us. Part of the sacrifice that comes with seeing through the delusion of this decadent corrupt cauldron that is Western society, of seeing clearly the duties and tasks of a jihadist Muslim, is to risk estrangement and even hostility from your friends, associates and your families.

"But remember the cause, for which you are struggling and fighting, is the most beautiful and radiant one as it is blessed by Allah and it is willed by Allah. Eventually, either in this world or the next, those friends and family will realise that you fought for them and you sacrificed for them because with Allah's help you *loved them*. But in the present..." Here he paused, stared deeply at both of them and took both their left hands in his. He resumed after a few moments, "here in the present, you may have to endure hostility from the ones you love most. It is part of the sacrifice, of the struggle of being in the advance guard of those creating a new world according to God's will. Of being a *holy warrior* in the building of that new world!"

He clasped hold of them and hugged them to him, like a father to two sons and said softly, "Praise be to Allah!" Still locked in the embrace they replied softly "Praise be to Allah!" When Qatib released them from the embrace, Sadeq reported later, both boys were tearful but re-enthused and reinvigorated in their convictions. Qatib had played it cleverly, almost teasingly, assessing their convictions, testing them and now beginning to build up to the point where they were entirely in his grasp and ready to move on to a new phase.

Meeting four developed this further. Qatib dwelt on the themes of sacrifice, of the necessity for the holy warrior to be apart from others, but not to attract too much suspicion. To Mohammed he spoke of the need to resume his studies, to go through the façade of going back to university. To Khaled he urged him to continue to stay out of trouble, to work hard in his father's butcher's shop as he had been lately. To both, he enjoined them to lay low, please their families and do nothing to attract attention.

During the fifth meeting, Qatib brought out a DVD which he played. It was a thirty minute film featuring in the main the tall, bearded figure of Ali al Hassan in flowing robes declaiming fervently and stridently in Arabic with English sub-titles on the subject of jihad and sacrifice interspersed frequently with dramatic footage of bombings and attacks from various theatres including Afghanistan, Iraq, Syria, Libya and Chechnya. Also shown on the DVD was the film of Mohammed Siddique Khan one of the 7/7

London bombers before the attacks explaining his motivations for the bombings as resulting from the West's attacks on Muslims. There were clips of other suicide bombers too and the film culminated in a rousing and passionate cry from al Hassan for young Muslims to get radicalised and join the holy warriors engaged in armed struggle – he rhymed off a list of conflicts – across the globe.

Ali al Hassan was often quoted as the rising star in al Qaeda after the death of Bin Laden. He was credited with ending disputes and in-fighting within al Qaeda and its various factions, of bringing a new sharper coherence and dynamism to the organisation; certainly al Hassan's rhetoric roused the boys who spontaneously applauded at the end of the DVD. Qatib spent the rest of the meeting elaborating on the issues raised in the film and "The brilliant work, inspiration, leadership and unity which Ali al Hassan has brought to the mujahedeen and which has sharply intensified the struggle recently."

We knew meeting number six was going to be the biggie and Qatib didn't disappoint. Right at the start he told the two boys it was to be the last meeting "for a while" as "he had work to do elsewhere", but didn't specify. The boys looked disappointed at this news but also concerned. He went on to sum up all he had spoken about over the last few meetings: jihad, struggle, devotion to Allah, the vanguard of the holy warriors and mujahedeen leading in that struggle for a new and better world and so on. After an hour he asked them what they were going to do for the struggle. They replied almost imploringly that they would do anything required to assist the struggle.

"Anything?" he queried.

"Anything!" Khaled replied stridently.

With a quizzical air Qatib asked, "Why, what do you mean by anything?"

"Jihad," Khaled responded."

"Sacrifice, martyrdom," Mohammed added even more stridently.

Qatib stayed silent for a few moments, while continuing to look at them closely. Finally, he asked, "Do you want to become holy warriors?"

"Yes," they both replied.

"Do you want to be part of jihad?"

"Yes!"

"To take part in the struggle?"

"Yes!"

"To sacrifice and embrace martyrdom?"

"Yes, yes!"

He clasped hold of them. "My friends are you prepared to help in the struggle here in Scotland, in this city?"

Mohammed spoke. "Doctor, this is a corrupt city, a very immoral place. Our people are being crushed in the lands of the Caliph, but here they are asleep and seduced into thinking they have a good life and turning their backs on their fellow Muslims. I would want to bring the armed struggle here to wake them from that and bring fear to the infidel!"

Khaled nodded throughout Mohammed's declaration and merely said when he had finished, "I totally agree with Mohammed."

Qatib's face broke out in a soft smile, he turned to Sadeq, "And your thoughts?"

"If I was their age over again, I would have no hesitation in becoming a holy warrior."

"Age is no barrier to martyrdom, Sadeq," Qatib said sharply. "But we're not expecting you to be a holy warrior, but you can be of valuable assistance to the struggle."

"Count me in," Sadeq responded almost lamely.

Qatib turned back to the boys. "I think both of you are strong and ready to carry out activities on behalf of the global struggle. You will need training and preparation and I will ensure you get that. Our war requires that warriors preparing operations in the West select their own targets and after training that is what I will help you to do. For now, from this moment onwards you must think, act and behave as if you were in an enemy country which is in fact what you are in. Trust and confide in no one but each other, myself and Sadeq. You are very privileged young men for you are about to enter the sacred calling of the holy warrior. Praise be to Allah the merciful!"

"Praise be to Allah the merciful!"

The recruitment had happened; the boys were in and eager to be on board with Sadeq there to assist. Result. From now on Qatib told them he would arrange to get in touch with them. They would use different locations to meet on each occasion. He would train them how to spot they were being followed and basic techniques to shake off a tail. There were to do nothing to arouse suspicion among family and friends just keep their heads down, no talking of jihad or martyrdom. They, of course, should still attend mosque, but do nothing to bring attention to themselves. "The eyes and ears of the British Intelligence services are everywhere," he sternly warned, which of course brought a smile to our faces when we read that in the transcript.

"Above all, and I cannot emphasise this too much, when you are on active service there has to be *NO* communication by mobile phone except for the ones I give you which are to be used once and then discarded immediately. Likewise, no internet activity. We meet up in safe locations, decide on what we're going to do, do it and meet up afterwards and so on. We take the war to the infidel, but we cannot use his technology for he has that under his control. We go back to basics and through that we will, God willing, always be ahead of him."

After the meeting and after the two boys had left energised and motivated with the prospect of the great struggle they were about to embark on, Qatib made it clear to Sadeq that he trusted him and would need him for "resources" and as a helper to aid Khaled and Mohammed. Sadeq said he was completely committed to this and would carry out any instruction the doctor asked of him. That was important for us. Sadeq had not offered to initiate anything, only to follow orders. It was then Sadeq's turn to be embraced by Qatib. They parted with Qatib promising to get in touch with him and the boys "soon."

*

My long-awaited meeting with Mulrooney was brief. I updated him on progress over the six meetings so far and requested that Grand Minaret be moved up to an 'Alert' status. There were four status levels. 'Notification' was when something had come to our attention, usually through an informer or 'Joe.' Something that piqued interest and might be worth pursuing. This had happened after Sadeq had informed us about the radical preacher Siddique's activities at the mosque and Dr Qatib's 'talks'. The next status level was 'Watch' where the Joe was recruited to literally watch a specific target and we could allocate a team to assist him. 'Watch' had been initiated after the meeting in Largs and Grand Minaret had been launched. Now activity was underway and the boys had been recruited as a potential terrorist cell the next level was 'Active' and meant I could request assistance from 'A' Branch, other sections of MI-5 and other agencies when needed such as CTC and SIS. The final level was 'Interdict' where a criminal and terrorist act was about to be perpetrated and we would move in to arrest. We in MI-5 never actually arrested anyone; that would be left to CTC, but all the background information and evidence that would hopefully lead to a conviction would be prepared by us and presented anonymously in court.

After studying the transcripts from the six meetings and the overall background summary I had prepared, Mulrooney said, "This looks good, Eddie, it looks solid."

"Thanks, Sir," I replied. We were sitting in his austere office in the Shields, the only personal touch in the room being three pictures each of his wife and two daughters.

"You're sure about your Joe, Sadeq?"

"Absolutely, Sir, he's been totally reliable for over twenty years."

"Drugs, money laundering, counterfeiting yes, but this is terrorism, perhaps a different league?"

"You're forgetting Possil, Sir and the connection with the Provos which he helped to nip in the bud!"

"Of course," Mulrooney remembered and conceded. "And he's not overstepped the mark, nothing that a good defence QC could pin our balls to the floor over re entrapment?"

"You've read the transcript. Everything Sadeq's done so far and everything he will do on this operation, should we proceed with it, Sir, has been at Qatib's request. He's a past master at keeping on the right side of entrapment."

"Yes, I agree." Mulrooney stayed silent for a few moments contemplating the transcripts and my background briefing before, a smile emerging from his twinkling hazel eyes, he said, "I am going to request Thames House (MI-5 head office in London) that we move Grand Minaret up to Alert status. Get me a brief paper on what you need."

"Sir, I've already done that." I moved a folder across the desk and extracted from it a three-page paper I had written outlining the resources I reckon we would need with a projection of the costs likely to be incurred. Mulrooney smiled ruefully at my presumption and rose from his chair. I rose with him.

"Ok, Eddie, I'll send all your material down with a request to go to Active. I should get a response in no later than forty-eight hours." He offered his hand. "Good luck, Eddie. It's not every day you get a chance to track an al-Qaeda terrorist cell in the making and then bust it before the swines commit an atrocity! The least you and your team will get after this is a commendation. No one out there will know what you did, but you will have the personal satisfaction that you saved countless lives and prevented appalling suffering."

As I left his office I felt a strange mixture of elation combined with the thought that Mulrooney's encouraging words were almost identical to the pep talk I'd given Sadeq in Largs. I walked along the corridor to my team waiting in the conference room and informed them of Mulrooney's backing. They were delighted. We all knew that with Mulrooney's recommendation together with the material we'd already gathered, that permission to proceed from London HQ should be virtually automatic, which it was just over a day later

*

Operations, like life, are comprised of long periods of tedium punctuated by short, sharp bouts of frenetic activity. Grand Minaret was no exception. Qatib would surface in Glasgow roughly once every six weeks. Sadeq would be alerted to his visit by a single, innocuous text message which Qatib had told him about at their previous meeting. This message was sent to a cheap Nokia phone which, Sadeq was instructed, was never to be used for any other purpose than to receive this text. If the text was in any way different from what Qatib had said it would be, Sadeq should assume the worst; that their mission had been infiltrated, make no attempt at any further contact and abort. If the text matched, which of course, it always did, Sadeq would then send a second equally innocuous text to Khaled and Mohammed on two separate phones supplied by Qatib to them again only for this purpose. At the previous meeting Qatib would have arranged with Sadeq and the boys the date and time for their next rendezvous. Sadeq's text to the boys confirmed that the meeting was on. The same principle applied: Should Sadeq's texts vary the boys were to assume the mission was compromised and abandon it.

On the appointed day of the meeting Qatib would turn up at the back entrance of the mosque two hours before and be driven by Sadeq to one of his many flats that were temporarily empty between lets. The choice of flat for each meeting was made by Sadeq, known only to him and was different each time. After depositing Qatib, Sadeq drove back to the mosque and fetched Khaled and Mohammed who were instructed to be at the mosque exactly an hour before the meeting. Sadeq would change vehicle and drive them to the flat he'd chosen for that occasion. Qatib, therefore, would have no direct contact with the boys between meetings: Sadeq would serve as the cut-out. Equally, neither Qatib nor the boys knew which flat Sadeq had chosen for the meeting. But by the same token, Sadeq and the boys knew nothing of Qatib's whereabouts or activities between meetings. He simply materialised in Glasgow on the day of the rendezvous and disappeared again after the meeting. At the meeting Qatib would collect the three primitive Nokia phones and hand out another three. He would inform Sadeq the content of the next message and the date and time of the next meeting. Before departing the meeting, Sadeq would tell the boys the content of his message to them. All three would memorise their messages; they would never commit them to paper.

The first four meetings after the 'recruitment' took on a regular pattern. Qatib, Sadeq and the boys would embrace each other and the doctor would ask Khaled and Mohammed how they were to which they responded fervently that they were "up for it" and still eager to embark on holy war and jihad. Qatib had already received an update on the boys from Sadeq in the hour before delivering them to the rendezvous flat as he was keeping a watching eye on them at the mosque. After the catch-up Qatib would show a DVD which invariably featured a mixture of Ali al-Hassan delivering another passionate oration on jihad and holy war interspersed with footage of the armed struggle. This was the only opportunity the boys had to watch these DVDs as Qatib had warned them not to keep or watch them at home or anywhere but the meetings. After the DVD Qatib would talk about practical issues such as counter-surveillance, watching for people tailing them while constantly reiterating the absolute imperative to avoid any internet activity that could attract suspicion to them such as visiting jihadist websites as these were scrupulously monitored by Western intelligence agencies and would be traced back to them. The meeting would end with Qatib reading passages from the holy *Koran* that appeared to encourage jihad and the duty of a good Muslim to commit to holy war. Afterwards Sadeq would drive the boys to the mosque. When he got back to the flat Qatib would have vanished.

The great paradox of terrorism and counter-terrorism in the 21st century was that just when anyone with a mobile phone, laptop, PC or IPAD could communicate instructions, access information and commit resources virtually instantaneously and to an extent unparalleled in human history, terrorist organisations were abandoning them precisely because they rendered their users vulnerable to detection and interception. Every one of those devices was a walking beacon allowing trackers to detect the user's location, even when switched off. Using the internet required a specific IP address that allowed any monitor to trace all website traffic accessed and build a detailed profile of the user's internet activity. Sure, terrorist organisations such as al-Qaeda had attempted through sophisticated encryption to disguise their member's online activity, which had worked in the short-term. But intelligence services had always been able to catch-up by employing equally sophisticated decryption methods.

The result: most terrorist organisations now restricted use of mobile phones to a bare minimum, effectively prohibited any internet activity relating to their operations apart from propaganda material and concentrated on person-to-person contact through cut-outs and prior arranged messages. In effect active terrorists were reverting back to a world prior to the internet and instantaneous global communications. And, in response, the counter-terrorist agencies charged with combatting and disrupting them such as MI5 had been forced to adapt by reversing the emphasis on Commint (Communications Intelligence) and Sigint (Signals Intelligence) which had prevailed since the 1960s. Instead, the focus was back on Humint (Human Intelligence). Good old cloak and dagger spies, infiltrators and narks, the lifeblood of the secret world for millennia, had proven their innate superiority over non-human and highly vulnerable technology. Sadeq was a classic case in point.

For all Qatib's clever attempts at security and compartmentalisation, it took only one human infiltrator in the set-up, i.e. Sadeq, to render all the security procedures redundant. As long as Qatib continued to send the messages to Sadeq and entrusted him to contact the boys and arrange the meeting places, the whole operation was exposed and we could watch every aspect of it unfold stage-by-stage. Of course before each meeting Sadeq would let myself or one of the team into the chosen flat to place some simple but undetectable bugs which gave us a complete account of what went on. After the first meeting we were able to follow Qatib walking out of the flat alone after the rest had left. By checking the street name where the flat was located he consulted a Glasgow *A-Z* and walked to the nearest main road where he hailed a taxi to Glasgow Central Station, the city's main-line rail terminus to the south.

But he didn't enter the station immediately. When delivering his 'talks' at the mosque Qatib had been dressed in typical male Muslim garb of long flowing white robes and turban. For the meetings with the boys he wore flannel slacks, casual jackets, trainers and no headdress on his thinning dark hair; apparel typical of a middle-aged to elderly man with a paunch. On leaving the taxi Qatib would go into a crowded coffee bar opposite the station. He would order a coffee, take a seat and after a few minutes get up and go to the gent's toilet, which was located in the basement and served as an overflow for the café but which was either invariably empty or had few people sitting there. This was clever because on leaving the gent's he would notice anyone new in the basement and clock the face. In the gent's Qatib changed into a business suit, patent leather shoes and a brown wig, his casual gear in a black hold-all which he was carrying.

Danny Mackay almost missed him the first time Qatib did this. He followed him into the café and witnessed the rather scruffy casually dressed figure of Qatib going down to the basement after ordering a coffee. Danny took a seat at the back of the café while 'reading' a paper and generally blending in when he espied, ten minutes later, an immaculately dressed be-suited businessman emerge from the basement. Danny was about to take his eyes off him but noticed the holdall; it was the same as Qatib's and radioed the details surreptitiously into his concealed mike. Tony Boyd, waiting at a bus stop across the street, picked him up and followed him through a side-entrance to the station onto a departing London-bound train. Tony kept an eye on the platform in case Qatib did a switch, while Tres Martindale quickly bought two tickets for her and Tony with five minutes to go before the train departed. At Carlisle, London based colleagues joined the train. They relieved Tony and Tres and followed Qatib to London and kept watch on him as he went to a nondescript apartment in Islington. The 'Activate' status level had brought in extra resources and we now knew where Qatib was based and were able to follow his movements before coming to and leaving Glasgow.

Qatib kept to the same MO throughout his visits to Glasgow. He would dress in a smart blazer or jacket for the journey up to Glasgow, change into the casual gear at the coffee bar in the station toilets and then change for a third time into a suit before leaving the city. The doctor was good at counter-surveillance and disguise; he was practicing his own MosBerBel rules and he even made a rudimentary sweep for bugs at each of Sadeq's flats. But he wasn't good enough for an expert counter-surveillance team and he never once cottoned on to our tails or found any of our bugs as I prided myself on the expertise and quality of my team.

There was a file on Qatib in MI5's voluminous Registry in Thames House. Qatib wasn't his real name which was Fayol al Haq. He was in his sixties and originally from Egypt where he'd obtained a doctorate in law from Cairo University, but where he'd also been arrested for activities with the Muslim Brotherhood. He'd spent time in prison there and been radicalised before, on release, being deported by the Egyptian authorities. He'd made his way to

Afghanistan and joined the mujahedeen fighting the Soviet occupation forces. This was the late 80s when the Afghan resistance were viewed as freedom fighters in the cold war struggle against communism. When the Soviets left Afghanistan the mujahedeen fell to fighting in internecine warfare among themselves and al Hag, who by now had adopted the alias of Qatib subsequently adding the Dr to the name, fled to London in the early 1990s.

'Qatib' was one of a huge influx of political activists and Islamic militants who came to London in the 90s. This was before 9/11 and just after the cold war when most of them had been feted by the west as good anti-communists. Britain had no war against Islam and at the time there was no suggestion that people like Qatib could pose any threat to the UK or the West in general. In those halcyon days just after the war on communism Western liberal democracy appeared to be in unassailable ascendancy having apparently seen off all competitors. The reality was Qatib and people like him regarded Western liberalism with as much enmity as communism; both were manifestations of the infidel, utterly corrupt and decadent. But this was before 9/11. It was only after that, that the wave of Islamic militants who had come into the country attracted interest. Qatib had made contact with radical preachers throughout the country and brought himself to the notice of MI5's informers (such as Sadeq). His MI5 Registry file noted these details, but otherwise, information in his file was quite sparse and Qatib hadn't really brought himself to our or seemingly any other intelligence service's attention. Now that Qatib's Glasgow activities were exposed, our London colleagues were surveilling him and 'A' Branch had been able to place a bug in his Islington apartment.

'A' Branch staff had also made themselves useful here in Glasgow. Both the Khaled and Mohammed households had experienced a sudden loss of all internet connections. Within minutes of the loss in the early evening, both households had 'British Telecom' engineers complete with ID badges appearing at their doorstep. Over each families' protests that BT wasn't their internet provider the 'engineers' explained that there was a "technical routing problem" at the local exchange which was disrupting both cable and Wi Fi internet connections irrespective of who the specific provider was and they needed access to the routers in the house to resolve it. Both families bought this and thus the 'engineers' wandered through the chaotic but friendly Khaled family flat in Govanhill and the more sedate and formal setting of the solid Mohammed villa in Pollokshields apparently checking and repairing a main cable connection in each household. They were in and out of both in minutes and of course all internet connections were restored; the suspicions of neither family, including Khaled and Mohammed, aroused. "Blink and you would have missed them; a class act," said Danny Mackay admiringly as we followed their radio traffic to each other back at the Shields. The 'BT engineers', alias 'A' Branch staff had placed a sophisticated all-encompassing tap in both households which would now capture all Wi Fi and cable internet traffic as well as all landline and mobile phone conversations emanating from both. Should anyone in either of the two houses phone BT's faults and repairs line about temporary loss of internet connections because of faults at the exchange and visits from engineers to those specific addresses, the operator would have directed them to a polite but authoritative second 'operator' who would have confirmed the authenticity of the faults.

The intercepts on both houses were a back-up precaution. Both of the boys complied with Qatib's instructions: there were no visits to radical Islamist websites least of all al-Qaeda linked ones, by either. Khaled stuck to a diet of martial arts, YouTube and porn while Mohammed hardly used the internet at all and when he did, did so exclusively for pious sites on the *Koran*. All phone conservations by either were also unrelated to Qatib, holy war and jihad; they never contacted each other by phone.

And so it went on routinely for months. Sadeq reported, and we were able to verify this from the intercepts, that in the brief snatches of conversation he had with the boys as he drove them to the flat, the boys were becoming frustrated at the lack of action, "fed up", as Khaled succinctly put it "with endless fucking videos and talks!" So it was to the boys' great relief that in November, six months after the meetings had begun, Qatib announced, without ceremony right at the start that he thought they were ready to embark on jihad.

The boys perked up, eyes filled with eager enthusiasm and even more alert than normal to Qatib's every word. He explained that if they were ready, then he was ready to send them for training to Muslim brothers who would teach them the arts of holy war.

"Are you ready?"

"Yes, yes, of course!" they almost screamed at him, Khaled adding a touch of Glaswegian directness:

"You fucking bet we are, doctor!"

Qatib smiled in satisfaction and went on to tell them there would be no more meetings for four months, because in two weeks they would be flying from Glasgow to Islamabad, the capital of Pakistan. From there they would be picked up and taken to the north-western province of North Waziristan, a tribal, mountainous area bordering on Afghanistan where the Pakistani authorities' writ was weak and the Taliban had strong support including bases and training camps. It was to one of these camps that the boys were to be taken. Once there, they would be given instruction in fire-arms, explosives procurement training and handling, counter-detection, self-defence close-quarter combat and further instruction in the true words of the Prophet, the venerable legacy of the Sheik (referring to Osama Bin Laden) and the teachings of Ali al Hassan. "All you will need to become a true holy warrior and engage in jihad and..." He paused, studying them both, before saying the single word slowly, "martyrdom."

That didn't faze the boys, they were too fired up and delighted at the prospect in front of them, but Mohammed did enquire, "Doctor, what will we tell our families?"

Qatib immediately replied, "Tell them you're going to study Islamic law and business practice in a Muslim country, Pakistan, the knowledge gained in this will assist you in a venture here in Scotland to establish an Islamic charity that will work with people from the Pakistani Islamic community who have fallen on hard times." The boys both looked perplexed at this. Qatib turned to Sadeq.

"You are vital to this. You must visit the families, you know the fathers, they go to mosque with you." Sadeq nodded in agreement. "And you must give this story real credibility the families must believe you and then they will believe the boys and put up no resistance to them travelling to Pakistan."

I had to admire Qatib. Not only was he a past master at stretching out the meetings, slowly building up the ante, tantalising the boys until, their patience nearly exhausted, he would suddenly push them onto the next phase and they would grab at it eagerly and unquestioningly, but he had also constructed an excellent legend or alibi for why they were going to Pakistan. Khaled's family wanted their wayward, directionless son to settle down. Mohammed's family desired that their suddenly withdrawn but studious son knuckle down and get involved in something serious. Sadeq, well known to both families, a good Muslim and family man, but also a successful businessman, would provide the patina of respectability for the legend, the aura of certainty, that would allow the families to wholeheartedly support it and endorse their sons' sudden, unexpected but positive moves towards settling down to a good, solid career. Of course, Qatib, wouldn't have to worry how, upon their return to Glasgow, the boys would be able to sustain the fiction of their non-existent involvement in a bogus charity for disadvantaged Pakistani Muslims in Scotland. If all went to plan, within weeks of their return, both boys would be dead.

The prospect of imminent death and martyrdom was, however, greeted by the boys with evident enthusiasm, as on the drive back to the mosque there was a lot of high-fiving and high spirits between them with the usually serious minded Mohammed joining in as much as Khaled.

*

We too engaged in our own form of high-fives. That is the team and I got pissed in a safe house in the west-end: it was important for us that we also celebrated this important milestone in the evolution of Grand Minaret, but not before I'd met with Mulrooney to update him. Predictably, he was delighted with progress. Following my meeting with him, he reported personally to his superior in London who arranged for him to report to the Joint Terrorism Analysis Centre (JTAC), the main body responsible for collating information on and co-ordinating responses to terrorist threats in the UK. As well as MI5, JTAC included representatives from SIS, the Government's communications agency GCHQ and Counter-Terrorism Command's HQ in London. JTAC were impressed at the level of control we'd established over the developing terrorist cell in Glasgow without, of course, crossing over that all-important line into entrapment.

They were particularly pleased with the extent of infiltration and intelligence we'd obtained. The hallmark of al-Qaeda operations in the west were their elusiveness. Like thieves in the night al-Qaeda operatives like Qatib would recruit vulnerable young men and occasionally women to carry out terrorist activities. Unlike organisations such as the IRA or the Basque group ETA, they would have no roots within the native Islamic community from where they were recruited, almost all the members of which would be repulsed if they knew what the fledging terrorists were up to and would condemn them in the strongest terms were they to succeed in carrying out their plans. Consequently, al-Qaeda cells were usually isolated, and removed from the native community operating completely clandestinely. Which meant, as with the Glasgow Airport or the 7/7 London bombers, they could appear to come out of nowhere and literally self-destruct, leaving carnage in their wake. Being ephemeral and having no base in their community meant it was absolutely imperative to have an informer in there at an early stage; which was why Sadeq was of such importance, and such a star. To match their appreciation JTAC allocated further resources to us if we needed it and commended us for the progress achieved thus far.

More importantly and practically for us, Mulrooney met with his counterparts at SIS (Secret Intelligence Service) to give it it's official name, Britain's foreign intelligence agency. It would be the SIS station or office in Islamabad that would monitor the boys' arrival in Pakistan and SIS 'assets' in North Waziristan and, hopefully, the training camp the boys would be going to, would keep an eye on them. Grand Minaret was becoming international. Not only were SIS involved now, but through JTAC the Americans would be alerted. And that meant not only the CIA, but the labyrinth of US intelligence agencies such as the NSA (National Security Agency - the US equivalent to GCHQ) - and the alphabet soup of outfits and agencies attached to the US Defense Department i.e. the Pentagon, all of whom would have counter-terrorism interests and assets in the lawless border region of Pakistan and Afghanistan where the boys were heading to. From Govanhill and Pollokshields the boys, unbeknown to them, were stirring up international interest in their activities.

In the weeks before their departure Sadeq continued to live up to his star billing by visiting both the boys' homes and talking to their parents about the venture they were about to engage in with the bogus charity. Sadeq gave the story life and talked with conviction about the project which required the boys to study Islamic law and business practice in Pakistan before coming back home and setting up the charity here. The boys would learn so much and assist such a good cause and the families bought it because they wanted to and because Sadeq was so convincing and they knew him and trusted him.

He admitted to me after the visits he felt uncomfortable about deceiving the families and setting the boys up like this. I consoled him by reminding him that without him, Qatib and the people behind him would almost certainly have the boys killed by completing their mission. This way, in spite of the shame that would befall them, the families would still have their boys alive, albeit they would be many years in a cell.

In the second week of November, Khaled and Mohammed were driven by Sadeq to Glasgow Airport where they boarded a flight to Islamabad. In the departure lounge they were surrounded by fellow Pakistanis heading back to family reunions or vacations or business trips or a combination of all three. Apart from a certain aloofness, they did not look out of place. They used their own passports as they had no record of subversive, least of all terrorist activity, behind them and after their return they weren't going to be leaving the country again. At their last meeting Qatib had handed out paperwork which seemed to verify the bona fides of the charitable 'foundation' the boys were allegedly going to including an office address in Islamabad and an address and name of a contact they would be staying with if asked the purpose of their visit either here or in Pakistan. It was this same documentation that Sadeq had flourished when he'd went to see their parents about the good endeavour their sons were embarking on.

They boarded their flight unimpeded and the plane took off into a wan Scottish autumn sky heading for South Asia.

*

They went to a training camp run by a combination of Taliban and al-Qaeda fighters located twenty miles from the Afghanistan border. Their progress, from arrival in Islamabad where they were met with 'officials' from the charitable foundation, an overnight stay in the city and three days' long journey to the camp was uneventful. They stayed in the camp for three months. I got regular brief updates, usually weekly, on what was happening from Mulrooney who in turn was getting them from SIS and their various sources.

Life at the camp, based on the sparse information from the briefings, was very like what Qatib had said it would be. Very early rise, an ascetic diet, prayers, readings and interpretations from the Koran which of course emphasised jihad and martyrdom and exposure to talks and associations with Taliban and al-Qaeda fighters who were veterans of various conflicts: Syria, Iraq Chechnya, Libya, Bosnia in the 90s, Palestine etc. The real meat was the firearms and explosives training. They were taught how to assemble, maintain and fire handguns as well as basic training in machine guns and heavier weapons and target practice. But the real focus of their training, apart from constant immersion in religious instruction and al-Qaeda ideology, was in explosives. The boys were taught the ingredients and exact measures required to bring fertilisers and chemicals such as acetone peroxide, the infamous "mother of Satan" which had caused such devastation in the 7/7 London bombings and other attacks, together. For security reasons they were taught the necessity of purchasing the chemicals in small quantities from different stores, while minimising exposure to CCTV cameras when visiting those stores. They were shown how to handle and mix the various chemicals when brought together and how to reduce the inherent instability of the chemicals, particularly acetone peroxide, when transporting them in back-packs. They were shown a number of gruesome videos of suicide bombers from either CCTV footage, mobile phone cameras or other cameras that happened to be in the vicinity. The footage had been edited to illustrate in vivid close-up during the seconds before detonation, how the "holy warrior martyr soldier of jihad" had set about pulling a cord on the back pack which detonated the bomb. They practised carrying backpacks and familiarised themselves with attaching and subsequently pulling cords for when they would be carrying out the real thing. Complimenting this they were given lessons on counter-surveillance particularly in crowded locations such as railway stations.

Although SIS informers watched over them from a distance during the three months the boys were in the camp, they could only really report on the content of their training. They couldn't get close enough to them to assess their morale or how they were coping and fitting in with the strict regimen of the camp. I was concerned that exposure to unremitting prayer, poor diet, endless talks and constant instruction might put Khaled and Mohammed off so that when they returned home they would abandon the whole thing and flit back to a normal life and the bosom of their families. This had happened before and months and sometimes years of patient surveillance work was nullified overnight as the fledgling holy warriors unceremoniously fled the cause the moment they arrived back on home turf.

I was also concerned that Grand Minaret might be literally blown apart by an American drone attack. There had been quite a few drone attacks on similar camps in the area and in spite of informing the US agencies about Grand Minaret, the imperatives and opportunity of taking out a fully operational terrorist training camp might have greater priority for any of up to half-a dozen US intelligence agencies than the need to look-out for two Glaswegian wannabe suicide bombers. I could only hope that the need to protect and maintain the flow of information from their own presumed assets in the camp would stay the Americans' hands.

Finally, I was also worried that our surveillance and interest in the boys would get back to the main local Pakistani intelligence service, the ISI, or Inter-Services Intelligence agency which had a reputation of working both sides: the West and al-Qaeda. If word leaked from ISI that the boys were in fact unwitting assets of the British they would be eliminated, but not before being savagely interrogated to see what they knew. I wanted Khaled and Mohammed locked in a cell in a Scottish prison not blown to pieces, tortured or more prosaically, bored to death and deterred from martyrdom.

I needn't have worried. In the second week of February, Mulrooney got word from SIS. The boys had left the camp. Three days later they were back in Islamabad. SIS Passport Control at the airport had noted tickets had been bought for them on a Glasgow-bound Air Emirates flight. Unmolested by drones or leaks, the boys were coming home and the team and I would resume control.

*

On the day the boys boarded their return flight in Pakistan, Sadeq received a terse text from Qatib on one of the primitive phones he'd been told to keep at his side. The message simply read *"Friends coming home"*. Sadeq immediately looked up the Emirates Airlines arrival times at Glasgow Airport on the internet. He also alerted me who instructed him to meet the boys. Their flight landed in the late evening of a crisp, cold late winter day, but the boys would be accustomed to freezing, biting weather after their time in the camp amidst the mountains of north-west Pakistan. Unimpeded through customs, Sadeq with little fanfare greeted them and drove them home to their families.

Any doubts I'd entertained about their commitment or dedication to the cause of jihad after their time as guests of al-Qaeda were unfounded. Though they said little on the drive back from the airport, mainly owing to tiredness, what brief answers they made to Sadeq's enquires about their time 'away' made it clear they were both profoundly affected by the experience and eager to get on with a 'mission' now they were home, or as Khaled put it back in "the heartland of the infidel." He dropped them off at the mosque and noticed in his rear view mirror that they firmly embraced each other before parting.

At their last get-together before the journey to Pakistan in November Qatib had arranged a follow-up meeting for the three of them in late February, some two weeks after the boys' return. As usual Sadeq drove them from the mosque to the meeting with Qatib. Sadeq reported that they were more voluble about their journey and experience abroad this time. They were proud to have been among holy warriors, to have been taught by them and were desperate to fight for Islam. They were especially disparaging about their 'so-called' fellow Moslems in the West who'd gone soft and been corrupted and even made some contemptuous remarks about their own families which made Sadeq, a proud father and grandfather, bristle. At one point on a busy street while waiting for traffic lights to change on the way to meet Qatib, Khaled gestured at the bustling throng of people on the pavements beside them:

"Look at those fucking sheep, doing what they're told, we'll fucking show them!"

"Yeah," Mohammed joined in, "we're going to wake this city up, by the will of Allah."

Qatib embraced them when he arrived and spent most of the meeting debriefing them about the camp. He was especially interested in what they'd learned about preparing, assembling and carrying explosives and asked some detailed questions about this. He appeared satisfied with their answers and said they'd "learned very well" and were now ready "soon, very soon" to undertake a mission for jihad. When both implored him to say how soon that would be, he merely asked them for forbearance and patience. When I met Sadeq after the meeting he said the boys had become very serious, there was an austere gleam in their eyes and any residual quirkiness or humour Khaled may have had left-over from his tear-away days had vanished, until he and Mohammed acted like clones of each other, He summed this up by remarking, bitterly:

"They've taken these boys and turned them into fanatical zealots!"

"Listen Sadeq," I responded to him, "prison will get that out of them, we'll get them back. They'll probably be released when in their late forties' and get back a few decades of their lives, mebbie they can even warn other kids of the danger of falling for this claptrap."

"I hope you're right, Mr Lomax."

We waited another month for the all-important next meeting which we sensed would be the critical one where the boys would be asked to embark on a 'mission' for jihad. As usual, there was no communication between them. We still had intercepts from the boys' homes which showed nothing unusual or in the slightest related to terrorism. Even Khaled's downloading of porn ceased. The only topic of interest that was picked up was the two families' enquiries about when their respective sons would start work with the charity for destitute Pakistanis, to which they both gave the rehearsed response that they were waiting for an important official from the charity to come to Scotland sometime in the next few weeks, which for now appeared to appease the families.

Meanwhile Ali al Hassan's ascendancy in the ranks of al-Qaeda continued. He was credited with bringing together and unifying all the various regional branches of the group such as al-Qaeda in the Maghreb, the Arabian Peninsula, al Nusra in Syria and Islamic State in Iraq which had tended to drift away and become effectively independent, steadily back towards coming under a unified command. If he wasn't the de facto leader already, he soon would be. His video appearances on Western media were becoming more commonplace, reminiscent of those of the 'Sheikh' i.e. Bin Laden. He was single-handedly revitalising al-Qaeda's image and appealing to many, young disaffected Muslim men in the Middle-East, the West and elsewhere.

On a rainy Tuesday night at the beginning of April, almost a year since their first meeting, Qatib, Sadeq and the boys met for the last time. It was held in the same Battlefield flat the doctor had held his first meeting with the boys outside of the mosque. There was a tangible air of expectation, which the transcripts didn't do justice to. Qatib reiterated old themes of martyrdom and the necessity for jihad to bring about the restoration of the caliphate and the paramount importance of striking at the soft underbelly of the infidel in the West. He asked them if they were ready to do this. They replied fervently that they were.

"Here in Glasgow?"

"Yes, here in Glasgow!"

"And to become martyrs for jihad?"

"It is an honour and a duty for a holy warrior to die for Allah," said Khaled. "Allah has willed it. We have travelled far and been trained by the holy warriors, Allah has chosen us."

Mohammed took up the theme. "There is no life for us to go back to."

Satisfied, Qatib then asked them to consider what the best targets would be in a city like Glasgow that would cause maximum disruption and damage. They talked through various options, including bars and nightclubs, shopping malls and sports events but they kept coming back to transport. Qatib explained that Muslim men, either together or singly, might stand out in clubs and bars. Similarly, being seated or standing in, say, a football stadium with backpacks or bags might attract attention from bystanders or CCTV operators before they had time to detonate their loads. Buses, trains and stations were a different matter where backpacks and bags were normal. Qatib thus steered the deliberations towards a suicide bombing on the transport system. The next question was when and where. Qatib asked, though he almost certainly knew the answer himself, which were the mainline train stations in Glasgow. Like most Glaswegians who holidayed or travelled abroad but rarely ventured around their own country, Khaled and Mohammed knew the answers, but had only a vague notion of where the trains from those stations went to.

"Queen Street for eh," Khaled began before Mohammed put in: "Edinburgh."

"And the north, the Highlands," Khaled finished.

"And then there's Central for England, London and that," Mohammed added.

And that's how the targets were selected. Queen Street and Central Stations, both mainline termini for destinations to the north and the south respectively, but also major hubs for Glasgow's extensive commuter services to its suburbs, the largest such system in the British Isles outside London.

It was agreed that two suicide bombings or 'acts of vengeance against the infidel that afforded entry to paradise' would occur on the second Wednesday in April. Khaled would set his off in the concourse of Queen Street while Mohammed would detonate his amidst Central Station. Sadeq would drive them to the stations. Qatib advised them to carry out a reconnaissance first: each man wearing a backpack to do a walk-through each station, becoming familiar with pulling the ripcord that would set off their bombs. But he instructed them sternly to purchase the ingredients for the explosives in small quantities at various shops. He asked Sadeq if they could use the Battlefield flat to store the equipment and assemble the bombs, including the acetone peroxide, electronics and circuit boards.

I remember blanching at the sheer recklessness of this. Two young lads having spent only a few hours being taught bomb-making in a training camp in Pakistan were going to assemble two bombs in a flat on the top floor of a tenement in the middle of a busy residential district of Glasgow! I resolved there and then that as soon as they'd brought the first batch of acetone peroxide to the flat, we'd go through the door team- handed and nab them: with the transcripts, the intercepts and the physical evidence we'd more than enough on them.

The reconnaissance was arranged for the following Wednesday, a week before the attacks. The meeting concluded with recitations from the *Koran*, drinking cups of sweet tea and much embracing as they said farewell to Qatib, their al-Qaeda recruiter and erstwhile mentor, for the last time. On the drive back to the mosque the boys stayed mainly quiet but exuded a clam and firm conviction: they were about to make their contribution to jihad and enter into eternal paradise.

I updated Mulrooney who let London and JTAC know and also set up a meeting with CTC. We would need them as back-up for surveillance of the reconnaissance and as the actual arresting officers once they'd bought the components for the bombs. My team and I were buzzing: the months of patient surveillance were almost over and we'd been on top of it all the way. Grand Minaret was about to progress from 'Active' to 'Interdict' and reach its successful conclusion.

5: RECCE WEDNESDAY

The first inkling I had that things would not go to plan with the end of Grand Minaret was when Sadeq contacted me two nights before the reconnaissance day or 'recce Wednesday' as the team, or more precisely, Wattie were calling it.

"Qatib's coming up and joining the boys for the reconnaissance," he spoke hurriedly to me by phone using a secure line. I asked how Qatib had got in touch. Qatib had handed out a further three throwaway phones to Sadeq at their 'final' meeting in Battlefield and instructed him to check them every day up to the bombings in case he needed to get in touch; after the bombings they were to be discarded. Sadeq had checked the phones routinely earlier in the afternoon and, to his consternation, saw a text had been received on one of them which read simply: *Call box Glasgow Cross 6.15.* Telephone box to telephone box, I thought; still the safest method of communicating by phone, as mobiles were effectively walking tracking devices.

Sadeq arrived at the telephone boxes amidst the old Mercat Cross and distinctive mediaeval baronial Tolbooth Steeple of Glasgow Cross, the oldest part of Glasgow. At 6.15, the receiver rang in one of the two booths. Qatib was brief and told him he was coming up on Wednesday for the reconnaissance and would meet him at the mosque as usual an hour before he was to pick up the boys and then rang off. Sadeq sounded panicky, so I arranged to meet him at the busy Bothwell motorway service station on the M74 outside the city.

I was on high MosBerBel alert at this critical part of the operation, but there was nothing suspicious among the medley of travellers at ten on a Monday evening in the service station. Sadeq looked flushed and excited at the same time and I could empathise with him. He was participating with the same outfit that had given the world 9/11, 7/7, Bali, Madrid and a bevy of other headline grabbing outrages and was about to be the main factor in getting their newly created Glasgow 'franchise' busted. No wonder he was nervous.

"Why he's coming up, Mr Lomax?" he asked in an agitated tone, "the meeting in the Battlefield flat was supposed to be his last contact with us before..." he gestured with his hands and let the sentence trail while looking worriedly around him. We were in a secluded corner of the large cafeteria. In a newsagents', opposite the cafeteria, Tony Boyd was 'browsing' through some magazines while staying in line of sight of the café: outside in the car park Danny Mackay was strategically located in a bogus BT service van watching every vehicle entering and leaving the service station. Any hint of anything untoward from either and they would alert me through the ear-set I was wearing. There was nothing. I endeavoured to reassure him.

"Calm the jets, Sadeq, trust me, we're on our own here except for friends watching out for us!"

He appeared to calm down, but then suddenly became agitated again. "I mean do you think he's rumbled something; that he's on to us?"

"Wheeeeeee!!" A small boy rushed past flapping his hands in the air pretending to be an airplane, pursued by a harassed mother frantically demanding he return to her side. Completely innocent, but it caused Sadeq to almost jump in the air. I grabbed hold of his arm.

"Now take it easy, Sadeq! Immediately after your call I contacted colleagues in London. We've been watching Qatib for months, monitoring his calls, observing his movements and there's been nothing out of the ordinary the last few days. Nothing," I emphasised. "Why's he coming up? He wants to see how the boys perform on recce Wednesday. Will they bottle it? Have they got what it takes to go through with it? God knows Khaled or Mohammed could wake up in the middle of the night before 'Bomb day' screaming after realising what they've got themselves into, confessing all to their fathers before heading off to reveal everything to the authorities! That's what's probably going through his mind. He just wants to come up and make sure his boys, who he's spent nearly a year grooming, are still up for it."

It was disingenuous bullshit, but if it calmed Sadeq down it was worth it. He had enough to worry about before adding this to the mix. In truth I was slightly alarmed at this development. It was highly unusual, in the tightly compartmentalised world of international terrorism, for someone like Qatib to get his hands dirty with the foot soldiers on active service, even on reconnaissance. Qatib was officer material, a professional recruiter and groomer whose skills could be used elsewhere now the Glasgow operation was in its final phase. Moreover, if Qatib was arrested on the recce with the boys, he was the only contact with the next rung in the al-Qaeda hierarchy and could endanger that. So why *was* he coming up to Glasgow? Was it off his own bat or had he been ordered to? If the latter, it almost certainly meant al-Qaeda were suspicious and would send someone else up as well. And that *was* alarming.

I was being truthful about Qatib's activities in London. But the reality was the months of observation by our colleagues down south had produced meagre results. Qatib scrupulously refrained from using the internet except when he visited the offices of several radical Arabic magazines run by exiles, though having no links or sympathies with al-Qaeda, where he worked in some editorial capacity, though as far as we could ascertain, he never contributed any articles himself. All his mobile phone calls, except for his terse text messages to Sadeq, were ostensibly related to his work on the magazines.

For a social life Qatib would venture out to Middle-Eastern or North African cafes or shisha smoking bars in Bayswater or the Edgeware Road where he would mingle with the regulars, frequently discuss Arab and Maghreb politics volubly, but never endorse al-Qaeda or related groups. There were Friday prayers and other regular visits to a 'conservative' mosque in Haringey which had never had any association with radical Islamic groups. And that was it. No woman in his life and in bed by ten. A typical middle-aged, somewhat pious Arab gentleman, except of course that he occasionally preached jihad and martyrdom at various mosques which radical preachers had invited him to. And, over the course of the past year, visited Glasgow to recruit, radicalise, groom and mentor an active al-Qaeda terrorist cell.

We knew that among the thickets of Qatib's apparently uneventful and conventional activities in London there would be the trail leading to his al-Qaeda contact. But so far London hadn't uncovered it, nor had JTAC or SIS produced anything more than we knew already.

As for the notion that Qatib was coming up because of apprehensions over the mettle of Khaled and Mohammed to go through with the Glasgow suicide bombings, this rang hollow too. Any sign of wavering or doubt by either of them would have become apparent when they arrived back from the training camp. But there was no indication of this: indeed the opposite. These boys were in it to the dreadful end, fully signed up as martyrs and holy warriors. No, whichever way I looked at it, I reluctantly had to concede that the news of Qatib taking part in the reconnaissance was a disturbing development. Up to now, Grand Minaret had progressed almost like a textbook case of how a terrorist cell was recruited, radicalised, trained and activated. The cell's recruiter and mentor joining the recce wasn't part of the textbook. Looking at the worried, perspiring figure of Sadeq in front of me I made a sudden decision. I placed a hand on his arm.

"Sadeq, we're going to be watching your back all the way from now to next Wednesday. If we see anything worrying we'll get you and your family out. I promise you."

He smiled weakly, Thank you, Mr Lomax," but I knew he was unconvinced.

"Listen to me, Sadeq," I looked him straight in the eye, "we've come this far, we're almost there. I can assure you right now there's not another al-Qaeda unit or sympathiser active in this city, nothing. The police, CTC, ourselves at MI5: there's nothing around al-Qaeda on any of their radar: not another thing. Qatib, the boys and you are the only game in town where al-Qaeda is concerned. And we'll be following Qatib all the way as soon as he leaves for Glasgow. If he brings anyone else, we'll know and I'll let you know." I held his arm more firmly.

"There's only a few more days to go, Sadeq. There'll be recce Wednesday. Qatib will more than likely fuck off immediately after that. The boys will want you to drive them around to buy the 'ingredients'. As soon as they've bought enough stuff to make a bomb and brought it back to Battlefield, you're out and we and the Branch will pile in and nick them before they've tried to assemble it and possibly blow themselves and any other fucker in that tenement up. We're all the way with you on this, Sadeq, I'm not going to hang you out to dry."

Suspicion seemed to leave him and relief took over as he visibly calmed down. "I trust you, Mr Lomax, I always have and you've always looked after me. It's not me, it's my family."

"I know, Sadeq. I know, you're a family man first and foremost" (his occasional visits to Glasgow's lap dancing establishments notwithstanding, this was largely true) "and we'll ensure your family are safe." I reached into my pocket and retrieved a small bottle wrapped in plastic. "Inside this are nine sedatives. I suggest you take one at night. They'll calm you down, reduce the stress and anxiety levels, and most of all allow you to get some sleep. Take them till this is all over."

I proffered the tablets. He hesitated for a few moments before slowly taking them from me. I stood up. "I'll see you this time tomorrow night. Are you going to use the blue van for the reconnaissance?"

"Yes."

"Ok, I'm going to leave you now, but you will have protection from here on. Give it twenty minutes and then go from here."

I turned and walked resolutely out of the cafeteria. In the service station car park, through the secure radio system I instructed Danny and Tony to shadow Sadeq all through the night. At seven the next morning, I'd get Tres and Wattie to relieve them. There were groans from both of them. Beginning late on Tuesday night, when we'd place the intercepts in Sadeq's van prior to the reconnaissance, they'd be on continuous surveillance duty until we made the arrests, with only a few hours' sleep each day. Today and tomorrow were scheduled to be their last free days for a while. Danny was enjoying a day out with his wife and young child and Tony was preparing to go out to dinner with his fiancée when I'd called them with Sadeq's disturbing news and told them to get to the service station for back-up. Once the meeting with Sadeq finished they'd assumed they would be able to get back to their loved ones for at least one last night. I heard out their protests before stating firmly:

"Sorry, boys, but our friend from London coming up is not part of the script. I'm bringing forward full alert status on Grand Minaret by twenty-four hours. Ok?"

Reluctantly they both radioed back, "Ok boss."

I'd already alerted Mulrooney to Sadeq's news about Qatib which he had to concede was 'interesting'. Now I contacted him again and told him I was putting the team on full watch status a day early. He didn't argue with that decision and said he would inform CTC. They were due to join us as soon as Sadeq went to pick up Khaled and Mohammed for the recce. London would follow Qatib up and I also had access now to other MI5 assets in the Glasgow area who could provide further assistance as the team would likely be stretched over the next week or so. Apart from the development around Qatib, everything was going smoothly; even the normally fraught meetings with CTC had gone well.

Predictably, they'd made protests about not being brought in earlier which I ignored and equally predictably they tried to take over which I was having none of: they were confined to back-up surveillance for recce Wednesday and then the arrests. I was adamant; the rest was ours. They were led in their protests inevitably by DI Dougie 'Hammy' Anderson in full-blown nose-out-of-joint, 'whatever happened to the spirit of partnership working' mode. Fortunately, Danny Mackay was one of his ex-CTC sergeants, who after getting over his initial anger at Danny jumping ship to join the over-rated spooks in MI5, who never actually did anything really dangerous like *arrest anyone*, figured that he could use Danny as his 'man' in the Glasgow MI5 camp. So I could use Danny in return to manipulate Hammy into thinking he knew more about what we were doing than we were and thus be in a position to tell him only what we wanted him to know.

As I drove back to Glasgow the sense of excitement and anticipation I felt was palpable. We were almost there. The only nagging doubt was Qatib: why *was* he coming up? But I wasn't going to let that spoil my overall feeling of satisfaction that things were progressing well. I put on Miles Davis as a sudden rain shower poured onto the darkened motorway.

*

Sadeq was a lot more relaxed when I met him twenty-four hours later. Whether this was due to the sedatives or he was just a lot more chilled about things or a combination of both, I didn't know. We were in the back of his van in a residential side street a few blocks from his home The street was quiet with a small park on one side. The sight of Sadeq loading and unloading his van was a common one here, even after ten on a weekday and would go unremarked by neighbours.

Across the park, in a street parallel to the one Sadeq's van was in, a white transit van bearing the insignia for a firm of plumbers was parked. In the back, screened off from passers-by, were Tony and Danny. A camera was attached to a small aerial protruding slightly from the front of the van and feeding pictures to a colour TV screen in the back which afforded excellent viewing of Sadeq's vehicle, or by clicking on a mouse allowed the operators in the van to rotate the camera enabling them to observe the entrance to the street Sadeq's house was in. Anyone in a car or on foot could be observed going in or out of the driveway.

At eleven Tony and Danny would be relieved by Tres and Wattie. They were working in relays. Tony and Danny had set up the van and watched all through the previous night. Tress and Wattie took over at six and stayed until three followed by the lads doing the back shift. Tress and Wattie would act as watch through tonight and Danny and Tony would take the morning shift, allowing Tress and Wattie some sleep. They would be back at one ready to observe Sadeq drive the van to pick up Qatib and the boys for recce Wednesday. Each member of the team would arrive separately in nondescript hired cars which would be parked a couple of minutes' walk away from the 'plumbers' van'.

The arrangement was that at one the next day Sadeq would walk to the van with a white Marks & Spencer's carrier bag, open the back of the van, throw in the carrier bag, close the door and go back to his house. This was the signal that in five minutes Sadeq would be leaving for the pick-ups allowing Tony and Danny time to leave the van, walk back to their cars and take up position in the city centre. Meanwhile Tress and Wattie in one surveillance car and Hammy Anderson and a CTC colleague in another would follow Sadeq's van to the pick-up. Other MI5 colleagues would collect the 'plumbers van' and its cargo of observation footage back to the Shields.

I was in the back of Sadeq's van installing several small transmitters in the ceiling and side walls of the van. In spite of their diminutive size, these intercepts would transmit powerful audio signals allowing us to record all conversation taking place as the van brought Khaled and Mohammed into Glasgow. Sadeq's van was a dark blue five-seater Volkswagen Transporter. The back space contained wooden shelves and space for Sadeq to transport produce and other stuff between his various newsagents and restaurants. Hopefully I'd made a good job of concealing the transmitters, but unless Qatib was going to make a full in-depth sweep of the van which was unlikely given there had been nothing to indicate he was proficient in the technical aspects of counter-surveillance, we didn't need to have much concern.

As I finished installing the last of the transmitters I delivered some good news to Sadeq which I'd deliberately held back from him until I was finished and about to leave.

"I meant to tell you, London contacted me about an hour ago. Qatib left his flat *alone*, went to Kings' Cross and boarded the overnight sleeper for Edinburgh again *alone*. It looks as if he's coming up all on his own. As I said he most likely just wants to check out how the boys are, assess if they're still up for this."

It was still the same disingenuous bullshit it had been twenty-four hours' earlier in the service station. We were still none the wiser why a good operator like Qatib was breaking all the rules of compartmentalised insurgency security at this late stage and at this critical moment, but it worked for Sadeq.

"Good, great!" he said, plainly relieved, then more plaintively "I just want this over, Mr Lomax and I want out after this."

I replied firmly, "You have my word, Sadeq, if need be we'll put you up in Monte Carlo. The wife can go shopping all day, the grandkids can go on the beach, and you can play the casinos."

"Mr Lomax, the entire resources of the British Intelligence community could not afford that."

"You playing the casinos?"

"No, my wife shopping!"

We both laughed, before I resumed the theme: "Seriously, though, we'll look after you and your family. I promised you protection and you've got it round the clock."

"Yes, I know, thank you," he responded.

We both exited the van. From a holdall I was carrying at my side, I brought out a handset about the size of a large android phone with a screen on the front. I bent down and aimed the handset at the underside of the van beneath the chassis. "What are you doing, Mr Lomax?" Sadeq asked.

Somewhat reluctantly, after a few moments aiming the handset, I stood up, checked the screen and said, "Its' part of MosBerBel. This is an explosive detector. It can tell if there's explosive material hidden beneath the van and," I pointed at the screen on the handset, "there's none. So no one has tampered with this and the guys over there," I gestured discreetly towards the van across the small park, "will watch this van until recce Wednesday is over. And if you chose to use this van to take the boys round for their, how shall I put it, *shopping*, then this wee beastie will tell us if there's something nasty around the van before you go near it. It's a standard precaution in these circumstances."

"Why would they want to kill their own people?" he asked, perplexed.

"Not al-Qaeda, perhaps rivals and enemies but," I moved on quickly, "there's not an iota of evidence for that and I'm just going by the MosBerBel rules. So don't worry about it." I smiled at him.

He shook his head. "I'm beyond worry. The sooner next Wednesday comes the better."

"Ok," I said. "I'm going now. Tomorrow will go quickly. You'll be followed, discreetly, throughout. After tomorrow the boys will ask you to drive them about to get the 'shopping'. That might be two or three or four trips. As soon as they've bought a decent enough amount, we'll arrest them. And you're out, apart from a heavily disguised appearance in court to give testimony. You'll never be in any danger. Good God you were always at far greater risk with the likes of the drugs gangs and the IRA and all the muscle they could put up in Glasgow compared to two mixed-up fanatics and a sole recruiter with no other back-up in the city!"

"If you say so, Mr Lomax, I trust you."

"I'll be back here tomorrow night, same time, for a quick debriefing."

I walked a few feet away from him, then turned round and made one last comment. "If it's any help and you can't sleep tonight in spite of the sedatives, think of your grandkids and your wife and what you're preventing." I turned away, and headed down the street towards my own hire car. Behind me, I could sense a solitary figure staring intently at my back. It was at times like this, I thought, that you realised you wouldn't change places with your Joe for the proverbial million dollars: it was a terrifying, lonely and dangerous place to be, in spite of all the soothing reassuring words we tried to calm them with. I should know, I was one for years. Still, I reflected, as I approached my own car and carried out a quick MosBerBel sweep with the handset, we had him well covered and protected: we weren't throwing him to the al-Qaeda wolves and I would move heaven and earth to ensure he and his family were safe after Grand Minaret.

I put the car radio on as I made my way back home and found a station playing some jazzy Frank Zappa. As the uplifting strains of *Peaches en Regalia* filled the car I felt a mounting excitement. I too would find it difficult to sleep tonight, but for different reasons than Sadeq. Grand Minaret was in its final phase and all the pieces in place, the evidence mounting. There was only one nagging worry which I couldn't clear from my head: why *was* Qatib coming up?

*

I awoke at 6.30, having caught a few hours' sleep. For the duration of the last phase of Grand Minaret, as officer commander, I would be sleeping in what was described as an 'operational bedroom' in the Shields. Which meant after a shower and shave, I could immediately read all the update situation reports on a secure laptop over a breakfast of hard boiled eggs and toast. Qatib's sleeper had got into Edinburgh at six and, after his usual quick change act, was now ensconced in a coffee shop off Princes Street, smart but casually dressed, eating a croissant and sipping a latte while reading *The Times*.

Back in Glasgow, on the south side, Wattie and Tres had had an uneventful night in the 'plumbers van' watching Sadeq's van. They gave way to Tony and Danny who took over just after six, with nothing to report. All was well.

The rest of the morning went that way. At eight I met with Mulrooney and Hammy Anderson from CTC for a brief update in the former's office. All the procedures that had been agreed in advance were confirmed. The plan was for Sadeq to drive to a café on Victoria Road in the Govanhill district where he would collect Khaled and Mohammed. Hammy Anderson and a CTC colleague in one car and Wattie and Tres in another would tail Sadeq from the café into the city centre. Once he reached George Square where Queen Street Station was located and one of the two targets for next Wednesday's intended bombings, Sadeq would let Khaled off. Tony Boyd, on foot, would follow him through the station. On the day of the bombings, of course, there would be no need to worry about a get-away strategy as Khaled had every intention of blowing himself up and hundreds of people with him in the station concourse during the morning rush hour. So the intention today was for Khaled to sedately, discreetly, but not too slowly, walk through the station while pulling on the ripcord attached to a backpack filled with a brick encased in newspaper wrapping simulating the activation of the deadly explosive that would be in the backpack the following week. After walking through the station Khaled would get a bus to the Battlefield flat where all three would rendezvous. Tony Boyd would tail him through the station and back to the flat.

I would be watching Khaled's progress through the station on a TV screen with a link to the bank of CCTV cameras that covered Queen Street courtesy of British Transport Police (BTP) under whose jurisdiction security for all railway stations in the UK was entrusted to. The camera footage of Khaled's movement's in the station including the all-important hand movements as he simulated activating his device in preparation for the real attack the following week, was vital evidence for the court case. I would view the footage in an office located in a building round the corner from the station while communicating with a BTP officer called Mike who was specifically trained to work with the security services on operations like this. I would instruct Mike to select the cameras needed to follow Khaled from the array that covered the station the moment I espied him coming into the main entrance.

Outside, Sadeq would drive Qatib and Mohammed the short distance across the city centre to Central Station, the second target for next week's bombings, where Mohammed would alight and make his way through the much larger concourse of Central, again simulating the attack that was to come the following week. Across the road from the bustling front entrance to the station, Danny Mackay and an MI5 operative named Carl, or 'Carl the geek' as he was more commonly called, would be ensconced in a hired office with a similar set-up to me: a link up to a BTP officer controlling the CCTV cameras in the station.

As Sadeq drove away from George Square, I would alert Danny who would leave Carl with the TV link to the CCTV, cross over to the station entrance and await Mohammed, before following him through the station and back to the flat.

There was satisfaction at the briefing in Mulrooney's office that Grand Minaret was proceeding to plan; even Hammy Anderson was positive: "Aye in the next few days we'll have these bastards wrapped up and I'm looking forward to that!" Everyone was buzzing, maybe too happy. At the risk of lowering the party atmosphere I asked the boss if anything more had been gleaned as to why Qatib was going along with the recce.

Mulrooney responded firmly. "Yes, Eddie, we may have shed some light on that. SIS, through JTAC, have analysed this move and though they can't be certain, so it is just speculative at this stage, it probably reflects recent events in four European cities." I looked at him quizzically.

"Since the start of last year, four attempted al-Qaeda attacks have been pre-empted by counter-terrorist operations in Dortmund, Germany; Cracow, Poland; Lyon, France and Genoa, Italy. In each case the respective al-Qaeda cell was infiltrated and rolled up after cell members had purchased and assembled enough material to make explosives. All the targets in the four cities were the same: train stations, bus terminals. Very similar MO to what we have here."

I asked an obvious question. "Was Qatib involved in any of these failed operations?"

"Yes, in all four cases," he replied tersely.

"Were any of the other recruiters picked up?"

"Apparently not, though we can be certain it wasn't Qatib in any of them."

"So, what bearing has this on Qatib breaking the rules today?"

"Good question, Eddie and I asked that of SIS. The planned attacks on the four cities are, it seems, closely connected to the rise of Ali al Hassan, the favourite to succeed Bin Laden. As you're aware, he's manoeuvring to get firm control of all the al-Qaeda affiliates in North and West Africa and the Middle-East; no small achievement by any standards if he manages this. But he's also extremely keen to strike in the West; it would be the icing on the cake that would confirm his leadership and control: a firm statement, as it were, that al-Qaeda is back under new and strong management and able to strike at will. So a big push has been on to recruit cells to attack targets in Europe and so far all have been thwarted. So the smart money is on the recruiter for the Glasgow operation being instructed to take a risk and go out with the cell at the reconnaissance stage, but keep an alert eye out for infiltrators. It's likely he may stay for a few days and watch everything that's going on. He'll need back-up for that, though we've got nothing on any other al-Qaeda related contacts or allies assisting him in Scotland, least of all Glasgow. You'll need to be very careful, Eddie, when meeting with Sadeq, get your team and their support to go on maximum alert before the target and you move against the two terrorists."

"Have you just found this out, Sir?" I was concerned that Mulrooney had known this earlier and had not bothered to let me know. But he assured me, "Eddie I've just received it this morning from Thames House."

Anderson added, "Well that explains why your man's came up. Don't worry, Eddie, we'll help your team out. If Qatib's got help to watch your Joe and the two guys we'll flush them out for you!"

Christ Hammy Anderson could be a patronising, condescending git. My team was more than capable of detecting any back-up with

Qatib without relying on CTC plods! But I smiled wanly at Anderson and said: "Thanks, good to know."

The briefing broke up shortly to reconvene after the transcripts from all the day's activities, including the rendezvous meeting back at the Battlefield flat had been prepared. Mulrooney's news did make some sense. I had been aware of the arrests in Europe, but hadn't connected them to Grand Minaret. Al-Qaeda had been noted, post 9/11, for letting each local branch or 'franchise' operate independently with only minimal oversight through the recruiter, who would usually leave the scene before any planned attack. Ali al Hassan's rise to the top indicated a more co-ordinated approach. I pondered whether to let Sadeq know, but it would probably add to his worries so I decided not to tell him and rely instead on raising the surveillance on him and the others to an even higher level. My concern was if Qatib stayed around after the reconnaissance how would Sadeq cope with that? I cast that aside for the moment as I knew we had to focus on a detailed, trouble-free watch of today's recce.

*

I stayed in the Shields for the rest of the morning. In Edinburgh Qatib left the coffee shop after an hour and took a leisurely stroll up Princess Street. He walked into *Waterstones* and spent some time browsing there, mainly in the fiction and arts sections. At eleven, he boarded the train for Glasgow at Waverly Station and arrived in Queen Street Station, which one of his protégés was going to blow-up a week later. On leaving the station his predilection for coffee continued as he made his way to the nearest Starbucks and changed in the gents' into some faintly dishevelled, but unremarkable casual clothes.

I left the Shields at twelve and drove to the city centre to the hired office next to Queen Street where I made contact with Mike from the BTP. We tested the equipment and after a short while I was able to get Mike to give me close-ups of any part of the station covered by CCTV upon demand. The quality was excellent and we would make an unwitting star of Khaled as we would of Mohammed at Central.

Sadeq came out of his house at one, down the driveway, into the side street carrying the white Marks and Spencer's bag; the prearranged signal that he was going ahead as planned. Tony and Danny left the 'plumbers' van'. There had been nothing unusual to report during their watch. Just the usual morning routine coming and goings of a residential street: people going to work, kids, sometimes accompanied by parents, going to school, one or two workmen keeping appointments at resident's homes and the postman making his rounds; a typical, mundane slice of everyday life in suburbia. Apart from his wife going to the nearby shops and returning with milk, bread and a tabloid newspaper, there had been no activity at Sadeq's house. Sadeq went back to his house for exactly five minutes before coming out again and driving away in his van.

Before he drove the van away, Hammy Anderson and his CTC colleague drove by. At the other end of the street Tres and Wattie took up position. The two cars followed Sadeq as he headed for the first pick-up: Qatib at the mosque. After leaving Starbucks the doctor, who evidently knew Glasgow's public transport system well after all these months of clandestine visits, took three separate buses and then walked the last twenty minutes along very quiet, leafy streets to the mosque; our back-up colleagues remaining unobserved throughout.

After driving back into the city centre with Danny, Tony Boyd joined me for a short while at the command post watching with an almost hypnotic fascination the flow of people through Queen Street. After confirming to me that the morning spent watching the van and the driveway from the back of the 'plumbers' van' had been one of unremitting tedium, the most unrelentingly monotonous part of the life of an intelligence officer in any service anywhere on the planet, we went on to chat over a sandwich about his forthcoming stag night in Dublin and all the frenetic preparations for his wedding like two normal guys on their lunch break. Meanwhile Danny Mackay went to his command post opposite Central Station.

Sadeq waited at the mosque for ten minutes until Qatib arrived. They drove immediately to the pick-up with the boys. The intercepts in the van were clear and came through distinctly over my headphones linked to an 'A' Branch detection facility back at the Shields' operated by two technicians with Mulrooney sitting in. On the drive to the pick-up we could hear Sadeq saying to Qatib: "I wasn't expecting you to come up doctor? I thought your role in this had finished?" It was quite a few moments before Qatib replied.

"Well, I wanted to see how the boys were, let them know I'm here to support them. Besides, it's good for an old warhorse like me to get a feel again for what frontline struggle is like."

If there was a prize for lame responses, Qatib would have easily won it, but Sadeq and he drove the rest of the way in silence. The drive from the mosque to the pick-up venue was at most ten minutes, but Sadeq took nearly thirty going through the pretence of trying to spot surveillance vehicles, all for the benefit of Qatib. Of course Sadeq's manoeuvres posed no challenge to Hammy or Tres and Wattie, nor were they meant to.

At a quarter-to-two Sadeq pulled up outside the café on Victoria Road. Khaled and Mohammed were waiting for him. The café, which was owned by a local man and not part of the big chain coffee shops, was reasonably busy for this time on a Wednesday afternoon, mostly regulars and almost all of south Asian origin. Over the last few days a young Asian couple of Pakistani origin had taken to coming in with a young boy of about three. The proprietor was getting used to them as they always bought lunch and plenty of coffees; he even had a high-chair ready for the child. They told the proprietor they'd just moved into the area, the young man remarking that he was waiting for word to start work in a software company run by a cousin in the west-end. Today they'd taken up a table at the wide window looking out onto Victoria Road. They'd finished their lunch and were on their third coffee, the child fast asleep, when first one, then a second young Asian lad, both clad in denim, trainers and baggy tee-shirts and both with back-packs, entered the café, ordered Cokes and sat in silence at a table set in the middle of the café.

Sadeq walked in and Khaled and Mohammed, the two youths sitting at the middle table, visibly tensed. There were no big greetings or high-fives, just a laconic "Hi" from both. Sadeq looked around him, still playing pretend MosBerBel, this time for the boys' benefit. "The van's outside," he said, sitting down beside them and "Dr Qatib's there as well."

This raised eyebrows from the pair.

"Why?" inquired Khaled.

"He was supposed to be finished with us," added Mohammed.

"Is something wrong?" Khaled asked with an urgent tone.

Sadeq shook his head and smiled benignly at the pair. "I've asked him. He assures me he's just up to support you and get his hands dirty a little bit."

Khaled couldn't help the old cheeky, irreverent side of him come out. "He should try and do what we're fucking doing next week, that's a lot more than getting your hands dirty man!"

Sadeq looked quickly at his watch and said wearily, "Have some respect now, come on." The two boys stood and made to leave, but not before Sadeq asked to see the backpacks. They both handed them over for him to see. He unzipped them, looking in and saying in a low voice, "Two ripcords attached to paper wrapping around a brick, and some underwear and toiletries above in case you're stopped by the cops." Zipping the packs back up he smiled and said, "The doctor will be pleased. That's exactly what he asked you to do."

"Come on, Sadeq," Khaled said impatiently, "let's move!" Sadeq rose from the table, giving them back their back-packs and the three of them left the café just as the young child with the Asian couple woke and proceeded to bawl.

We knew the details of what was said because in the handbag of the young Asian woman with the child and her husband was a mobile phone that served as a mobile interceptor and once aimed at a specific object such as the table where Sadeq and the boys were sitting, could filter out all background clutter and focus exclusively on their conversation which was transmitted straight to the Shields and relayed onto me. On the man's side of the table was a white plastic bag hiding an explosives detector similar to the one I'd used around Sadeq's van the previous night, pointed at the table where Sadeq was going through the backpacks and similarly obtaining a negative reading.

After Sadeq and the boys had left, the couple settled the child down and finished their coffee. They left after twenty minutes saying goodbye to the proprietor who hoped that "your cousin phones you today," which they thanked him warmly for and went out into the street with the child in his buggy. They were never seen again in the café or the area as, of course, they were part of the assistance we were getting from London and they would now go back there, ready for another cameo part in some other surveillance operation. Nobody else on my team could have fitted in to that café like that 'couple' had.

Back in the van Qatib greeted the boys. "Do not be alarmed I thought I would lend some support, everything is going well. Shall we proceed?"

"Sure Doctor," Mohammed agreed.

Qatib moved to the back row of seats while Mohammed and Khaled with their backpacks got into the front beside Sadeq who started the van and drove out of Victoria Road.

*

They drove in silence by a circuitous route into the city centre, the surveillance cars tracking them unobserved all the way. It was a typical mild, cloudy April day in Glasgow; a leaden sky punctuated with occasional shafts of sunlight. Tony Boyd left my side to take up position in George Square ready to tail Khaled through the station. The Square itself, though busy as always, was in that calm post-lunch phase prior to the frenzy of the evening rush hour.

Sadeq was driving to the Square from the east end of the city which meant, given the one-way system round it, he would enter on the south side of the Square before turning right into the west side in order to drop Khaled off. He would then drive round the Square again before making the brief drive across the city centre to Central Station. Tony Boyd took up position at one of two bus stops on the west side directly outside the entrance to a suite of offices and a Greek restaurant. This stop was for regular bus services while the next one along catered exclusively for the open-topped scarlet double decker tour buses that drove people round the landmarks of Glasgow. Sadeq would have to stop between the two stops to let Khaled off. An open-topped bus was waiting at the tour bus stop taking on board a collection of sight-seers.

I had two open radio connections: One to Tres in the MI5 surveillance car and another to Tony at the bus stop in the Square. In addition I had two mobiles for communicating with Mulroney at the Shields and Danny opposite Central Station. I was also able to monitor the relay from the Shields of the intercepts from the van and then there was the TV screen in front of me linked to the bank of CCTV cameras in Queen Street Station. Total coverage of every angle, I thought, with no small amount of pride. They might well use Grand Minaret as, to use the modern jargon, a good practice case study for future counter-terrorism operatives in the Service: Christ they might even get me to lecture the trainees like some counter-terrorism guru! I allowed myself a slight chuckle at the notion before being distracted by a noise coming from the intercepts in the van.

Sadeq was approaching the Square. Apart from Qatib's remarks when the boys had entered the van, they'd stayed silent through the rest of the journey. Indeed I'd had to be assured by the 'A' Branch technicians on the link that the intercepts hadn't stopped or malfunctioned. Now as the van entered George Square there appeared to be a humming noise. It took me several seconds of intense concentration on the sound to realise it was a low chanting noise, like a mantra or the recitation of a prayer. Two young male voices chanting in unison. Then it struck me: Khaled and Mohammed were reciting verses, possibly from the *Koran* before they engaged in martyrdom as holy warriors for jihad. This is how they would do it next week. Each one going into their appointed railway terminal at rush hour with a fully primed backpack, reciting to themselves verses from the *Koran* like a soothing balm as they walked among the throng, their twisted interpretation of the Prophet's words fortified with a zealous belief in vengeance, redemption and salvation for the world fully justifying their ideological righteousness as they pulled the ripcord on the backpacks and...

One of the radios crackled into life. "Van indicating right turn, stopped at lights," it was Tres in the MI5 car, three vehicles behind Sadeq on the south side of the Square.

"Spotted, van about to turn right into Square," Tony confirmed at the bus stop through his concealed earpiece.

For what seemed like eternity the lights stayed at red, Sadeq's van behind a black taxi. The van was perfect for this job: a slightly dirty dark blue van which attracted zero attention in busy streets unless you were looking for it. The lights changed. A bus pulled up at Tony's bus stop depositing a stream of passengers. All the sight-seers had boarded the tour bus at the next stop which was about to depart on its tour of Glasgow.

"Van turning right," it was Tres again.

Tony spoke into his earpiece, "Van's turned right, slowing down, he's letting a motor cyclist go past before moving into the side, overtaking a bus at my stop. Coming into the pavement now, van slowing down, I can see front right passenger about to open…"

The explosion was like a crack of thunder, a deep bass rumble, then vibrations and movement and then silence and then me frantically screaming into the radio connection "Tony? Tony, Tony, can you hear me? What happened? Are you there? Tony? Tony?" before the screams and the silence. I looked at the timer on one of the bank of CCTV screens covering the railway station in front of me.

It was 2.26 pm.

I later saw some CCTV footage of the explosion. You can see Sadeq's van slowing down in front of the bus at Tony's stop. The tour-bus has started moving away from the curb and a motor cyclist scoots past the van. Sadeq's almost at the pavement when there's a flicker on the screen as a shock wave seems to ripple from the van before flames burst out and the van appears to lift in the air, the roof detaching. But then everything, the van, the buses, the people, the Square is completely obscured by thick dense smoke which billows out rapidly, enveloping the west side of the square, hiding the flying debris including fragments of statues, masonry, vehicles and human beings.

Operation Grand Minaret and recce Wednesday had come to a catastrophic end.

6: BLOWBACK

"You should have let us in on this at an earlier stage! You should have taken those bastards and Qatib long before they were able to drive a van round Glasgow with a bomb; that's what we'd have done!"

Hammy Anderson's accusatory chubby finger was pointing straight at me while his florid face revealed anger, fear and an urgent desire to rescue his own backside from the horrific mess that was Grand Minaret,

I'd finished summarising everything that had happened from the meeting with Sadeq in Largs through the evolution of Grand Minaret up to the dreadful denouement at George Square. I'd been listened to in silence as I recounted events; the only sound being Fiona, the admin furiously typing my every word into her laptop. I stayed silent in the face of Anderson's imprecation but thought of the saying I believe was attributed to Oscar Wilde and later recounted by John. F. Kennedy: that success has many fathers, but failure is an orphan! In that case Operation Grand Minaret and all associated with it were fully contagious plague carrying lepers.

"Detective Inspector there'll be plenty of time for recriminations later. An appalling disaster has befallen this city at the hands of international terrorists. All of us in this room are tasked with preventing such acts against our country, our people and our way of life and yet, under our noses, it has happened. There'll be queues of people lining up to give us a kicking so let's try to work together and get a fix on this awful situation." Mulrooney spoke commandingly and shut Hammy up.

"Now the last time you saw Sadeq in person Eddie was?"

"Tuesday night, Sir."

"You checked out the van with a hand-scanner and did an obs beneath it," it was a statement not a question, but I confirmed it anyway.

"Yes, Sir, nothing from either."

Mulrooney, looking at me directly, concurred. "I got A' Branch to check out the scanner's memory; it has a reading from the time you were at the van at about eleven pm on Tuesday night and its' negative. So there's nothing in the van then. Remind me who was on night watch Tuesday into Wednesday?"

Tres and Wattie raised their hands. "And nothing to report?" Mulrooney inquired. "Not a zilch, Sir." Wattie affirmed.

"The street was completely quiet the entire night, Sir," Tres added. "The only thing of any note that happened was a taxi pulling up in Mr Sadeq's street at about ah," Tres checked a small notepad in front of her, "at about 2.30am. A girl got out of the taxi which had pulled up on the opposite side from Mr Sadeq's residence. She appeared tipsy to me by the way she left the taxi and walked to what I presume was her own house. She fumbled in her handbag and retrieved some keys, unlocked her door and went in. The camera managed to pick up a light in the front bedroom of the house she must have gone into for a couple of minutes and then it went out. I assumed she'd gone to bed." Tres looked up from her pad, "and that was it, nothing else the whole night." Wattie nodded in agreement.

"No cars hovering around, cruising slowly by?" Mulrooney asked.

Tres shook her head while Wattie added "That street was as quiet as Stirling Albion's ground on a Saturday afternoon." The reference to the crowd-drawing ability of a lower ranked Scottish football team was either lost on Mulrooney or ignored by him, for he merely said tersely:

"OK, the girl will be interviewed and the taxi traced for elimination purposes. Danny your watch?"

"As I said previously, just routine; kids heading for school, folks going to work, Sadeq's wife getting provisions. Nobody hanging around. Sadeq himself didn't surface till he was supposed to at one," Danny stopped there.

"A' Branch are analysing the footage from the surveillance camera, but I know that'll just confirm what the three of you have said," Mulrooney said reassuringly. "So if there's no device in the van when Sadeq drove away, it must have got into the van somewhere between there and the Square. Let's start with the mosque and Sadeq picking up Qatib. Detective Inspector?"

Hammy blanched as if he'd been shaken out of a reverie. "Eh, well, all we saw was Qatib get into the van with the informer, Mr Mulrooney, but Miss Martindale and Mr Craig were sharing surveillance with us."

Wattie looked at Hammy with contempt before saying, "The doctor guy just got into the van and they said a few words to each other and then drove away."

"Qatib wasn't carrying anything?"

"He left the hold-all with his change of clothes at the mosque," Wattie replied, "he'd need at least a backpack for the amount of explosive that went into that bomb; besides why would a recruiter act as the trigger man? That's wrong MO for al-Qaeda!"

"Everything's fucking wrong with this operation," Hammy almost growled at Wattie who shot back another look of disdain.

"Enough Inspector, please!" Mulrooney said curtly. He moved on.

"That leaves the rendezvous in the café with Khaled and Mohammed. They had backpacks?"

I spoke up. "We know from surveillance that Sadeq checked the packs in the cafe and there appeared to be just bricks and paper in them. We had people in there with a detector and that read negative." I looked at Mulrooney for confirmation of that and he nodded in agreement. "So the backpacks had no explosives either. But even forgetting that for a moment, if Sadeq is a double-agent for al-Qaeda and he's either acting alone or colluding with the boys in a double-game, that means, of course that we, or more specifically *me* have been duped completely by Sadeq. Now that's not impossible I grant you but he certainly kept his fanatical Jihad tendencies well under wraps while he played the worldly businessman, gambled at the roulette tables and hung around the lap-dancing clubs: Sadeq liked the sins and pleasures of this world, not the usual CV of a holy warrior eager to immolate himself to get a VIP place in heaven.

"And then there's the boys. They were recruited over a year ago at the mosque. Since the first meeting at the Battlefield flat, we've had them on tape. What, eleven odd meetings over twenty-two hours and not one hint or slip either that Sadeq was deceiving us on behalf of al-Qaeda or that the boys, even possibly Qatib, knew this and were playing along, that they were working to a script during all that time! A' Branch pick up nothing on them from their homes, SIS gets nothing when they go to Pakistan. Before this, before last April, before they got radicalised, Khaled was a young Govanhill tearaway and Mohammed was a serious and austere young man. Through Qatib they were groomed and turned into lethal suicide bombers. But for the two of them to be colluding with Sadeq into deceiving and stringing us along through all those hours, days and months is assuming a level of sophisticated deception which I don't believe those guys were capable of. There's nothing to suggest at this stage, that the two of them didn't sincerely believe they were carrying out the recce before buying the materials, assembling the bombs and carrying out the acts. Nothing."

"So," Mulrooney inquired, "if the explosives weren't put in the van by Qatib or Sadeq or the two boys, who did put them in the van? And why?"

There were blank expressions on every face round the table in the conference room. Somehow and sometime between me checking the van out with the scanner and Sadeq driving away from the café with the boys and Qatib to their final destination at the Square, someone got to that van and placed the deadly material which caused carnage. And, apart from being emotionally drained and tired beyond words, I could not figure out the answer as to whom, why and how, but neither could anyone else in that room and Mulrooney sensed that.

"All right," he said "we're all too tired and too close to today's calamitous events to think straight just now." He consulted his watch again. "It's gone 6.45. I'm absolutely dreading looking at my mobile or checking my email for all the urgent messages I'll find, but," he said resignedly, "needs must. I'm meeting with," he cast a sideways glance at Hammy, "Superintendent McAllister from CTC in a few minutes followed immediately by a conference at police headquarters. The First Minister and Criminal Justice Minister will no doubt be there. As best as I can I'll do a holding job on this, say we're making thorough enquiries on what's happened and try and avoid an answer to the question: did we know or have any indication that a terrorist attack was planned in Glasgow this afternoon?

"But I can only do that for another seven, eight hours at most. At some point early tomorrow we're going to have to admit to what we know, or what we all thought we knew of today's events. And when news gets out that officers from MI5 and CTC tailed that van into George Square as part of an operation to *forestall* a terrorist atrocity on the city, then," he shrugged, "God help us all! For now, if it's possible for any of you, I want you all to get some rest. But I want you all back here at three am and I want you to think carefully about everything that's happened over the past twenty four hours, no matter how trivial, stupid or absurd it may seem, that might, just might, have some bearing on what's happened. Eddie I want you to go to the Art Safe House. The rest of you go back to your homes. Needless to say, nothing to anyone outside of this room, you're still active Security Service officers on her Majesty's service no matter what happened today."

Mulrooney rose from the table and, with Fiona, went to the door where he paused while she walked on. He said: "Eddie, can I have a few moments please?" before exiting the room.

I looked around at the team. Wattie had put his head on the table, Tres continued to look ashen and Danny consulted his mobile. Hammy left the room but not before saying in a conciliatory tone, "I'm sorry you lost the young fella Boyd."

"Thanks Dougie, that's appreciated," I gave the best attempt at a smile I could muster which he returned with a nod of his head before departing.

"Has anyone contacted Tony's family?" it was Tres.

"They won't have officially identified the body yet," I replied. "He's not supposed to be finishing the tour till next Thursday, week tomorrow, so his folks and his fiancée won't be expecting to hear from him till then." Tres put her hand over her face and shook her head and said almost inaudibly:

"The poor girl, it's dreadful."

Tony's cover was as a civil servant in the Home Office Statistical Branch specialising in drugs. For operations like Grand Minaret which could require him to be out of circulation for days or weeks, the story was he was on a liaison tour with colleagues in equivalent departments, this time in Latin America, and he would be incommunicado for a few weeks.

"Tony is a huge loss," I spoke to them all, "apart from all the other shit that's hit us today and all the thousands of questions that'll be racing through your minds right now, but the boss is right, you all need to get some rest, but I'm conscious you can't go back to your families yet. Wattie what will you do?"

"Get a few hours kipping at my old SAS pal's gafe in Yorkhill." Like Tony, we all had cover stories that plausibly kept us apart from families and friends. Wattie lived with a woman in Paisley who by now was inured to his long absences. "Danny?"

"I'll use one of the rooms upstairs, boss if that's ok with you?"

"Sure," I replied. When Danny left CTC to join MI5, he officially left the police to work as a 'security consultant', which again required him to be out of touch for long periods. His wife, familiar with his long absences during his days with the Branch, wearily put up with it and concentrated on looking after their five year old son.

Without being asked Tres said "I'm going back to my flat." Tres lived alone. The last boyfriend or 'companion' as she liked to call them was a year ago. He'd lasted only eight or nine months and was the third since she'd joined my team. It seemed that men more than women couldn't stand long periods of no contact with a partner with only minimal explanation for their absences and a job, ostensibly as a 'Home Office Administrator liaising with the Scottish Government', which she refused to elaborate on or invite them to office parties or meet colleagues.

"Ok, all of you get some rest and get back here for three." I shook hands with Danny and hugged both Tres and Wattie.

"What the fuck's going on, gaffer?" the big fellow implored after I separated from him.

"I genuinely don't know, Wattie but it'll not be for the want of finding out." I left them and went to see Mulrooney in his office. It was a brief meeting. Mulrooney asked me a more polite version of Wattie's question as he fidgeted with his phone and looked at the emails on his laptop. I made a similar reply as I had to Wattie, namely I didn't know, but was desperate to find out, adding that I was convinced Sadeq was innocent. I was going on further, trying to collect my thoughts and about to ask if there was any further update on Qatib and why he went on the recce when, suddenly, Mulrooney exclaimed:

"Oh fuck, fuck, fuck!"

It was so unusual to hear Mulrooney depart from his authoritative, but polite patrician middle-class Scottish brogue to indulge in profanities. "What's the matter, boss?"

He looked away from the email in front of him, his face a mask of concern. "It's Thames House. An hour ago a *Guardian* reporter contacted the Service's press desk. The reporter quoted an Arab news agency based in Beirut that sources close to al-Qaeda were saying that the Glasgow bombers were under surveillance from MI5. He, the reporter, was asking for confirmation which the press people naturally denied. This reporter, incidentally, was one of the journos that was close to Snowden when he was leaking the Washington NSA intercepts, so he not only has form and motivation for upsetting the intelligence community, but also credibility. Fuck! I thought I would get another few hours' grace to prepare us. Just when you think it couldn't get worse, it does!"

"Was there anything else the reporter revealed about his sources?"

"No, nothing, but there's about a dozen emails and texts coming in from Thames House and Edinburgh. Yep," holding aloft his mobile, which was vibrating, "there's the Chief Constable of Police Scotland. Perfect!"

"He said bombers," I commented oblivious to his concerns.

"What?"

"The reporter said 'bombers'. Not a bomb, but 'bombers'. Whoever told the Arab news agency must have been told by someone in al-Qaeda who knew details of Grand Minaret. There's an insider leak, Sir, somewhere in the system, JTAC, 'A' Branch, CTC, *Us*, there's an informer!" It hit me like a force of revelation. I went on, "We thought we were infiltrating and controlling them and they were infiltrating us."

Exasperated, Mulrooney said, "Yes, agreed, they could have *turned* us, but they could have used Sadeq to do that, it needn't be an actual UK intelligence operative."

Mulrooney was clutching at straws and we both knew it: if the operation had been turned, infiltrated, better it be the Joe, the Muslim informer, than one of us, for the implications were terrifying. I didn't argue with Mulrooney; I just stared impassively back at him. There were more vibrating sounds emitting from his phone. "Eddie, I really must answer this. I'll see you at three."

I stood up, "Of course, Sir," and left the room and the Shields without saying another word.

*

The Art Safe House was so-called because it was situated close to Glasgow's world famous School of Art designed by Charles Rennie Mackintosh and situated in the Garnethill district which was located across the steep slopes of another of the city's Ice Age legacy drumlins.

And by safe house standards the Art Safe House was luxurious. Not some grotty, sparsely furnished flat, but effectively a penthouse on the top floor of a recently built apartment complex finished in blond sandstone tastefully in keeping with the neighbouring buildings. The apartment was well-equipped with two bedrooms, both ensuite, a kitchen and an expansive living/dining room that afforded a view over the north side of the city. Both MI5 and SIS jointly ran and paid for (through a London based estate agent) the Art Safe House. Its five-star status was owed to its role as a holding base for high ranking defectors from regimes abroad, agents and informers from foreign intelligence services or domestic informers that we wanted to treat quite sumptuously. It was located in an area that adjoined the city centre and all its facilities while retaining its own anonymity.

I let myself into the safe house and slumped into a comfortable dark leather armchair and watched the lights of the city through the large window as dusk approached. My head was buzzing, thoughts and images and scenarios racing through my psyche. I felt completely gutted and washed out. I got up, went to the kitchen and retrieved a bottle of Chilean merlot and poured a good measure into a glass. Christ, I thought, was that the best we could do wine wise? I sat back in the chair, put a light on, located a remote control and switched the large wall-mounted TV screen on. I quickly found the news channels.

All of the satellite news stations: BBC, Sky, CNN, Euro news, even the London outlets of foreign news services such as RT (Russia Today) and TV France were concentrating on the Glasgow bombings.

Whatever the channel, the scenes were horrific and this after the most gruesome footage had been edited out for the news bulletins. Moving shots of buses with their roofs shorn off were interspersed with clips revealing the Squares' statues on the west side reduced to their plinths, somehow the most evocative of the images of the violence done to the Square. While the BBC and Sky managed to avoid any shots of bodies by skilful editing, the other channels had blurred those parts of the footage where bodies lay. Grainy mobile phone footage, taken from behind the entrance to Queen Street Station by a passer-by, graphically showed people covered in blood in panic, terror and confusion rushing into the station, dense, thick smoke behind them flowing into the station obscuring everything.

A woman, in her forties, was interviewed with police barriers behind her and spoke tearfully but eloquently, quiet anger mingling with her shock and fear. She told of how she had been standing outside the station waiting for her friend when 'the bombs' had went off and all around her was flying debris, smoke and a blast wave that threw her to the ground, but she had emerged, at least physically, unscathed. Her friend had texted her minutes before to say the bus she was on was just coming into the Square and to wait for her at the station entrance. The woman spoke of how she saw that bus her friend was on drawing to a halt at the stop eighty yards in front of her when… She finally dissolved into tears.

There were more interviews with by-standers and survivors recounting what they'd witnessed interwoven with comments from police and rescue commanders updating the latest casualty count which at this point was fifty-six dead and rising and numerous injured, some critically (the final death toll from the George Square bombing was eighty-two, apart from Lockerbie, the worst ever terrorist act carried out on Scottish soil). Various political talking heads popped up, including the First Minister of Scotland and the Criminal Justice Minister and spoke of their 'revulsion' at what had happened and their 'absolute and resolute determination to apprehend the perpetrators of this vile act and bring them to justice'.

At the bottom of the screen on each station was the proverbial banner strip streaming the same few snippets of information about the bombing prefixed by the legend in block capitals: BREAKING NEWS! I happened to have flicked onto Sky News interviewing another distressed witness when there was an update to the breaking news stream declaring: 'Reports that British intelligence agents were trailing terrorists who carried out Glasgow George Square bombings' with no further elaboration.

I switched off the TV as I knew the news stations would indulge in feverish speculation about this with various pundits and experts cropping up to discuss it, which I couldn't stomach. I rose from the armchair, stretched my arms and then, taking the glass of merlot with me, went to one of the bedrooms. After taking a generous draught of the indifferent wine I lay on the bed fully clothed in the darkness trying to focus my swarming thoughts.

Blowback. That was the one word that kept recurring repeatedly in my head. Blowback. All intelligence services were haunted by it. You infiltrated a group, got them to carry out activities which benefit you and the side you support and the consequences came back to bite you nastily on the backside. Afghanistan is always cited as the classic case study of a blowback situation. One of the last acts of the Cold War was the Soviet Union's invasion of Afghanistan in 1979 to bolster the pro-Soviet regime there whose hold on power was increasingly shaky and to destroy their 'reactionary' Islamist opponents. In response the newly emboldened hawkish conservative administrations in the West led by Thatcher and Reagan armed the Afghan Islamists (now known collectively as the mujahedeen and designated 'freedom fighters') to the teeth with devastating weaponry that was able to grind the Soviet occupying forces down in a remorseless guerrilla war which eventually forced them to throw in the towel. People in the West now heard of and became familiar with terms such as 'jihad' and 'holy warrior' which duly entered the political lexicon for the first time.

Out of this maelstrom emerged groups such as the Taliban (who eventually took power in Afghanistan in 1996) and, of course, al-Qaeda. Having seen off one super-power these groups now turned their enmity to the very people who had armed and financed them in the first place: the West. These groups' virulent hatred of all secular values wasn't confined to communism, but was equally antipathetic to all manifestations of Western life including liberalism, democracy, women's equality, gay rights and everything else taken for granted nowadays in the West. And this animus towards the decadence and corruption of the West was to culminate in the attacks on the Twin Towers on 9/11 and all that had happened since: the invasions of Afghanistan and Iraq, the overthrow of Saddam Hussein, the rise of ISIS and all the various bombings from 7/7 in London, through Bali, Madrid, Paris and now Glasgow. All stemming from initial support, including supplying weapons, to 'freedom loving' jihadists' fighting communism.

Blowback; it was clear to me now that Grand Minaret had been victim to blowback; there had been a mole and al-Qaeda informer who had penetrated the operation probably from its inception. In a way it was devastatingly clever; use all the surveillance, interceptions and informants your adversary has assembled against you to *guarantee* that your bomb has a safe escorted passage into the heart of a Western city. Masterful I had to admit. But precisely how did they do it? And who did they do it through? I tried to focus, to concentrate, lying on top of the king sized bed in the darkened bedroom of the Art Safe House.

The earlier initial debriefing back at the Shields had effectively eliminated Sadeq, Qatib, Khaled and Muhammed as suspects in their own deaths. Which left only one line of inquiry.

Think Eddie think. The thinking was horrendous in its implications, but it had to be done. I tried to bring all my analytical and forensic rigour to it. Forget the history, forget the names, think it through, try and be detached. The van was explosives free when I left it at just after eleven on Tuesday night. Thereafter it was exclusively and solely watched over by, yes, go on think it, the *team*. Wattie and

Tres on Tuesday night into Wednesday morning until about six, then, Danny and Tony until one.

I rose from the bed sharply, switched on one of the bedside lamps and took one of my mobiles from inside my jacket. After the fifth ring the phone was answered. It was Carl the Geek, one of the technicians watching the Central Station today. Carl and I went back a long way; in a way he was one of my discoveries and he'd proved indispensable in far too many surveillance and counter-terrorism ops. I'd plucked him from mind-numbing tedium writing voice recognition software for BT's extensive wiretapping outfit in the nineties and let him flourish for the Service's Glasgow activities. He was twenty years younger than me, was mightily irreverent and had a fondness for the wacky-backy which wouldn't do him any favours if random drug testing was brought into MI5, as had been threatened recently. Despite this, he was first rate when it came to analysing intercepts, audio or visual, which he appeared delighted to spend vast amounts of time on, which along with his wire-framed specs, tousled fair hair and dishevelled, absent minded appearance earned him the moniker: the Geek. And, no doubt because I rescued him from the 'tyranny' of voice recognition he liked me and was always ready to do me a few favours.

He gasped in astonishment when he realised it was me. "Eddie man! What the fuck's' going on?" Technicians in the service were outside the formal ranking structure of intelligence officers and their superiors and Carl had therefore no need to address me formally as 'sir.'

"Carl, I'm trying to find that out. Listen I haven't time to gab, I take it you're still in the Shields?"

"Yep."

"Are you working on the intercepts from the OP targeting the van?" The OP was the 'Observation Post' i.e. the 'plumbers van' watching Sadeq's own van.

"You bet. Mulrooney's been in here three times in the last hour looking for an update!"

I had to think and act fast now. Even if he initially resisted the idea that the infiltrator who sabotaged Grand Minaret was one of us, Mulrooney would be forced to confront that dreadful scenario or have it forced upon him very soon. Whatever, I suspected that our freedom to come and go would soon be severely restricted.

"Well, I'm going to have to add to your misery. Is there anything you've got from the tapes, something that doesn't gel?"

"Eddie, there's a total of nearly forty hours of the fuckers!" He was referring to the entire period the team were watching the van.

"You can forget the first twenty-four hours," I told him. "It's after I leave on the Tuesday night until Sadeq drives the van away on the Wednesday lunchtime that's the real interest."

"Yeah I get that," he replied briskly, "and that's what I'm concentrating on."

"Are you on your own there?"

"No, there's two other techies with me, but it's cool so far. I can talk."

"So, allowing for the fact that you've still got a lot of work to do on them, is there anything that's caught your attention?"

He sighed slightly. "Nothing really gaffer. The OP camera's fixed on the van almost the whole time during the night. It's a different story from seven in the morning when the street comes alive and the camera hops between the van and the street where your man lived, but it's all just routine, though we're going through it minutely."

"Ok, Tres told us there was only one time the entire night that the OP camera shifted from the van and…"

"No two times." Carl interrupted.

"Sorry, what?"

"There's two times the camera is away from the van during the night," he confirmed.

"All right," I said perplexed, "the first would be when a taxi comes into the street and lets a young girl off, agreed?"

"Yeah that was about 2.30am."

"And the second time?"

"Well," he paused while thinking, then said "hold on a second," Carl's voice trailed away and I could hear him talking to one of the other technicians. He came back on the line "The second time was 5:20 to about 5:40-45, about twenty minutes."

"And what was the reason for it going off the van, what was it looking at?"

"Nothing."

"What? Say again?"

"Sweet Fanny Adams. It goes to the guy's street and stays there like it did when the taxi arrived a few hours earlier. Only this time there's no activity, absolutely nothing. Just darkened houses for about twenty minutes."

"What was on the audio?"

"Nothing, the operator didn't say anything."

"But there's audio when the taxi came into the street earlier, yes?"

"Correct. Tres gave a full commentary."

"But nothing the second time?" It was more of a statement than a question from me.

"That might mean nothing, Eddie," Carl came back. "Operators move cameras like the OP one for lots of reasons, especially at that time in the morning when there's nothing else happening. Tres or Wattie could have thought they'd seen something in the street on their peripheral vision, moved the camera, but there's nothing and they didn't want to make a song and dance out of it, thus no audio commentary."

"Agreed Carl, but there's a problem."

"What's that?"

"You said the camera stayed on the street for about twenty minutes?"

"Yeah, about that."

"So why did the operator spend that length of time fixing the camera on a quiet empty street and not revert back to the van earlier? That must have seemed like an eternity at that time in the morning!"

"Beats me."

"Unless you were trying to *divert* the camera's attention away from something that was happening at the van."

There was a long pause before Carl came back. "Oh fuck yes, I see what you're getting at! But that means…"

"Carl shut up!" I interrupted him sharply. "Not a word to Mulrooney, you hear? I'm back there at three, I'll talk to Mulrooney then. Meanwhile, if there's anything else you come up with on the intercepts, anything, phone me first before you speak to anyone else.

You really have been a great help as usual." I hung up. I knew I could trust Carl to stay silent until I told him otherwise.

My mind was racing. Tres and Wattie had never mentioned the camera being off the van the second time at the meeting back in the Shields earlier. True, there appeared to be nothing to report on, but what had caused them to shift the camera for an entire twenty minutes and why was there no audio commentary on it?

I switched the bedroom light off and paced up and down the darkened bedroom. Sometime between Eleven pm on Tuesday and one the following day, someone places a bomb underneath or in the back of Sadeq's van despite that van being under observation by two MI5 surveillance teams. Which meant that one or more members of my team either placed it there themselves or connived with someone else to do so by, for example, diverting the camera away from the van. And the ideal time to do that would be in the quiet of the early morning, a dead time, rather than in the midst of the hive of normal routine activity through the morning hours.

The thought that any one of the team I'd recruited and worked with so closely and intensely over the past few years could be an al-Qaeda spy, mole, informer, infiltrator (the words all merged into the one that screamed *traitor* in my head) was not only appalling but also felt like staring into a dark abyss that left a churning, sickly feeling in my stomach. These are the worst times in the secret world. The times when any residue of certainty and normality in what is an intrinsically uncertain and abnormal profession evaporates. The times when friend and foe cannot be distinguished and when paranoia and fear become rampant. In such situations entire sections and teams within intelligence agencies implode and destroy themselves. And that, from the point of view of your adversary, is precisely the intention. I'd been in a similar situation once before, just after the Possil disaster, but it didn't have the same intensity or ramifications as this; least of all because mass civilian casualties hadn't been the consequence, just seven dead junkies!

I had to be careful not to race ahead too quickly, to go pointing fingers and making accusations in what was an already out-of-control situation. There was nothing definitive, *yet*. But the accumulating circumstantial evidence was that the terrorist atrocity committed today in George Square was aided and abetted from within MI5.

Think Eddie. Don't let the magnitude of it overwhelm you. What could be the possible motivation to cause any one of four white, Scottish, non-Muslim individuals with a good career path and earning reasonable money, living in a liberal, tolerant and open society to help and support an outfit committed to a zealously rigid, fundamentalist interpretation of Islam and the imposition of a bigoted, intolerant, mediaeval, puritan, misogynistic, homophobic way of life? What could possibly be the attraction in that?

Treachery and betrayal of one's own side or cause is normally stimulated by one of three factors: money, blackmail or ideology. Taking these in turn, none of the team had suddenly come into money or was living a lifestyle way beyond their means. And al-Qaeda had no track record of buying Western intelligence service personnel; this would be a first, though that wasn't to rule it out.

Blackmail, but what was there to blackmail? All of the team lived in a secular society where stern moral sanctions and prohibitions had long gone or had very limited traction. Being gay, having an affair, living a heterodox lifestyle in early 21st century Scotland were no longer a threat to one's livelihood, even within the security services. The one exception to this was any hint or whiff of paedophilia which, rightfully, was completely beyond the pale. So unless al-Qaeda had stumbled upon one of the team members being involved in child porn, blackmail seemed unlikely, though again it could not be conclusively ruled out. In any case blackmail is always a risky and precarious way of recruiting infiltrators. The stresses and strains on those being blackmailed usually become overwhelming leading to a breakdown, suicide or the blackmailed making a clean breast of it and confessing all to their own side, thus the useful productive career of an infiltrator recruited through blackmail is invariably short-lived.

Ideology or firm conviction and belief in a cause were far more solid grounds for recruiting informers and maintaining them in place to spy or carry out activities against their own sides. Much the most formidable spies and infiltrators in history have been motivated by supreme belief in the righteousness of what they were doing exemplified in the 20th century by Kim Philby and the others in the

Cambridge Five spy ring, who were convinced that communism, epitomised by the USSR, was the wave of the future and a perfectly legitimate cause and faith to spy for against a reactionary and decadent British imperialism. And, whatever its manifold faults, communism with its promise of a classless utopia to come held a positive secular attraction for many in the West. That couldn't be said for al-Qaeda's programme to reinstate a theocratic Islamic caliph based on an ultra-strict interpretation of Sharia law.

None of these: money, blackmail or ideology, were for me convincing reasons why any member of my team should actively seek to work and support al-Qaeda. Nor could a fourth: revenge. What motive was there for any of them to work for al-Qaeda in order to achieve revenge?

For the umpteenth time images of each member of the team flickered through my mind in a fast moving sequence and I could not associate any of these usual motives with this team I had developed, worked with and got to know over the past five years. All had been rigorously vetted before joining MI-5. Any dubiety in their past should have emerged then, but nothing had raised concerns. I should know. As the receiving senior officer they were assigned to me after recruitment, training and induction into the service. I had, or thought I had an intimate in-depth knowledge of them and their backgrounds, reinforced by working closely with them on ops over five years. Sure, no background check, however detailed, can ever be foolproof. But what could possibly attract any of the team to al-Qaeda's fanatical, apocalyptic radical Islamism?

I thought of each team member in turn. Tony Boyd, the 'wean,' fresh faced, two years out of university and about to be married. His father was an accountant with a small financial services firm and his mother a primary school head teacher: impeccable middle-class professional backgrounds. Tony had went to Glasgow University and studied Politics and Philosophy where a left-of-centre lecturer had, to use that archaic term, 'talent-spotted' him for his academic ability, his prodigious memory and forensic attention to detail combined with his overall affability, sociability and ability to motivate those around him, which could easily morph into manipulating them.

Tony, of course, had effectively ruled himself out as a suspect by being a victim of the George Square bomb.

Then there was Danny Mackay. Danny was classic 'plod': a foot-soldier, a watcher, in for the long-haul on interminable surveillance ops; he could blend into the background anywhere. It was said of Danny that he could follow you the whole day and you would never notice him. He had begun as a beat-cop, gravitated into the CID before being assigned to CTC under Hammy Anderson where he'd spent several years. I needed a good patient, solid, reliable watchman and Danny came with all the right skills, plus I could use him as a good source of disinformation back to Hammy in the relentless, internal MI5/CTC turf war. He had the policeman's typical cynical sense of humour but he wasn't 'political' either in the office sense or driven against the right or left. He was loyal, did as you asked, got on with the job and asked no questions. His only interests outside work were his family: wife and five year old son who he was devoted to. I could see no way al-Qaeda could entice Danny to work with them.

Tres had come to us from nursing via the mind numbing tedium of MOD procurement. She had went into nursing straight after school and spent fourteen years on the wards, rising to the position of Staff Nurse. Her stints on the wards had included periods working in the war zone that was the Accident and Emergency department of a major Glasgow City Centre hospital. I had often reflected ruefully and occasionally said directly to her that enduring the ordeal of working a Saturday nightshift in the city's busiest A & E with its assortment of volatile drunks, injured people and general organised chaos was probably the best training anyone could have for working on fast moving, potentially dangerous undercover intelligence operations.

According to her background papers Tres could have been promoted to Sister as she had specialised in working with spinal injuries at a Glasgow children's hospital and was regarded as an excellent nurse, quick-witted, intelligent and able to motivate and inspire colleagues: all qualities that would stand her in good stead in the secret world. But she quit nursing in her early thirties. Why? She was open about it to the assessors. She was disgruntled to say the least, about staff shortages on the wards and the increasing workloads being imposed on the nurses. She had finished her shifts sometimes feeling distressed that she not had time to really care and do all that was needed for her patients, and this was happening more often. She felt she was 'fire-fighting' most of the time and this was seriously undermining her professionalism and her ability to discharge the best treatment for the patients. Compassion was being increasingly replaced by a remorseless tide of paperwork, bureaucratic procedures and cuts to staffing. She had enough of nursing after endless attempts to draw attention to shortcomings on the wards were ignored by the hospital management and, with a heavy heart, left the profession.

It would be fair to say that up until the late 1990s, Tres would have had no hope in hell of joining MI5. Not only was her background not 'right'; she was the daughter of working class parents of Irish Catholic descent; her father a labourer in the Lanarkshire steelworks, her mother a shop assistant in Hamilton, though there was absolutely no connections with the Troubles in Northern Ireland. But in the feverish Cold War atmosphere that prevailed in MI5 in those decades anything less than a military, police, ex-colonial or unionist family background was frowned upon. Compounding this would have been her disaffection with the cuts in the health service which would have been seen as 'political' and possibly indicative of a 'subversive' attitude. This would have automatically ruled her out for recruitment.

Come the late 90s a wind of change swept through the service. The Cold War was over, the service was put on a legal footing, the revelation that some of the most damaging spies had been from the old boy public school background, allied to the new spirit of equality and diversity that swept through all public agencies in the UK meant that a former nurse, a woman, with a good background in a highly thought of public service with excellent inter-personal and professional skills was exactly what the assessors were looking for to give the service a more rounded, inclusive and representative profile. So when, after passing her civil service exams and being posted to the MOD offices in Glasgow, Tres saw an internal staff notice for 'opportunities to work in assessment and collation of intelligence material' and duly applied, she was viewed favourably by the recruiters; her reasons for having left nursing in the new environment now regarded as reflecting an assertive, 'sparky' dynamic personality which allied with an ability to think quickly in a fast moving situation as she'd had to do daily as a staff nurse, would neatly match the requirements of the service. Tres was in.

And she hadn't disappointed. She was quick-witted with a mischievous sense of humour which stopped short of the perennial cynicism the rest of us indulged in which was really only a form of insulation from the stresses, strains and sometimes absurdities of the job masquerading as gallows' humour. Tres was good company and a solid grounded agent able to combine objectivity and realism with a warmth and empathy the rest of us lacked, probably because, with the exception of young Tony, the rest of us were classic repressed West of Scotland males. Certainly the world that Tres inhabited and that of al-Qaeda couldn't have been further apart.

And then there was Wattie. Man mountain Wattie who told you it as it was: irreverent, cynical and, unsurprisingly given his military background, the most reckless of the team. Wattie wouldn't stop unless you clearly commanded him to. But he was nobody's fool and had a sharp line in observation schooled on many undercover operations with the SAS. He came from a military family. His father was a sergeant with the Argyll and Sutherland Highlanders, a regiment which Wattie also took the colours with. After several tours with the Argylls, including two in Northern Ireland as the Troubles were coming to an end, Wattie applied to join the SAS.

We only ever got clipped anecdotes about his time with the SAS. I knew from his records he'd spent time back in Northern Ireland on joint undercover liaison ops with MI5 surveilling dissident republican terrorists. Later he'd served in the invasion of Iraq and his last tours of duties were in Afghanistan. He was approaching his late thirties; old for the army generally, geriatric by SAS standards. The proliferating and lucrative world of private security agencies beckoned as it did for many of his comrades, but Wattie decided for much less money and glamour to work with British Intelligence. He'd had enough travelling in world trouble spots and if you could ever settle down after working with the Special Forces, then routine undercover surveillance work with MI5 on your home turf was it.

Wattie applied, was recruited and brought his vast experience of undercover work and a military outlook to our civilian group.

Wattie never spoke about it, but the record tells the story of a three man SAS unit in Helmand province accompanied by an Afghan intelligence officer, all of them dressed in flowing robes, wearing head-scarfs and bearded, one of them being Wattie. They'd materialised at the edge of a small town which had been cleared of Taliban fighters allegedly a few days before. There was a small checkpoint manned by two local Afghan police who'd held up three cars to let an army Land Rover with soldiers from the Black Watch through. The Black Watch vehicle stopped and three soldiers, one of them a major who was the commanding officer, got out to speak to the local cops at the checkpoint. Across from the checkpoint, there was a small general shop which also sold tea with some tables and chairs outside it. Wattie's SAS unit with the Afghan officer sat down there and ordered tea while watching the activity at the checkpoint. Something caught Wattie's eye.

Three men, probably in their early twenties also bearded, wearing robes and headgear passed quickly by the side of the Land Rover. Almost imperceptibly, and certainly without catching the attention of the cops or the Black Watch soldiers, the man in the middle of the three bent down as if to check his trousers or his shoes while stretching out his right arm towards the Land Rover before straightening up and moving on. It was over in seconds, but Wattie caught it, rose up from his seat and softly but firmly and audibly declared, to his two colleagues: "IED, Land-Rover, Taliban," before rushing over to the vehicle, his two mates in tow. The soldiers and cops at the checkpoint were surprised to see this tall bearded man running up to them speaking authoritatively in a Scottish accent:

"Those three guys are Taliban," pointing to the three receding figures heading into the surrounding scrubland, "and one of thems' just placed an IED under the Rover," turning to the cops he ordered "call them back!"

That galvanised everybody. The major glanced under the Rover then shouted to the rest of his men "Move away! Now!" while the two police commanded in Pashto for the three men to stop. Upon hearing this they broke into a run prompting the two cops, one of the

Black Watch soldiers and Wattie, who produced a sub-machine gun from under his robe, to open fire on them. All three fleeing Taliban were hit and killed instantly while the checkpoint area was evacuated until an army bomb disposal unit arrived to neutralise and remove the IED. The device would have been triggered by a remote control mechanism as the Rover left the village killing all the Black Watch on board. Wattie received a citation for his actions that day and, at the invitation of the Black Watch soldiers, got absolutely pissed with them, back at their base in Camp Bastion.

IED, Improvised explosive device. It was, to use the cliché, the proverbial elephant in the room and always had been from the moment I had to think the unthinkable: that one of my team was an agent in some form for al-Qaeda. Although we all had rudimentary training in small firearms handling and identification of explosives, Wattie was the only one of us who had actually handled and worked with bombs and bullets on a virtually daily basis. Again, I was trying not to run ahead of myself but trying to put together the conceivable reason, the motivation, for why a former British soldier and Special Forces agent would work with the Taliban or al-Qaeda.

It was not unknown for soldiers in theatres like Afghanistan or Iraq, like comparable combat zones such as Vietnam where the focus was on counter-insurgency and anti-terrorism action rather than conventional warfare, to become confused as to what the aims of the campaign were, especially if there was high 'collateral damage', that is lots of civilian casualties: women, children and old people in particular. Groups like the Taliban operated in the heart of local communities, amongst local people and, despite every effort to avoid it, military action against such a foe always carried the risk of causing civilian deaths. Airborne drone attacks were particularly notorious for this. Entire families had been wiped out by such assaults at wedding feasts or tribal gatherings just because intelligence had been received about the whereabouts of a Taliban commander but without the background information that said commander was amidst a civic event or the intelligence was just wrong with appalling consequences. This was a world away from the targeted, focused work on IRA and dissident IRA activists that

Wattie would have taken part in as part of his SAS duties in Northern Ireland.

Did Wattie see some dreadful after-effect of a drone attack wreaking havoc on a civilian village or convoy? Had he come across the mutilated remains of women and children as a result of indiscriminate firing or a revenge attack from his own side? Had he gone AWOL for a day or so, been captured by a Taliban or al-Qaeda unit and been 'turned' to work for them before being released back?

All this was highly fanciful and speculative, but having assessed in my head the characters and personalities of my team, Wattie was the only one who possessed the practical skills and the hint of a possible motivation for becoming an al-Qaeda operative. It was still difficult to picture the Wattie I knew with his humour, irreverence, fondness for a beer and the women as an austere, fanatical jihadist and traitor, but then that was what good deep 'cover' was about. And besides, it was on Wattie's watch, admittedly with Tres, that the surveillance camera had been mysteriously diverted away from observing Sadeq's van in the dead of night; the only opportunity by my reckoning for an explosive device to be placed in it between my own checking of it and the catastrophe in the Square.

I picked up another of my disposable mobiles and phoned Vincent in Registry on his private phone. Registry was MI5's vast archive of records, hundreds of thousands of files on anyone who had ever come to the attention of British or allied intelligence agencies: suspects, 'persons of interest', informers, agents and deep background information on all MI5 personnel including assessments and the results of all enhanced vetting exercises. Access to Registry was gained only through the Registry Information Officers or RIOs. In a previous era and a different cultural world they were known as the 'Registry Dragons' or 'Queens' as they were then virtually all middle-aged females and usually spinsters, which in the old boy philosophy that prevailed previously apparently rendered them less vulnerable to blackmail.

In the cultural revolution of the 90s Registry, along with the rest of MI5, had been opened up and new RIOs from diverse backgrounds recruited; Vincent was one of them. Now in his late fifties, he came from the town of Bellshill in North Lanarkshire not far from my own home town of Motherwell, both just outside Glasgow. Vincent had spent most of the 80s after leaving school on the dole, until a quick retraining course rescued him from a lifetime on benefits by giving him the basic skills to successfully apply for a clerical administration job with an electronics firm based in Watford where he moved to. The firm had defence contracts which also involved admin work so he was required to sign the Official Secrets Act and be vetted. Vincent took to the work with aplomb and before long was a senior admin officer. Then, like Tres, after eight years with the firm he saw a vacancy in the 'Home Office civil service' for 'administering the collation of classified material' which was intelligence speak for a vacancy in Registry. He applied, was successful and had been there ever since.

I'd first encountered him on a particularly tedious day-long refresher training course in Thames House on 'Updated Procedures and Regulatory Protocols for Accessing Registry Files' which was jargon for how to pick up a phone or send an email requesting a RIO to access a file for you. Vincent had been reluctantly assigned to 'co-facilitate' the day with a senior Registry Manager who in stark contrast to Vincent epitomised zealous bureaucratic pedantry in all of its glory. I clocked his still strong west of Scotland accent when he was allowed to make his only short input to the training in the first hour which was a model of precise succinctness compared to his superior. I made a beeline for him during the first coffee break and immediately identified a kindred spirit when, within the first ten minutes and out of earshot of everyone else on the course, Vincent said direct to me: "This whole fucking day could have been condensed into an hour! That clown," pointing to his erstwhile boss, "could spin out telling you how to open and close a door last a bleeding week!" I recognized there and then that day that Vincent and I were two Lanarkshire boys amid an ensemble of Home Counties bureaucrats. We clicked and I knew I'd made a good and useful Registry contact and I hadn't been disappointed.

Vincent wasn't at work when I phoned but by good luck was going on night shift in the Registry at ten. "Has this shite at the Square got anything to do with you, Eddie?" he asked in his usual direct way.

"Vincent I can't go into that man, but I need your help." There was no reply but Vincent was a man of few words. "I want you to go into three agency personnel files: Daniel Mackay, Teresa Martindale and Walter Craig."

"That's your squad Eddie, minus Tony Boyd."

"Tony died at George Square."

"Oh right," typical Lanarkshire male bluntness and absence of surface emotion.

I resumed, "I want you to go into each file and subject them to a rigorous cross-referencing analysis. I want linkages with every other database that you can access to: CTC, SIS, Police National Computer, NATO, Army Intelligence, and Interpol, anything that my clearance level will let you into."

"And the APRO will be you?"

I paused. APRO stood for Authorised Personnel Requesting Officer; no Registry officer, even at the most senior level, could access any file without authorisation from a ranking MI5 officer. The problem was if it hadn't already happened, my clearance to authorise access would likely be withdrawn after today's events. "No, the APRO is Stu Hutchinson." Stu was a fellow Glasgow-based MI5 operational team leader. He would double for me and take charge of my team if I was on leave or ill or whatever, likewise I would double for his team. It was likely that Stu would be put in temporary charge of my team. "Ok," Vincent replied.

I asked him how many RIOs were meant to be on duty tonight. "Four, but after what's gone on today they might bring in more."

"Vincent, I need to ask you a big favour. For all I know when you go on duty tonight up to ten RIOS will be going through my team's files, including mine. And if that's the case don't do anything. I don't want you to get into any shit. But if there's still time use Stu's name and get in there. If Stu or Mulrooney or anyone else requests access then abandon it. You understand?"

"Don't worry I can watch my back. How do I get back to you?"

I picked one of five disposable mobiles at random. "Use this one", I read out the number.

"Ok Eddie, take care," he rang off. I had to trust him that he wouldn't let his Registry bosses know and I didn't think he would.

The phone I'd used to call Carl the Geek earlier rang; it was Carl. "You had company, all the way from the mosque," he announced.

"What?" I said, confused.

"We've spliced together all the available footage: the CTC surveillance car, your team's car and all CCTV coverage. Everything from the mosque to the Victoria Road pick up at the café, into the city centre and onto the Square. You were being followed."

"*What*?" I almost bellowed.

"Your team's car and the CTC car and, of course, ultimately the van were being followed by a silver grey 2002 Nissan Bluebird, bought at a second hand car auction in Edinburgh. The car was bought on Tuesday by a white guy who paid cash and gave his name as John Parkinson with an address in Newcastle. There's a real John Parkinson at that address but he knows sweet Fanny Adams about owing a 2002 Nissan Bluebird and he's been driving a bus all day aroond the toon (Carl affected an awful Geordie accent), so he's got dozens of passengers and colleagues to verify that he was nowhere near Glasgow at any time today. He did, though, recently sell a car through an online auction, but it wasn't a Bluebird. Looks like a wee bit of identity theft."

"Any update on the whereabouts of the Bluebird?"

"None," he replied firmly.

"You definite about this, I mean how did we miss them?"

"Absolutely," Carl warmed to his theme. "We've put it together as a continuous sequence. Your guys and the CTC guys are concentrating on the van and the van driver's probably concentrating on sussing if there's any surveillance (Carl wasn't privy to Sadeq being our agent), so nobody's looking for a third party. But when we look at the back cameras on the CTC car and your car, you can clearly see the Bluebird following on. Add the CCTV footage and it's even clearer. To be fair the driver's good, in fact he's a pro and you would never see it until you combine it all together."

The back cameras were positioned at the rear of the surveillance cars and fed into the dashboard, but the focus would be on the van in front, so unless the third follow-on car made it obvious, whoever it was could avoid being spotted, as they all drove towards the Square. But to avoid being spotted tailing two cars driven by CTC and MI5 agents was not easy; they had to be good, which meant they had to be trained professionals and that somehow didn't click with al-Qaeda's style.

"What happens to the car after the Square?" I asked Carl.

"Well, we've got CCTV footage tracking them out of the city centre, across the Clyde on the Kingston Bridge and then we lose them."

"You'll find the car abandoned and burnt to a cinder, if it's not already in a breaker's yard," I said wearily. "Any close-ups of who's in the Bluebird?"

"No, the footage is too grainy, though we're working on it, but not expecting too much. It looks like two guys, driver and a front seat passenger. Eddie," Carl had lowered his voice to a more confidential tone, "I'm in a loo at the Shields. This place is buzzing. Top brass are up from London; there's talk that the DG himself is in the building." He paused for a few seconds. "We've been told that if any of you guys: Wattie, Tres, Danny, you, contact us we're to inform House Security right away."

"Which you haven't done in my case, Carl?"

"No, Eddie and I won't either."

"Thanks Carl appreciated. We're all due back there in a couple of hours but keep this line open if there are any developments."

"Sure, Eddie, but watch yourself, the media's full of talk about MI5 following that van into George Square and a massive fuck-up!"

"I know, Carl you just keep me informed of any updates. That's the best way you can help me." I ended the call.

I lay on the bed, head buzzing. Though invaluable, Carl's new information felt like the final gratuitous kick to a man already lying on the deck. Not only had Grand Minaret (a name I harshly reminded myself that Wattie Craig had inadvertently come up with) been apparently fatally compromised from within, but even the final moments, as most of my agents groped in blissful ignorance towards the bloody denouement, were being watched, though by whom I didn't know. We had been used, manipulated, even humiliated. I felt utterly depressed and useless. Then the doorbell rang.

I got up, went through to the hallway and looked at the monitor. There were three cameras: one on the street outside, the backcourt and the landing with the monitor switching between the three. Tres was outside on the landing. She rang again and I opened the door to let her in.

I put the lights back on in the living room. I sat in the chair opposite the leather sofa which I indicated for Tres to sit down on. Reaching to the coffee table between us I picked up the bottle of merlot lying there, picked up two fresh glasses, poured some wine into one of the glasses and was about to do the same into the other when she put out her hand and said sharply, "No, I'm driving and I'm going to the Shields later. If you want me to, I'll drive you there."

"Thanks that would be good."

I sat back in the chair, drank some wine. We stayed in silence for some time. Not surprisingly, the sparkle and the lustre had gone out of her sensuous green eyes. She looked pallid and drawn, her brown hair crumpled. After a while she said:

"I couldn't relax. My mind's jumping from one thing to another. I can't even cry anymore!"

I shook my head. "Tres, I know, it's beyond comprehension, or at least my limited comprehension."

She opened her arms wide, seeking explanation: "What happened?" I knew her question was more rhetorical and she didn't really expect me to have the answer.

I looked her straight in the eye. "I don't know Tres. All I do know for certain is that we've been turned inside out and the consequence is that al-Qaeda, for I have to assume it is they, has been able to rip out the heart of Glasgow, which of course we were supposed to, were paid to, protect." Tres put her head in her hands. I felt like reaching out to her, taking her in my arms, hugging her, but I couldn't, instead I said:

"Sorry, Tres but there's no point in soft soaping a calamitous situation. The media are already onto us tailing the van."

She looked up and nodded her agreement. "I've heard," she said.

"And it gets worse. Carl the Geek's just been on the phone. The Shields is full of brass, so I'm expecting to get put through the ringer, in fact," again I looked her straight in the eye, "I'm expecting us all to be put through the ringer. Anyway Carl and his techie buddies have put together all the camera footage from yours and Wattie's car, the CTC car and CCTV. It appears we were being tailed, somebody else was watching us watching Sadeq and company."

"What?"

"Exactly what I said when I heard it. But, no it happened. Pros by the look of it who knew what they were doing. Did an ID theft from some poor bugger in Newcastle and bought the car using his *documents* at a car auction in Edinburgh on Tuesday, which means they knew the recce was going to happen on Wednesday."

She shook her head, her brown hair flailing over her shoulders, hands palms up in front of her. "But this is crazy," she protested, "How could they know?"

I put my wine glass firmly on the table between us. "Work it out, Tress." I waited for a few moments, but as there was still incomprehension written on her face I went on. "The only possible solution to your question, how did *they* know is…" I waited for a few more seconds, then concluded "that one of us assisted them or to put it another way, one of us was an informer for them, an agent."

As recognition dawned, she sighed: "Oh my God!"

I decided now was the time to ask her the burning questions that I needed some answers to. "Tres, could you take me through Tuesday night into Wednesday morning again?"

"I've already been through this Eddie!"

"And there'll be plenty more times when you're going to have to go through it believe me, but now just between us, tell me again." I picked up my glass and sipped the wine, listening intently to what she had to say.

"Wattie and I took over the van from Danny and Tony at eleven. You'd just left. We settled in. There was absolutely nothing to report and we kept the camera on Sadeq's van until the girl arrived home in the taxi about 2.30. She…"

"Who was operating the camera and moved it onto the girl away from the van?" I asked interrupting her.

There was a blink of her eyes, a fleeting movement of them from left to right and back before she resumed. "I saw the taxi and told

Wattie. I was working the camera and moved it onto the taxi arriving."

"You *told* Wattie! So you weren't sitting beside him?" Again there was the flickering of her eyes.

"Yes he was beside me, but he was reading a magazine, so I had to alert him to the taxi and he watched it with me, you can hear both of us narrating on the audio."

"So the girl leaves the taxi, tipsy, goes into her house and goes to bed while the taxi leaves?"

"Yes, as I say, that was it."

"And there was nothing the rest of the night until Tony and Danny relieved you at six?"

"No absolutely nothing, as usual, boring as fuck!" she said with apparent conviction.

"Tres, techies like Carl the Geek are probably among the most scorned people on the planet, but by God they do come in useful. Who else would sift through forty hours of the equivalent of watching paint dry all to get shots of a pissed lassie coming home and then, a couple of hours later, another twenty minutes of Sadeq's street with nothing happening. Oh, by the way, what caused you to shift the camera from the van to the street? This would be about 5.20 and why didn't you tell us about it?"

She stared back hard at me, apparently perplexed, confused and anxious in equal measure. Finally, she replied. "I don't understand what you mean?"

"It's simple, Tres. For some reason you, either *you or Wattie*, moved the camera away from the van for twenty minutes, but there's nothing to see on the video, nothing to justify that length of time away from the van which was our prime focus and there's no audio commentary on it and neither you nor Wattie saw fit to mention it which happens to be a flagrant breach of elementary surveillance tradecraft. I wouldn't expect two experienced field operatives on my team to do that, especially on so crucial an anti-terrorist operation such as this! So again, what caused you to move the camera away from the van and why didn't you tell us about it?"

Anxiety and fear had now overtaken every other emotion on her face, her eyes were flickering wildly and her cheeks were bright red.

Finally, after what seemed an age, she said softly, but audibly, "I didn't know about the camera being moved away at that time."

"Why didn't you know?"

She looked away from me, shook her head then looked back at me firmly, saying "Because I was sleeping."

"You were houring?"

"Yes Eddie, I was houring, we've all done it, Christ you and I have done it!"

'Houring' was the unwritten practice where on long two-person nightshift surveillance operations, one person slept for an hour while the other kept watch. It prevented two people succumbing to fatigue and they would alternate the hours through the shift. I did a quick mental timetable in my head.

"So, if you were on the monitor screen observing the van when the taxi arrived with the girl between two and three that would mean Wattie was 'houring' or sleeping then. You presumably woke him to alert him to the taxi entering the street and you were moving the camera, yes?"

"Yes."

That would explain why she shifted her gaze when I'd asked her why she'd had to let Wattie know of the appearance of the taxi as he'd been sleeping beside her.

I continued, "So, fresh awake, Wattie stays up and covers 3 to 4 am, allowing you an hour's sleep. Then you're on 4 to 5 while Wattie sleeps. Nothing happens in those two hours?"

She nodded in agreement.

"Wattie takes over from 5 till 6 and you go to sleep?"

Softly she said, "Yes."

"But he doesn't awake you during that hour, doesn't draw your attention to something that's alerted him and makes him move the camera away from the van at 5.20 in the morning for an entire twenty minutes?"

"No."

"When did Wattie wake you?"

"Just before Danny and Tony arrived, just after six."

"And Wattie never said anything to you or the guys about why he moved that camera away from the van?"

"No, nothing."

Tres's face was ashen as the consequences of this sank in.

"Why did we did provide surveillance, allegedly *protection* (I emphasised the word in a sarcastic tone) for nearly forty hours over a day-and-a-half for Sadeq?" I answered before she had time to think about it. "Because Sadeq was spooked about Qatib unexpectedly coming up to Glasgow; it was to provide him with *reassurance*. 'Look we're here, your friends are looking after you'.

"I checked that van at eleven on Tuesday night and it was clean. Nothing out of the routine happens on Danny and Tony's watch and they wouldn't have been 'houring'. Then Sadeq drives the van away at just after one. So the only chance for someone or some people to *place* an explosive in the van or to put it another way, an *IED*, was on the Tuesday nightshift. The techies have shown us there were only two times during that shift the camera wasn't on the van. One of these we can account for. The second we can't as you were sleeping and Wattie was at the screen controlling the camera on his own.

"Those twenty minutes would have been enough for a former Special Forces officer, experienced in handling and dealing with explosive devices, to place an IED in or under the van either timed to go off when it did or triggered by him in the Square. Alternatively, while you were asleep he could have signalled to another party outside the van to move in and place the device while he diverted the camera. I take it you heard or witnessed nothing strange in Wattie's behaviour all during this time?"

As I had been speaking to her, Tres still white-faced had been focused somewhere in the middle distance. As I finished my last question she refocused and looked sharply at me, her green eyes staring intently. "You know you're going to have to give Wattie Craig an Oscar after this!"

It was my turn to look perplexed. She went on, "I'll tell you why. I sat with that man on two night shifts and he never cracked a light, never the slightest change in character to indicate he was helping out al-Qaeda and sabotaging his own operation. Granted we were all high as kites because of Grand Minaret and so were *you*. But he was the same man, the same jokes, the same cynicism, as he always was. I was on the phone to him before I came here. Do you know what he said to me? He said 'Tres we're gonna get flung out the service after this, so why don't the two of us open a bar in Ibiza and play 90s old Skool dance tunes to all the old ravers who go there.' Now that doesn't strike me as someone who's just helped to blow up a city centre square killing hundreds of people, does it?"

"Tres, I hear what you say, but the fact is he moved that camera when you were sleeping and didn't tell you, nor has he informed anyone else, me for example. And that was the only chance for someone to get at the van to place the explosives. Clever, almost perverse genius: use the very people meant to be watching your target, to place the device!"

"But, why, why would Wattie do it? I mean, Jesus that would mean he's been instrumental in killing Tony, his friend and colleague!"

"I've no idea, Tres, I could guess, I can speculate, but I don't know; only Wattie will be able to tell us that. And who he worked with; who his contacts were with al- Qaeda."

Tres put her head in her hands and leaned forward heavily. I moved over to the sofa and sat beside her. I gently put my arm around her. Suddenly she lifted back her head, mangle of brown hair falling back. "But surely," she said, "Wattie would have known that people like Carl and the techies would have spotted the shift in the camera and known that could only be traced back to him, why would he be so stupid?" She said this as if it would deliver a fatal blow to any assertion of Wattie's guilt. It would be incredibly difficult for Tres to even begin to contemplate that one of her fellow agents who she's had to trust and depend on, spent hours on surveillance operations with, enjoyed the highs and lows with, was all along working on behalf of terrorists; as it was hard for me to take in.

I kept my arm around her shoulders. "Tres, for al-Qaeda Wattie would be expendable. If he's not done this for money or blackmail, then he's done it because he believes in it which means, despite all the front which he's hoaxed us with these last few years, that he's a fanatic. So, and I'll need to alert the service to this, whether he's caught or not is irrelevant as long as there was a gap that could be exploited to place the explosive device in the van, which he was able to do. As far as al-Qaeda are concerned, job done. Wattie will either go on the run or if they come for him, he'll go out literally with a bang; after all he's possibly bought into the whole jihadi notion of the martyr getting the key to heaven and eternity in heaven, no doubt with a few virgins to help him pass the time. And he'll be able to rationalise Tony's death as necessary; in that mind-set all those killed in a jihadi act also go to heaven, so Tony will be in paradise along with him."

I realised I would need to speak to Mulrooney urgently about Wattie, including how to bring him in. Al-Qaeda operatives had a track record of spectacularly blowing themselves and their erstwhile captors up when cornered.

For now I really began to feel tired. I kept my arm around Tres who had laid her head against my shoulder. We stayed like that in silence for a while, only the sound of a clock ticking in the room. Eventually I gently pulled her face to mine; her face was still slightly pallid and she was clearly shocked and exhausted, but a gentle smile played around those wonderful green eyes. I said softly to her, "Let's try and get some sleep, there's still a few hours till we're due back at the Shields."

She smiled then moved her forehead against the bridge of my nose before moving her head back, still closely watching me. The lustre in her eyes had returned, the white pallor of her skin receding. I moved further towards her and meeting no resistance kissed her, softly at first. She responded fully and we engaged in a passionate snog. After a while we came up for air and went to the bedroom. We tenderly undressed each other until naked and we made love. She had a fantastic body, trim and toned. She worked out a lot which was essential when the bulk of your job was desk bound or sitting and driving around in cars for long periods on surveillance. By contrast I didn't exercise at all and this showed in my mid-fifties' portly frame or to put it more unkindly, 'beer gut'. Tres had fantastic long legs which she could wind round you like a sinuous snake and her body practically enveloped you in its warm sexy embrace.

We were tired, we were exhausted. We were shocked, we were profoundly disturbed. We thought we were in charge of something and about to reap generous rewards and accolades, but 'it' was in charge of us and we were about to get severely punished for our conceit; careers and reputations in tatters. Around us appeared only treachery and betrayal. And it was almost assured that we would be cast out into oblivion; apart from death the final destination at the end of the (self) deception road.

Maybe it was because of or in spite of all this that the sex was frantic and energetic; a last pleasure before the hangman's noose. We tore and tagged at each other, chanted fulsomely "fuck me!" at each other a dozen times, screamed and ranted and finally climaxed in an orgasm of sighs before collapsing into each other and the soaking sheets.

We lay in silence afterwards. Tres seemed to doze off and I would occasionally lapse into a short, fitful sleep before awaking abruptly. At one point when I awoke with a start, the bed beside me was empty. I rose up and saw the hallway light streaming through the bedroom door only for it to be extinguished and Tres to come in and get back into bed to the sound of a toilet flushing. She lay with her back to me and resumed her sleep. It was only later that I realised she could have used the ensuite bathroom in the room, but I put that down to her unfamiliarity with the layout of the Art Safe House.

Our 'affair' if that's what it was, had lasted for about a year now. It had not begun, as many usually had, during the long interminable hours and in the cramped confines of a surveillance post. I was Tres's boss and was very scrupulous to keep things 'proper' and 'appropriate' between a superior officer and his subordinate. Indeed I believed I had acted quite reserved around her and certainly wouldn't engage in the ribald humour that I would do with the men, particularly Wattie. Not that Tres was reserved. She had a sharp tongue and could hold her own in the mutual banter and 'slagging' that went on between the team.

Though I did regard her as an attractive and sensual woman, I did not regard Tres as someone I would be likely to have a relationship with, mainly because I was her boss and it might prove too complicated for both of us. Indeed I'd considered Tres and Wattie more likely to get involved with each other. They got on very well and more often than not were paired together on surveillance jobs. As for me, well I'd been married twice. Once, for seven years which had produced my only child, my daughter Louise studying business management at university in London. Louise was the only positive legacy from a marriage that was already over by its second year and only spluttered on until my wife got fed playing second fiddle to MI5 as the 'third woman' in our marriage and sought a divorce. The second marriage lasted just over two years, until my second wife moved out and moved in with the teacher of her Spanish evening class. Good luck to both of them. How I ever thought I could be the married type was a mystery to me and, even more mysteriously, that the two woman could have believed it as well.

I could blame the service and the job: the long hours, the inability to confide anything of depth to your partners, all the strains and tensions of the secret life, all of which had produced far too many 'MI5 widows'. But it was more than that. Give me a routine office job and I would probably end up the same: lacking commitment, singularly lacking in romance, married to the job and unable to give the emotional depth that a loving, healthy relationship needs. Add to that mix the profession I'd got into was a world immersed in deception and betrayal, of manipulation and treachery. To shut that off, to try to compartmentalise my life so that a relationship was based on honesty and openness was for many in the secret services difficult, for me it was impossible. So, for most of the last ten years, after the failure of my second marriage, there'd been long periods of nothing interspersed with short, intense relationships (if you could really dignify them with that name) which had rapidly fizzled out. And, in truth, that is probably what I really hankered after.

Tres and I happened on a night out. Planning a night out can be a pain when you're in a secret intelligence agency. You can't simply phone a restaurant, club or pub and book 'a table for MI5!' You have to be careful where you go, not just in case you meet people you don't want to rub shoulders with, but so you can have the space, the privacy of relaxing and unwinding without strangers, non-secret service people around, especially when alcohol, the great disinhibiter, loosens the tongue. Consequently our team nights out were always held in out-of-the-way venues.

Just before the critical meeting with Sadeq in Largs over a year ago, which got Grand Minaret underway, we'd organised a team night out at a hotel-cum-diner on the Fenwick Moors to the south of the city. We'd booked it for a quiet Tuesday in April and we virtually had the place to ourselves, which was ideal. The food was good and the bar was our own, so we could talk and play in comfort. We got to use that lovely Glaswegian expression, 'wired' into the booze. Young Tony was the first casualty and crashed to his bed around midnight. After getting him to his room the rest of us continued dancing, singing, drinking until after an arm-wrestling match between Danny and Wattie (predictably Wattie won), the guys announced they were going to their beds. This was around four am and after much dishing out of 'wimps' and 'part-timers' as Danny and Wattie left us, Tres and I stayed drinking for another hour.

Inevitably, alone between a man and a woman at that time in the morning, the conversation turned to relationships or the lack of them in our lives. But it wasn't morose as we both agreed that neither of us were suited for a full-time committed relationship. Like me, Tres was married to her job, as she had been in nursing. And despite working with children in the highly charged atmosphere of a children's ward, she'd never really wanted children herself, even though at thirty-five her clock was ticking away. We both agreed that if the right person came along anything was possible, including children.

Tres had stretched her arms, yawned and rose from her seat. "I'm done in", she said, "I'm going to bed."

I put my glass down as well. "So am I. Don't think I'm going to make breakfast in," I checked my watch. It was well past five and I shook my head, "In about three hours!"

"Me neither," she agreed.

We climbed the steps to our rooms, laughing and giggling on the way up. Tres's bedroom was the first we reached just by the landing. "That was a great night. I thoroughly enjoyed it," I said.

"Yes," she replied those mischievous, sparkling green eyes darting from side to side, a playful smile on her lips, "but it doesn't have to end now."

I looked carefully at her and weighed up the desire to have her versus the complications that might ensue if I spent the night with her. What clinched it was her opening the door and gazing lustfully over her shoulder at the room inside with the bed beside the window prominent. Without waiting any longer she walked into the room. I followed, shutting the door behind me and spent a beautiful early morning sunrise having very fulfilling sex in spite of all the booze consumed.

Nobody made breakfast that morning; indeed Tres and I were the first to rise at around eleven. The upshot being that nobody was aware we'd shared a bed. Over the next year we continued to meet up for regular, very satisfying sex, with nobody else on the team any the wiser, or if they had cottoned on, they were discreet enough not to talk about it. Neither Tres nor I saw the need to let anyone know. We were both in agreement that if anyone else came along that one of us took a deeper shine to and heaven forbid fell in love with, then we would end it. And that's how things between us had stood over the past year.

I must have fallen asleep again but not pleasantly as dreamy images of what I'd witnessed in the Square: torn statues and people, ripped off roofs of buses and shards of glass dripping with blood cascaded by in a lurid kaleidoscope of vivid colours, until I heard a deep vibrating, throbbing noise which brought me back into wakefulness. It was the mobile phone I used exclusively to communicate with the Shields, vibrating and lighting up on the bedside table. I picked it up. There was a text from Mulrooney.

Urgent report immediately to base. Your team have been instructed to do the same. Do NOT phone or attempt to communicate

That was serious. Something big had happened. I checked my watch; it was just after midnight, a couple of hours before the scheduled meeting at three am. Tres was sleeping beside me. I shook her gently awake. "The shit seems to be hitting the fan already. We've just been ordered back to the Shields, immediately, all of us," I said to her.

Through sleep-loaded eyes she looked up at me. "This is a nightmare," she said.

I kissed her on the lips, "We'll get though it somehow," I said, trying to be reassuring, but the look on her now limpid green eyes told me I wasn't being convincing.

7: RATLINE

Tres and I drove to the Shields in silence. Even though it was past midnight during midweek the city was unearthly quiet; the shocked, still afterglow of a city in trauma. Apart from a few police vehicles we were alone on the roads. By contrast, the Shields when we arrived there was a blaze of activity, every light was on in the upper two storeys which made the unlit and apparently empty ex-service man's club on the ground floor stand out in distinction.

Two Rovers were parked on the street outside, two men in each, and I recognized them as CTC cars. That *was* a turn-up for the books: CTC providing security for MI5. Or was it more likely to be surveillance? Tres brought our car to a halt on the busy gravel driveway. As we walked up the short flight of steps that gave on to the entrance which afforded access to the upper floors, the imposing doors opened and two tall, slim men, shaven headed and both wearing leather jackets blocked the entrance, saying nothing, faces stern, watching us closely. We produced our IDs which were examined intensively by one of the men. He gave us back the IDs before taking out a radio handset and talking to someone inside the house.

Over the static we could hear a disembodied crackly male voice say "Keep them there, someone will be down in a few minutes." Replying "Rodger" into the handset the shaven headed man replaced the radio inside his jacket and resumed his fixed, blocking position at the entrance, his non-verbal expression saying 'you heard the man', which we clearly had. The four of us stood there in silence in the mild April night in the midst of Glasgow's suburbia until a dapper figure, sporting a moustache and a dark suit came from behind the two men and announced in a cut glass accent:

"Ah, Mr Macintyre and I do believe Ms Martindale. Sorry to keep you but we're on Alert Red and everyone's being stopped. Do come through." The men gave way and let us past, but then followed behind us, belying the notion that they were just security doorman; the dapper figure walked in front.

We ascended the narrow staircase to the first floor with prints of Scottish highland and wildlife scenes on either side. Two more security men, dressed similarly to the first two were at the top. As the dapper man moved into the corridor, the two men stood in front of me while the other two from downstairs stood behind. A female security officer appeared, dressed entirely in black with a radio set and gun hanging from the belt of her trousers and took gentle hold of Tres who offered no resistance. The dapper man spoke again:

"I apologise again, but this is procedure in Alert Status Red." Tres and I were given a close body search. My crumpled suit and trousers were patted down revealing nothing more than my wallet, ID card, keys, money and two mobile phones, all of which I was allowed to keep. Tres was subjected to the same routine by the female officer, including an inspection of her handbag, but again nothing appeared to cause alarm.

Cursory search over, the dapper figure bade us follow him along the corridor, this time unescorted by the security detail. "The last time I remember it being like this was in Thames House during 9/11," he said almost jovially. "I missed the 7/7 bombings, I was on annual leave, but it was probably not unlike this too."

We arrived at Mulrooney's office. The dapper man stopped and spoke directly to me. "You don't recognize me Mr Macintyre do you?" Without waiting for a reply he went on: "I'm Harry Perkins, you've been on a few training courses over the years I've organised." As soon as he said his name I knew who he was, though in truth I'd only seen him for a few minutes each time on busy training sessions over the last thirty odd years in the service. Harry Perkins was second in charge of MI5 Security; those who watch the watchers. I knew that his casual, upper class public schoolboy appearance was a façade. He had risen from organising counter-intelligence training courses to No 2 at Security by dint of a razor sharp mind. Though he could cover it with a certain cultured bonhomie, he was probably as stern and ruthless as the security detail he was in charge of. I'd only seen him fleetingly in all those years because, outside training updates, we'd had no need to get to know each other as I'd never come to the attention of his department: until now.

"Well it would have been better to be reacquainted in nicer circumstances," I responded to him dryly.

"Indeed. Now, if I could escort Ms Martindale to the conference room, Mr Mulrooney and the DG are waiting for you," he knocked on the door and opened it, indicating for me to go in.

I said "See you later, Tres," as Perkins took her gently by the arm.

"Take care, Eddie," she half-turned with a look of care mixed with anxiety as she was led away. I entered Mulrooney's office.

Seated behind his desk was Mulrooney, still in his bespoke suit, but what a contrast to the urbane, confident figure who strode into the conference room only a few hours earlier. His face was waxen and his whole appearance belied a man who looked washed out and frazzled. The mask must have begun slipping when the *Guardian* journalist started the inquiries about MI5 tailing the Glasgow bombers, which had caused him to engage in an uncharacteristic bout of swearing. Since then he'd probably been chewed out by a bevy of Scottish Government senior officials, Home Office permanent civil servants and Cabinet Office secretaries, not to mention his own boss the DG and that was before he was thrown to the politicians and the media.

Any illusion that he could ride this out, engage in some form of damage control and somehow survive was by now irremediably shattered. A lifetime of behind the scenes manipulation and riding the wave of MI5 office politics to retire on a good pension and a possible knighthood or at least a CBE and a well remunerated set of consultancies and directorships, was now destroyed and within a few hours Colin Mulrooney would be forced to resign in disgrace as Scotland National Co-ordinator of MI5. And while I had some degree of sympathy with my (for now) boss, disgrace and resignation might not be too bad an option compared to the shit I was to face. As it was, it was evident in that room that all power had evaporated from Mulrooney and was focused on the man in the immaculate pinstripe suit sitting beside him: the DG of MI5.

In front of the desk was a chair which the DG indicated for me to sit on. It was only when I went to sit on the chair that I became aware of a third man in the room, sitting very quietly in the corner with a laptop; he was bald with a high forehead, jacketless wearing a cream shirt with red braces. I glanced at him, but apart from his piercing blue eyes, he remained expressionless. I knew who he was even though again I'd only seen him a few times at conferences and updates; it was Algy Hunter, Head of MI5 internal security, Perkin's boss.

Fuck's sake, Macintyre, I thought, the top brass of MI5 all the way up to Glasgow to see you: for all the wrong reasons!

Seated I looked straight at the DG. He appeared of medium height with close cropped brown hair turning to grey in spite of the best efforts of hair dyes. His eyes were deep inset which together with his overall composed demeanour made it nearly impossible to discern what he was thinking or what his emotions were. It was said that he could be bawling you out or praising you with the highest accolades and his expression would remain exactly the same. He consulted some papers in front of him before looking up at me. Clearing his throat he said:

"We are all in the service very saddened and affected by the loss of the young officer Mr Boyd. He died on active service and I've ordered Mr Hutchinson to pass on our condolences and anything we can do for his family."

The accent was, like Perkins, pure Oxbridge out of Eton. While the lower and middle ranks of MI5 might have been opened up to the hoi polloi, the upper echelons were still the preserve of the aristocracy. But it was the import of what he said that struck home. I was Tony Boyd's officer-in-charge but Stu Hutchinson would be informing and no doubt meeting the family rather than me. Okay it was small beer compared to the rest of the crap that was about to come my way, but indicative of the fact that I was persona non grata.

Turning briefly to the waxen-faced Mulrooney, the DG said, "Ms Martindale and Mr Mackay are here, but we seem unable to contact Mr Craig," he turned away from Mulrooney who merely briefly nodded in agreement and looked enquiringly at me.

I'd also glanced at Mulrooney and for the first time noticed that the framed pictures of Mulrooney's two daughters and his wife were no longer on his desk: symbolic of the brute fact that he was on his way out.

Replying as best as I could to the DG's blank face I said, "I've had no contact with Mr Craig since our last briefing here a few hours ago."

"But you had been in contact with Ms Martindale?"

"She came to the Art Safe House, Sir."

"Why?"

"To give me support," you could almost feel the three males in the room saying "oh is that what they call it these days!" But there was only silence for a short while.

"So you've no idea where Mr Craig is?" the DG pressed on.

He was either focusing on Wattie because he was keen to get the surviving Grand Minaret team in one place as soon as possible or anxious that he wasn't here because he was already a suspect; probably both.

"No, Sir," I replied. "If he wasn't at his flat I wouldn't know where he is."

An authoritative sharp voice spoke from behind: "Contact him, Macintyre. Now!" It was Hunter barking orders like an aristo army CO to a subaltern.

I reached into my jacket pocket and retrieved my office mobile, found Wattie's name under the alias of 'Richardson' and phoned, but it rang on to voicemail. "There's no answer," I said.

"Text him," Hunter ordered. I typed a short text: *Wattie get your butt into the Shields NOW!*

I held the phone aloft for the three of them to see the message, sent the text and replaced the phone in my jacket.

"I don't need to tell you, Mr Macintyre, of the sheer gravity of the situation that we're faced with here," the DG resumed. "Over 80 dead, among them a serving officer, many more injured. Dreadful enough for us if we hadn't known it was coming. But we actually escorted the bombers into the heart of the city to commit their diabolical act. How do you explain that, Mr Macintyre? How do I explain that to the media, the public, the PM, the First Minister? How did Grand Minaret go so badly wrong?"

I took my time answering him. The room was in total silence in stark contrast to the buzz of activity in the rest of the Shields. Eventually, I said succinctly:

"The precise details of what actually transpired, I don't know, Sir. But what I do know is that the operation was compromised."

"And what exactly, Mr Macintyre do you mean by 'compromised'?"

"Somebody got to the van and placed the explosive device on it. And the only way they could have done that is by knowing what our specific surveillance details were and evading or diverting away from them. This was not a suicide bombing," I said firmly. "None of the people in that van were carrying a bomb."

Hunter spoke again from behind. "So if the operation was compromised, who compromised it? Who placed the bomb?"

I turned to face him. Just be honest, I thought, he probably thinks the same. "It shatters me to say it, but possibly one of the surveillance team."

"You mean *your* surveillance team?"

"Yes, *my* surveillance team. But," and rather too quickly, but almost impulsively, I added, "they couldn't have acted alone; they would have had to had help."

Hunter retorted, "Well that would be obvious wouldn't it?"

There was a long, heavy silence eventually interrupted by the DG who spoke to Hunter: "Algy, I think it's important that Mr Macintyre has a chance to see the latest update."

Hunter stood up, extinguished the overhead lights and took up a remote control bringing a large plasma screen on the wall to the left of Mulrooney's desk to life. The DG spoke again:

"Al Jazeera TV's Beirut station received this tape sometime in the last two hours. They were kind enough to get a copy to our Beirut embassy who dispatched it to JTAC who've circulated copies to us, SIS and GCHQ, as well as the FO and Downing St. Al Jazeera haven't broadcast it yet, but they will soon, probably in the next hour or so and the repercussions are likely to be serious as you'll see."

The screen came to life and revealed a desert landscape with low hills and some bushes in the background. In the foreground was a tall slim man in long flowing Arab robe and head-dress reading from notes, flourishing the papers widely from side to side as he addressed the camera. He was in his mid-thirties with a short beard, no moustache and a wide sharp-featured face. Certainly, in spite of the fact that he was speaking or rather orating to the camera in Arabic, he was a handsome man with a striking presence. From reports and briefings I guessed who he was, but the DG confirmed it, "Ali al Hassan presumed new leader of al-Qaeda and successor to Osama Bin Laden."

However much you may have reviled Bin Laden and the horrors he was responsible for, he had a telegenic profile which made him instantly recognizable. Ali al Hassan, though a younger man, was in the same mould; he had a perverse charisma and, watching him on the screen, it was easy to see how he had managed to rally the disparate factions and elements that were loosely affiliated to al-Qaeda and make a serious bid to unite them under his leadership. I watched him closely as he spoke to the camera and followed the English subtitles at the bottom of the screen. He was speaking about the Glasgow bomb.

"Today we have struck once again in the heartlands of the West. They had written us off, that we were incapable of striking in the middle of their cities, amongst their own people, just as they have done to our people for decades. Today in Scotland, which like the rest of the world, will come to live in peace, universal brotherhood and equality under Islam, jihad was carried out. Our brothers, our holy warriors sacrificed themselves for Allah and Islam and they are not alone; there are hundreds of thousands of brothers prepared to become martyrs for Islam." He waved a finger at the camera.

"You in the West can never relax; can never know when we will strike next. Yes, you may be lucky and your dirty cowardly informers, who will face unmerciful, unspeakable tortures for eternity in hell, can stop some of our missions. But I assure you for every person or group that belongs to us who you break-up and capture, there are many more to replace them.

"And we have another weapon which, Allah willing, will make us impregnable and help to ensure the final victory of Allah's will on earth. We have managed to infiltrate to the heart of the West's intelligence services. Our brothers have put on the face of decadence and imperialism and have infiltrated their way into the intelligence services. Yes, those who thought they could destroy us through informers and spies, well two can play that game, my friends. Today in Scotland our holy warriors attacked, but they were assisted in this by our brothers who have penetrated the secret operations of the Western intelligence agencies who conspire against our people and Islam. Now we conspire against them to the highest levels with our infiltrators and our spies who will bring the CIA and the MI6 and the rest of them to their knees. Jihad goes on, the holy war goes on stronger and more resolute than ever! Praise be to Allah!"

The image faded abruptly, the screen darkened as Hunter switched the set off. I resumed facing the DG who was staring straight at me. He said: "The probable new top man in al-Qaeda has just told the world that he has agents in our intelligence services who helped him to blow up a British city! Do you realise what impact this will have when Al Jazeera broadcast it?"

Yes I did. It wasn't only Mulrooney who was on the way out. The public revelation that al-Qaeda had penetrated MI5 to help them commit terrorist atrocities meant that all of us in that room: the DG, Hunter and, of course, me were all on our way out. In a strange way, that made me feel less isolated. But there was something puzzling me and I expressed it to the DG.

"Sir, why would al Hasan reveal that, reveal he had infiltrated agents into the West, surely he would want to keep silent on that and exist on the take those informers can give him?"

It was Hunter who answered from behind me. "It's politics, Macintyre. Since the death of Bin Laden, al-Qaeda has been on the back foot. All the big operations of the noughties: 9/11, 7/7, Madrid, Bali haven't been replicated, or as you're no doubt aware with the thwarted attacks on European cities this past eighteen months, have been stopped by good intelligence work. ISIS have made all the running especially with their devastating attack on Paris. Yes Hassan has rallied all the regional groups that were breaking away and is on the cusp of unifying them under his command, but he has had to fight every inch to achieve that and there's a lot of commanders in the regional groups that are either still not sure of him or even mistrustful of him. Remember it's those regional groups, in North Africa, Mali, ISIS in Syria and Iraq as well as the Arabian Peninsula that do the actual fighting, the holy warrior and martyrdom stuff.

Hassan has to show he has the cojones and the ability to pull off attacks in the West just as good as ISIS appears to be able to.

"One Glasgow is worth a hundred operations in Syria, Iraq or Yemen in terms of publicity. Add to that claims, or rather the *actuality* that he has been able to infiltrate Western intelligence agencies and that puts his credit rating even higher. There are probably people in al-Qaeda right now cringing that he's revealed this, because they think like you and I would; keep your agents in place for the long run. But Hassan at the end of the day is a politician and like all politicians he wants all the glory and the triumph *now* revealed for the entire world to know, particularly those he's trying to win over in his own camp. Besides, look at the chaos, the paralysis, which will now ensue in Washington, London, all over Europe," he paused, those piercing blue eyes penetrating me like laser beams, "here in MI5, as the investigations and the accusations get under way." Hunter shook his head, almost sadly and conceded to his terrorist foe: "Though it pains me to say it, credit where credit's due, this is a coup for him and will consolidate his leadership of al-Qaeda."

The DG took up the flow. "There's good intelligence that all the top commanders of the regional al-Qaeda affiliates are all getting together for a meeting in North Africa sometime in the next few days. The timing of the Glasgow bomb and his announcement today is, therefore, perfect, as it gives Hassan all he needs to claim his place as Bin Laden's rightful successor. What's even more alarming is that if all the regional groups do agree to come under his command, the potential of a co-ordinated, well-armed al-Qaeda is a much greater threat to the West than it was even after 9/11. But, Mr Macintyre, that will be for others, not us, to fight. What we have to deal with here, with very little time to do so, is how al-Qaeda were able to infiltrate our service and who was their agent or agents amongst us." His voice lowered almost to a whisper, but was still firm in its conviction. "That is what I wish to do before I depart, which will be very soon." He glanced over at Hunter who stood up, which was the cue for the DG and Mulrooney to do so as well. I got up, but before Hunter could say anything I said:

"You know that our surveillance were followed from the rendezvous with Qatib (and we still don't know why *he* came to Glasgow), the pick-up at the café and into the city-centre, to the Square? It was a professional team; we never detected them." I knew I was risking Carl here, but I wanted to see their reactions. Hunter responded, "Yes, we are aware of that."

"Any idea who they were?" I asked.

There was a fleeting, almost imperceptible, rapid movement of Hunter's eyes, a quick glance at the DG before Hunter replied, "No, we're still working on who that might be."

Lying bastard! All my career, when asking critical questions and the eyes of those being questioned dart and blink like that, I know without fail that the answer's going to be a lie, like Tres back at the Art Safe House trying to cover up the fact she was sleeping during the hour the camera was moved away from Sadeq's van. Hunter was lying and, by implication with his glance over to him, so did the DG. I started to think rapidly so had to concentrate hard as the DG spoke to me.

"Mr Macintyre, Mr Hunter's department will be leading a full inquiry into the aftermath of operation Grand Minaret, at least initially," the DG couldn't help himself making another fleeting glance at Hunter, they both knew that at any time they themselves could be under investigation or suspended and an inquiry handed over to another agency. "Mr Perkins will accompany you to the facility in Troon where we can carry out a thorough investigation into what has happened, I trust with your full co-operation."

"Of course, Sir," I replied. Hunter opened the door. I gave one last look at Mulrooney, from whom all life seemed to have drained. He just nodded sadly at me and I nodded back in kind. Twenty-three years he'd been my boss and like all good bosses he'd been a combination of guide, mentor, supporter and, occasionally, pain in the arse. I liked him, as he'd given me the right balance of freedom and control to get on with the job. This was a really terrible way for that relationship to end. I felt sad for him and me.

Perkins was waiting in the corridor, his good natured, casual act still to the fore as we walked along the corridor. "I'm to take you to Troon to try and shed some more light on this," he said amiably as if we were going for a quiet discussion on who might have nicked an office laptop. 'Troon' was a house which doubled as a 'farm' outside the Ayrshire seaside town of Troon, best known for its proximity to the world famous Turnberry golf course. It was one of the Service's investigation centres which meant it was used for interrogations of suspected double-agents.

"Danny and Tres coming too?" we were going past the conference room.

"Maybe later, Eddie, I'm only accompanying you just now." I got the impression that Perkins struggled to refrain from uttering 'old boy' or 'old chap' at the end of most sentences lest he reveal himself too much as an unreconstructed, anachronistic upper-class public schoolboy in these supposedly more egalitarian times.

By the conference room we turned right. At the end of this corridor was another exit where two more leather jacketed, well-built security guards waited, silent and motionless.

"I take it the goons are coming with us?" I asked him.

Almost apologetically, he replied, "They will be along with us, yes."

I stopped halfway to the exit. "Listen, Harry," I pointed at myself, "I've only got what I'm standing up in. Any chance I could go up to the overnight room I was staying in last night? I've got some shirts, trousers, underwear and toiletries up there I could pack in an overnight bag. After all I suspect we're going to be a wee while in Troon."

He smiled. "Of course, Eddie." He made a 'don't worry, everything's fine' expression to the security men at the exit as we retraced our steps back to the main corridor. As we climbed the stairs to the second floor, there was a discernible vibration noise coming from one of the mobiles in my jacket pocket. I tried to ignore it, but Perkins remarked: "You not answering you're mobile, Eddie?"

"Of course." The vibration had stopped. I fished out the mobile, it was the office phone and there was a text from Wattie which said:

Fuck off boss, not getting thrown to the wolves. Not doing an Oswald for any bastard.

I switched off the lit screen and tried to put the mobile back in my jacket. We'd reached the top of the stairs and were only a few feet from the overnight room. "I think I should take that Eddie." We stopped. Perkins' face still held a smile, but the eyes were steel, a window to the real Harry Perkins and what I should expect more of shortly down at Troon. Without a word I handed over the mobile. "Thank you," Perkins kept the mobile in his hand as we resumed our way to the overnight room.

My head was a whirling maelstrom of thoughts of which three were uppermost. Wattie was on the run and, as a firm believer that President John. F. Kennedy was assassinated as part of a conspiracy, was comparing himself to the 'patsy' that he was strongly convinced Lee Harvey Oswald, Kennedy's alleged assassin, had been made out to be. The second thought prominent in my head was that, after the summons for us all to report earlier than scheduled to the Shields, Wattie had sussed that he might be a suspect either because he *was* an al-Qaeda agent or he'd worked out that his military background and time in Afghanistan and Iraq might bring him under suspicion. Alternatively, he might have been tipped off and the only person that could have done that was Tres to whom I'd revealed the movement of the surveillance camera away from the van. Finally, what was the DG and Hunter covering up by lying about whoever had been tailing us into George Square; what did that imply and why wouldn't they tell me? Wattie's phrase in his text resonated strongly in my mind: *not getting thrown to the wolves*.

What I did next was completely unplanned and totally impulsive. Stopping at the door of the overnight room, I turned to Perkins.

"Listen Harry, I'm dying for a crap, I've not been all day, I don't want an accident on the way to Troon, so could you give me ten minutes?"

There was a small ensuite bathroom attached to the overnight room. I figured that Perkins wouldn't want to wait in the room and listen as I attended urgently to nature.

Somewhat disconcerted he replied: "Of course, but no more than ten, eh?" He flashed ten fingers, palms upwards at me, "Or I'll have to come in and get you."

"No problem, I'll be finished before then, thanks Harry." He gave me a 'too much information look' as I went into the overnight room and closed the door behind me.

I looked around the small overnight room with the compact bathroom, which also contained a shower. I moved to the window and looked outside. The room looked onto the back of the house with a short gravel path and a garden behind with some flowerbeds, greenery and, more importantly a large, gnarled oak tree, some of whose branches jutted out across the neighbouring garden. There was another solid two-storey red sandstone villa behind the Shields which itself had originally been only two stories until it had undergone a major refurbishment and conversion to create a third floor, after the service had acquired it. Some twelve feet below the overnight room window an extension to the ex-servicemen's club on the ground floor meant there was an almost flat, gently sloping roof made of pitch tar immediately below

I tried to remember the layout of the first floor of the Shields and was fairly certain the room below me was a storeroom which meant it would normally be empty. At the edge of the building was a parked car, but I could only see the back of it, the rest of it was out of sight, but I couldn't see any sign of life from it, nor from the lack of reflection did the rear lights appear to be on. There was a wooden bench at the side which I knew staff who smoked used regularly, but there was no one there now.

Moving away from the window I picked up the overnight shoulder bag I'd brought with me. I'd brought enough clothes to last a couple of days as I reckoned that after recce Wednesday I'd have to stay on operational duty at the Shields for a few nights so I'd crammed some shirts, sweaters, a pair of jeans and socks and underwear into the shoulder bag. Going into the bathroom, I looked at my reflection in the mirror. Not a pretty sight, unshaved, eyes heavy with stress and lack of sleep and clothes crumpled: I looked dishevelled. I quickly got out of the clothes I was in and washed my face in the basin. I even very quickly brushed my teeth. Grabbing a towel I covered up my crotch with it and went to the door. Perkins was completely taken aback by the sight of me naked except for the towel hiding my manhood.

"Sorry Harry, but I was minging. Give me an extra five minutes till I finish a quick wash and put some fresh clothes on. That alright?"

"Sure, Eddie, sure, five more minutes." I shut the door again on his startled, but now relieved face.

After attending to my toilet needs, putting some sweet smelling deodorant on and changing into fresh socks and underwear, I changed into a casual grey jacket, white sweatshirt and blue jeans. Riffling through the compartments of the shoulder bag I retrieved two false passports with my photo on each. One, known to the service, was under the name of 'Gary Carson'; the other, not known to anyone else was issued to a 'Jack Donaldson'. I also took out two credit cards that belonged to the Donaldson alias as well as six disposable mobiles I kept up to date on credit. Finally I took out a wallet stuffed with £2,000 in cash which I kept for emergencies and 'contingencies'.

'Jack Donaldson' was a real person, born in Glasgow, who would have been my age, but died in a car crash in the Highlands when he was eleven. I had created many aliases in my career as an MI5 officer, all known and sanctioned by my superiors, but the Donaldson alias or legend was my own private creation for contingencies and emergencies such as this. Life as an intelligence operative, whether you're an officer/agent handler or informer is a dark one, full of intrigue. In 'normal' routine situations you need to rely on your team and your bosses to support you and you for them. But, in the twilight world of the secret service, where treachery and double-dealing is only a stone's throw away, you have to plan for a time when the routine collapses, when you really can't trust anyone and trying to distinguish between friend and foe becomes blurred. This was such a time.

Over the years I'd been on training courses with SIS agents. A routine part of those courses was what we'd call 'enhanced MosBerBel'; basically as an intelligence agency working abroad this was standard rules for conduct and survival for SIS agents in unsafe, hostile environments where reliance couldn't be placed on the local British embassy either because it was too dangerous to try to approach it or the operation you were engaged on was 'deniable' by official government sources: i.e. you were on your own if things went wrong. SIS agents, in such cases, were encouraged to develop their own 'ratlines'.

A ratline was a set of informers, agents, contacts, sources, some on the official books, more importantly some not, who you could turn to in an emergency. They could be used to provide shelter, food and other essentials, acquire documents and get you to the embassy, or if that was too risky, help to exfiltrate you out of the country. Outside the official training sessions, on get-togethers, drinking sessions and similar set-ups, a young intelligence officer, even though operating in your own country on behalf of Her Majesty's government, is encouraged by colleagues, especially veterans, to set up their own private home-grown ratline of contacts and informers for whenever a situation of enhanced MosBerBel arises. That is when your own home turf becomes enemy country and nobody can be trusted.

I didn't subscribe to conspiracy theory; in the main. Even though the essence of our work as secret agents was a conspiracy, I'd seen too many cock-ups and fuck-ups over thirty odd years to know that the grand master conspiracies beloved of the conspiracy theorists were too clever, too well planned to reflect reality which was mainly dull, grey and punctuated by the odd horror or calamity. Human error, cock-up and the completely unexpected would blow apart any grand design. Though we tried to infiltrate and manipulate people and organisations it never did quite work out the way you intended and I'd seen nothing in counter-subversion, counter-intelligence, counter-terrorism and even anti-drugs work which came near the grand machinations that we are constantly led to believe lie just 'behind the scenes'. In my experience behind the scenes only reveals chaos and defensive cover-ups. That's where ratlines came in: your own private network that you could turn to when official sources are likely to have been compromised or betrayed.

Ten minutes had passed. By my reckoning I had another five before Perkins would rap on the door. Was I ready to do this? Was it not madness? I probably would have complied with orders and went with Perkins and his goons to Troon were it not for the fleeting glance exchanged between Hunter and the DG. They'd denied knowing who'd followed us yesterday into the Square, but I was certain they'd lied. And even though I didn't believe in conspiracy theories the whole scenario with my immediate team allegedly being infiltrated, the new CEO of al-Qaeda openly telling the world he had spies in MI5, the mystery around who followed us into the Square, the clamour to find the culprits and traitors in our midst, meant in that cauldron the search for truth would give way to half-truths, evasions, distortions and compromises. Whatever, I could languish in Troon and places like it for a long time falsely accused of being part of a terrorist conspiracy or reviled as an incompetent, neglectful officer, which neither reflected the reality of my career and was totally unfair. Ok it looked as if one of my team did assist terrorists to commit the heinous act today. But they had to have had help and where did that come from? Incarcerated in Troon at the mercy of Perkins and Hunter (or whoever replaced them) wouldn't help me get the answer to that and would probably be extremely harmful to my wellbeing.

I had three minutes left. "Just changing into new Cary Grants, Harry, be with you in a couple of minutes," I shouted through the door.

"Sorry?" I heard him respond baffled.

"New pants, Harry, cream boxers to be precise. You don't want to be sitting beside a guy in a car with dirty pants do you?"

"Sure, sure, just hurry." his perplexed voice urged from behind the door.

I went to the bathroom with one of the disposable mobiles and phoned Andy, a taxi driver and one of three ratline contacts I had ideas of using, for in truth apart from getting away from MI5, the Shields and the prospect of Troon, I had no definite plan. The phone seemed to ring for eternity. At last Andy answered.

I tried to remain calm. "It's Gary Carson, Andy. I need a hire immediately."

His voiced changed a gear. "Where are you?"

"Southside, could you get to the middle of Nithsdale Road quickly, I mean *very* quickly!"

"You're in luck. I'm in Pollok and I could be there in ten minutes."

"OK Andy, that's great, halfway up the road, I'll get you there."

I came out the bathroom, did a final check of my jacket pockets: phones, credit cards, passports, all there. I didn't want to be encumbered so I left the shoulder bag and went to the window. There was a catch which I easily unlocked and opened the window gently. I checked my watch; it was just past two am. I waited for any alarm to go off. There was nothing and nothing stirred below. Reaching out I could confirm the rear lights of the car parked at the side were out. This gave me the final confidence to reach up, climb over the sill, crouch and jump to the pitch tar roof below. I landed with a thud but otherwise comfortably and unhurt. I crawled towards the edge of the roof. The back was empty, not even a nightshift smoker on the bench. The room on the first floor level with the roof was also in darkness.

Again crouching down I jumped from the low roof onto the gravel path. Apart from a few scratches on the palms of my hands from the gravel I landed easily. Still nothing stirred. I walked quickly to the oak tree. Grabbing a low hanging branch I got my foot on a crevice between the trunk and a couple of sturdy branches and climbed slowly upwards. The silence was uncanny until I remembered the windows at the Shields were reinforced thick glazing to disguise any sound from within. I reached the start of one of the branches that jutted out to the neighbouring villa, which was in pitch darkness.

As I climbed along the branch I looked up and saw the open window of the overnight room; Perkins had still not come in, but could do so any second, especially if I wasn't responding to him. I reached the wall that divided the Shields from its neighbour. There was razor wire fencing on top of the wall and presumably some sensors installed there. What I didn't know was if there were any sensors on the tree. I moved forward across the wall, above the wire fence. No alarm sounded. The branch began to get thinner and appreciably lighter. I swung from under it and let myself fall to the grass below. I landed on my side, but the grass absorbed the impact. I picked myself up, shook the grass off me and walked round the side of the villa.

I froze as a security light came on but it wasn't accompanied by any alarm and allowed me to see clearly to the front of the villa, which was a circular driveway that gave on to a sloping road leading onto the main road and, to my immense relief, was not blocked by gates. Suddenly a loud, distinctly old Etonian voice rent the air: "Macintyre, don't be so bloody silly!" It was Perkins who'd entered the room, saw the open window and began shouting desperately into the night knowing he would cop it from Hunter for losing me.

I ran across the circular driveway down the sloping road onto Nithsdale Road. No lights came on in the villa, but how long would it take Hunter's people to scramble cars or chase after me through the gardens? I stopped at the open gate, breathing heavily, heart racing, face flushed. At my last medical check-up about six months ago I was told I was generally ok, but not super-fit, to get some regular exercise and lose weight. Of course I'd done nothing about it, probably put on a few extra pounds and was now even more out of shape and boy did I feel it. Getting my breath back and pulse slowing I looked along the street in both directions. There was nothing; just stillness and silence.

Suddenly I heard the distant but unmistakable sound of a helicopter. No way, I thought. How could they scramble a helicopter that quick? That *was* James Bond style! But the sound of a motor engine heading my way distracted me. It was coming from my right. I hid behind the open gate door, hopefully not visible against the dark foliage. The vehicle was approaching slowly; I crouched further down behind the gate. It drove slowly by revealing itself to be a cream white Network Rail van. I got a fleeting glimpse of both the driver and passenger wearing fluorescent high-visibility jackets. I relaxed slightly as the van drove away. The helicopter was still whirling in the distance and hadn't come closer. Come on, Andy, where are you? The roads between the Shields and this villa it backed onto were long and parallel, but it shouldn't take long for cars from the Shields to get here.

There was a sharp cracking noise behind me followed by a dull thud then someone uttering loudly "Fuck!" The security light came on and I could hear footsteps on the path beside the villa. Hunter's goons had climbed the tree and probably broke the overhanging branch with their weight which explained the sharp crack followed by the oath. Those guys were fit and in their twenties, at most early thirties. I was in my mid-fifties and had no chance of outrunning them or even attempting to fight my way past them so I walked into the middle of the road and started shouting "Fire, fire!" at the top of my voice, repeating it again and again as I saw, between shouts, two guys at the top of the sloping road from the driveway who had stopped, caught by surprise at my incessant shouting and unsure what to do. I was conscious of lights coming on, curtains being drawn and at least one door opening in the villas around me with an elderly gentleman in a dressing gown approaching down the front path of a house to my right asking plaintively: "Where, where's the fire?"

Then, to my indescribable relief, the familiar sound of the diesel engine of a hackney cab prompted me to abruptly curtail my shouts as a black taxi came into view hurtling along the road at a surprising speed. The old gentleman just got to the pavement and more doors opened as the taxi slammed the brakes and I recognized the driver as Andy who brought the cab to a halt right beside me. The goons realised what was going on and started running down the sloping road, but by the time they reached the street, I'd jumped into the taxi which swung round and accelerated away leaving the goons frustrated and the Shield's neighbours bemused.

I'd first heard it on a training course thirty odd years ago. It was a Special Branch detective telling us that in a really tight corner, on your own with no back-up and none remotely near, the best chance, at least in a street setting, of drawing a crowd and possibly deterring your attacker/captor was to holler as loudly as possible 'Fire!'. People could choose not to hear cries for help or screams lest they get caught up in something that would endanger them or was beyond their ability to cope with. Shouting 'Fire!' at the top of your voice relentlessly has a better chance of provoking people to move, in case it was them, their family or their property that was threatened. And just that simple act of lights flicking on and curtains twitching might just give you time to get away or slow the chasers as the good burghers of Pollokshields had just demonstrated.

Andy was driving at a furious pace. Above the noise of the engine and some country music he asked: "Where to, Mr Carson?"

"Royston, but avoid the motorways and any cops."

"We'll be alright with the cops in the south side cos they're all up at the riot, but the city centre's buzzing with them after what happened today."

"Riot? What riot?"

"At the edge of Govanhill where it meets Strathbungo before coming into Pollokshields, an Asian guy was attacked there last night so a whole gang of Asians went up to Victoria Road and they ran into a white gang that'd came up from the Gorbals and Toryglen and they've been boxing each other the last hour or so with the cops in-between. Fucking mental! The Square getting blown this afternoon and now rioting!" He shook his head, "What the fuck's going on?"

I realised now why the helicopter was in the air. It was obviously a police helicopter which had been scrambled to assist with riot control in Govanhill which was over two miles to the east of the Shields.

"I take it those two fuckers in the leather jackets were chasing you, Mr Carson?"

"Aye Andy, they wanted a word with me. Do you think they would have clocked your plate number?"

Andy chuckled to himself as we drove sharply around another tight corner, "Probably not in the darkness, but in any case whenever you phone, Mr Carson, I put the special plate on and I know for a fact there's no taxi enforcement bandits on duty the night!"

I smiled back at him clutching onto the passenger handrails at the back of the speeding taxi. Hiding in plain sight is a term that has come into popular use in the last few decades and it perfectly defines the use of vehicles like taxis for undercover purposes. Like utility vans and trucks which are superb for stationary surveillance purposes, black cabs can be used up and down streets, to ferry people and things across town or just even to wait, outside a house or venue and no one would question it, except of course if you were engaged in undercover work yourself in which case nothing you ever hear, see or smell is ever hidden in plain sight.

Andy was a squat, small man, overweight, with a mop of black hair and a slight fading scar on his left cheek. Like many Glaswegian men he physically went into middle-age very early and you could place his age anywhere between late thirties and mid-fifties (he was in fact forty-two). He had the typical cabbie's backchat and belligerence, but was also loyal and in spite of a strong aversion to being called sentimental, had a heart of gold. The old, the young, the infirm and the helpless would have a champion in Andy. Many an old biddy laden with shopping and unable to pay the full fare would get a free ride and assistance into the house with the shopping from him. But don't be funny and try not to pay your fare; then the wee stout man would give you a lesson in how angry a Glasgow cabbie can get.

I'd come across him back in the 90's drug war days. He'd been couriering for one of the big North side drugs gangs and was also on the edge of Sadeq's outfit. He knew a lot, saw a lot and heard a lot and he could relay it all back with high fidelity: no embellishments, no wishful thinking, no gaps; just as it happened which was a gift for people like us. I used him as an informer and paid him generously, but kept him off the books because I didn't want him being exploited by us or traded onto other agencies leading to burn-out and worse; that I'd witnessed too often. Andy was mine and mine alone: he became part of my unofficial ratline network.

Then, in spite of my protective urges, it must have become all too much for him. He'd split up with his wife, had a disastrous affair with a married woman which ended in a really tough fight with her husband (thus the scar) while informing for me and couriering for the gangs, not to mention a couple of other shenanigans he was involved in. One day in the middle of all this, having a sparse day fares wise, he parked the cab outside a pub at noon where a lot of his mates drank, went in 'for a pint' and ended up there in a binge session, including a lock-in, for fourteen hours. Loudly and aggressively refusing any help to get home he staggered to the back of his cab, got in and fell asleep sprawled across the seats only to be woken several hours later by the traffic police, still very drunk and arrested. He faced losing his livelihood until I intervened, pulled a hell of a lot strings and much use of the magic talisman of 'national security' and got the PF with great reluctance, to drop all charges. Ever since Andy has been one of my most loyal but unofficial informers and I could count on him without him asking too many questions.

"How you thinking of getting up to Royston, Andy?" I asked him over the dreadful sound of a country and western singer lamenting the fact that his wife who had been his childhood sweetheart had ran away with his best friend who he'd been in the army with.

"I was out earlier on," Andy replied, "all the bridges over the Clyde had cops on them stopping what few cars were on the road except for the Squinty Bridge, so we'll use that then up the west-end up to Maryhill, go past Springburn and across to Royston."

The 'Squinty Bridge' was officially known as the Clyde Arc. It was a relatively new bridge over the Clyde, but crossed the river at an angle rather than straight across and hence had inevitably been dubbed by Glaswegians as the 'Squinty Bridge'. There was no sign of any pursuers as Andy took tight corners employing his encyclopaedic knowledge of the city streets to avoid busy roads that might have police checks. When we got to the Squinty Bridge, though, there was a lone patrol car at the south entrance to the bridge.

"Sorry, Mr Carson," Andy apologised as he slowed down to the approach to the bridge and the police car. "The bridge was cop free earlier, will I turn round?"

"No we'll take our chance. We'll attract their attention if we turn round and every cop tonight will be on maximum terrorist alert. Besides every crossing will be the same."

As we came to the bridge a policeman came out of the car and waved us down to come to a stop. We were the only traffic on the bridge; the streets were deserted. Andy rolled down his window and the cop stooped to talk to him.

"Morning, can I ask where you're heading?" He was young, early twenties, though of course I was at the age where most policemen and women look ridiculously young. He appraised Andy and looked over at me.

"Just taking my fare to Partick," Andy replied.

"Can I see your documents?" the cop asked. Andy's taxi plate was false but he had two sets of documents; one of which would confirm the false plate number. This would be fine, but if the cop decided to radio into the Licensing Police for verification, we would be in trouble. He took the documents from Andy and with his torch read them. Andy looked at me in the rear view mirror and I gave him a brief nod: if the cop went on the radio we would bolt; there was only one police car here with another cop at the wheel and the chances are these two wouldn't have Andy's knowledge of the back roads and we'd probably be able to shake them off. But it would mean, given today's events, we would have all of Glasgow's finest looking for us which is the last thing I needed.

The cop went to the back of the taxi and checked the plate number with the documents. He came back to Andy and gave him back the documents. "Thanks, where did you pick up your fare?" the cop again looked at me and I stared back at him impassively.

"Govan," Andy replied.

"Why didn't you use the Clyde Tunnel if you're going to Partick?" It was a reasonable question; the Clyde Tunnel went under the Clyde and would have been the shortest and most obvious route from Govan to Partick.

Andy didn't hesitate. "I thought it was shut!" he protested.

"Aye, but they reopened it an hour ago."

Andy pointed to the small screen to his side which updated him on possible hires and any obstructions on the road. "These bastards tell you nothing!"

The cop smiled and straightened up. "Ok mate on your way."

Still muttering about the ineptitude of taxi controllers Andy drove across the bridge with its steel arch above us. As we drove away from the bridge and towards the west end Andy's face lit up in a big smile.

"That was a fucking guess, Mr Carson. I had no idea the Tunnel had really been shut!"

"No problem, Andy, it worked!"

We made our way without further incident through the eerily empty west end and on up to the north of the city. I asked Andy to make a diversion to an area called Port Dundas, so-called because it had once been a genuine inland port servicing the canal that linked the Clyde with the river Forth and provided a waterway transport connection across the central belt of Scotland and a vital artery at the start of Glasgow and Scotland's industrial revolution. It had been rapidly eclipsed by the onset of the railways and then, of course, motor transport and had fallen into disuse and decayed. Now it had been turned into a leisure and arts development with the massive bulk of the former warehouse known as Speirs' Wharf transformed into upmarket flats and penthouses as wells as offices for small businesses.

Andy parked the car on a small layby just past the Wharf; there were a few lights on in some of the apartments. The canal and M8 motorway which snaked through the city like a mainline cable loomed in front of us. Port Dundas was on raised ground above the city and the entire city-centre was in full profile in front of us beyond the motorway. It was an impressive array of modern office blocks in concrete, solid stone- built 30's office blocks, Victorian red sandstone edifices and the occasional strutting church spire attesting to the former piety of this once great commercial and industrial city. Almost defacing this amazing combination of styles and designs was the hideous gaudy structure of the large multi-storey Cineworld complex which dominated the view from here.

I left the cab while Andy played Kris Kristofferson and walked to the canal and stood on the side of the bank. Taking out one of my disposable phones I called the second of the three ratline contacts I intended to use. Even though it was now coming up for three am I had a hunch he would still be up: and I was right.

Shaban answered the phone within two to three rings. I apologised for the lateness of the hour and asked if I could come over as I was wondering if he was able at very short notice to assist me. I was only a few minutes away and would be over soon. That was no problem, Shaban said and he would look forward to seeing me. I rang off and threw the mobile into the canal. That was the easy call: now the hard one.

Using another mobile I phoned one of three numbers for Wattie I had memorised for emergency situations or enhanced MosBerBel, as I had with each member of the team. The first number rang out with no answer. I tried the second with the same result; ditto the third. Going back to the first number, I texted:

It's Macintyre. Like you I've went AWOL. Believe me or not. Need to talk, urgently.

I sent the message to all three numbers, and waited. After fifteen minutes I was going to give up when the phone rang with the second number. I answered, but there was silence at his end.

"Wattie, Wattie speak to me." Still silence. "We need to talk, Wattie. The new top man in al-Qaeda is telling the world that he's got agents that helped him to do what happened in George Square yesterday afternoon. That means we're all under suspicion, you included. They were about to take me down to Troon when I did a bunk. I'm running around Glasgow right now just like you, on the loose and wanted. From heroes to zeroes in one day, eh?"

At last Wattie responded. "You're full of bullshit, boss!" It was a weary and tired voice.

"How's that?" I asked.

"You're probably sitting with Mulrooney, the DG and that head security geezer from London, saying give him the come-on. Tell him you're in the same boat as him, you're on the run too. Get him to agree to a wee meeting with you. Do me a fucking favour, gaffer, do you think I'm buttoned up the back? And your Carl the Geeks and the A Branch techies are probably getting a fix on where this phone is so I'm just gonna hang up right now, but not before telling you all to kiss my sweet arse and take a flying fuck!"

"Listen, Wattie, you're absolutely right and you got the names spot on. I was with the three people you mentioned. But they're yesterday's men and on their way out. I've genuinely ran out. I'm using my ratlines, cos I don't think in the panic, hysteria and paranoia that's engulfing the service either you or I or anyone connected with Grand Minaret will get a fair hearing. Wattie, I'm in Port Dundas using a disposable mobile phone. Listen." I put the phone in the air. Even though there were only a few cars on the M8, there was the general background urban noise of a large city centre. I put the phone back to my ear. "Still there?"

"Yeah."

"Ok I'm going to take a selfie." I could hear the click of the camera and I sent the photo to his phone. After about a minute, which seemed like eternity, I asked him if he'd received the picture.

"It's just arrived," he confirmed.

"What do you see?"

"Your ugly coupon, the M8, Glasgow Caley Uni, the Cineworld and the rest of the city centre. But look, for all I know that's one of your gizmos; you could be sitting in the fucking Shields making all this up."

"Aye I could Wattie, anything's possible, but I'm not. I am where that picture was sent from at 3.15 in the fucking morning!"

Abruptly Wattie said, "Ring off and phone me on the third number you tried." I complied and dialled the third number. Wattie was moving about, trying to prevent any fix or trace on him, but I couldn't make out whether he was in a building, outside or driving.

Wattie resumed speaking to me in a controlled but angry voice: I still didn't know whether he believed me or not. "You know what makes me really fucking angry, boss?"

"No, what?" I asked.

"I'm the only cunt among the lot of you that's had to fire a gun in anger, that's actually been in a war zone, no make that war zones!" (Now that wasn't strictly true as I had been in a few hairy, life threatening situations, but this wasn't a time to point score with Wattie who, in the army and SAS, would undoubtedly encounter dangerous environments far more frequently than I ever would).

Wattie resumed, warming to his theme. "Aye that's right I'm actually fighting for Queen and country while you lot are sitting in cars, watching people or in front of a computer screen *analysing situations* (he pronounced this with much vitriol and contempt) while I've been out there facing real terrorists in Iraq and Afghanistan with real guns and real fucking bombs! And who's the first to get the finger pointed at as a terrorist suspect? Why of course it's the guy that actually fought for his country, who's blown away Taliban and al-Qaeda on their home turf. Aye stupid, thick army type, soft Wattie, sees his comrades getting blown to pieces by IEDs, but can still be turned by the Taliban! Fuck off! I'm no al-Qaeda man and I don't get civilians blown up!"

"I hear what you're saying, Wattie," I responded to him calmly. "But there's a reason why, apart from your military experience, that suspicion has fallen on you first."

"Oh aye? Entertain me, how's that?"

And I did. I told him about the camera on his watch, his hour, being moved away from the van to the street for twenty minutes, but he was ready for that and as I suspected it was because Tres had already told him.

"Ok, it's my fuck-up, I'll admit it. I was zonked. I don't know what it was but I could barely keep awake the whole night. When Tres went to sleep at five, I really tried to stay awake, but the next thing I know it's ten-past-six, Tres is still asleep and Tony and Danny are due to relieve us any second. So I woke Tres and, well, I thought nothing had happened, so just went on as normal."

"You didn't think to tell Tres that you'd both slept through the same watch period?"

"No because that would upset her; she'd worry that she'd be in the shit because she'd been sleeping on surveillance duty. Everybody does houring gaffer, but it's not official and nothing had seemed to happen so there didn't seem any point in telling her."

"Why did Tres let you know when I'd asked her to keep it confidential?"

The question was routine and I'd expected a reply along the lines of she was a close friend and two frontline workers were looking out for each other, plus yes they would both be in the shit for not complying with official procedures so it was better they were both aware, but his answer took me aback.

"Tres and I are really close. In fact if you don't know already we're an item."

"Going out with each other?" I asked immediately.

"Yeah for the last six months. She's about the only thing that's keeping me sane right now."

I had a great struggle both to keep hold of the phone and prevent it slipping into the canal and to refrain from saying "*What?*" for the umpteenth time in the last twelve hours. My head was reeling, but somehow I kept it together to ask him: "But I thought you were living with a woman in Paisley?"

"Ach that finished at the start of the year. You know what it's like, it's difficult to keep a relationship going in this line of work. Look, Tres and me have been close for the past few years, become real friends, she's a soul-mate, so I suppose it was just natural that we'd take it to the next stage. Christ I never thought this shit would happen to us! Now, gaffer leave her alone, she just tried to help, to warn me. I would have done the same for her and you probably would have as well."

Should I tell him that I too on a regular basis have been sleeping with his new girlfriend, though in my case I had no notion that I was in love with her or that she and I were 'soul-mates'. My head was still floundering. I couldn't believe I had pangs of jealously, or was it more vanity that the older boss was being upstaged by a younger subordinate. Get a grip, Macintyre, you're talking to a guy who's on the run and might, just might, be an informer for al-Qaeda who's assisted them to kill over eighty people and maim God knows how many others, a man you were in charge of and an operation you were in command of and here you are pissed off and feeling sore over a women! Even in the midst of catastrophe the everyday emotions can still run high.

"You kept it well hidden," was all I could think to say.

"Well, out with work we hardly see other." I realised that Wattie wasn't aware Tres and I were occasionally sleeping with each other which gave me a small morsel of comfort. I changed the subject:

"I take it Tres told you that you were followed all the way into the Square?" There was silence and I realised I'd hit a sore point. Wattie prided himself on his counter-surveillance skills honed as a Special Forces officer.

Finally, he said, reluctantly, "Aye, they were good, very good, never picked up a whiff of them."

My next question to him I would have made anyway to test his response and reactions to it, but it was probably mingled with a dose of spite as a result of the revelation about Tres.

"Unless you knew they were there all along, Wattie, all part of the set-up?"

"Fuck off!" he responded vehemently. "I'm not a fucking terrorist or a fucking terrorist accomplice! Why, why would I do it, help to kill women and weans? My whole family are army, why would I do that to them?"

"I don't know, Wattie, if truth be told I'm completely confused and ripped apart with this, but that camera did move on your watch.

Twenty minutes was more than enough time for an experienced military man to place a powerful IED underneath the van. And, apart from any other consideration, that is what's attracting attention to you!"

"Aye, but those cameras can be remote controlled from outside, an external operator can take over the camera, could have moved it away at that time and pinned the blame on me."

I hadn't thought of that. It seemed complicated, maybe a bit too complicated, but it might work. I remained non-committal.

"Look, Wattie, I'm going to hang up shortly, but I want to keep a line open to you. Do you trust me?"

"I trust nobody, boss, but I'll give you one more chance if you have genuinely gone on the run."

I continued: "How do I get back to you?"

"Use the third number you rang."

"And you're ok you'll be able to avoid getting caught?"

Wattie's response spat contempt. "Do me a favour, after Iraq and Helmand province, hiding in Glasgow is a piece of piss. You've more chance of getting busted than I have!" I deserved that, but it did suggest he believed I was also on the run. He added:

"Mind, keep Tres out of this."

"That's out of my control, Wattie. She'll either still be in the Shields or they'll have taken her to Troon."

"No, she and Danny are at the Art Safe House."

"How do you know that?"

"She's got a phone stashed somewhere they haven't found yet. Two security people are with them."

"Ok I'll use the third number." I switched the phone off.

I stared across the dark shrouded cityscape in contemplation. Was Wattie innocent? Was he bullshitting? What about Tres? Was there anything left I hadn't been deceived about or deceived myself? Would this road of deception ever end? All this whirling through my head until my reverie was broken when I became aware of a police van cruising eastwards along the M8. There were no CCTVs here, apart from those on the motorway which had a short range and personal security cameras covering entrances at Speirs Wharf, so I wouldn't be noted by the city's CCTV system which would be looking out for any suspicious activity. But the cops could look out their van window, spot a lone guy standing by the canal bank with a waiting taxi forty yards ahead at this time of the morning and after yesterday's events, decide that's worth taking a look at. So I moved swiftly, but not too swiftly, back to the taxi.

Once inside I said to Andy, "Royston now Andy." The police van continued its cruising eastward; we hadn't attracted their attention.

I had Andy drop me off at the Charles Street flats in Royston: an array of five red and cream painted multi-storey tower blocks that straddled most of one side of Royston. The area had once been home to a dense warren of tenements whose tenants had worked in the heavy industrial factories and workshops, most significantly the large sprawling railway locomotive works of St Rollox and the Caledonian Railway which had dominated the area, employing tens of thousands of people. Only a tiny residue of that once great enterprise was left and the land had been turned into a retail park.

I walked the distance of the flats noticing the distinctive Royston Spire a landmark church steeple on the hill across the way, then retraced my steps. I was performing basic MosBerBel of course, but I also didn't want Andy to see which block I went into, not because I didn't trust him, but because I didn't want him to have the added burden of having the precise flat I'd entered interrogated out of him should that happen on top of what he could divulge transporting me in flight across the city.

I came to the controlled entrance of the third flat and pressed the buzzer for 21/3 which was on the third floor from the top. There was no concierge visible and I was confident I hadn't been tailed. I'd noticed the security CCTV trained on the entrance, so looked away from the camera, though that would only protect my face not my bald profile. A tinny voice came through the entry panel: "Hello?"

"It's Mr Carson, Shaban." The door clicked open and I quickly made my way across the foyer to the lift bay, one of whose doors opened straightaway and I ascended to the twenty-first floor in the small grey claustrophobic lift.

Arriving at the twenty-first floor I walked across the landing and rang Shaban's doorbell. He answered after the second ring, a man of my own medium height, with a dark pitted complexion, ruddy dark hair and deep brown eyes with flecks of white in them. He ushered me in to the hallway while with his fingers to his lips he urged: "Please, we stay quiet, the children and my wife are in bed." I immediately apologised for ringing the doorbell, but he directed me to the living room. I had been in Shaban's flat on only one other occasion five or six years back, but it hadn't changed much.

The living room was cluttered with an assortment of different clothes, various props such as wigs and costumes, children's tops and, in one corner, what looked like a printing press attached to a PC which Shaban appeared to have been working on. I knew Shaban was a chronic insomniac so felt comforted that I wasn't disturbing him at this hour. He offered me a cup of tea which I accepted gratefully. He disappeared into a small kitchen off the living room. In the few minutes I was left alone I began nodding off and nearly sank into a deep sleep, so exhausted was I, but was prevented from this by Shaban gently shaking me and giving me the cup of tea. I thanked him for the tea and sat in silence for a few minutes.

There was a blank plasma TV screen on the wall. Shaban pointed to it and broke the short silence:

"It is a terrible thing that has happened today. Lots of people dead. It is horrible. Glasgow is such a nice city." This was probably both a conversation opener from Shaban who like most people couldn't do silence, especially when a relative stranger connected to the British intelligence services descends out-of-the-blue on your house, and as a means of trying to establish whether there was a connection between my visit and the earlier event without asking too directly.

I shook my head sadly, "It's awful and the first time since the Glasgow Airport bombings of 2007 that Glasgow's been involved in a terrorist attack, utterly appalling!" I resumed sipping the delicious tea which I commended him for. Then, placing the cup on a low table by my side got down to business.

"Shaban, I wish you and your family well and good health, but I'm in a bit of a hurry, though I would request if I could stay until about six o' clock, or until such time as your wife and children get up?"

Shaban put his hands in from of him imploring: "Six o' clock is fine, Mr Carson, but you can stay longer if you need."

"Thank you, but that won't be necessary. Shaban I am a bald man as you can see. I need a wig. But I need a wig that won't make me look ridiculous, particularly to young observant security people. I also need a passport that would be able to get by those same kinds of people. Can you help?"

The slight tension and apprehension Shaban was displaying which was really only a concern about the purpose of my visit and what he would be asked to do, visibly lifted. He smiled and rose to his feet. "Of course, Mr Carson, that would be a pleasure. Shall we begin with the wig?"

Over the next couple of hours Shaban proceeded to try on different wigs with me. At first I thought he was having a laugh at my expense as some of the wigs were clownish if not outright grotesque, but he explained he was just trying to find the best fit for my large head. There was obviously an art or science to wig fitting and I let Shaban take his time as he fitted lots of wigs on, from a considerable supply, until we got progressively closer to one that he and I thought suitable. The key was getting the wig to match the eyes and the residue of hair around the ears so that the ensemble appeared natural. When we got there, with a smooth-fitting but firm greyish-brown wig, I couldn't believe the transformation. It took about five years off me and appeared perfectly natural and made me regret, and not for the first time in my life that I'd gone bald in my early thirties.

Shaban made me put the wig on and off a few times until I was familiar and comfortable enough with it to be able to put it on and adjust it myself so that it continued to look natural. Shaban explained: "People leave wig-makers and they are happy. Then they come back after a few days saying the wig makes them look terrible! But it does not, they just don't how to adjust and get it to fit right with their head, which is why I spend so long with people so that they know how to put the wig on and off correctly."

Shaban then moved onto the passport which was to be in the name of 'Lenihan': first name 'Thomas'. He took a series of photos of me in the wig and then got to work at his computer and printing press creating the actual passport. He made me more cups of tea, which I was grateful for, because not only was it refreshing but it helped to keep me awake, all the while we conversed with each other, but both of us scrupulously refrained from mentioning the bombing or, of course, why I was needing the wig and passport. Shaban spoke of his wife and two young daughters, one of whom had started primary school.

His conversation about his wife and children was like a soothing balm to me, a pleasant distraction on routine family life which for a few hours until the passport was ready allowed me not to think of what I was actually involved in. I suspected it was also a pleasant distraction for him, given who his clients were. Shaban had worked as a designer and tailor in his native Albania and had made a good living, including turning his hand to producing good quality forged documents. All was well until one of his biggest customers, effectively one of his patrons, was charged with corruption. Shaban explained that in the context of Albanian society at that time, charging someone with corruption was akin to accusing someone of bad singing at a karaoke disco as corruption was embedded everywhere in that country. It really meant that his patron had fallen foul of and/or not sufficiently paid off rivals, contacts, the authorities and the police. The new people that came to replace the patron viewed Shaban with suspicion and paid him a fraction of what he'd been earning previously. Complaining was not an option and Shaban felt he could be charged with corruption and thrown into prison, there to languish for years, at any moment. He fled to Britain as an asylum seeker in the early 2000s and ended up in Royston.

An Albanian community, largely made up of asylum seekers, had emerged at the same time in Glasgow. Some elements of this community were involved in people smuggling and trafficking, prostitution as well as drugs and Shaban's skills in tailoring, disguise and forging were exactly what they needed. Naturally, he came to various law enforcement agencies' attention and he was quickly beholden to a few of them to provide information. His chances of getting his cover accidently blown or discovered or just getting stressed out, which is usually the fate of the informer in these circumstances, was saved when SIS and us needed him to inform on the Glasgow end of an Albanian expatriate drugs and arms network that straddled militants in Kosovo and links to Islamists in Chechnya and down to the Middle-East. His new role as an informer for MI5 and SIS meant the other agencies were warned off him and he had virtual immunity, within limits, to provide disguises for people and forge documents, provided SIS and us got the take and there was no straying into drugs or trafficking. I'd also resolved to use his skills as part of my unofficial ratline network in Glasgow if ever I needed to.

Just after six, we'd finished. The passport was a professional job that only an expert could uncover as a fake and the picture was an excellent photo of me in my new guise of 'Thomas Lenihan' with medium-length medium-brown hair. Shaban also gave me a couple of casual shirts as well as socks and pants which would be useful if I was to be on the run for at least the next few days. He packed the clothes into a small black shoulder bag, watched me attentively as I put the wig on again and then walked me back to his front door.

"Thanks Shaban," I said to him, "I greatly appreciate this." I reached into the inside pocket of my grey jacket, brought out my wallet and counted out four hundred pounds which I handed over to him, but before actually putting them in his hand, stopped and looked him straight in the eyes. "Shaban, this is between you and I. I wouldn't want anyone else to know of this."

"Of course, Mr Carson, I will tell no one."

I continued to stare at him, the money in my hand still stationary above his outstretched palm. "No one means absolutely no one Shaban, that includes anybody else the Security Service MI5, or SIS. Do you understand?" His eyes opened wider as the significance of what I was telling him got through. "Yes of course, Mr Carson absolutely no one." I let the notes fall into his hand which he quickly drew into his pocket before opening the front door for me. We parted in silence.

Sporting a good-fitting, natural-looking wig I left the Charles St flat, head turned away from the entrance security camera and walked along towards the end of the street fortified by the many cups of tea provided by Shaban. I felt invigorated at least momentarily. I still had no plan apart from keeping going and eventually meeting up with Wattie somewhere and somehow.

I was still unsure of him, but a remark Tres made in the Art Safe House the previous evening kept repeating itself in my head. It was when, incredulous at the concept of Wattie actively conspiring against us for al-Qaeda and helping to perpetrate the massacre at George Square, she had said strongly that over months of working with Wattie on Grand Minaret and then immediately after the horror of George Square and the magnitude of what had transpired there, he 'hadn't cracked a light', meaning there'd been no change in his character or demeanour. Indeed I could still clearly discern the same old Wattie in the telephone conversation I had had with him in the early hours of this morning.

Maybe *I* was being naïve, delusional even, but I couldn't in all consistency stick my neck out for Sadeq being completely innocent of placing the device in his own van or even knowing about it, precisely because his character hadn't changed all through the development of Grand Minaret and not accord Wattie the same benefit. And then of course there was the possibility, which I hadn't considered, that the control console operating the camera in the surveillance van could be remotely controlled and operated *externally*. That would achieve the twin objectives of diverting the camera for enough time to allow someone to place the IED on or beneath the van and deflect suspicion onto my team, specifically Wattie with his special forces and combat zone experience.

Was I clutching at straws? Is this what I wanted to believe: that it was none of my team's doing? That I, *we*, had been set up, been made dupes, by wider forces we could barely get a hint of. Possibly, but if Wattie had been part of it, he had performed the best cover performance I'd ever encountered. The only way to definitely find out was to meet Wattie in the flesh. I was convinced I would know once I met him again and that's what I resolved to do at some point today but first I needed a safe place to get some sleep.

I had five phones left: one for Andy, one for contacting my third and final ratline contact and three others each for Carl the Geek, Vincent in London and Wattie. I phoned the final ratline contact (I had more ratline contacts, but these three were the ones I thought were the best to use for the purposes of disguise, forged documents, transport across the city and now a safe bolthole to rest). Again it was three attempts, only on the same phone this time, before the third contact answered.

"Sorry, I had my phone on silent. I only noticed it when I picked it up there just now; I'm just getting dressed." She spoke very quietly, almost in hushed tones as if not to awake someone. My face broke into a grin as I asked her if it was ok if I stayed at her flat in Possil. Fortunately, that was she where she was heading to. She was in a city centre hotel and would be getting a taxi back, so should be at her flat just after seven at the latest. That was fine for me as it was just gone six-thirty and I should be in Possil for then. I thanked her and rang off. I toyed with the idea of phoning Tres, but, apart from injured male pride, there was no point in that and it could implicate her with the two guys on the run. Besides, she was under guard at the Art Safe House and there was nothing she could do.

The last vestiges of morning twilight had gone and daylight was in ascendancy. It was a typical dull, grey, but mild spring morning with birds singing and not a soul in sight. At the end of Charles Street I turned onto a narrow pavement which had a thick outer wall comprising the boundary of the last remains of the old railway engine works and on the other side a dual carriageway, which even at this early time, would normally be busy leading up to the morning rush hour, but very few vehicles were on the road this morning.

As I walked past the end of the railway works revealing the large open space of the retail park, I felt invigorated, primarily because, however illusory it could turn out to be, I felt I had some control of my life again; that I wasn't just reacting to events and was now working to the beginnings of a plan, namely to meet with Wattie and, if I thought he was being truthful with me formulate a plan together: a former SAS soldier and an MI5 team leader; that should be a formidable duo. I had no regrets now that I'd fled from the Shields and wasn't confined in Troon. Passing the edge of the retail park, the sun broke through the grey clouds and lit up the morning. I felt calm and relaxed.

*

I arrived in Possil in just over thirty minutes. People were starting to surface and go about their business as best they could after the trauma of what had happened to their city yesterday. As I passed them by, mostly early morning shift workers and two nurses, I could only wonder what their reaction would if they were aware that the middle-aged, casually dressed 'brown-haired' guy walking past them with a bag slung over his shoulder, for all the world like them, a regular guy about to go to work, was in fact twenty-four hours earlier a senior MI5 officer in charge of the team that escorted the van into George Square when... Before that I really thought my pension was about to be considerably enhanced as the consultant 'go-to' man on how to conduct textbook anti-terrorist, surveillance and interdiction operations to a plethora of agencies in my retirement.

Possil looked distinctly better than I knew it during the dark days of the early to mid- 90's drug wars. New buildings, including a large all-purpose Health Centre, had sprung up. Where once there were shabby grey-stoned council tenements, some of which were boarded up, derelict and had become shooting galleries for Possil's prolific numbers of injecting heroin users, there was now new build houses, many of which were privately owned. As I looked across and up one of those streets, I recalled with a shudder that two-thirds along that street, where a new two-storey house was now with a garden and children's swings outside, had been the location of the four-story tenement where the 'Possil Disaster' had occurred. We'd come across seven bodies in a flat on the top floor killed outright through over-dosing on heroin which had not been cut properly. And the reason for that could directly be attributed to our actions in taking out three levels of the normal distribution process.

We'd taken out the people who normally cut or 'stamp' the heroin with impurities in our keenness to get to a top drug-gang leader and his developing paramilitary connections with the result that a bag of nearly 80% pure heroin had got through to street level with calamitous results that quickly became known as the 'Possil Disaster'. That had been covered up as it was only 'dead junkies' and all the parties to it, me included, survived with careers and reputations intact. No career or reputation would survive Grand Minaret.

I put those thoughts aside as I walked into the heart of Saracen Street, the main thoroughfare of the area. This hadn't changed much; sturdy red sandstone tenements towered on either side of the street here. At ground level were rows of shops that indicated a not too healthy and wholesome lifestyle prevailed locally as a collection of betting shops, fast food takeaways, bargain discount stores, pharmacies, firms of lawyers prominently advertising their legal aid and criminal defence services, and pubs predominated: this in spite of all the new 'initiatives' which had attempted to 'regenerate' the area.

I walked past the pedestrianized areas that surrounded what had been Saracen Cross, before parts of it had been blocked off to traffic and was still referred to as such. A large colourful mural on the gable end of a tenement which had once faced onto the 'Cross', but was now partly hidden by an office building, depicted the old ironworks known as the Saracen Foundry and the products it made: a representation of a bygone era the only remnant of which was a cast-iron shelter that had become notorious as a venue for dealers to hang-around to ply their trade. I went past the shelter, up a short hill and doubled back along a street which paralleled Saracen Street. At the far end of this street was the flat where my third ratline contact lived. Since leaving Royston I had been keeping a careful watch around me practicing basic MosBerBel. As far as I could see there were no tails on foot or by car. My third contact's flat was on the top floor of a tenement at the corner of the street on a slight hill and afforded a view onto Saracen Street and a good way along the street paralleling it: excellent for counter-surveillance purposes.

'Amber Chantel' was at home and gave me a peck on the cheek as she ushered me across the landing into her neat living-room. "Check you with the wig; could hardly fucking recognize you there! You look good in it too!"

In truth I was starting to feel uncomfortable in the wig; having something on your head when you've been hairless for over a quarter-of-a-century, didn't seem right, so I took it off as soon as I entered the living room.

"That feels better," I said placing the wig on Amber's leather settee.

"Don't put that there, I've just bought that sofa!" she cried. "Here give it to me!"

I handed the wig over to her which she placed in a plastic bag.

"Breakfast?" she offered.

"That would be lovely," I agreed.

Her kitchen was across the landing and I joined her there as she prepared breakfast. She offered bacon and eggs, but I asked her for boiled eggs and toast with lots of butter.

"That was horrible what happened up the town yesterday," she said, "all those people and bits of kids killed. Hanging's too good for the bastards. Fucking monsters!" She looked up at me with genuine sadness and anger, but I knew, like Andy and Shaban, she would refrain from asking me what I knew about it or if I had had anything to do with it.

"I take it you didn't get much in the way of business last night?" I asked.

She gave a dry laugh. "Gary Carson, men are men! My first client cancelled at four, then phoned me an hour later to say that he'd like to see me after all; said he needed some 'comfort' after the horrors of the day." She shook her head, "men, what are you like? After that it was the same as normal; one penthouse trick and two hotels all of them wanting 'comfort'. Aye all right whatever! A tricks a trick whatever excuse you have for it." I merely nodded in agreement with her.

"As I said on the phone, Amber, I just need a place to sleep for a few hours." She fixed me with a friendly stare from her large hazel eyes.

"Gary you can stay as long as you like, I never bring punters back here."

"Thanks Amber I appreciate that." As she put three hard boiled eggs into eggcups (two for me, one for her) I thought how beautiful she looked. Black curly hair complimented her dark, almost Italianate complexion which with the striking hazel eyes gave her a very sexy demeanour even when she was making toast. She was wearing a pair of faded jeans and a casual, white sweater, but having seen her fully dressed up for 'work', I imagined how alluring she would be for men prepared to pay lots of money for her: Ye Gods! I thought to myself, the night after the worst terrorist atrocity in Glasgow's history and she still manages to get four clients!

Amber Chantel wasn't, of course, her real name; she'd chosen that because she thought, despite her Italianate looks, it made her sound exotic and French. Her real name was the decidedly un-exotic Aileen McPherson and she was as French as pie and chips. She came from the local area and, in spite of, as she admitted herself coming from a 'decent' family background she went off the rails at an early age, got in tow with a 'bad crowd' and before long was injecting heroin. Very quickly her already chaotic life spiralled further out of control. A heroin habit, which she quickly acquired, requires high support costs, and, for an attractive young woman there was one tried and tested route that would supply her with the cash to feed her habit: Amber went on the game.

At the point when Amber started selling her body in the early 2000s' the internet was coming into its own: as a result prostitution in Glasgow, as elsewhere, shifted from the streets to flats. There, it was more easily controlled by criminals and pimps and the girls could be closely supervised. Amber, like other women in her situation, lived a twenty-four unrelenting cycle of servicing up to a dozen men per day punctuated by occasional snatches of sleep and injecting heroin four-times-per-day: the latter being the narcotic that allowed her to keep going.

A police raid on the apartment she was working in freed her from both violent, psychotic pimps and heroin. She was put onto a methadone programme and with that help weaned herself off heroin. But she didn't give up the game. Instead, she went solo. The smack and the beatings from the pimps hadn't taken away her looks or her toned physique. Using the limited amount of money she could save from her meagre earnings as a barmaid in a city pub (her first and so far last 'proper' job) she rented a flat, and got enough money together to advertise in a sleazy down-market Sunday tabloid under her new nom de plume of 'Amber Chantel'. In her own terms the money paid for that advert was a good investment as her phone never stopped ringing and she gained a steady stream of regular clients. Soon, she was able to break into the lucrative escort market working the city's four and five-star hotels.

It wasn't all smooth. She'd been arrested several times and, without the excuse of being controlled by violent men and having a heroin habit, had received increasingly stiff fines. She'd also been beaten a few times and once was nearly thrown out of a car at 80mph on the Erskine Bridge by a wealthy Canadian coked out of his brain. After that episode she'd resolved never to go out with her punters but stay exclusively in the hotels, whether the foyer, bar or punter's room.

She came to the attention of the intelligence world when a Chinese businessman on a trade delegation to Scotland who SIS identified as an agent for the Chinese Ministry of State Security happened to choose Amber to keep him company in his hotel suite one evening. Mulrooney was approached by SIS, who normally have strict rules prohibiting them from operating in the UK: he assigned me to the task. Amber walked into the hotel, made her way to the bar, bought a vodka and Coke, sat at a table, made a quick call on her mobile and waited.

When Mr 'Chan' a middle-aged man of dignified appearance, came down to the bar and walked up to Amber, I knew who the escort was. We'd already bugged Chan's room with audio and video taps. As Amber left about four in the morning I stopped her outside the hotel. I told her I worked for the Home Office, that I knew what she was up to and that she was in a whole pile of shit unless she walked with me to my car and told me everything "and I mean *everything*," they'd talked about before, after and in-between their physical exertions. We didn't really need Amber. There was enough from the take on 'Chan' elicited by the audio and video surveillance to allow SIS to blackmail him into working for the Brits back home, which he duly did, though only for a year as, burnt out and stressed, the poor bastard didn't cover his tracks too well, was picked up by his own side and was thrown into prison or shot. No, I saw a recruitment opportunity with Amber and when other opportunities arose for potential entrapment of foreign businessmen, dignitaries, the occasional celeb or diplomats, Amber was one of several working women we were able to use.

Then one day there was a purge as anti-trafficking agencies in liaison with local police and welfare agencies swamped the city's hotels looking for exploited and trafficked girls. Amber was netted as a by-product. Unfortunately, she was up against the same magistrate who had already given her increasingly severe fines on two previous appearances, and with absolutely no mitigating circumstances, was given a custodial sentence. Through her lawyer Amber got in touch with me and, as usual, I played the national security card and got Amber out within twenty-four hours. At that point she was as beholden to me as she had been to any pimp. I resolved that she would become one of my ratline network contacts and gave her my Gary Carson alias. Like Andy the cabbie and Shaban the forger, Amber was in a profession that straddled the twilight zone between the legit world and the underworld. Intelligence agencies and their operatives like me also inhabited that same terrain.

I looked across at her over the dining table at the bay window of the living room, the two of us munching eggs and toast washed down by coffee. She was now in her early thirties, but looked about six years younger. She had come out of addiction and abuse and had a wealth of experience in manipulating men. But she knew and I knew she was still vulnerable. If she was smart, as I'd said to her before, she'd be putting money aside or investing it, ready to get out. But could she leave the game? I don't think she was anywhere near knowing the answer to that and that made me all the more worried for her as I genuinely liked her.

She finished the last of her toast, sipped her coffee and reached for her handbag beside her. Producing a packet of cigarettes, taking one out and putting it to her lips, she inquired:

"Ok, if I smoke?"

"It's your house, Amber," I replied, "no I don't, on you go."

Lighting the cigarette, she asked: "Did you ever smoke, Gary?"

"Gave it up years ago. It's about the only bloody bad habit that I have managed to give up."

Her next question took me by surprise. "You married Gary?"

I laughed and shifted in my seat. "I've been married twice, but it was all long ago, a long time over."

"Any kids?"

I looked at her straight. "Amber, I might not be your punter and I never will be, but let's stick to punter's rules, all right?"

'Punters rules' were a set of conventions working women adopted with their clients. They included never initiating a conversation, except to talk about the weather or how nice or good the punter was. The punter must always lead the way and if it's clear the he doesn't want to talk about a particular subject, then, clam up, immediately. A lot of money and, often, a girl's personal safety, were dependent on this.

Amber smiled through clouds of cigarette smoke. "I don't see you as a punter Gary, in fact," she shook her head and blew out more smoke, "I'm not quite sure how to figure you," she had a quizzical look in her eyes.

"Don't try to figure me out," I responded.

There was a long silence while she studied me carefully. Finally, stubbing her cigarette out, she said, almost with a sigh: "All right, Mr Carson, punter's rules. But I can ask you how long you intend to stay for, not that there's any rush for you to go."

"Just a few hours Amber, probably till this afternoon."

"Well that's fine cos I'm off to bed now. I'll probably kip till about four or five. I've got lasagne in, enough for two so you can get your tea."

"Thanks Amber, but I'll probably be gone by then."

"No worries, but it's there for you anyway." She rose up, yawned and stretched her arms. "The spare room's just across from here. I changed the linen on Sunday so it's' fresh."

"Thanks again Amber, I really do appreciate this."

She came round to my side of the table bent down and gave me another peck on the cheek, then stood back and said: "Get a good sleep Gary, you look as if you need it." I nodded my head in agreement as she turned and headed out the door.

I looked out the bay window onto the street below as it slowly came to life. I was, of course, on constant MosBerBel alert, as my eyes perused the street, but there was nothing out there to cause me any concern. Most of my thoughts were on Amber, who I could hear rummaging around. I was aroused by her and not for the first time. Having a relationship with her, assuming she would allow me, broke every rule in the book, though that's not to say officers hadn't done so. I was still too linked in to the system, too cautious to cross that boundary, but oh after twenty-four hours like I'd had, what I'd give to lie beside a women like Amber. Ok there had been Tres the night before and that was great, and I was still feeling pissed at Tres sleeping with Wattie as well as me. But that was all. I had no deep feelings for Tres; it was mainly, if not solely, sex mutually agreed upon by both parties and we both said to each other often enough, if somebody else came along who we had strong feelings for… And I had harboured feelings for Amber for some time.

I had no issues with Amber's lifestyle. When you deal only in intrigue, deceptions, lies and outright chicanery as we did for a living, then you'd no right to morally judge anyone else also pushing the envelope to earn a crust. No, what was disturbing me beyond my arousal was that I had deep feelings for Amber, probably greater feelings than I'd had ever had for Tres. I could smell the delicate aroma of her perfume even through the lingering odour of her cigarette smoke and the image of those luscious hazel eyes stayed with me.

I rose abruptly from the dining table, collected the breakfast dishes and took them back to the kitchen where I cleaned and dried them: it was the least I could do for Amber as I tried to dispel my ridiculous notions of romantic love with a full-time hooker on the secret-service payroll.

There was a small portable TV in the corner of the living-room. I found a remote control, switched the TV on and was in time for the BBC 8 o' clock breakfast news. Predictably, the headlines were dominated by yesterday's bombing including Ali al Hassan's claims to have infiltrated UK intelligence services, which had first been aired on Al Jazeera. But the major new development, heralded inevitably by the continuous 'breaking news' banner stream at the bottom of the screen was the announcement that the Prime Minister had instructed Scotland Yard's Counter-Terrorism Command to lead, in liaison with Police Scotland the investigation into the George Square bombing and all related aspects of the case including 'the conduct of the Security Service in relation to this and other cases'.

This, of course, unleashed an orgy of speculation as to the future of MI5. The BBC reporter was broadcasting live from outside Thames House and commenting wryly on whether there would be a 'for sale' sign affixed to the building soon. Less than thirty years ago the BBC would barely even have mentioned MI5 which until the early 1990s didn't even have any official legal status. Now there were camera crews parked outside its headquarters! As the reporter was speaking live to air, he suddenly clutched his earpiece and informed viewers that he'd just got news of two further developments.

"I've just been told that the Director-General and senior members of MI5 staff will take temporary leave until the results of a full and rigorous review of allegations that MI5 had been infiltrated by al-Qaeda have been completed, allegations incidentally which the Prime Minister is at pains to point out he does not believe are founded. This review will be led by the National Crime Agency (NCA) which up to now has focused on economic crime, cyber-crime and organised crime. Assisting the NCA, the Prime Minister has also announced, will be the police Counter-Terrorism Command who, for a temporary period, will lead, in active co-operation with MI5 staff, ongoing anti espionage and counter-intelligence operations. I've also been told, though this is not official *yet* that the Secret Intelligence Service, that's MI6 to you and me, the country's foreign intelligence service, will also be assisting in this. So, major developments coming out of Whitehall this morning in the aftermath of yesterday's Glasgow bomb and al Hassan's accusations of al-Qaeda moles in Britain's intelligence services. Now, back to the studio."

I turned the volume down as I tried to take all this in. Forget all the talk of a 'temporary period' and a 'review'. MI5 was finished. I suspected that all of our anti-terrorist and related operations would be parcelled out to Counter-Terrorism Command and NCA, in other words the police, while all the counter-espionage, counter-subversion and counter-intelligence operations would go to SIS. Throughout its history since its inception in 1909, MI5 has always struggled to maintain its independence. After the First World War, first the military, then the police followed by SIS all had eyes on taking over the domestic intelligence service and creating an integrated national spying agency. Assisted by the threat from the Nazis then the Second World War, MI5 had successfully fought off all such attempted incursions. The Cold War had sustained the need for an agency like MI5, but ever since the fall of communism the agency had been struggling for an identity. It had dabbled in drugs, counter-terrorism, organised crime as well as traditional spying operations. The problem was MI5 was in a busy marketplace: all of its various functions were either being replicated by other agencies or could be. For over twenty years the Service had fought a vigorous rear-guard struggle to deny this and attempt to carve out a niche for itself. Well, Grand Minaret appeared to be the dodgy door slamming shut that had brought the whole MI5 house down. Christ I thought, I've unconsciously helped to blow up my own city and now greatly assisted in the demise of my own intelligence service! What the hell would be my next trick?

I kept watching for another half-hour. It was mainly rehashes of the footage from the Square shown earlier interspersed with Ali al Hassan's video and lots of talking heads discussing the bombings and the momentous consequences, not least for MI5, of there being terrorists in the British security services. Only the short, local Scottish news bulletin picked up on the riots in Govanhill the previous night. There had been a few injuries and some damage to property but the rioters had dispersed after a few hours and local community and religious leaders were calling for calm, tolerance and respect in these worrying days. Neither the local nor the national news mentioned anything about two MI5 officers based in Glasgow being on the run. As to who the bombers were, there was still no indication as to their identities. Whitehall would hope that in characteristic British fashion the announcement of an inquiry and the suspension of the DG would deflect too much attention from the media gaze.

I switched off the telly, had a quick look out of the bay window, before crossing the landing to the spare bedroom. It was small and sparse but tidy with a window onto a deserted backcourt of bins, washing lines and occasional patches of grass. Virtually every window in the row of tenements opposite had blinds drawn. I duly did the same, undressed and flopped into bed. I thought I would struggle to sleep after all that had transpired, but within seconds I was fast asleep.

I awoke, startled to find myself in a strange room, until everything flooded back into my psyche. The time on my watch on the bedside table was twenty to four: I'd slept for seven hours. Rising from the bed I yawned and stretched and pulled the blind up slightly. The backcourt was still mainly deserted except for a woman hanging out her washing and two small children playing on bikes. Pulling on a pair of jeans to protect my modesty lest Amber was up (though why I should do so in front of a professional hooker was anyone's guess) I went to the loo then to the front room, checked outside from the bay window, reassured myself there was nothing untoward and put the telly back on to the BBC 24 hours news channel. The major development was that the DG had resigned along with his deputy: the head of Counter-Terrorism Command would temporarily take over the DG's role while a former head of SIS would take over the deputy's functions. The carve-up had begun. Still no mention of agents on the run.

I sat back on Amber's sofa and yawned. Despite the long sleep I'd had, I was still feeling shattered and I knew I had to keep moving, keep focused. A shower would get me fully wakened and refreshed, but before that I went back to the bedroom and got the mobile for Carl the Geek from the shoulder bag. With the all-knowing wisdom of hindsight I should have showered first and then fully conscious would never have phoned him, but we are all wise after the event. It took five attempts before Carl answered.

"Eddie, you shouldn't have phoned man, Christ!" He sounded jangled and very frightened.

"Ok Carl," I tried to calm him, "where are you?"

"I'm at the Shields. We've been called in to go through the tapes of every operation your team have been involved in since you were formed. Everything. That's why I couldn't answer the phone. I told them I wanted a smoke break and I've came out to the bench to take the call. Your name's mud by the way; beyond mud, you're the bubonic plague times a hundred!"

"Who's in charge, Carl?"

"We're all getting grilled about how close we worked with you. The DG's resigned, Mulrooney's gone, Hunter and co left with their security people hours ago!"

"So who's running the show?"

"Cops, CTC, the place is swarming with them, and guys in suits that rumour says is SIS. And there's photographers and TV crews outside the gates. Unbelievable! We've to be escorted out in cars with tinted windows!"

It was difficult to comprehend. The MI5 offices in Glasgow, supposed to be one of the most secretive locations in Scotland were being door-stepped by the media! Carl went on: "Look man if they knew I was speaking to you I am beyond dole, I am in Troon! Everybody knows you fucked off and the ex SAS guy's on the loose though we've all been told to keep it zipped and…"

"Carl," I interrupted him, "it's ok, I'm only going to be a few more seconds with you, then I'll hang up and I swear I'll never let anyone know I phoned you, ok?"

He appeared to calm down. "All right, yeah."

"Fine, I just want to ask you a question."

"What question?" his nervousness was increasing again.

"The surveillance equipment in the vans, the type used on the night we were watching the van, can that be remotely controlled externally? I mean like say we've got two operators in the van, would it still be possible to control the movements of the cameras from outside?"

"Yeah, of course," he replied as if it was the most natural thing in the world. "It's like have you ever had any problems with your PC or laptop and you phone a maintenance company and they take control of your machine to detect what the problem is. It's the same principle. You could be at the Shields or anywhere and control the vans."

"And you've done that?"

"Yeah, remote control surveillance, plenty of times, mostly for back-up on Northern Ireland ops."

"Anything in Glasgow recently?"

"Nothing Eddie, and there was nothing in the Shields two nights ago; you guys were on your own." He said this with conviction and I believed him.

"But nothing to prevent anyone else taking control of the cameras?"

"As long as they knew how to access the cameras, yes someone else could have."

"Remember Carl you and your colleagues stumbled across the fact that we were followed all the way to the Square by a professional bunch who knew all about us, so if they had access to that information then there's no reason they couldn't have had remote control of the cameras?"

"No, there's no reason. Listen I better get back, there'll be wondering why I'm so long."

"Ok Carl, thanks again."

I took a long, leisurely shower and felt strangely elated as well as refreshed as the hot water and soap poured over my skin. Wattie, I was now sure had nothing to do with al-Qaeda or yesterday's bombing. We had been set up with Wattie taking the role of the patsy because of his Special Forces background. Why and by whom I didn't know. The only way forward I resolved was to team up with Wattie and the two of us to come in from the cold.

After showering I put some fresh clothes on still feeling high, positive and determined. I picked out the mobile for Wattie and walked back across to the front room. Before phoning I looked once more out of the bay window. Two women, one with a pram and a baby were at the corner of the street which gave onto Saracen Street; both were talking animatedly. On Saracen Street six young teenage boys walked along the pavement, two of them jostling each other in a friendly way. They passed a newsagents', from out of which a young man in his late twenties appeared. He wore a black jacket, blue jeans and trainers and had dark-tousled hair and carried a newspaper which he opened after a quick glance up at the street where Amber's flat was, before moving on out of sight. On the opposite side of the street where the two women were talking, two pensioners, one with a walking stick and appearing to struggle with the effort passed by.

Looking away from the window I was just about to dial Wattie when I heard Amber get up so, not wanting her to come in and overhear my conversation, as much for her protection as my privacy, I moved back to the spare bedroom. On the third attempt, as he had instructed, he answered. There were strange discordant noises in the background, which I ignored as I went directly to the point.

"Wattie we need to meet up. A lot's happened since we last spoke: the DG's resigned, the agency is finished, al-Qaeda have told the world they've got spies in British Intelligence and I believe you were right about the camera and the equipment being remotely controlled." He kept silent, I went on. "New regime, new people, we might not be hung out to dry after all. What do you say?"

When he replied, he sounded tired, but I probably did too. We were both living on our nerves. "Where do you suggest meeting?"

"Somewhere public, but with no CCTV and where we can see what's around us but still have a chat and not city centre, somewhere where there's unlikely to be too much security."

There was a few moments' silence before Wattie replied. "East end, Parkhead Forge, let's go for that."

It was a good suggestion. A busy shopping mall, but far enough away from the city centre not to be crawling with cops. I even thought of the best location within the complex. "You know the entrance at the Gallowgate end across from the Eastern Necropolis next to the multiplex cinema? Just there, there's no cameras there."

"Ok," he agreed, "when?"

I looked at my watch. It was four-thirty. "I can be there in an hour, six at the latest." I had no idea where Wattie was, there seemed to be traffic noise in the background around him.

"All right, boss," he agreed "but I swear to God if you're fucking about…" He broke off before resuming "Let's just say I'm angry, pissed off and if I get messed about any further I'll not be responsible for my conduct!"

I knew that was no empty rhetoric from Wattie. Despite the threats, evidently directed at me, his controlled anger and emotion made me even more convinced he was telling the truth.

"Wattie, I'm on the run like you, it's just the two of us. I'll see you at the Forge in just over an hour." I rang off and phoned the mobile reserved for Andy. He could make Saracen Cross by five. Business was 'shite' he bitterly informed me so he wasn't missing much earnings, though I had every intention of paying him generously for his services as he well knew. I told him I'd be wearing a brown wig and the clothes I'd be wearing, which he took in his usual calm stride.

Amber was in the kitchen cutting up vegetables. "Sure you don't want some supper?" she asked.

"Amber there's probably nothing in the world I'd rather do now than have dinner with you, but I really have to go."

"Oh Gary your patter's like water!" We both laughed. She still looked sleepy and was wearing a night gown, but she looked beautiful and sexy, her dark complexion accentuating those sensual hazel eyes. She was looking up at me. I had put the wig back on. "Actually I prefer you bald." I didn't respond but put my hand in my pocket and took out £100 from my wallet which I was about to offer her for letting me stay when her expression changed dramatically and she said angrily:

"Fuck off, now!" Her hand waved the knife she'd been cutting vegetables with in front of her.

I put the money back in the wallet. "Sorry." Her expression relaxed and she resumed cutting the vegetables, potatoes started boiling in a saucepan on the hob. By way of breaking the awkward silence that had descended I asked her: "Working tonight?"

She looked over at me and broke into a beautiful smile which made me feel immensely relieved. "Not till eight, so I'm gonny get a bite to eat, a long bath, watch a soap on the telly, then the war-paint on and back to work."

"I better go," I said moving closer to her. "Listen, I was never here, you never saw me, right?"

She put on a frown. "Who you talking about?" Never heard of you mister."

I smiled and bent towards her intending to give her a peck on the cheek, but she moved her face full to me and I ended up kissing her briefly full on the lips, which were soft and beautiful. I broke away.

"Bye, Amber."

"Bye, Gary." She gave me a gentle wave as I turned and left her flat.

Saracen Street was going about its business as usual as I walked along it heading to the Cross my head full of thoughts about Amber while still keeping a careful MosBerBel eye around me. Halfway along the street, the young guy with the dark tousled-hair and black jacket who I'd seen earlier from Amber's front room window leaving the newsagents', came out of a bookies, the newspaper folded under his arm, studying a betting slip in his hand as he passed me by. An aimless existence, I thought; probably heading now towards the pub.

I bought a newspaper myself, more to kill time and to make myself as inconspicuous as possible. I leaned against the steel barriers at Saracen Cross perusing the paper while waiting for Andy, bag over my shoulder: a guy reading his paper and minding his own business while waiting for his lift to work or home. Around me was a hive of activity: people crossing the busy street, women were out shopping while most of the men were either hanging about the pubs smoking, or loitering outside bookies or at the iron shelter across the way engaging in lively conversation.

The newspaper was entirely devoted to the bombings but from what I could discern had nothing new to add, though I did enjoy the speculation about the future of MI5. A black cab coming up the road caught my attention. I folded the paper and started walking beyond the barriers to just in front of a crowded bus stop where Andy's cab pulled up.

Apart from a predictable caustic comment about the wig, Andy drove in silence most of the way which suited me fine as I was thinking of Amber and the feelings I had for her and the futility of those feelings as they couldn't go anywhere for me, assuming for a moment she had any reciprocal feelings for me. It was good to delegate most MosBerBel duties to Andy (though he would never have known them as that) as he drove a circuitous route through north Glasgow. He only broke his silence to inform me that the city-centre was still off-limits, that it was best to avoid the motorways as they were '"crawling with cops," but the rest of the roads were relatively fine.

Unsurprisingly, rush-hour traffic was light given that almost all offices and shops were closed in the city and, despite the convoluted route we were close to the Parkhead Forge shopping mall within twenty minutes. As we drove through Shettleston on the approaches to the Forge, traffic was heavier and we got slowed down at a succession of lights. Still thinking of Amber, Andy interrupted my thoughts:

"See that red VW Passat ahead, he's kept ahead of me the whole way from Springburn since I first saw him." I looked ahead at the car in question. "And behind," Andy went on. "The grey Megane's overtook me once then let me overtake him and now he's staying behind."

I looked behind and saw the Megane behind us. We were coming to a set of lights that were green and allowed the Passat to go through. Andy slowed down sufficiently for the lights to turn to amber then red. The road ahead was visible all the way up to the major junction that was Parkhead Cross; the Passat stopped two-thirds of the way up the street.

"This doesn't look good, does it?" I said to Andy, but he remained silent. In the distance across the city a helicopter was hovering but that was almost certainly in relation to continuing security and the clean-up operation from yesterday. The lights changed. Behind us the Megane cruised. A single-decker bus was ahead of us and it was coming to a halt at a bus stop to take aboard about a dozen pensioners. Andy stopped behind the bus as the pensioners slowly boarded. He took advantage of this to get out the cab and apparently check his wing mirror. The Megane which had been behind us had disappeared. Andy came back into the cab and I asked him if he'd seen where the Megane had gone. He just shook his head.

"No, it was too quick but the Passat's still up the road." He turned to face me. "I can smoke these bastards out easily Mr Carson, if you're all right with that?"

"Do what you have to do Andy."

The last of the pensioners were getting on the bus as Andy started the cab up, drove into the outside lane and went past the bus. Almost immediately the Passat's right indicator light came on and it moved onto the outside lane ahead of us. As we passed a side street on our right, the Megane was clearly visible parked a quarter-way down it.

"Fuck!" We both uttered in unison, our worst fears confirmed, emphasised further as the Megane turned into the main road behind us. I racked my brains trying to figure out how the hell they'd tailed us. How had they uncovered Andy as he wasn't an official contact? And, official or unofficial, were they going through all of my team's contacts and just putting surveillance on them all? That would be absurd as the resources needed for that would be colossal, unless they thought, in the most negative way possible, that I was of sufficient threat to national security to be 'worth it'.

We were approaching Parkhead Cross, a busy junction at any time with five main roads intersecting, some at right angles to each other. The lights were at red and four cars were in front of us on the outside lane, the Passat being the second with the right indicator flashing; Andy had his right indicator flashing too: about five cars behind us was the Megane. I waited for the lights to change, unsure what Andy was going to do.

As the red and amber lights came on the front car in the right lane accelerated and turned to the right, followed by the Passat. Andy followed the other two cars in the right lane until he was just past the lights at which point he suddenly turned sharp left cutting across the left lane, forcing cars on that lane to break sharply or swerve confirming everyone's prejudices about taxi drivers and initiating a cacophony of horns, gestures and strong language from the other drivers and their passengers. Unperturbed, Andy drove on in reverse direction from the Passat.

At the second turn on the right by the Cross, without indicating he turned sharp right again almost colliding head on with an oncoming driver who, after braking sharply, stared in furious disbelief as Andy, after turning right, executed a half-circle, reversed and then drove back out onto the street, past the driver now on his right who was shouting at him out of his window.

Both lanes on the near side main street leading back to Parkhead Cross were full, so Andy shot across to the far side and ploughed ahead causing more oncoming cars to brake sharply and swerve onto the pavements forcing pedestrians to scatter. One of those cars was the grey Megane and as we flew past it I caught a glimpse of the young guy I'd seen in Possil with the dark tousled-hair and the black jacket in the back. I gave him the middle finger and shouted "Fuck you!" as we drove past. The lights ahead were at red but Andy stormed through narrowly avoiding a bus, regained the near side of the road and got us past the opposite lights for oncoming traffic at the other side of the Cross into relative safety and in the right lane.

Andy slowed down as we went past the Cross. "Where did the Passat go?" I asked him as I reached for the Wattie mobile.

"The minute he thought he saw me turning into the side street by the Cross he went down the left street there at Springfield Road to catch up with us down there which is exactly what I wanted him to do!" I smiled with satisfaction well pleased that Andy had masterfully wrong-footed our two tails.

We were driving past the Gallowgate entrance to the Forge next to the multiplex entrance of the cinema where I'd arranged to meet Wattie. I asked Andy to slowly drive past the entrance, but there was no sign of him. Time was of the essence. The Passat and the Megane would be turning round and rapidly heading this way, their occupants determined to catch us up as there is nothing more frustrating and embarrassing for a surveillance crew than to lose their quarry. While Andy was brilliant at manoeuvring the cab a hackney was a slow vehicle in comparison to the other two cars and they would find us before long unless we moved away quickly. And if our pursuers were part of the official state security apparatus, they could call on lots of backup, not least the local cops. In any case Andy's antics would have alerted the CCTV operators covering the Cross, not to mention a few phone calls reporting the manic cabbie from irate motorists and pedestrians.

I had to make a quick decision: get out the cab and try and meet Wattie and risk the two of us getting nabbed or warn him via the phone, hoping to let him and me get away. There was no real choice; besides for all I knew they might well know in advance our rendezvous point: the Forge could be jumping with undercover agents from a cocktail of agencies.

"Ok Andy, let's get away," I instructed him. Andy sped the car away from the Forge as I furiously texted to Wattie:

Abandon. Unexpected company. I didn't invite them

It was unlikely Wattie would believe that last bit, but I had to type it anyway. We came to another set of lights at red, which this time Andy respected. The lights changed and we moved a short distance to a roundabout where we stopped to give way to traffic on our right. Suddenly Andy exclaimed:

"Where in the name of Christ did he come from?"

The Passat had moved up right behind us presumably having come up from the south road past Celtic Park. Andy shot the cab forward leading to the predictable screeching of brakes and howls of protest from the drivers who had right of way. Traffic here was less busy and Andy had two clear lanes to manoeuvre in, but it also meant the Passat had room to try to move ahead of us which it did and tried to clip us on the side but Andy moved the vehicle away: this was the vehicle that earned him his living and he was going to protect it as if it were a part of his own body.

Another set of lights loomed ahead. For once the lights were at green and Andy, just keeping ahead of the Passat moved to the outside and made as if to turn right and head onto the north road, but again at the last possible minute swerved sharply to the left and moved onto the southbound road. However, the Passat driver's learning curve was steep and he had predicted the move as he swerved to the left and then tried to cut across and block Andy going to the left, forcing the cab to mount the pavement and just miss the pole of a street lamp and the elderly man standing beside it.

Andy regained the street but on the wrong side of it forcing more oncoming traffic onto a, thankfully, empty pavement, before he was able to get into the south bound lanes, but the Passat was now level with us and trying again to clip us. Andy again managed to move away each time, but it was difficult to see how long he would be able to keep this up as the odds were running against him. An ice cream van was coming up the opposite lane. Andy suddenly veered right forcing the ice cream van driver to swerve straight into the path of the Passat who could only avoid him by steering left mounting the pavement and crashing into an iron fence at the side of the pavement which brought the Passat to a halt; the ice cream van also came to a halt in the middle of the road, but otherwise appeared unharmed.

Andy had turned into a narrow road with the grounds of a sports centre on one side and some factories and warehouses, a lot of them closed, on the other. Despite its narrow width Andy continued to drive fast through this street, but there was no traffic on this road apart from a few parked cars and vans which he easily avoided. Neither I nor Andy knew how much damage the Passat had sustained or the extent of any injuries incurred by its occupants, but even if it was a write-off, there was still the Megane floating around, so as Andy drove on past each street corner we kept a watchful eye out for the Megane's sudden emergence.

The narrow street gave way to a larger warren of streets in an area comprised almost exclusively of offices and warehouses, but with no people. I went into my jacket pockets and took out all the mobile phones I had: there was Wattie's of course, Amber's, Andy's and Carl's (Shaban's I'd already discarded in Royston). I had to assume the worst: that they were all compromised or could be, and were acting like the blips on a radar screen. Opening a side window, I unceremoniously threw them out onto the empty streets, but not before retrieving each SIM card which I kept in my hand.

We were approaching the end of a long road at the end of which was an estate consisting of semi-detached two-up residential houses which had been built on the site of an old railway station. Andy brought the cab to a halt.

"What do you want to do chief? I could try to sidle back up to the north side of the city or get us down south? You're welcome to stay with me."

I looked at Andy's open, honest face staring round at me from the front of his miraculously unscathed cab.

"Andy what you pulled off there was amazing. There's probably not a driver in the entire British intelligence services that could have done that. But lucks running against us, especially if we stay together. I don't know how they got to us, but it means anybody I'm working with, including you, is in danger. We need to split. Your cab's amazingly undamaged and that's testament to your ability so put your hire sign on, pick-up the first punter that waves you down or park at the nearest rank and moan like fuck with the rest of the cabbies; blend, mingle in. I'll bin the wig and find my own way out."

"Ok, chief, you take care!"

Taking my wallet out I leaned over to Andy and gave him £300 I had in it He tried to wave the money away like Amber, but wasn't as determined and eventually took it. I exited the cab and felt quite light-headed as I walked onto the pavement after all the jostling and swerving, but quickly regained my balance as I waved farewell to Andy.

I knew the area I was in well, as indeed I did of almost all of Glasgow and I followed the street beside the housing estate down to a tenement and onto a main street, on the way putting the SIM cards down a drain and ditching the wig below a pile of rubble. I was at Bridgeton Cross, another main junction, though less busy than Parkhead having been largely pedestrianized, with a wrought iron circular shelter pavilion, another legacy from a past industrial era, at its centre. I walked across the junction as if wading through a minefield, alert for everything, aware that I'd not tumbled the tousle-haired guy in Possil, and so looking at everything and everyone with maximum scrutiny; but there was no Megane, nor any tousle-haired chap.

Across the square was Bridgeton Railway Station where a commuter line went from the city centre out to Lanarkshire. I was unsure whether it would be open after yesterday, but the presence of an assistant behind the ticket window assured me it was.

"Return to Helensburgh please." I was the only passenger at the ticket box.

"11.10 is your last train back to Glasgow," he informed me helpfully as I took the tickets and my change.

"Thanks," I replied as I walked away. There were two stairwells to the platforms below; one eastbound, the other westbound. If I was really going to Helensburgh, a seaside coastal resort on the Firth of Clyde, I should have taken the westbound, but that was only to throw up a false trail. I looked behind me: the assistant had his back to me, head engrossed in some paperwork. I went down the eastbound stairwell.

The platform here was empty. I'd just missed one train and the platform screen told me the next train for Motherwell was fifteen minutes. I sat down on a bench in the middle of the platform allowing me to see either side. Across, the other platform was fairly busy with people waiting for a train into the city centre. After a few minutes a train pulled in to that platform I looked at my watch. It was ten-to-six. God it seemed ages since I'd left Amber in Possil. The train opposite started to move away revealing as it did an empty platform. There was still no one on my platform.

I racked my brains as to how they knew I was in Possil. Had Carl the Geek blabbed? Had they traced my call from his phone? Or had they saturated the Shields with an all-surrounding net and been able to trace the signal from Carl's phone from mast-to-mast back to my phone? What helped me come to that conclusion was that the phone I used to contact Carl had been issued within the agency unlike those for Wattie, Amber, Andy or Shaban as, with the exception of Wattie they were all my ratline contacts and those phones I'd purchased privately. I comforted myself with this thought as it meant that those contacts wouldn't immediately be associated with me, though they were still, apart from Andy on the agency's 'books'. I also reassured myself that the detection trail from the mobile phone masts would most likely have pinpointed the precise block or tenement I was in but not the actual flat.

But any reassurance I gave myself was short-lived superseded by the certain knowledge that it was my stupidity in contacting Carl the Geek that had revealed my position and could have endangered Andy or Amber. There was no need to have phoned Carl; it was obvious that the cameras in the surveillance van could have been remotely and externally controlled and that there was a good chance Carl would have been working at the Shields. An announcement came on the station tannoy system that the next train at my platform would be for Motherwell and that it would be due in ten minutes. The platform opposite now had a few people on it but mine was still deserted.

Motherwell was where I was heading. I would stay the night there in a cheap B & B before making my way to Edinburgh Airport. I would use the new 'Thomas Lenihan' passport Shaban had made for me and withdraw enough money from my 'Jack Donaldson' credit cards to get a flight out of the country. Where I was going and what I was going to do there I wasn't sure of, beyond a vague notion of opening negotiations with the new regime at whatever was replacing MI5; threatening to do an 'Edward Snowdon' unless I could get safe passage, though in truth I had nowhere near the clout or the information to trade that Snowden had. Furthermore Snowden had no links with terrorists whereas I was intimately involved with a full-blown terrorist attack.

I put my head in my hands sitting on the bench wondering should I just give myself up and take my chances with my, almost certainly, new bosses. How did it end up like this, getting chased through your own home city?

I thought, for the umpteenth time, of the grim litany of people who had died on this operation: Sadeq, Khaled, Mohammed, Qatib, and Tony Boyd. I thought of Tres, of Wattie on the run. Of Amber and my feelings for her. For the first time in a long time I thought of my daughter Louise in London who I hadn't seen in nearly eight months. God what would she think of...

"Buddy, would I get a train to Hamilton from here?"

My reverie was abruptly broken by this slim, well-built guy, straight back, with receding short chestnut hair, probably somewhere in his thirties wearing blue jeans and a white top. He just seemed to have materialised in front of me. I was about to reply when he pulled his left arm back and went on, in a friendly, reasonable tone:

"The reason I'm asking is..." and then, to my total surprise, his left arm shot a devastating blow to my solar plexus which completely winded me. As I slumped forward there was another sharp punch to my upper left jaw. I started to lose consciousness but not before I could feel him getting hold of me as I began to slide off the bench and also hear him say to someone else on the platform: "Could you give me a hand here, pal, this fella's taking a turn..." before obliviousness took over.

8: INTERROGATION

In movies whenever someone wakes up from being knocked out, they come around feeling groggy but in a short time they're up and away and back to normal. The reality, at least from my experience, couldn't have been more different. I awoke in pitch blackness with not a clue as to where I was. Then a searing pain began in my left jaw and seemed to spread all through my head and upper body. With a lot of exertion and much willpower, I managed to turn my head around, but the effect was winding and, involuntarily, I began moaning in pain and utter discomfort.

I was aware of a small light coming on which even though it was quite dim still felt harsh after the intense darkness. There was a movement to my side and I saw a woman standing there at the edge of the bed. She had a serious expression on her face and I thought I recognized her from somewhere, but couldn't place her. Then I realised she was holding a plastic cup and was speaking to me in a soft voice which I wasn't able to make out. It was only when she clutched hold of my head and pulled me towards her that I realised she was trying to get me to drink water from the cup, which I duly did along with some pills which she made sure I swallowed. I was dimly aware of her turning around and the light being switched off. I lay there still for some time until I fell asleep again.

The next time I regained consciousness, the darkness was still impenetrable but the pain was less intense, more a dull throbbing which allowed me space to think about where I was and how I'd got here. Slowly and fitfully it all came back to me, not in a linear sequence, but in stabs so that talking to Amber in her kitchen would be followed by me talking to Sadeq at the Bothwell service station, then the fit guy asking me if a train was due for Hamilton before his vicious, devastating two punches, then the horror of the Square, then Mulrooney's face etched in worry, all in a jumbled sequence until it was just getting too much.

Suddenly the dim light came back on. The woman was back at my bedside with a tray. The light seemed brighter now and I could hear what she was saying: "You'll start to feel better now and you'll give yourself a great help if you take some soup." She propped some pillows behind me and she helped me to get upright while she put the tray across me on the bed. Her voice was soft but clear now, middle class English probably from the south-east: an accent sometimes referred to as 'estuary English'. "Take some pills first," she urged as she passed me the plastic cup and handed two green pills which I swallowed without resistance. "Now the soup!" She handed me a bowl and spoon. It tasted pretty bland, but in the state I was in a cordon bleu delicacy would have tasted bland. I had difficulty in swallowing at first but this subsided and I was able to finish it all. Satisfied, she took the tray, switched off the light and went out. It took a while longer this time to resume sleep but eventually I did.

I was awakened by the woman saying softly to me, "We need to get you up and get you walking about." The bed-sheets were rolled back and to my surprise I became aware I was dressed only in my underpants. She put her arm under my arm and started to gently pull me out of bed; I didn't resist and worked with her in getting myself standing up. I realised there was someone else in the room and looked over to see the dark, tousle-haired chap standing at the end of the bed. He came round to my side and with the woman on my other arm they started to walk me around the room. I was unsteady at first but slowly regained my balance and gait. After a few moments they were able to let me walk unaided. The pain had subsided to a dull ache. I looked at the tousle-haired chap and said: "No offence about the Vicky, mate, it was a fair cop." He merely smiled, as did the woman but he didn't say anything.

"Ok, we'll get you back to bed now," the woman said as I walked unaided back to the bed.

They left, but didn't switch the light off so I could study the room, which apart from the bed, the table beside it and the lamp on it, was completely empty and featureless. I could make out the edges of a door in the wall opposite the bed. I got up slowly and went to the door and confirmed my suspicion that it could only be opened from the outside. I went back to the bed feeling stronger, but not before examining the lamp and switching it off. No one came into the room to scold me for doing so, so I reckoned I was allowed to do this at will. I could feel the tenderness in my abdomen and upper jaw where I'd been socked; this would turn to a nasty bruise soon.

It seemed I'd just got to sleep when I was shaken awake by the tousle-haired chap. "Ok mate, need to get you a wash, come on!" He helped me up and directed me to put some slippers on.

His accent I thought was northern, perhaps from Manchester. We walked to the door which opened automatically as we approached it so I guessed a camera must be in the room tracking my movements. The light in the very narrow corridor outside seemed very bright, but this was only because my eyes hadn't adjusted to it yet.

The tousle-haired chap walked behind until we came to a corner at right angles. He opened a door to the left to reveal a windowless bathroom with shower. "Take your time, get a shower and shave, if you want one, and I'll wait for you here," he said.

I thanked him and went into the bathroom. I must have spent an hour under that shower; it was so reviving it felt luxuriant. Coming out of the shower I noticed my reflection in the mirror: not a pretty sight at the best of times, there was a livid gash on my left cheek; the only slight consolation was that I seemed to have lost weight and the middle-aged spread wasn't as prominent as it had been. There was a shaving kit lying beside the wash-hand basin and, carefully avoiding the nasty gash on my cheek, I gave myself a good shave.

Just as I finished shaving, there was a knock on the door. I opened the door and the young lad passed me some clothes. I recognized them as my jeans and white sweater. I thanked him, closed the door and put them on. Whoever these people were, I thought, they weren't (yet) about to put me through sensory deprivation or any of the other dark arts that add up to heavy physical interrogation. But they hadn't gone to these lengths just to have a nice chat either.

Refreshed, I left the bathroom and this time was led by the young chap to another windowless, featureless room which had three tables in it; there were two chairs behind two of the tables, and a chair in front and a chair behind the third table. The young chap directed me to sit on the chair in front of that table. The woman who had given me the pills and later the soup came in and sat at one of the other tables. She didn't look at me but concentrated on what seemed like a USB attached to a tablet in front of her; I noticed she also had a writing pad and a pen. With a start it came to me who she was. She was one of the two women I'd seen out of the front window at Amber's flat before I made the fateful call to Carl at the Shields. She had been the one with the pram and the baby talking to another woman while the tousle-haired chap had nonchalantly walked out of the newsagents' with a paper in hand. They'd all blended so naturally into the background, but that's what a good surveillance team were supposed to do. It's difficult to be natural when you're trying to be. MosBerBel training teaches you to look out for the contrived, the artificial, the forced in what's around you. These people were good as they managed to minimise artifice. Or my MosBerBel training needed refreshing. Probably a bit of both. One further consolation, I thought. I was in with a bunch of pros, most likely from our side of the desk, so I wasn't in the hands of some violent, psychopathic, fanatical terrorist group who thought delivering a blow to imperialism could be gained through systematically abusing and torturing me. But, again, that didn't mean it would be a pleasant conversation.

A third person came into the room and sat at the remaining desk. He wore glasses, a grey top, a pair of dark trousers, was of medium build, quite slim with close-cropped fair hair. He sat down and said, "Hello," civilly. I replied in kind, after which he remained silent, but watched me carefully. Another person entered and I sat upright in the chair and tensed as it was the guy who'd knocked me out in the railway station. He looked exactly as he had done then and sat at the table in front of me, hands in front of him saying:

"Don't worry, pal, there's no more boxing!"

I stared back impassively as he went on in a broad Glaswegian accent: "Where did ye get that cabbie from? We'll give him a job any day!"

"I picked him up at the taxi rank in Saracen," I replied to which he responded sardonically:

"Aye and I'm going out with Beyonce, but two-timing her with Rhianna!"

I stayed silent.

"Don't worry, Mr Macintyre, we're not interested in your cabbie, just you." He fixed me a straight glance to which I continued to stare back at him impassively.

"Ok, jihadi boy, when did you start taking al-Qaeda's money? Or did they have something on you?"

I stayed silent. After a few minutes my interrogator, for that is what I now saw him as, went on, "Big silent treatment eh? Not talking? So, jihadi boy, how you feeling about the great victory you've managed to pull off for your pal al Hassan? Eighty-two dead, hundreds injured, MI5 in tatters and al-Qaeda exultant! And who gave the bombers a personal escort into the Square?" His eyes were bright and his forefinger pointed straight at me. "You did! So how does it feel, jihadi boy, like victory?"

Wearily I spoke almost in a monotone: "I had no idea there was a bomb in the van."

There was another prolonged silence before he suddenly got up, shoved back his chair, came round to the front of the table and sat on it. I bristled for a moment thinking he was going to renege on his word and become physical again.

"Macintyre, you're either one of two things. A total fucking incompetent who lets his own team become infiltrated by al-Qaeda right in front of him!" He shook his head disdainfully. "In which case Security Service? I wouldn't give you a job on the door at Primark!"

He went back behind the table, up-righted his chair and resumed sitting on it. "Or behind the façade of ineptitude and incompetence there's a totally signed up jihadi boy that's bought into the whole holy warrior kick, a traitor to his country, a Philby wannabe for the new Islamo-terrorist age, who thinks that blowing people to smithereens in his home town is a great victory for jihad! Have you bought into jihad, jihadi boy, is that what it is? Converted to Allah but went for the full fucking terrorist option. Concocted this whole Grand Minaret thing with your pal Sadeq and your Special Forces buddy with the two boys as the sacrifice?

"And you know what? It's worked. Not only have you given Ali Hassan his biggest hit since London and Madrid but MI5 is finished and the rest of the world thinks the UK is riddled with Islamic spies and terrorists!? Well done, jihadi boy! And all behind that fucking front of '*I didn't know, I knew nothing, woe is me!*' Your SAS pal is still out there, Macintyre, but despite all that nonsense they spout about these superhero SAS guys being able to live off dog shite and eating grass, he'll need to come in for supplies at some point and we'll be waiting for him!"

It struck me as he delivered this diatribe that every time he mentioned 'special forces' or 'SAS' he almost spat out the words with contempt, indicating perhaps a military background, which his bearing and prowess with his fists would attest to but also the characteristic regular army disdain for what they regarded as the over-rated gung-ho warriors of the special forces. I looked behind at the woman furiously writing on her pad and at the other man still watching me carefully. Behind me, I was aware, was the young chap. I remained silent.

"You see, Macintyre," my interrogator resumed, "there's only really three options here. One is you're a total wank who can't see what's in front of him and is totally unable to sniff terrorist shite in his own team. Or, two, you're a jihadi holy warrior fully committed to the destruction of the decadent Western world, but oh by the way I don't want to be a martyr, I'll let other poor fuckers do that, but I'll organise it from the side-lines. Or, three, you're a totally corrupt shithead that's taken Al Hassan's money and turned a blind-eye to a mass atrocity. Or, let me think, is there a fourth option here? What if they've got something on you, Macintyre? Are you a pedo, Macintyre, fond of wee boys or girls?"

I'd had enough and despite my resolve to say nothing turned to the other guy sitting there in complete silence and who I vaguely discerned was the senior in the room and burst out:

"Was he born a wanker or did he get good training in it?" It was a pathetic riposte, a Weegie and a Lanarkshire boy jousting with each other, but I couldn't resist it. The senior guy made no response, physical or verbal.

My interrogator continued, completely unaffected by my juvenile outburst. "I actually don't buy you as a jihadi boy-come-terrorist accomplice. You're too much of a typical overpaid Security Service bureaucrat who thinks meeting a Joe in a West-End park is *dangerous*! No, my money is either you're an inept wanker or you've been blackmailed!"

A silence descended on the room. In truth the accusations of incompetence were stinging at me. It was on my watch that George Square happened and it was an unalterable fact that it could only have been when my team were surveilling Sadeq's van that the explosive device was planted. I had to hold on to the notion that we had been set up; otherwise what the interrogator was flinging at me seemed too close for comfort. Finally, after what seemed an age, I replied:

"You're forgetting, arsehole, that I lost an officer at George Square and you're discounting the possibility in your own incompetent and inept way, sunshine, that my team could have been set up. That Wattie Craig and I have been made to look like patsies in this!"

The interrogator opened his arms wide, and with a mirthless smile and mock confused look on his face he looked around him at the others in the room. "Where the fuck is this: the sixth floor of the Book Depository in Dallas during a JFK assassination conspiracy convention? Fucking patsies my arse! We know all about the incident where the camera is off the van for twenty minutes. Macintyre look at me straight pal: you can search for ages, but there was no other team in control of that camera. Your man Craig sneaked out while Tres Martindale was houring and placed the IED, a device with which, with his *Special Forces* background, he's very familiar. And he did that either with your complicity or behind your back, which means you're either a criminal terrorist wanker or just an incompetent wanker. In either case you're a wanker. Personally, my money's on Craig being turned by the Taliban in Afghanistan and him finding something on you: still makes you a wanker."

"And how do you know that?" I responded, riled, "How do you know that there was no other team operating that camera. If you know so fucking much then you'll know that there was a team following us into the Square from the time Sadeq picked up Qatib at the mosque! Or am I supposed to have organised that as well?"

"What about Dr Qatib?"

It was the senior guy, the first time he had spoken. I looked at him, surprised at his intervention. The voice was classic upper-middle class English: confident, commanding, used to being in control, with a warm superficial coating concealing the hard centre underneath, but without the patronising aristocratic tones exemplified by the likes of Harry Perkins or the more commanding strictures of Algy Hunter. I shook my head. "He was the recruiter, the main instigator. It was around him that Grand Minaret unfolded. Up to the point that Qatib unexpectedly came up to Glasgow before the planned reconnaissance, which I presume you know about, Grand Minaret was proceeding smoothly…"

"Perhaps too smoothly," the senior guy interrupted. I didn't argue, conceding the point, yes, maybe it had all gone too smoothly.

"So," the senior guy went on, "why did you think Qatib had come to Glasgow for the reconnaissance?"

I shook my head again. "I was stumped at that, we were all stumped. I don't know."

"Would it surprise you to know Qatib didn't know either?"

I felt the senior guy's eyes boring into me as I tried to take in what he'd just told me. "Yes it would very much surprise me," I replied staring straight back at him.

He rose to his feet slowly. "I think that'll be enough for now Mr Macintyre. We'll take a few hours' rest and resume later." He walked out of the room followed by the woman with her USB, tablet and writing pad.

My interrogator broke into a smile, not mirthless this time, before rising and saying: "Nothing personal in this, Macintyre," before he, too left the room. The young lad was left to accompany me the short distance back to the 'bedroom'.

A short time later, supper was brought in. It was a fish supper and my taste buds had revived so I devoured it; the first substantial portion of food I'd had since breakfast in Amber's flat. But when was that? I felt completely disoriented on two counts: I had no idea how long I'd been here for, how long I'd been unconscious, or what time it was: morning afternoon or evening. I also, of course, had no idea where I was being held or exactly by who. But I was also disoriented by the certainty of the senior guy's revelation to me that he knew that Qatib didn't know why he was being sent to Glasgow. How did he know that for certain?

I managed to get some rest for an hour or so. As well as being delicious and filling the fish supper had been accompanied by some fresh orange juice so, in spite of my disorientation, I felt reasonably well in the circumstances: the pain had now virtually eased altogether, though they were still giving me the green pills, which I assumed to be painkillers.

I was drowsing when the young lad woke me again. He let me use the bathroom and wash my face before taking me back to the room with the three tables for what I presumed to be the second part of my interrogation. The woman, who I now sub-consciously associated with the pram in Possil and thus dubbed her 'pram lady', came in first and gave me a brief smile which I returned before she resumed her place at her table complete with USB, tablet and writing pad. My interrogator came in next, gave a quick nod of recognition which I also returned and, to my surprise, sat at the table where the senior guy had been before. The latter came in last and sat at the table opposite me. The senior guy had a brown paper file in his hands which he placed on the table and rifled through. The young chap had left the room and returned with a jug of water and two glasses which he placed in front of the senior guy who poured water into each glass and offered one to me which I accepted and thanked him for. This was obviously going to be a more civilized, less abrasive session than the last one had been. After taking a sip from his glass, the senior guy spoke to me.

"Mr Macintyre let me say straight away that I don't think you're either a terrorist informer or agent and neither does my colleague," he glanced over at my previous interrogator who nodded his assent. "My name's Henderson. Who I am and who I and," he looked around the room at the others, "we represent, I'll leave to later." He contemplated the file before him and selected a single A4 typed sheet.

"You've had a very interesting career, Mr Macintyre. You were recruited to the Security Service in 1977 as an agent-informer within the Revolutionary Socialist Party or RSP, regarded at the time as the most active of the far-left Trotskyist groups. To be precise you were recruited after being arrested for occupying and attempting to set fire to a Job Centre in..."

"Paisley," I finished for him. I could still recollect the events of that day as if they were yesterday. I smiled as I recalled what happened. "It was the month in 1977 when the unemployment rate went over the one-million mark under the Callaghan Labour Government. We decided to protest by occupying the Job Centre in Paisley as we had a very active branch there. We walked in during the day and just sat in there, told the staff to leave which they did and started putting placards on the windows and on the walls. It was all actually quite good natured. Members of the public that were in the Centre found it bemusing and some were sympathetic to us. The police turned up and they were ok as well: they said we could occupy the place for an hour or so, make our point and go, and we agreed to that.

"Things went wrong when one of the branch activists who I suppose the term 'hothead' was coined for, picked up a sheaf of application forms and other information about the Youth Opportunity Programme or YOP. This was a programme for young people at the time that we regarded as pure exploitation as well as a ruse to keep the dole queues down, so our activist comrade, who just acts before he thinks, takes a match to all of these bits of paper relating to YOP. It was meant to be a symbolic protest but there's loads of paper on the desk. Next thing they've all caught fire and the desk is well alight too. Dense black smoke starts to fill the whole centre and we have to rush out only to be promptly arrested by the cops who called the fire brigade, who extinguished the blaze in minutes. I was taken to Paisley police station. I'd never been in trouble with the law before and suddenly was faced with a serious charge of being an accessory to wilful fire-raising. I was frankly terrified."

I remembered it vividly. The RSP had been fun: demos, occupations like the Job Centre, endless conferences and social events, girls, lots of girls. And all this at the heady age of eighteen while still living rent-free at home, getting meals put on the table for you, reading about revolution in a comfortable bedroom while my mother and father worked hard and just about to enter university free of charge in an era long before student loans. All this looked in jeopardy because of that idiot setting fire to the Job Centre with some lousy papers!

I was put in a cell for an hour or two and then I met a cool guy who changed my life. He arranged for my release. There were no questions asked about this. The hothead got the book thrown at him and two of the others received fines. My youth helped me; my comrades thinking the judicial system regarded me as a naïve daft wee laddie and that was why I was let go. But the fact that I had been 'active' at the Job Centre occupation, which began to take on arms and legs with stories of how the cops had stormed the building and waded into us with truncheons gaining currency, earned me a lot of status in the RSP. I was regarded as a 'battle-hardened activist' and gained respect, trust and status within the Party. The cool guy at the police station who, after arranging my release, met up with me again, was in fact an officer for MI5 who, to cut a long story short, had recruited me as an agent-informer, a task to which I committed myself with gusto.

Henderson resumed his narrative. "So you became an informer within the RSP. Over the next eight years you provided reams of information about the Party. You gave MI5 advance warning about demonstrations and occupations, about links with CND and details of planned protests at the nuclear weapons facilities at Faslane. You passed on details of all recruits, who was on the up and who was sleeping with who, which trade unionists were sympathetic to the Party or had actually joined. Then you became branch organiser of the, by RSP standards, *busy* Glasgow South Branch and, in that capacity you had access to everything.

"Then came the miners' strike of 1984-85 and your reputation with your handlers really took off. You successfully became Chair of a Miners' Support Group which was really an RSP front for organising support to pickets in the Lanarkshire and Ayrshire coalfields as well as trying to blockade the Ravenscraig Steelworks. More importantly it gave you access to National Union of Mineworkers activists who were organising flying pickets across Scotland and with it details of their planned movements all of which went to MI5 who passed it onto the police. Indeed you received an indirect commendation from a senior police commander who commented that the intelligence supplied on the movements of pickets had been 'invaluable' in allowing the police to pre-empt attempts to close pits where miners had been returning to work and blockading other facilities.

"The miners, as we know, were defeated. You made it clear you wanted out of being an informer and in any case the RSP were in steep decline and no longer regarded as a threat to democracy or national security. In an unusual move you asked if you could join MI5. At first you were refused. You appealed and there was a change of heart and you went through the normal civil service examination process and enhanced positive vetting or EPV. Finally, you were accepted and assigned to London on routine counter-intelligence tasks which you later described as," Henderson referred to the A4 sheet, 'dullsville personified'. In 1987, just as the Cold War was ending, you were reassigned to Glasgow.

"Back on your home turf you really struck gold when routine surveillance of a Communist Party member, or rather one of his relatives, uncovered a link with a US navy commander based at the then Polaris base at the Holy Loch. It was a classic honey-trap and the commander was passing on information to the Soviets on US submarine movements and the American's proposed alternatives to their fleet being stationed in Scotland. The network was rolled up and your star was in the ascendancy; you even got a mention in Washington.

"Subsequently, you were promoted to Team Leader and in the early 90s headed up an operation probing and infiltrating links between organised crime in Glasgow, particularly around the drugs trade, and Northern Irish paramilitaries' intent on scuppering the peace process. By all accounts it was an intensive period. There was a considerable amount of violence and some fall-out." I gathered this was Henderson's euphemistic reference to the drug wars and the 'Possil disaster' of 93 but he refrained from going into details. "This was also the time when you recruited Abdul Sadeq Hamid, always referred by you thereafter as Sadeq who later became central to Grand Minaret. The upshot was you played a pivotal role in preventing a drugs-for-arms pipeline becoming established between the west of Scotland and Northern Ireland even though, as is often the way of these things, the Belfast people took most of the credit."

Henderson put the A4 sheet back on the table. "Good, colourful CV," he continued, "unusual, a bit sideways in some respects, but nevertheless a positive upward trajectory. And then," he put his hands upwards in front of him, "there's nothing! From 1993 to 2015 routine surveillance operations, plodding counter-intelligence work, occasional anti-terrorist alerts, none of which leads anywhere: stolid fare after the halcyon days of the Holy Loch spy ring and the 90s drugs wars."

He took a sip of water and resumed. "In a way, Mr Macintyre, your own, to use that much overused word, personal *journey*, is rather emblematic of MI5 as an organisation. Forgive me if I appear to resemble one of the many vultures currently scavenging at the carcass, but post-Cold War, in the nineties MI5 makes a determined effort to move in on drugs, organised crime, links with terrorists and paramilitaries and, yes, there's some success, but nothing that's consolidated. All those areas are claimed now by others.

"And then came 9/11 and there's a real threat to national security followed by 7/7 in London and dozens of attempted plots which you guys, admittedly almost all in England, manage to abort. But MI5 are back, needed, despite the fact that anti-terrorism, at least domestically, is a crowded field. Until Grand Minaret and the horrors that have issued from that so that now you and your agency's fate, Mr Macintyre are rather intertwined."

It was a succinct overview of, as he put it, my MI5 'CV'. I couldn't fault him on that. I knew well that, until Grand Minaret came along, I'd felt stuck, treading water. Grand Minaret had appeared to offer the escape route; a revival of the glory days of the 80s and 90s, then retire on a high with a lucrative career in anti-terrorism consultancy waiting. Now the least of my worries was not having consultancies lined up when I retired.

"Grand Minaret must have seemed like a gift from heaven, something that fell right into your lap, yes?" Henderson asked me directly.

"In retrospect I suppose it did. But it appeared sound. Sadeq *was* a reliable informant for over twenty years. He reported what was going down at the mosque with the radical preacher and then Qatib appears grooming and recruiting. And then the two boys Khaled and Mohamed took the bait. Qatib arranges for them to go to Waziristan. They come back even more radicalised and it unfolds from there. I'm sorry, but it was standard operational anti-terrorist tradecraft right down to ensuring that Qatib requested Sadeq to do things for him and not the reverse in case we were accused of acting as agent provocateurs." I had my hands in the air now reflecting my exasperation. "I've racked my brains but I can't see where we conducted ourselves wrong. There was nothing in those hours of surveillance tapes that we recorded for over a year in the development of Grand Minaret to suggest that any of the people who got killed in the van on Wednesday were deceiving us. Yes, one of my team could have been an agent and," I looked over at my ex-interrogator, "you can call me all the incompetent wankers under the sun, but I *genuinely* had no inkling of that if it's true. This is bigger than just my team because you're conveniently forgetting that we were tailed going into George Square, by a professional outfit by the way, but who were *they*?"

"You're looking at them," it was my ex-interrogator.

"What?"

Henderson picked it up. "It was us that followed your team into the Square."

"And who the fuck are you?"

He produced a plastic card which he showed to me. It had Henderson's picture on it, but a narrow strip of paper blocked out his name so I presumed 'Henderson' was an alias, which didn't surprise me. What did get my attention was the logo with crown and heraldic shields next to the caption reading: Secret Intelligence Service (SIS) the official name for MI6, Britain's external intelligence agency who, along with the National Crime Agency and probably others unknown, were currently devouring MI5. Henderson withdrew the card but not before I'd had time to notice the name of the department of SIS he was assigned to in very small letters on the bottom right-hand corner of his card: Special Operations Branch.

I looked back squarely at Henderson. "This doesn't add up," I said firmly. "Grand Minaret was proceeding well until the van blew up in the Square. So, why would SIS be interested prior to that? It was on home turf and you guys are reserved for overseas. Besides, through JTAC, we were keeping you guys up to speed on everything!"

Henderson adopted a quizzical expression and parroted some of my own words back at me: "Grand Minaret was proceeding well until the van blew up in the Square?" He waved his left hand in front of him. "I'd go back a bit, Mr Macintyre, if I were you."

I wasn't sure what he was getting at, then I realised what he meant. "Qatib?" Henderson nodded in agreement. Of course, Qatib coming back to Glasgow after he'd set everything in motion; that's when Grand Minaret actually did start to take a wrong turn.

I continued: "We never did find out why Qatib came back to Glasgow, but it sure put the frighteners on Sadeq who up to then had been quite stoic about his role in this." Even as I finished saying this I suddenly saw a connection opening which I hadn't thought of before. Qatib's announcement to Sadeq he was coming up to Glasgow for Recce Wednesday had not only put the shivers on Sadeq, it had galvanised me into bringing the surveillance on Sadeq's van forward by nearly thirty hours thus *assuring that members of my team would have unimpeded surveillance and access to the van.*

Henderson caught the sudden look in my eyes. "What is it, Mr Macintyre?"

"Qatib coming back to Glasgow also caused a chain reaction. I'd only planned to place the listening devices on the morning of the reconnaissance. Sadeq was panicking, so to reassure him I put the surveillance on his van from the Monday night."

"And?"

"So what I'm saying is, originally the team would only have had limited access to the van with me on the Wednesday morning. After the news that Qatib was coming up the potential was there for thirty hours to allow one of the team the opportunity to place the IED." My voice trailed off in utter dejection at this train of thought.

"So," Henderson urged, "you're suggesting that Qatib was brought up to give one of your team members, who might be a mole for al-Qaeda a much better opportunity to place the device without being caught?"

I had my head in my hands. "I don't know, I'm just speculating. Why else would Qatib be coming up?"

Henderson repeated the remark he'd made earlier: "Qatib didn't know either."

Lifting my head I looked at him straight and asked him: "How do you know that?"

"Because he told us. He was our Joe."

I was speechless and if my jaw hadn't actually opened it felt as if it had. Henderson placed the A4 sheet in the folder, closed it and rose from the table. "That'll be all for now. We'll talk further later."

Back in the bedroom I lay with the lamp on in despair. Adding to the dreadful feeling in the pit of my stomach that the whole Qatib affair had been a diversion to allow a mole in my team the chance to place the bomb was this new information that Qatib was working for SIS. Was there no end to this ceaseless bombardment of revelations, this conveyor belt of deception? What a clueless clown I felt myself to be. Everything about Grand Minaret, which I was supposed to be in charge of, was a big deception. I or we had been manipulated throughout. There *was* a mole in my team: I now had yet again to confront, to face up to, that unpleasant fact and Qatib all along was working with the people across the river: SIS. And while I thought I was in some sort of a relationship with Tres, she was also seeing Wattie who might very well after all be an agent for al-Qaeda! How much worse could this get? "Oh Macintyre you are a *schmuck*". A Hebrew word meaning the disused tip of the foreskin or a useless piece of dick! How true.

I must have lay in the room in despair for some time when I heard the door open and Henderson came in. He had two bottles of Budweiser in his hands. "You could do with a drink and some fresh air." I rose from the bed and he handed me one of the bottles. "Follow me."

We went through the narrow corridor, past the bathroom and the 'interrogation room', further along until we went through an open doorway into a landing with stairs going down to my right and another set ascending to the left. We climbed the left stairs which went up two flights until we reached a steel door with an iron bar across it and two fire extinguishers on either side. A large notice on the door read: ACCESS FOR AUTHORISED PERSONNEL ONLY. Henderson pushed the already slightly ajar door open and walked on: I followed him.

It took a couple of minutes to adjust as I walked into the open air. Everything seemed to hit me at once: the open air, slight breeze, the height, the noise and the view. We were standing on the roof of a building in the heart of Glasgow. It was dusk and the lights of the city were coming on. To our left was the giant ramp of the southbound slip road leading off the huge edifice of the Kingston Bridge which linked the M8 motorway north and south of the river Clyde. Traffic was pummelling across the bridge while immediately in front of us as we faced north was the Clyde itself looking calm and clear on this mild spring night. Across the river were the canyons of the city's business and financial district and beyond it the glow of the city centre. To our right, or east, by the King George V Road Bridge was the magnificent iron colossus of the Central Station railway bridge leading out of the station itself. A couple of commuter trains were heading into the terminus while a long vividly red and cream painted train, probably heading to London, was rattling out of the station. Behind me, to the south, the slip road ramp ended at some waste ground and a collection of buildings which now housed a drugs crisis centre, a rehab service and a homeless unit.

We walked across the roof to the centre where my ex-interrogator was seated on a folding chair also drinking a beer and reading today's edition of the same evening paper which I'd last read waiting for Andy at Saracen Cross. I was eager to catch up on the news, but Henderson walked past him for another twenty metres until we reached two more folded chairs lying on the roof surface which he unfolded and bade for me to sit on one.

I sat down, swigged some beer which tasted quite gassy and thought just how surreal this all was as I sat on this riverside rooftop. It reminded me of the 60s movie *The Ipcress File* in which the kidnapped spy, Harry Palmer played by Michael Caine, is subjected to deep psychological interrogation augmented by the film's quirky, almost psychedelic editing and special effects. Palmer believes he's been imprisoned in some Soviet bloc Balkan country, so when he manages to escape he is stunned and relieved to find himself exiting a warehouse in central London surrounded by familiar landmarks. So it was here. I had convinced myself that I was miles away from Glasgow and in some special interrogation centre, but no I was on the banks of the Clyde in the middle of downtown Kingston.

I knew what this building was. It was intended to be a set of luxury apartments which had been built on the back of a property boom, but even though it was within walking distance of the town, because it was virtually surrounded by a busy motorway and next to waste-ground, with no immediate access to shops or amenities, the flats had never really sold. So they were let out as party flats to weekenders and students, which pissed off the few permanent residents who eventually sold up, usually at a loss, leaving the flats empty for most of the week. Again, a fleeting, transient population bereft of nosy neighbours: perfect for gangsters and intelligence services.

"I'd never have thought of this place in the middle of town as a holding centre," I said almost admiringly to Henderson. 'Holding centre' was intelligence speak for interrogation centre which in too many cases morphed into a torture centre.

"I believe another fashionable expression is 'hiding in plain sight'," he replied. "Well if this isn't it," his arm described a 360 degree circle around the crowded urban vista given greater emphasis by the sound of a train horn as it negotiated the Central Bridge, "I don't know what is." He went on: "This was intended for Qatib, for his debriefing," he waved his hand at my surprised expression, "I'll explain in a minute. We rented the whole top floor. Half of it we made into a holding centre, which you've just been in, with partitions and minimal sensory input and the other half is the luxury penthouse it was intended to be. We got it for a song, which will please the service bean-counters and the Treasury. When Qatib, to our very great surprise, met his demise at George Square, which wasn't in the script, we had a ready-made place to bring our suspect moles from MI5, which of course included you."

"Is that past or present tense?" I asked him directly, but he ignored me, instead saying:

"We need to bring Craig in *urgently*! We need closure on this."

"Are you going to tell me about Qatib and what he was doing for you?"

Henderson took a generous swig of his beer and appraised me carefully. "I need you to bring Craig in or all hell will break loose. My superiors are more or less in charge of the intelligence side of MI5 and are able to keep the cops, the civil servants, the military," he shot a quick glance at my ex-interrogator now doing the crossword in the evening newspaper and confirming my suspicions of his military connections, "the media and above all the politicians at bay, but only until tomorrow. If I don't have Craig in custody by the morning, he'll be named as the prime suspect to be the al- Qaeda mole and an all-points bulletin put out on him with orders to shoot on sight if necessary, which means almost certainly. Irrespective of if we get Craig, the bombers will be named tomorrow, but not Qatib."

"And Sadeq?"

He nodded in confirmation.

I put the beer bottle down on the roof surface with a bang which broke the ex-interrogator's concentration on his newspaper. "That is shite!" I said angrily. "Sadeq was only doing everything we asked him to do and he was reporting and trying to prevent a mass terrorist killing in the making. He was a loyal, good guy and he's as much a victim in this as those folk who died in the Square. It's a travesty! If he's named as a bomber or an accomplice his family will suffer total disgrace both from their own community and the wider Scottish community. On the contrary if he's named as helping us, they'll be at the mercy of a revenge squad from al-Qaeda. You've got to keep his identity hidden!" I implored him, "This is no way to treat twenty years' loyal service."

"All three families have been taken into protective custody."

"Yes, but that's only short-lived. As soon as that winds down its' open season on them!"

"If you help me to bring Craig in, I'll see what I can do."

"Then tell me about Qatib first."

"Deal." He clinked his bottle against mine on the floor, and took another swig.

"Before you tell me about Qatib I need to know two things," I said.

"Yes?"

"Firstly, how did you track me to Possil?"

"We had complete coverage of the Shields; every incoming call was monitored in a 300 metre radius either side of the building linked to GCHQ in Cheltenham. GCHQ also had voice recognition IT software set up so when you phoned the technician, the systems immediately kicked in and they were able to trace your connection back through the masts to within a 60 metre radius of a tenement block in Possil. Then we just sent the Team up there within forty minutes and waited for you to appear, which you duly did. Even with the wig we were able to ascertain your profile, through your build and your height. We obviously wanted you to lead us to Craig, but your very alert taxi driver put paid to that idea."

"But you didn't locate the precise flat I was in?"

"No, nor are we interested unless it can help us to get to Craig. And your second question?"

"That flat can't help you to get to Craig, neither can the cabbie."

"Then we're not interested in them. Your next question?"

"I know where I am now, but what day and time is it?"

"It's Friday evening at," he checked his watch "seven-thirty. You were brought here about twenty-four hours ago."

"How did you find me in that railway station?"

"The Megane driver spotted you from a distance as you walked across that pavilion section, kept watch on you and radioed to the rest as you made your way into the station."

"And how did you get me out of the station?"

"After our friend here," he again glanced over at my ex-interrogator who had now finished reading the newspaper and was reading from a Kindle; the light was fading fast but the reflection from the street and building lights combined with a cloudless night meant that we could still see each other clearly, "had knocked you out, the other younger chap with the dark hair was called upon to assist with getting you medical attention and taking you out of the station. When they took you outside I *happened* to be driving by and offered to take you to hospital. All very plausible."

I was satisfied with his response re Amber and Andy. Along with Shaban, they should be safe and untouched by this. "Ok, now tell me about Qatib."

"Let me walk you through this. It is of course highly confidential and completely deniable, you understand?"

"I understand." Two fire tenders were racing across the Kingston Bridge, sirens wailing. Somehow it seemed to lend gravity to Henderson's cautionary words.

"Ali al Hassan has had a meteoric rise within the ranks of al-Qaeda. That's not really surprising; he's youthful, charismatic and handsome. Not since Bin Laden have they had someone that could act as a rallying figure as well as be so perversely telegenic. The problem is that whereas Bin Laden earned his spurs in Afghanistan on the frontline and, more importantly, was in charge when 9/11 happened and could take the credit for it, al Hassan doesn't have any such comparable background. He's emerged out of Lebanon, talks the talk and looks the part in front of a camera, but he hasn't got frontline experience anywhere near the same as Bin Laden.

"Now all these different 'branches' or 'affiliates' of al-Qaeda: al Nusra in Syria, ISIS in Iraq and Syria, the groups in Yemen, Mali, Libya even Boko Haram in Nigeria, all have fought their way through armed struggle to seriously threaten the regimes they're fighting and are serious contenders for power. They're just not going to roll over and let some guy lead them no matter how good he is on the TV. And more importantly, while they have been very active, there has been hardly anything on the so-called 'western front'. All the spectacular mass killings of the noughties have not been replicated, with the appalling exception of the ISIS attack on Paris. Almost every attempt by *al Qaeda* in the past eight years has been thwarted by Western security services, including your agency and mine.

"So al Hassan has a serious deficit if he wants to be the heir to Bin Laden, or not to be upstaged by ISIS, he has no significant history of engaging in armed combat and he cannot take credit for organising any attacks in the West. Enter his number two, al Sharjanah. This guy has more street cred. Ok he lacks al Hassan's charisma and presence, but he's fought in Gaza, Syria and Iraq and talks the same language as the various military commanders: they in turn respect him. He's also led cells in Germany, France and Spain and so has experience of clandestine terrorist operations and networks in Western countries. Finally, he's also committed to unifying al-Qaeda and making it a formidable military force that can seriously make a claim on gaining power politically and trying to create their vision of a renewed caliph in the Middle East. And, at the end of the day, that's what the regional commanders want as well. So al Sharjanah has been tasked by al Hassan with delivering a 'spectacular' in the West. The equation is simple: al Sharjanah hasn't got al Hassan's charisma to lead al-Qaeda, but needs him if he wants to be his deputy and, someday, take over the leadership. And al Hassan needs al Sharjanah and his networks to stage a spectacular in the West and thereby pave the way for him to consolidate his hold on the leadership of al-Qaeda.

"And who does al Sharjanah delegate the task of carrying out a mass attack in the West? Enter our friend Dr Qatib. He had a good track record in Egypt, Syria and Lebanon of grooming and recruiting militants to the fighting cells that would become the nucleus of the groups like al Nusra and ISIS. He was multi-lingual and comparatively unknown to the Western authorities so could travel around Europe relatively easily. Two years ago al Sharjanah met with Qatib in the eastern Libyan Desert and put him in charge of a project to recruit 'clean skins' in European countries. Not the capitals, but large cities in each country where a cell could be recruited and trained. Qatib travelled through Europe, with a different alias and legend in each country of course, and succeeded in his remit. He would find out about radical preachers based at mosques in various cities in each country who had already begun to radicalise people, especially young men, and hone in on them, just like the preacher Siddique here in Glasgow. In Dortmund, Cracow, Lyon and Genoa he struck gold. The MO was almost exactly the same as Minaret here in Glasgow. Disaffected, disillusioned young Muslim men groomed for over a period of a year, radicalised further and trained either in Waziristan or Yemen and sent back to their home towns to carry out jihad on targets that were likely to cause the most loss of life and create maximum publicity. Like a travelling salesman, Qatib flitted between the different cities delivering the same programme almost to a standard template.

"Except, of course, that they didn't succeed. All were rolled up before they could carry out the attacks. Why was that? Well, in two cases, Cracow and Genoa, there were already informers at the mosques where Qatib in league with the local preacher had successfully begun to recruit, just like your man Sadeq Hamid here in Glasgow. That helped, but doesn't tell the whole story and certainly can't explain what happened in Dortmund and Lyon where there were no informers.

"The explanation lies in the fact that a week after al Sharjanah met with Qatib in Libya, the latter walked into the British embassy in Rome and offered his services to us. Why? We'll probably never know the whole story and what the full motivations were, but it began with a personal animus against al Sharjanah and developed into full-scale disillusionment with the whole project to the extent that he wanted out and the best way to do that was trade with the West. He also happened to love London and wanted to settle there. Whatever the motivation, we took him on and within a short period he was starting to deliver with excellent results from our perspective.

"Al Sharjanah instructed him to recruit in Britain too, which of course he did. And after contacting preachers in major cities across the UK, except London, he made a hit in Glasgow, where there was an informer and that led to Grand Minaret the development of which we knew all about through JTAC.

"With the arrests and detention of all the cells in the European cities, al Hassan was putting pressure on al Sharjanah. He was desperate to convene a meeting of all the regional commanders of al-Qaeda in Libya to confirm his position as leader but he needed an attack in the west to succeed to give him the credibility and authority among the commanders to ensure that. In turn, al Sharjanah was putting pressure on Qatib and starting to question what was going on, why were all the operations getting blown? Suspicion and acrimony were flying back and forth between the parties.

"Glasgow was still to go ahead: the last to do so. Qatib was asked to attend a meeting with al Sharjanah at a location just outside Tunis on the day the reconnaissance was meant to have went ahead; that meeting was going to be extremely important." Henderson, who had been cradling his bottle of beer in his hand, put it down beside him, sat straight upright and looked at me closely.

"This is where you have to be very discreet and I have to trust you!" I returned his gaze equally as straight, without speaking, as if to say: 'Go ahead, you can trust me'.

He picked up his beer and resumed drinking from it, before continuing, "We knew, through Grand Minaret that Glasgow would be rolled up too and at that point Qatib might in in danger and brought in for, shall we say, 'questioning'. This meeting outside Tunis was before Minaret was due to be busted. So we reckoned that the meeting was for Qatib to assure al Sharjanah that the Glasgow operation was still going ahead, but also to let Qatib see the whites of al Sharjanah's eyes and make it clear to him that if Glasgow didn't happen and the guys he'd recruited for it are arrested, then he'd be accused of being a spy for the infidel. It's likely that once he met with al Sharjanah, the latter would have had him detained and brought to Libya where Qatib's fate would have been completely dependent on Grand Minaret's progress.

"Understandably, Qatib didn't want to go to that meeting. We managed to persuade him to attend."

"How?" I asked.

"By promising him it was the last thing he'd have to do for us, as during the course of that meeting we'd exfiltrate him and get him to a safe place, with a new ID, a new post and generous funds to sustain himself, for all the services he'd rendered to Her Majesty."

"You were taking a chance letting your man go to that meeting," I cautioned, "you would have needed to have been pretty well team-handed to 'exfiltrate' him during a meeting with al-Qaeda's number two in North Africa!"

"We would have had assistance," Henderson replied curtly.

"From whom?"

The sharp sound of a car horn from the bridge penetrated through the dusk and reminded me of what a surreal situation this was: an MI5 officer who was AWOL and on the run being briefed by an SIS special ops team on top of a roof in the midst of Glasgow city centre about the events leading up to one of the worst terrorist attacks in

Scotland! Unfazed by the car horn, Henderson addressed my question.

"As soon as Qatib walked into the Rome embassy and told us of his meeting with al Sharjanah, the Special Operations Branch of SIS, which I'm assigned to, took charge of him. This was needed as Qatib's operation crossed frontiers and no one country based SIS station could handle that on its own: that's why the SOB was set up, particularly in relation to anti-terrorist ops. SOB can also call on the resources of other departments, including the military", Henderson glanced over at my ex-interrogator, still reading his Kindle, which further confirmed my suspicions that he had armed forces' connections.

"But, of course, what Qatib had to offer, concerned our European partners and we liaised with security agencies in all the affected countries as we would expect them to do if it involved potential attacks on the UK. And, as a matter of course, we involved our American allies, as again we would expect them to do."

"So you involved the Cousins?" Cousins meant the CIA.

"Yes, and with them we could call upon far more resources than we could have on our own," Henderson said almost defensively. "So when Qatib was summoned to the Tunis meeting SOB and the CIA hatched a plan, not just to exfiltrate Qatib, but also capture al Sharjanah."

I raised my eyes involuntarily at this bombshell. Qatib, the man instrumental in the development of Grand Minaret and, unknown to us, an SIS asset, was also going to be the bait to capture al-Qaeda's number two.

"It was a glittering prize," Henderson went on. "Not only would Grand Minaret prevent the Glasgow bombing happening but al Hassan's hopes of a 'spectacular' in the West would be in tatters. And with his deputy captured his credibility would be destroyed, the meeting of regional commanders would be unlikely to go ahead and al-Qaeda would continue to have no unified command: it would be less than the sum of its parts and far less of a threat and al Hassan would be finished.

"What an opportunity! The CIA assigned a full team to us and they were able to call upon US Special Forces back up. They even managed to get part of the Sixth Fleet diverted off the coast of Tunisia to assist. The plan was for Special Forces to storm the venue where Qatib and al Sharjanah were meeting, exfiltrate Qatib and capture al Sharjanah, preferably alive, but dead if need be and take both to a Sixth Fleet ship." Henderson pointed back at the roof entrance from where we'd come out "this was where we'd intended to debrief Qatib, but as you are aware, it has not entirely been a waste of resources. If al Sharjanah had been taken alive, we, that is SIS, would have gotten first bite at him, before the CIA would have taken him back to the States for *questioning*."

"But it never happened," I interjected.

"No, it never happened. Qatib was preparing to travel to Tunis when he got the call on Monday afternoon to travel to Glasgow."

"Call from whom, precisely?"

"A cut-out from al Sharjanah."

"What exactly were the instructions given to Qatib?"

"To be with the recruits in Glasgow as they went about their reconnaissance and to wait in the safe house in, in…" Henderson struggled to remember the name.

"Battlefield."

"Yes, Battlefield. To wait there until further instructions."

"Against all normal operating procedures for terrorist cells. Qatib must have been baffled and worried."

"Yes, he was alarmed, but he had no option but to go ahead and travel to Glasgow. We were with him all the way, kept out of the way, and ensured we were unobserved by your Security Service tails, watched his back, or so we thought, into George Square and… The rest is history."

"So," I decided to outline what Henderson might be reluctant to highlight, "You were aiming for a quartet of 'glittering prizes'. First, foiling the latest of a series of attempts at a Western terrorist 'spectacular'. Second, the capturing of al-Qaeda's number two al Sharjanah. Thirdly, as a result of one and two, destroying al Hassan's credibility and almost certainly snuffing out his attempts to wrest control of al-Qaeda resulting in, four the prevention of the organisation forming a formidable unified command. Instead, you've ended up with a terrorist spectacular in the West bolstering al

Sharjanah's credibility with al Hassan, allowing al Hassan, to be accepted and crowned as leader at this coming meeting of the regional commanders and al-Qaeda having a unified command structure with all that could flow from that. Oh and let's not forget, your asset, Qatib, has been terminated. That's some fucking result, some fallout!"

Henderson nodded his head wearily. I went on: "I take it the Cousins are not happy bunnies?"

"No they're not. They are currently quote: 'revaluating and reassessing the situation' and will be in touch with us imminently. They're expecting us to find out what went wrong and why urgently, otherwise," Henderson put his hands in front of him in a gesture of despair, "the entire range of Anglo-US anti-terrorist operations and attendant cooperation are in jeopardy. They would never trust us again, ever!"

A silence descended on the rooftop, which I eventually broke.

"It's' blowback, it's obvious. Al Sharjanah somehow found out, or knew all along, that Qatib was an informer and played him back and performed a complete reverse flip."

"Reluctantly, I would have to agree with you," Henderson replied. "Al Sharjanah has apparently played a brilliant hand. But the key to it is here in Glasgow. All the other plots in western Europe were foiled because al Sharjanah didn't have what he so obviously does have here: an asset in a local intelligence service."

Bastard! I thought. That was a straight bat back to me. But I had to concede he was right. The whole plot had unravelled and the reverse flip could only have occurred by someone at our end allowing that bomb to go onto Sadeq's van.

Henderson continued: "We need to find who that asset is. I don't believe it's you. I think you've been duped and I think it's a fair chance its Craig and we need to get him. I'd like him alive but I'll take him dead if need be, but after tomorrow morning that'll be out of my hands anyway."

I shook my head. "I can't believe its Craig. He's never changed his demeanour, he's always been the same way; he just doesn't fit the profile!"

"Come on, Mr Macintyre!" Henderson replied exasperated. "You know as well as I do that 'profiles' are averages generated by geeks with computer programmes that allows politicians and intelligence agency chiefs to reassure the media and the public that they've got a handle on who's likely to be a terrorist or spy or whatever. Bullshit! The best spies are those who shock us when they're revealed. Good spies compartmentalise themselves. They become the legend until they need to act. Your man Craig is probably in that category."

I was still reluctant to concede the point. "I still can't believe it, but it's academic as I wouldn't be able to get to him now especially after yesterday's keystone cops' shenanigans! He'll never trust me again!"

Henderson looked at me squarely: "Who would he trust?"

I knew the answer to that the minute he asked it. "I might know someone."

"Then ask them."

"What? Ask Wattie Craig to give himself up to spend the rest of his life in prison? Do me a favour!"

"All right, but if he's not the al-Qaeda spy then this is his only chance to give himself up to prove his innocence."

"He won't buy it."

"Then try and persuade this person that he trusts and ask them to request he meets with you."

I looked away and thought deeply. Wattie's only chance to prove his innocence was to give himself up, but that he wouldn't do voluntarily. If I, through someone he trusted, could persuade him to meet me, I could try to persuade him to turn himself in, or failing that, SIS and the rest would move in and attempt to capture him. It would be sneaky and very underhand, but if they were successful in that endeavour - and that would be a big *if* - and managed to bring him in alive, it was the only opportunity he would ever get now to disprove he was a spy, assuming they would give him a fair hearing, which was another big assumption. And if he was the spy then fuck it: he deserved everything that was coming his way.

I looked back at Henderson. "Ok, I'll give it a shot."

He looked relieved. "Thanks."

We both rose from the fold-up chairs and made our way to the stairwell entry. It was now completely dark, but we could still see well on the roof from the reflected lights. My ex-interrogator stopped reading his Kindle, rose from his chair, stooping only to retrieve his evening newspaper and followed us. As I made to follow Henderson back into the covered gantry that gave on to the steps leading downstairs I felt a prod on my back. It was my ex-interrogator with a grin on his face. He proffered the evening newspaper to me pointing at a small inset article on an inside page: one of the very few pieces in the paper that wasn't about Wednesday's atrocity. "Have a quick read of that, you might find it interesting." There was a bright light in the gantry which allowed to me to read the headline: *Police probe East End car chase incident!* The article continued:

"Police are probing reports of an incident in Glasgow's east end yesterday afternoon involving a black taxi and two cars. Witnesses spoke of a manic car chase involving the vehicles yesterday afternoon through Shettleston, Parkhead and the Gallowgate. Motorists had to take evasive action and pedestrians were put in danger of their lives as the vehicles mounted pavements and swerved between cars. The three cars were reported to have headed in the direction of Bridgeton. Police refused to comment on any connection between the incident and a VW Passat later found abandoned and burnt out in the Rutherglen area. However, a police spokesman firmly ruled out any link between the alleged incident and the terrorist attack in George Square. Inquiries are continuing.

I handed the newspaper back to him and descended the steps while he followed behind me. "Was anybody injured in the Passat?" I asked. "No, all in a day's work," he replied casually.

Back in the apartment we walked into the luxury penthouse side of the top floor where Qatib was originally intended to commence the enjoyment of his rewards for services rendered to the UK. My ex-interrogator, the tousle-haired chap and the pram lady all joined us in the main room. It had a large triple glazed window affording a panoramic view of the Clyde.

Sitting on a deep leather sofa, Henderson asked: "So who do you think he will trust? I really have to know that before I let you contact them."

"One of his colleagues: Teresa Martindale."

"One of your *team*," Henderson sounded almost incredulous. "They're never going to allow that! Your team and anybody that's had any connection with them are in quarantine."

"Who's they?"

"My colleagues in SIS have taken over all house-minding and security functions at the Security Service, temporarily of course."

"Precisely, your colleagues! And you are SOB with ranking priority status in an anti-terrorist investigation with sensitive diplomatic and international ramifications."

Henderson smiled, as if to acknowledge that I could trundle out the official verbiage with the best of them. "Assuming I was able to let you contact Miss Martindale, what would you want her to do?"

"Contact Craig, tell him I want to meet him. If he's innocent his only chance to prove that will be to meet me and give himself up, otherwise he's going to die, simples. Wherever he is I'll go and meet him on my own. Obviously you guys will be in the background, but I'll meet him face-to-face. He might take me hostage, he might kill me, but he also might give himself up. Otherwise it's a manhunt living rough, with the odds shortening by the day, with only one end. Yes, he could tell me to fuck off, but believe me this is your only hope of getting Craig alive."

"And why would he trust her?"

"He might not. Like me, he might tell her to piss off. But he might listen to her. And, they're an item."

"Lovers?"

"How prosaic, but yes I suppose so, or at least he believes it to be so." I couldn't resist an inflection of sarcasm on that last comment.

"And you trust her? No suspicion she could be involved?"

"Anything's fucking possible in this mental situation we're in, but no I don't think so. She tried to cover for him. They were houring and it was during her hour off that the camera in the surveillance vehicle was moved. Craig claims he fell asleep. No, after your little intervention yesterday he'll probably never trust me again if I attempt to make contact with him once more. Only Tres, Teresa, has a chance of getting through to him."

"How do you know she can get in touch with him?"

"We're spooks," I looked around at all of them, "all of you! She'll have a number or numbers memorised for him."

A silence enveloped the room. I could feel all eyes in the room on me, but especially Henderson's. Finally, he rose from the sofa and said: "I'll need to make a few inquiries," before leaving the room. His departure was the cue for the rest, including my ex-interrogator, to relax. The TV was switched on. *Eastenders* was on and we sat down to watch it with tea and coffee. Incredibly, in spite of the crazy scenario we were in the midst of, we all got absorbed in the soap.

After about forty minutes Henderson reappeared with a landline phone which he plugged in while someone switched the TV off. He said: "She's at the Art Safe House. She was taken there from the Shields this afternoon. You know the number?"

I nodded in the affirmative. It was just before ten when I rang her. She must have been waiting for the call as she answered it on the third ring.

"Eddie where are you?" Her voice sounded firm, with no trace of anxiety.

"It doesn't matter," I replied. I went straight to the point. "I want you to contact Wattie."

Tres was a good operator, but I could tell she was feigning surprise. "Wattie? Like you he's on the run, I've no idea where he is or how to get in touch with him."

"Come on, Tres, he'll have plenty of mobiles with him and you'll have memorised at least one of those numbers!"

"But why would I want to get in contact with him, why would he even listen to me?"

"Cos you're an item. And he thinks you're the only thing that's keeping him sane just now. I think he's in love with you."

There was a pause. "Did he tell you this?"

"Yes."

"When?"

"Earlier. He agreed to meet with me, but I fucked it up by phoning the Shields and they traced me."

"You're not still on the run, then?"

"No. But look that doesn't matter. What does is that time is running out for Wattie. He'll not take a call from me, but he will from you. I need for you to talk to him and persuade him to talk to me, otherwise sometime in the next two or three days Wattie Craig will most likely be shot dead, cut down like a stray dog."

"This is absolutely crazy, Eddie! How the hell did all this happen? One minute we're on top of these guys about to commit a massacre, the next we're getting treated like criminals and terrorists! Jesus, I mean..." Her voice broke off, straining with emotion.

"Tres I can't even begin to work out what the hell's going on, but I tell you this..." I stopped, carefully measuring what I was going to say next. I decided I needed to be hard on her and keep her focused. "You owe me, you owe the service, you owe those that were killed yesterday and you owe the country."

"Eddie, what the..."

"It was on your watch that that camera moved. You were 'houring', both you and he have admitted that and the only possible suspect that could have moved the camera, unless it was done remotely which I now reluctantly have to accept is unlikely, was Wattie."

"Eddie I feel bad enough as it is, you don't need to rub it in my face!"

"And it was you that alerted Wattie of the suspicions about him after I told you at the Art Safe house." There was silence. It was just after we'd last made love that she'd sneaked out of the bedroom and called Wattie. I tried to resist my next comment but it was welling up in me and I couldn't contain it. "And you cheated on me."

"Ah God, Eddie, that was purely sex, you made it clear that you wanted nothing more!"

"Really oh! Did you offer the same to Danny and Tony?"

"Och that's pathetic! Tony's not even cold you bastard!"

I instantly regretted that remark and I knew I was in danger of losing her. How could the tragic and the petty mingle so easily? Treachery, jealousy, vanity: emotions were running wild in this incredibly stressed situation.

"I'm sorry, Tres; that was unforgivable."

"But you said it!"

"I know, but please forgive me. Look the point is you're the only person that has the remotest chance of getting Wattie Craig to speak to me. And if he is innocent, this is his only chance to prove that. Please, Tres help?"

There was another long pause which seemed to last for ages. Finally, she said, "All right. But I want out of here. I want to get back to my flat, get a wash and a change of clothes. Then it has to be call boxes only, picked by me at random, basic MosBerBel. Deal?"

"Hold on." I conveyed her request to Henderson. It was good tradecraft. Tres would use telephone call box landlines which she would select completely at random to phone Wattie. She would spend no more than a minute talking to him before hanging up. This would make it virtually impossible for us to trace him. It was likely that Wattie would want time to consider whether to meet me. So Tres would move around the city to another call box to make the next call to him. This would likely go on for a number of times until Wattie agreed to a meeting or not. Henderson chewed over Tres' requests for a minute. "I'm not letting her leave the Art Safe House on her own," he said firmly.

I passed that on to her. She insisted that she didn't want to be followed around 'mob handed' and after some batting back and forth with me in the middle, it was agreed that Tres would leave the safe house with two female SIS officers in one car and a back-up car behind: nothing else. With reluctance Henderson also agreed to let her go to her flat first before beginning the phone box routine.

"Thanks, Tres, I really appreciate this," I said when all the arrangements had been finally decided and approved by both parties. "It might be the only chance we'll ever have to get to the bottom of this."

"Aye all right, Eddie, don't labour it." Her next comments were a devastating return serve for my crass remark earlier. "Don't forget, Eddie, you started all this. It was you who jumped when Sadeq informed you about what was happening at the mosque. It was you that got us all hyped up and totally committed to Grand Minaret. I can't believe Wattie Craig would help out al-Qaeda and assist in committing mass murder, but, without absolving him of responsibility, if he did you gave him the opportunity to do it. At the end of the day you're the boss, you're the one that's supposed to asses us and spot if there's anything that's not right with us. Ok I'm away now. I'll do what I can." I heard an abrupt click and then the dial tone that announced she'd terminated the call.

Her last sentences coursed through me, wounding me. Thanks Tres, I thought. That was all I needed. The others in the room looked away while Henderson unplugged the landline. Someone switched the TV back on. It was now just after ten and I could have done with watching the BBC news, not least to try to deaden the impact of those last stinging comments from Tres, but it was thought more appropriate to watch a music programme on BBC4. It was a repeat about guitar heroes. About twenty minutes into it, as the immortal black and white clip of Jimi Hendrix reducing the Lulu show to anarchy by performing a totally unscripted and impromptu live version of Cream's *Sunshine of your love* and going way beyond his allotted time was being shown, pram lady, who I had not noticed leaving the room, came in with a mobile, turned down the sound and informed us that "Martindale has left the safe house."

Thereafter she updated us on Tres' movements. She spent about an hour at her flat in Dennistoun just by the city centre, getting a shower and changing her clothes. She requested that she was able to take a bag with some clothes and toiletries, which after a rudimentary check was approved. She selected her first call box at Tollcross in the east end of the city and spent no more than a minute on the phone. Pram lady reported that Tres had not used any sheet of paper to make the call, so she'd obviously memorised a number for Wattie. The detail with Tres drove back into the city centre and cruised around for a while until she instructed them to drive to the south side where she had them drive around further until suddenly she instructed them to stop at a call box on Paisley Road West. Again she spent no more than two minutes on the phone. Pram lady looked up at me and offered me her phone. "She wants to talk to you."

I took the phone. "Hello," I said.

"He's agreed to meet with you." Her voice was calm. I felt a strange relief surge through me.

"That's cool," I replied, mentally chastising myself for breaking my self-imposed rule that no one over fifty should use the word 'cool'. "Whereabouts does he want to meet?"

"There's one condition, before he tells me where he is."

"*What* condition?" The relief turned to frustration. Could nothing ever be straightforward?

"He wants me to go to first, before you do. He wants to see me on his own."

I looked up at Henderson who was monitoring the call on an earpiece. He nodded in agreement.

"Ok, but you will be accompanied there."

"Yes, but there're not to come into the actual building he's in." Once more Henderson nodded his assent.

"You've got that as well, Tres."

"Fine. Now I've to make a last call."

She made them drive around until she ordered them to drive through the Clyde Tunnel, across the west end and up to Anniesland Cross, before again making them stop while she jumped out and used a call box there. After two minutes she was back in the car. Pram lady passed me the phone.

"LN117," Tres said, sounding quite excited.

"LN what?" I asked.

"He says you've to meet him at a place that you would know as LN117. You've been there. But, remember, you've to let me go before you."

"Has he told you where LN117 is?"

"No, but if you remember it, you're to tell me. Then I'll phone him one last time and I've to be taken there to him."

I racked my brains, but couldn't recall. "Tres, I can't think what or where LN117 is!"

"Well you're just gonna have to, Eddie." She went off the phone.

I handed pram lady back her phone. I looked at Henderson, still with his earpiece. I shook my head. "I can't think what that is."

"Give yourself time. Craig wants to meet you so it's a real place. Give yourself time," he repeated and left the room. I went to the panoramic window and gazed at the silhouetted buildings across the Clyde.

Just what the hell was LN117?

9: LN117

The more you try to think or remember about something the more your memory resists. Such was it with me and LN117. I just couldn't think what Wattie's reference meant. I thought of encrypted agent names and code names for operations, but nothing remotely resembling LN117 cropped up. I could feel the pressure to recall it from Henderson as well as Tres out there cruising with the SIS detail waiting for my call, as well of course as Wattie holed up in whatever and wherever LN117 was, no doubt having a laugh as I tried desperately to figure out where he was: field agents never make life easy, not least for their bosses.

My eureka moment with LN117 came precisely when I was slightly more relaxed and not focusing on it as much. It was about an hour after Tres' last call and the others had come back into the room. Someone switched the TV on again. There was a movie on that was set in the American mid-west, the exact plot of which I wasn't really getting into. It was about two young boys coming of age in this rural town. In one scene they were larking about on the outskirts of their small town at a water tower about forty feet in height built on four thin columns topped by a bell-shaped dome enclosing the water tank. I was reminded of an identical water tower that once used to supply a large tractor factory in North Lanarkshire. Predictably, the factory and its American owners had long gone, to be replaced by shops and houses, but I'd passed it many times in my youth as I lived not far from it and when I was a teenager I had a girlfriend who lived in a house with her parents across from the factory. Images of the tractor factory, its water tower and the girlfriend and her house cascaded by and then it crashed vividly into my head and I remembered exactly what LN117 was.

Both the former tractor factory and my former girlfriend's house were located in a district called Tannochside. The factory had been a huge sprawling complex employing thousands of workers and had its own water tower to service it. But there were two water towers at

Tannochside: the one for the factory and a much larger one built for the area as a whole.

Tannochside was situated on top of the steep north escarpment of the Clyde Valley, so the larger water tower sat on top of a hill and could be seen for miles around and was a local landmark. Built from reinforced concrete the Tannochside Water Tower was about 100 feet high. It had a large round tank containing up to 600,000 gallons of water which was supported by a thick middle column that contained the extraction pipes and a concrete stairwell leading up to an observation platform and control room on top of the tank. Nine further, but much thinner support columns surrounded the middle column at the edges of the circular tank. Above the observation platform was a large antenna. The whole ensemble with its columns and radio tower looked like some 1950s science fiction writer's idea of a prototype space shuttle and as a young boy I used to have fantasies of being the captain in charge in the observation section as we blasted off into the night sky.

Tannochside Water Tower was one of a number of such structures built around the Glasgow area in the late 50s to supply drinking water from Loch Katrine at the southern end of the Highlands to new housing and factory developments. There were about half-a-dozen of them all located on high-rise land and, therefore, prominent across the city skyline, though Tannochside was, arguably, the tallest and most impressive of them.

Its significance now was its association with a NATO military exercise set in Scotland three years ago called Hard Landing. This exercise was supposed to simulate an international political crisis during which guerrilla forces supported and supplied by hostile powers were to attempt to capture and sabotage or destroy key infrastructure targets such as railways, supply depots, power stations, and weapons bases and so on. Each designated target was allocated a number prefixed by the initials reversed of the local government area in which the target was located. Thus the two main targets were the UK Government's nuclear submarine base at Faslane designated BA1 (for Bute and Argyll1 – the actual name of the local authority was Argyll and Bute) and BA2 for the adjacent warhead depot at Coulport. There were nearly two hundred supplementary infrastructure targets scattered mainly across the west of Scotland. One of these was Tannochside Water Tower given the title LN117 or Lanarkshire North no. 117 (the local authority in whose area the Water Tower was located was North Lanarkshire Council). MI5 personnel were to work closely with their armed forces counterparts in either preventing attacks on the targets or recapturing them.

As a former SAS man Wattie was selected with Danny Mackay from my team along with a member of Stu Hutchinson's team to take back LN117. This had been 'occupied' by a 'radical terrorist group affiliated to militant Islam and supported by a hostile international power', which was newspeak for an al-Qaeda type group. The al-Qaeda group were played by Dutch marines and in a night manoeuvre oblivious to the local population Wattie, Danny and the other officer had managed to infiltrate the tower, capture the al-Qaeda' guys, keep them prisoner and hunker down for two-three days until the exercise was completed.

As usual NATO won. The exercise was supposed to highlight the effectiveness of civilian security forces such as MI5 working effectively with armed forces to combat insurgents in a crisis situation and prevent wholesale internal sabotage of vital supplies. Whatever, Wattie would have gained an intimate knowledge of the structure including how to get round the security arrangements and how to enter and leave it without being too obtrusive. There were shops nearby for supplies and he would have access to cash probably for up to several weeks. So he could hole up there for a while; hiding in plain sight on top of a bloody big water tower; that was typical Wattie! His real difficulties would emerge when his face was plastered all over the media, which would certainly start to happen tomorrow. He was a big man and a distinctive character and I didn't know if he had any disguises with him such as wigs or hair dye, but the odds were against him unless I could persuade him to give himself up.

"I know what LN117 is," I suddenly announced. Everyone else in the room, including Henderson turned to look at me. "It's a water tower," I continued, "in a place called Tannochside, about eight miles to the east of Glasgow. It's a straight road to it on the M8 from here. Where's Tres?"

"In an all-night McDonalds in the city centre waiting for you to recall what LN117 is," pram lady replied in her sweet southern accent. I stretched my hand out for the mobile which she'd already called Tres on.

"Hello," I spoke into the phone, "LN117 is the Tannochside Water Tower, the one you can see for miles when you're heading out that way."

"You mean towards Bellshill and Uddingston?" Tres enquired.

"Yeah. It was one of the targets in a NATO exercise Wattie and Danny took part in a couple of years ago. He'll know the building inside out. That's where he is."

"Ok, great. I'll phone him straight away.

She phoned me back five minutes later. "He says you took you're time, your slipping, but he thinks it's out of your control anyway as there's cops all around the tower."

I exchanged glances with Henderson, who was listening in on the earpiece. "Say again?" I asked her.

She clarified. "Wattie's been in the tower for about twenty hours now. He knows the security arrangements well. It's all covered by cameras, but he knows where they are, the areas they cover and their blind spots, so he knows how to get round them. But he reckons he's accidently set off a sensor in the control room above the tank because an hour ago two security guards with dogs entered the tower and came up to the control room. The dogs sniffed him out and he had to chase the two guards away with a pistol. Result, the place is now swarming with cops and there's a helicopter above. He doesn't want me near him in case I get hurt."

Henderson immediately left the room. I knew he would be contacting Police Scotland to lay off entering that tower. "Listen Tres, we'll make sure those cops don't go in. Just wait there till I get back to you." I handed the phone back to pram lady.

Henderson was only gone five minutes but it seemed like ages. "CTC have ordered the inspector in command of the local police at the tower not to go in. There's only one armed unit there at the moment. CTC are on their way and there'll be more armed units heading out there. The cops will be concentrating on evacuating the local residents in case something goes wrong at the tower, but they won't go in. Tell her to tell him that!"

I took back the phone and relayed that to her. "Get back on the phone to him, Tres. Reassure him. Tell him SIS is in control." Henderson looked askance at me. I put the phone aside and barked at him: "Apart from Tres and possibly me he'll have no trust left in MI5. Whether he's innocent or an agent for al-Qaeda, he might think he has a better chance with you guys if he wants to talk." I went back on the phone. "They know where he is now, Tres. You and I are his only chance if he lets us talk to him."

She agreed. I told her to discard the whole call box routine as it was now redundant and to use one of the SIS team's mobiles. "Do your best, Tres or else it'll be a standoff at that water tower and, no matter how good a Special Forces soldier he's been, he's outgunned and outnumbered."

"I'll do what I can, Eddie," she replied. Using one of her detail team's mobiles in their car parked off Sauchiehall Street she was on the phone to Wattie for fifteen minutes. Through pram lady's phone I could hear her in the car speaking to him. He did most of the talking and by the way she kept repeating "I do too" and "of course, Wattie, you know that," I gathered he was telling her his feelings for her. Finally, she came back on the phone to me. "He's agreed to let me go to him. He's not too sure of you, though."

"That's ok, Tres." I replied. "At least it's a start with you. Go ahead. They'll take you out there to him."

"No tricks mind," she said urgently. "He's too cute for that!"

I looked at Henderson, but without waiting for confirmation said to her. "I assure you, Tres they won't put you in danger. You go in there on your own first and when, *if*, he's ready to see me, phone me on this number."

I asked pram lady for the number which she gave to me and I passed it onto Tres. She then asked me directly: "Do you really think he's working for al-Qaeda?" It was a perfectly legitimate question. I had asked her to go alone to a former SAS soldier, holed up in a giant water tank with at least one gun, who might have been partially responsible for the worst terrorist atrocity on Scottish soil apart from

Lockerbie, and backed into a corner he might be capable of anything. I answered her as honestly as I could.

"I genuinely don't know, Tres, I really don't. My mind veers from yes it is him to, no it couldn't possibly be and then back again. But, somehow, I don't think he would harm you."

"*Somehow*! Thanks, boss, that's really reassuring!"

"It's the best I can give you, Tres, for the three of us if we want to try and get out of this."

"All right, I'll go to him. I'll do the best I can."

It only took the SIS detail fifteen minutes to drive Tres out to Tannochside on the deserted motorway. All the houses around the tower were being evacuated and the road off the motorway was full of hired buses, cars and vans taking residents to local community centres, schools or friends' houses for the night, but Tres's SIS car was given a police escort past the tower to a small shopping mall; the car park of which had become an improvised command and control centre with a mobile police command vehicle parked there, about two hundred yards from the tower. Once all the residents were evacuated Tannochside would be a complete exclusion zone apart from security personnel and police. The inner core of that zone was a circle from the shopping mall car park all around the tower.

While Tres waited in the car, there was the inevitable tussle and brief turf war between SIS, uniformed police and CTC as to who was in command of Tres, which SIS won, though the cops would make the decision about any attempt to go in after Wattie should 'negotiations' break down. CTC would defer to SIS's commands. I heard all this from Henderson who was in touch with his SIS superiors on his phone and earpiece beside me.

Turf war over, Tres left the car, but only after requesting that she take her bag with her toiletries and clothes in it as she "might be some time in that fucking tower!" This was allowed, though one of the uniform police inspectors wanted the bag searched, but one of the SIS team assured him it had already been examined and just contained 'woman's things'. Carrying the bag with her Tres walked the short distance across the road from the shopping centre-cum-improvised command post. She went past a garage and followed the perimeter of the iron fence that enclosed the tower which sat in its own grounds surrounded on three sides by houses and on the remaining side by the road which separated it from more houses across the other side.

Tres had a phone in her hand and kept in touch with Wattie who could obviously see her from the control room in the tower. Pram lady kept me and everyone in the room, including, Henderson, up to speed with a running commentary which she was getting from the SIS detail.

In the middle of the enclosed fence on the road side was a large gate which gave access to the tower. Tres paused here for a minute before walking to the gate and pushed open the unlocked door. As she made her way up the short road to the Tower she went out of sight of the command post in the car park and observation switched to a CTC observation post which had been set up in one of the evacuated houses. They watched her walk under the brim of the tower by the outside support columns on to a wooden door set in the centre of the stout middle column. She pushed open the door and, phone in hand and, with a last look around, entered and went out of sight.

"Ok let's move," Henderson ordered and we all leapt to life in the penthouse apartment. We were on the motorway and out to Tannochside in fifteen minutes. As we came off the M8 onto the road leading to Tannochside we were stopped at a police checkpoint. Henderson left the car and spoke to a sergeant; within minutes he was back in the car and a marked car, light flashing but with no siren, escorted us up the road, while behind us an unmarked car, CTC I presumed, followed. I looked behind to see if I could recognize any of the occupants, but it was impossible to see. On the other side of the road there were still vans, cars and an occasional minibus taking the last of the residents. As we drove past a roundabout, the tower came into view, looming above the surrounding houses. There were lights on in the round control room above the tank which made it even more noticeable than usual. Henderson explained that Scottish Water, who owned and operated the tower, had been instructed to switch these lights on.

The SIS car proceeded up the road and we went past the illuminated tower with the iron fence and the gate open. I could briefly see the short access road leading up to the wooden door embedded in the large middle column; the door was slightly ajar. I looked up at the lit control room, but could see nothing. I checked my phone, but there were no texts. At the end of the road from the motorway was another roundabout. We turned left here and skirted the side of the shopping centre. At yet another roundabout we turned left again and went into the shopping centre which was just a row of shops at the end of which was a supermarket. We'd doubled-back and it was in the car park of the supermarket, which afforded a good view of the tower, that the police command vehicle, a long white caravan, was parked. The car came to a halt alongside the command vehicle. Henderson, who was sitting in front of me in the passenger seat turned and said. "I'm going into the mobile command van, stay here." I nodded in agreement. The driver, the tousle-haired chap, and my fellow back-seat passenger, pram lady, also got out, both saying 'goodbye' and accompanied Henderson to the command vehicle.

I looked over at the tower. With the lights on at the top it looked more than ever like a strange spacecraft ready to lift off. There were four other cars in the car park. Two of these were marked police cars. From one of the other unmarked cars a man got out and walked across to the SIS car I was in. The glare from the supermarket entrance lights added to the reflection from the streetlamps made it difficult to make him out; just a figure walking across and approaching the car. I tensed as he opened the car door, got in and sat in the seat in front of me which Henderson had been sitting in until a few minutes ago. He turned to face me and I could see he was wearing thick dark shades. He had jet black hair which could have been described as crew cut, only the fringe at the back was ragged. What really distinguished him was his craggy, lined face as he gave me a long, penetrating stare which I attempted to return with equal hardness but I felt a cold shiver come over me.

In my career I'd met spies, gangsters, thieves, conmen, opportunists, bent cops, corrupt hacks; you name them I've met them. Every once in a while I'd met one that really put the shake on you, sending a cold sensation down the spine. They weren't all necessarily psychopaths, torturers or sadists, though a few were. No, the common characteristic was the feeling of complete control that wafted off them. A sense of a total right to command and secure complete obedience from all around them. And this guy in front of me right now with that craggy face, of medium height, wearing a casual polo-necked sweater exuded that same sense of effortless domination. He cleared his throat and spoke in a soft but firm American accent which I guessed to be east coast, possibly New England.

"I am a Cousin," he said, still looking at me from behind those impenetrable dark shades, "and if we haven't already done so I want to thank you for the assistance you gave us over the Holy Loch spy ring in the eighties."

In any other circumstances I would have been flattered. Within the space of twelve hours both Henderson of SIS and now this guy had praised me over my, in all modesty, admittedly crucial role in detecting and braking up a spy-ring whereby a US navy officer was giving military secrets to the then Soviet Union.

Apart from the praise, my mind was racing. 'Cousin' combined with the American accent almost certainly meant CIA. Henderson had told me SIS were working with the CIA to entrap al Sharjanah, al-Qaeda's number two, through the meeting with Qatib in Tunisia. Grand Minaret for these guys was a sideshow, though of course that was unknown to us; it was meant to prove Qatib was actively recruiting jihadists in the West who we would of course roll up without ever knowing the wider picture. Qatib was the lure, the bait to capture al Sharjanah whose detention by the Americans would destroy Ali al Hassan's credibility and any chance to take control of al-Qaeda and create a unified terrorist command. The Glasgow bombing had scuppered all that. Now I knew I was facing a senior guy in charge of the American end of the operation who had had a major anti-terrorist coup in his hand and had just seen it snatched away, in large part through what he believed to be the treachery of one of the agents I had been in command of. I felt his pressure on me. He continued.

"So you've helped us greatly in the past. We'd like to you to continue helping us, Mr Macintyre. I'd like you to persuade the man up there," he pointed at the tower, "to come down and speak to us. I very much want him alive to be able to do so. The scribblers who write about our profession would probably describe this as a 'cluster fuck'. Things seem to have gone badly wrong here in Glasgow. Words like 'blowback' are being thrown about. Well we need to get to the bottom of it. There are some people in Washington, Mr Macintyre, even in Langley, who are talking about never trusting the Brits again; some of the older hands are talking about Philby all over again. If these guys, and they are powerful men, Mr Macintyre, are not to get the upper hand, then we need to start getting at the truth and a part of that truth lies here."

He stretched forward further, his head only inches from mine. "You've heard of Winston Churchill, Mr Macintyre?" I nodded slightly in agreement. "He made many a memorable phrase. One of them was when he was criticising an inept general who, Churchill said, had managed to, quote 'snatch defeat from the jaws of victory'. In a way that's what we have here. We had al-Qaeda's number two just in our grasp and we were going to fuck up al Hassan's victory party in the Libyan Desert. Now al Sharjanah has disappeared, obviously knowing more about us than we did of him, your city's suffered a major terrorist attack, al Hassan's crowing about having assets in Western intelligence services, MI5 has been brought to its knees and Hassan is a genius in the eyes of all those regional commanders ready to let him take over the mantle of Bin Laden. That is not at all what we intended."

He moved his head back and resumed: "I don't find anger or revenge, except of course when served cold, to be of any use in these situations, Mr Macintyre. We need to find out what went wrong and you and your team are crucial to that process."

A silence had descended in the car and I realised that this was as much as the CIA man was going to say. A tinny piano sound indicated I had a text message. I looked at the mobile screen:

OK Boss. Ye can come in but on your own. I'll blow your fucking head apart if you've brought any company (again)!

"The man's ready to speak to me," I said to the CIA man. He offered his hand which I took. It was firm, but also rough and slightly sweaty.

"Lange," he said "Herb Lange." He withdrew his hand and got out of the car. He walked towards the unmarked car he'd emerged from. This was the cue for Henderson accompanied by a tall uniformed inspector to come out of the command caravan. I got out of the car and approached them. "He's ready to see me."

"It's the same routine as Tres," Henderson explained. "Walk across the road, past the garage, enter the gate, up the access road and through the wooden door." The Inspector stayed silent at his side. "How long have I got up there?" I asked.

Henderson checked his watch. "It's just after four. Probably till ten this morning. Take this." He gave me another phone. "That'll get you straight to me; the number's on redial and taped on the front." I put the phone in my pocket.

"Good luck, Eddie." It was the first time he'd called me by my Christian name. The inspector remained impassive.

"Cheers!" I replied, turning and walking across the car park to the road, glancing briefly at the car Lange had went back into, but there was nothing to be seen behind the tinted window.

Obeying Henderson's instructions I retraced Tres' path to the gated entrance to the tower. I could hear the sound of a helicopter far away and hoped fervently, as I walked up the short access road, that they wouldn't attempt to storm the tower before I had done my best to persuade Wattie to come out of it, but I had the certain feeling that command and control at this stage was still in the hands of the cautious suited bureaucrats and their uniformed police counterparts. After ten tomorrow would be different; then, if I wasn't successful in extricating Wattie, and possibly Tres and myself, the eager anti-terrorist boys would go in and blood would flow.

I reached the edge of the wide brim of the tower and paused for a second and checked the phone I'd used to keep in contact with Tres and which Wattie had texted me on. There was nothing, but no doubt he would have seen me approaching. I moved below the brim and saw the wooden door ajar. When I got to the door, as Tres had done, I took one last look around. Tannochside was literally deserted of its residents. All the houses across the road were in darkness, though I knew that in one of them, a CTC detail was watching: one clandestine symbol of the fact that, not a few hundred yards from us, hundreds of police and security personnel were surrounding the tower. I checked the phone again: still nothing, and entered the tower.

From behind the door a bare concrete staircase rose sharply beside the circular steel hulk that enclosed the tubes which delivered the water to and from the tank. The stairwell was brightly lit with orange lights at regular intervals, but that didn't detract from the dankness and the damp odour, nor the vibration of the tubes and the steady pinging like giant water-drops hitting an empty sink, all combining to produce a claustrophobic effect, relieved only by the frosted glass windows that were positioned at twenty foot lengths as I climbed the stairwell. Behind the frosted glass was just darkness interspersed with the refracted lights from the streetlamps.

By the time I had climbed about sixty feet my body was painfully reminding me yet again of how out-of-shape and overweight I was as every hard step taken was becoming more onerous and exacting. If I survived this, I thought, I promised I would go to the gym and get fit. This thought together with fleeting and jumbled images of the carnage in the Square, the car chase through the east-end, Herb Lange's craggy CIA face and, incongruously, Amber's sulky, sexy features all mixed together in an erratic stream of consciousness, served to distract me and helped me get to the top of the stairwell.

Here a narrow passageway with the ceiling barely above head-height, led to the right as the steel casing housing the water tubes now expanded overhead and, I assumed, became the base for the water-tank whose vibrating thrumming and throbbing could be clearly heard above me. I paused to recover my breath then moved along the narrow passageway. To my dismay this ended at another staircase which was at an even sharper gradient than the previous one and which gave access to the control room over the tank some thirty feet above. Standing at the foot of the staircase I shouted up:

"Wattie! Tres! It's Eddie. I'm alone." My voice echoed upwards and while I waited for any reply I checked the Tres phone, but there was nothing. I wondered if it was possible to get a signal here as I used the phone Henderson had given me to text him that I was almost at the control room. The text didn't bounce back and was sent successfully so I decided to press ahead despite no reply from the control room. This staircase was even heavier going compounded by the sharp right-angled turns every ten feet or so with only a small level surface at each turn and a thin wooden handrail to hold onto. I had just reached the second turn of the staircase when, to my stupefaction, the muffled and tinny sound of a pop song that I vaguely knew echoed in the corridor.

The tune went on muffled and echoey until it reached some high pitched tones and then just as abruptly as it had started died off. Where the hell did that come from? I wondered, dumfounded and then it started again. Until I realised it was coming from a ringtone broadcast by a phone concealed in the poacher's pocket of the casual jacket I had been wearing ever since leaving Amber's flat on Thursday afternoon. I felt in the pocket and had to put my hand deep into my jacket as the phone had fallen into the lining. Finally retrieving it I brought the phone out by which time it had stopped ringing. I was amazed because this was neither the phone pram lady had given me for Tres nor Henderson's, both of which in either case were in another pocket. This was one of my ratline phones, all of which I thought I had discarded from Andy's cab during the melee of the car chase yesterday. This one I'd missed because it had slipped into the jacket lining of an already deep pocket. Once I'd brought it out I looked at the screen. It was my MI5 Registry contact Vincent. I was about to phone him when it erupted into life again and I answered it: "Vincent? You picked one fucking hell of a time to phone!"

Vincent's straight and urgent tone cut across any banter or small talk. "Something's come up. I need to tell you about it."

"Vincent you're not psychic so you would never know this, but I'm actually virtually at the top of Tannochside Water Tower; as a Bellshill boy you'll know the one just next to the old tractor factory?"

"What you doing there?" he asked.

"I've always liked water towers Vincent from a small boy onwards, so I just took a notion that I'd climb it this morning!"

There was a short pause, then completely ignoring my smart-arse reply, he repeated: "It's really important that I get a word with you."

"Fuck's sake, Vincent!" I almost shouted, exasperated. "I really am in the Water Tower, there's…"

"..Teresa Pamela Martindale." He cut me off and got my attention.

"What?"

"You asked me to do a cross-referencing analysis of three of your team, see if anything cropped up from any linked database?"

"Yes, I did," I agreed.

"Well something's come up against Teresa Martindale."

"Which is?"

"I need to take you through it. I need a few minutes of your time. It might be totally innocent, even coincidental, but you should know about it."

As I stood there in the narrow passageway, phone at my ear, the deep rumblings of the massive water tank vibrating all around, I was intrigued and not a little apprehensive. "Vincent, a few minutes ok?" I urged him.

"A few weeks ago a guy was picked up by Belgian intelligence at Brussels Airport. He was calling himself Syed Ghazani and he claimed to be a doctor, a consultant paediatrician to be precise, but the Belgians didn't like the look of him and reckoned he was using a forged passport, so they detained him. They put out an ISIR notice on the name and got a hit back from the Israelis, MOSSAD to be precise. They informed the Belgians that the name, Syed Ghazani, was an alias that had been used by a Palestinian Sunni Muslim whose real name was Jalal Asaf. This guy had been killed in a gun battle between rival Syrian factions in a Palestinian camp outside Tripoli in Lebanon in 2008. Asaf was a real doctor who was working in the camp hospital when he died.

"But, under the name of Ghazani, he had been working in the UK as a doctor in the NHS. He'd worked in a few British children's hospitals in London, Manchester and Aberdeen. Mostly, however, for the last six years of his stay in Britain he'd worked in Glasgow: at the Glasgow Royal Children's Hospital."

I suddenly felt quite tense, a dryness developing in my mouth as I made the connection, familiar from the personnel file: The Glasgow Royal Children's Hospital was where Tres had worked for the last seven years of her nursing career!

"Is that how the connection was made?" I asked. "I assume you'll know that Tres worked at that hospital before she joined the firm?"

"Aye I know that, but that's not how the connection was made, Eddie. Ghazani was an alias mind being used by Asaf. Until the Israeli notification to the Belgians the name was clean, it was on no services' registry anywhere: Us, SIS, the yanks, Germans, French, nobody. The reason the name came to the attention of the Israelis was because they had a source close to an ISIS commander called Amir Asaf. This guy was Jalal Asaf's brother and he, Amir, *is* the real deal: a one-hundred percent full-on jihadi warrior, i.e. terrorist. Not only he is a senior ISIS militant, but he's been the main driver nudging ISIS back towards al-Qaeda which they were originally affiliated to until 2006. He's reckoned to be particularly close to a guy called al Sharjanah who's Ali al Hassan's deputy."

"Ah, for the love of God!" I exclaimed involuntarily, as my mind raced with the ramifications of all this.

"Sorry?"

"Nothing Vincent, please continue."

"The Israelis also informed the Belgians that there was a third Asaf brother named Ahmed. The three Asaf brothers were originally from Gaza. Jalal, the doctor guy who worked in Glasgow, moved to Egypt. That's where he adopted the alias Ghazani and got his medical qualification. Ahmed and Amir stayed in Gaza and the two brothers joined the al-Qazzam Brigades, the military wing of Hamas in the Gaza Strip. Ahmed was caught leading a commando raid against Israeli settlers in the Strip; this was in 2003 before the Israelis withdrawal and they were the occupying force there. Two years later in 2005 the Israelis left Gaza and there was a prisoner-of-war exchange; Ahmed was released and went straight to Lebanon, to the port of Tripoli where Amir had fled to earlier.

"The two brothers took over a radical Sunni Palestinian group in Tripoli which was inspired by Bin Laden, al-Qaeda and 9/11. Amir moved onto Iraq where he fought against the Americans, the Shias and the Kurds, while rapidly rising up the ranks of what is now ISIS. Meanwhile, back in Tripoli, Ahmed was killed when the Israelis invaded Lebanon in 2006 during a raid on the camp where he was based. Even though the Israeli's main target then was the Shia

Hezbollah group, they took advantage of that to hit their Sunni Palestinian enemies their too.

"It was after Ahmed's death in Lebanon that Jalal gave up being a doctor in Scotland, in Glasgow and moved away, apparently to work in a hospital in Cyprus where all trace of him ends. In reality he resumes his real name of Jalal Asaf and works as a Red Crescent medic in a Palestinian camp in Tripoli until he too is killed during fighting between different factions for and against Syrian President Assad two years later. We know this because the Israeli source is told this by Amir Asaf. It seems that Jalal was the non-militant in the family but got radicalised after Ahmed's death because it was after that that Ghazani/Asaf gave up his Glasgow post and went to Lebanon.

"The Israeli's warning to the Belgians following their ISIR based on intelligence gleaned from a source of theirs close to Amir Asaf was that ISIS and al Qaeda were attempting to activate a legend around the name of Syed Ghazani. Basically the guy detained in Belgium was claiming to have worked in Cyprus after practising for many years in Britain and now wanted to practice again in Western Europe, but he wasn't too good in the role and the false passport wasn't up to the job either. So, after the Israeli response to the ISIR the Belgians threw him back on a flight to Tunisia where he'd departed from. That's reckoned to be where al Sharjanah is based and the operation has all the hallmarks of his modus operandi. The new 'Ghazani' would almost certainly have been instructed to work in a hospital in Belgium and either set up or join a cell ready to carry out an attack in Brussels or someplace else in the country. Ghazani was a classic clean skin with no previous and a legit cover as a doctor; good material for al Sharjanah and Amir Asaf would have regarded it almost as a double-martyrdom and revenge for his late brother Jalal."

"So how was the connection made to Tres?" My voice was almost a whisper, conscious as I was that Tres was only about twenty feet up the staircase.

"Once the Belgians had deported the fake Ghazani, the name was flashed to all friendly intel agencies on an alert status. When I put Teresa Martindale's name through a cross-reference check to link with any terrorist suspects her name came up in connection with a flagged subject, Ghazani."

"How? In what context?"

"Ghazani had co-authored an article with two other consultants on some research they'd carried out on a new treatment or drug for children with spinal injuries. It appeared in a medical journal called *Journal of Paediatric Pharmacology and Therapy* with a title, typical of these things, which takes up half a page. Anyway there's a whole cast of contributors listed who assisted with the research and one of them is a 'Teresa Pamela Martindale' Staff Nurse at the Glasgow Royal Children's Hospital in a year in which, according to her personnel file, she was working there, same time as Ghazani."

"And before the Belgian and Israeli alert on Ghazani, there would have been nothing to link the two names?" I asked.

"No. As I said until recently Ghazani was a cleanskin with nothing against him. And he wouldn't be mentioned in her employment record as he wasn't her line manager or supervisor. There's no mention of him in her background vetting. The only point of contact they have on record is that medical journal."

"Were you able to access the Team files ok?"

"I used Stu Hutchins as the ARPO; there was no problem. Stu's still in the land of the living as far as the new bosses are concerned, whereas you and you're team are the undead. For now anyway."

"How's Thames House?"

"Fucking mental, full of paranoia and under new management! I'm playing the part of the minion, keeping my head down, obeying orders and seeing and hearing nothing I'm not supposed to: except for this."

"Thanks, Vincent, I really appreciate it. Leave it alone now; you've done everything you could. I'll alert the new management without grassing you up. Where are you now?"

"Just outside an all-night greasy spoon on the Caledonian Road. I'm going in there in a minute for a very early fry-up and then to bed. By the way what *are* you doing up in the Tannochside Water Tower?"

"That's a very good question and the answer could be very relevant to what you've just told me, but I can't go into it just now."

"Ok, but on Teresa Martindale there was just one other thing."

I prepared myself for more bad news. "Let's hear it."

"Using Stu Hutchinson as ARPO cover I got deep into her enhanced positive vetting or EPV file. Everything seems fine and above board. However, her past holidays might be of relevance to you."

"Why?"

"Well, for three consecutive years she went to Cyprus on holiday, on each occasion for three weeks."

"What years were they?"

"2006, 2007 and 2008. Each time she apparently went alone and booked into a self-catering apartment in Ayia Napa, a resort famous for clubbing on the south-east of the country. There was a routine check carried out as part of the EPV and the apartment records indicated she did stay there. She was asked why she went to Cyprus so many times (her last holiday there was just before she joined MI5) and she replied, quote 'I'm a geriatric clubber just turning thirty and I still love partying till dawn, so Ayia Napa is ideal for me. I'll probably grow up in the next few years'. 2008 was the last time she holidayed there."

"Was there any other verification, apart from the apartment records, that she hung around in that resort?"

"Yeah she gave the names of three girls. One was a nurse who'd worked beside Teresa in the past. She was called and said that she'd met her in a club there once or twice. That was apparently regarded as good enough because the other two names weren't checked out. To be fair, before Cyprus she'd holidayed in Majorca, Ibiza, the Algarve and Florida, so there would have been nothing to call attention to Cyprus; just an ordinary lassie enjoying herself abroad."

"Too true, Vincent there wouldn't have been," I concurred. "But it's a jumping off point for Lebanon."

"Absolutely. It might all be one big fucking coincidence, Eddie, but I thought you should know."

"You've done brilliant, Vincent, thanks. Now get that fry-up. If I get out of this I'll stand you a few pints."

"Aye ok, so you say. Just take care."

"And you." I ended the call.

It might all be one big fucking coincidence, sure, but coincidence is something that's regarded with healthy scepticism and not a little suspicion in the world of the spook. I was trying to absorb Vincent's information. For at least six years before she joined MI5, Tres had worked in the same hospital as a guy using an alias who turns out to be the brother of an ISIS militant who himself is close to the al-Qaeda number two al Sharjanah. I knew now, courtesy of Henderson and SIS that al Sharjanah, was in control of Qatib who recruited and groomed Khaled and Mohammed to carry out the Glasgow attacks. Qatib was in fact, after his walk-in to the British Embassy in Rome, an SIS and latterly CIA informer, though of course no-one thinks to tell the lowly counter-intelligence foot-soldiers at MI5 this; we were too far down the food-chain on the need-to-know principle.

The assumption was that through Grand Minaret surveillance we would have put the kybosh on Khaled and Mohammed while Qatib would have went to his meeting in Tunisia with al Sharjanah who would have been captured by the Americans. The upshot: there would have been no Glasgow bombing capping a run of attempted attacks on western European cities which had been rolled up by the security services, the al-Qaeda number two in captivity, al Hassan's credibility and pretensions to lead the organisation in tatters and, above all, a renewed attempt at achieving a unified command and leadership for al-Qaeda, over.

The reality: al Sharjanah knew that Qatib was an SIS/CIA asset and played him right back like a violin string. Through a cut-out, al Sharjanah orders Qatib up to Glasgow which panics everyone and we brought the surveillance on the van forward. George Square is bombed, Qatib is among the victims, MI5 is ruined and, as I stood here in the cramped staircase astride the giant water tank of LN117 in Tannochside, al Hassan is about to take over a stronger, more formidable al-Qaeda. Disaster! And linking all that was the amazing 'coincidence' that Tres, an agent on Grand Minaret, who was one of the surveillance team on Sadeq's van worked beside the brother of a senior Islamic commander who is close to al Sharjanah who controls Qatib, who… It was full circle.

Tres had to have met Ghazani at least a few times in order for her to get her name in that journal with him and if it wasn't for that journal we would never have made the connection between them. Often in intelligence it is the most tenuous, leftfield links that unravels connections that wouldn't otherwise have been revealed.

Of course, it was important to remember what Vincent had just told me. Ghazani/Asaf only became radicalised after his brother's death during the Israeli raids on Lebanon in 2006. When the research was being carried out he may have had no intentions of becoming involved in terrorist activities and the relationship between himself and Tres then could have been purely professional and innocuous. Only later, when he became active and, perhaps he had recruited Tres, would the published research article come to haunt both of them.

But was that not to push the other side of the balance sheet too far? It was all very well in my profession having a healthy distrust of suspicion. But the danger was you could see conspiracy and false, lurid connections in what was a simple straightforward coincidence: they do happen in life. It was getting that balance right that was the tricky bit and the judgement call to be made on it. Tres could all along be a nurse who got fed up and disillusioned with the health service and gravitated via an admin job with the MOD into the secret world: that again does happen. The fact that she worked in the same hospital and collaborated on research work with the brother of an al-Qaeda linked terrorist could just well be coincidence. But what were the chances of that same nurse going on to become an integral part of the MI5 team on Grand Minaret which went so catastrophically wrong and the links between her and the former doctor went right through the main characters of the events of the last forty-eight hours like a main circuit connection?

Tres-Qatib-al Sharjanah-Amir Asaf-Jalal Asaf alias Syed Ghazani-Tres! Could that loop really just be coincidence? What were the odds on that? And there was Cyprus.

It was a 'jumping off point' for all manner of terrorist, smuggling and clandestine activity in the Middle East, especially Lebanon. It was only a few hours by boat from Cyprus to Lebanon. Tres spent nine weeks over three years ostensibly on holiday in Ayia Napa. She stayed at a self-catering apartment so there would be no hotel reception staff or porters to see her coming and going nor chambermaids to witness she actually stayed in the hotel. She need only have spent two, at most three nights in the resort clubbing with the other girls to lay down a legend: 'the geriatric clubber partying till dawn', while the rest of the time she jumped a ferry to Beirut or Tripoli and joined Ghazani/Asaf, not forgetting his brother.

Certainly the timing is instructive. Tres starts holidaying in Cyprus in 2006. That's the year the doctor's brother, Ahmed Asaf, is killed by the Israelis in Lebanon and he quits his post in Glasgow. Her last holiday in Cyprus is 2008, the year the doctor is killed. There is every chance that Amir Asaf, rising up the ranks of the fledging ISIS, would have attended his brother's funeral in Lebanon and met her, and possibly not for the first time either. 2008 is also the year Tres leaves nursing and takes up a post with the MOD. Within a year she applies to join MI5 and after routine EPV is accepted.

I shook my head more in sadness than anything else. No, reluctantly, I had to concede that if I had to put on my analyst's hat and I was sitting in the cold light of day in the Shields or Thames House and reviewing this background, I would have to conclude there was a strong case that Tres had been recruited as a sleeper by al-Qaeda and activated when the opportunity arose. Conceivably, when Qatib struck gold in Glasgow through the medium of Khaled and Mohammed, Amir Asaf would have activated Tres. Sadeq being my informer and alerting me to Qatib's activities and the subsequent evolution of Grand Minaret with Tres on my team would have dovetailed beautifully with this, allowing her the scope to sabotage the operation when the time was right and divert suspicion to the ex-SAS and Afghan veteran Wattie Craig. The key now would be to establish what went on in that crucial hour when Wattie fell asleep at the same time as Tres was supposedly houring and the camera was diverted from Sadeq's van. Did Tres go out and place the IED there and then? Or did she signal to a third party to place it? But how would she have known that Wattie would be sleeping? Yes, there were details and residual doubts but it did look increasingly plausible that Tres was very much in the frame to be the spy and the saboteur in the ranks.

If this scenario were true then the published research article, unbeknownst to all parties at the time, was the weak link. There was probably only one written document in the entire world where Tres and Ghazani's name were together and linked and the software Vincent had used was explicitly designed to scroll through millions of pages of published and unpublished sources, open and closed, to find that link and he had.

So what was I to do now? Walk out the tower, go back across to Henderson and the American Herb Lange and tell them to refocus on Tres and try and retrieve something from the disasters of the last forty-eight hours? Or do I go on, up to the control room and confront them both? At the end of the day, those two above me were on *my* team. Scores of innocent people, including women and children had died, because of a van that we, my team, had escorted into Glasgow city centre. I could never ever forget that and the guilt would stay with me forever. And the two suspects were only feet away. I had to deal with it. I couldn't walk away. It was also personal; I'd had a relationship with Tres and the fact that I could have been taken in so badly combined with the horror and tragedy of the bombing added to my determination to get some, to use that other over-used term, closure, on this.

Besides, if it was Tres, she was unarmed. She had been searched back at her flat and was clean. She had requested an overnight bag, but that had been searched too and was cleared. When I joined them upstairs there would be two guys and one woman; ok I was out of shape but Wattie was a big guy, he was probably armed and he was ex SAS: Tres posed no real threat. Indeed, if anything, it was the uncertainty around what Wattie, who was likely to be armed, would do and what state of mind he was in that probably posed the biggest threat. No, I had to go up there and see this through to the end. After all, there was still the lingering possibility that the whole thing with Tres was just coincidence, that Wattie was still the guilty party or that neither of them were. Like a good detective I had to eliminate all the possibilities.

Before resuming my ascent up the staircase, I used the phone Henderson had given me to text him a message:

We might have been looking in the wrong place. Check agent Teresa Pamela Martindale, look for connection with Syed Ghazani alias Jalal Asaf, late brother of Amir Asaf of ISIS. Will explain all when (if!) I come out. Now going up to the control room. Restrain, repeat RESTRAIN any commandos in vicinity. Will be out ASAP.

"Eddie are you there?" It was Tres.

"I was resting, Tres, need to get exercise. Coming up now."

Putting Henderson's phone back in my jacket after I had turned it to silent mode, I resumed my climb. I came to the last right-angled turn of the staircase and looked up to the top of the stairs. Tres was standing there. She was on her own. I moved on up to her and confirmed that she couldn't possibly be carrying any explosive as she only had on a sweater and was wearing a pair of blue jeans. As I ascended the final stair and climbed into the control room, she came towards me and gave me a warm hug. I was disarmed and felt the warmth of her; she kissed me on the cheek and then on the lips, a kiss that seemed to linger, then she moved back and looked at me, her large green eyes shimmering. Could I be wrong? Could it all just be a coincidence?

She patted my stomach. "You need to get rid of that beer belly! I'll take you to the gym I use; they won't rip you off."

I laughed briefly, but then indicative of the rapid swings in thoughts and feelings I was currently subject to, I wondered if the warmth of the greeting, the deep kiss and the hug and apparently affectionate patting of the stomach, was a ruse to ascertain if I was armed. A sudden breeze of cold air brought me out of this and I said:

"Bloody hell, it's perishing up here!"

"It's Wattie," she replied, moving away from me. "He's opened one of the windows to have a look outside. You took so long coming up, he was wondering what was up."

I looked around the control room. My first thoughts were that it resembled the updated set of the interior of the TARDIS from Dr Who. The room was circular with a narrow path looped around a steel cover on top of the tank which had various dials and switches on it. I started walking around the steel cover which had some glass covers embedded in it at intervals allowing you to see the gently vibrating water below. Tres followed me. It was still dark outside but a faint sheen of light blue sky in the east signalled the approach of dawn through the thick glass panes of the windows which were divided into smaller squares of glass. Though it was dark and the windows were grimy, there was a panoramic view from up here and on a clear day would be spectacular. The control room was a third of the width of the tank below so outside the windows the control room was surrounded by the top of the concrete brim on the roof of which I could see the unmistakable tall figure of Wattie coming towards the control room. One of the windows on the south facing side of the room was ajar and Wattie moved this forward and climbed into the control room.

As the window opened and closed briefly I could again hear the sound of a helicopter outside, but now it appeared to be closer. I assured myself that I had until ten in the morning to get Tres and Wattie out or...

Wattie had a submachine gun, a standard SAS Heckler and Koch MP5, which he had swung over his shoulder and which he placed against the inside wall of the control room below the window he'd just shut. He sat down beside the weapon, his back resting against the low wall.

"A souvenir from your SAS days, which was never handed back to the quartermaster?" I commented sardonically on the weapon. There were strict rules in the British Army about soldiers handing back all weapons upon leaving the service, but the reality was that many ex-servicemen, especially those from what were regarded as the more elite regiments such as the Paratroopers and the SAS, kept some weapons as both a memento and an entitled gift or trophy for their service.

Ignoring my question, Wattie responded: "This is a fucking antique now boss! The UMP is the new standard issue submachine gun, replaced this in the SAS in 2014. You'd be lucky to get rid of the MP5 on the *Antiques Roadshow* now!"

I shook my head in acknowledgement of my ignorance of most guns and weaponry. Though I'd been around guns and ammunition most of my professional life and had been in the middle of gun battles and fire fights on a few occasions, I had only rudimentary training in firearms and had only ever actually had to use a firearm once in my thirty-odd years in the service; others like Wattie, far more proficient in this were always on hand to act as back-up and to assist when the bullets started flying. This was true of almost all MI5 officers, who rarely used weapons or had cause to do so, contrary yet again to the public's perception of our James Bond lifestyle. I did notice as Wattie sat against the wall that he had a pistol tucked into the back of his jeans.

"How did you, Danny McKay and the other guy from Stu's team ever capture the Dutch Marines up here? I'd have thought this would have been impregnable." I remarked in admiration as the tower swayed slightly in the breeze.

"Actually it was quite easy," Wattie replied. "Danny distracted them by pretending to negotiate with them outside. That bloody big brim of the tank means you can't see directly below you from this control room or these windows and, like today, the CCTV cameras had been disabled. So you need to place men at regular intervals all around the edge of the brim. There were three of us mind against fifteen of them, but we created diversions and feints that allowed me to climb up the columns and the edge of the tank to the north side which was weakly defended. I took out took two guys there, then ran over and threw about a dozen stun grenades into here. That incapacitated the Dutch marines in here, but as I expected, their colleagues took up positon at the south side there." He pointed behind his shoulder to where he'd just come from. "Waiting for us to defend or come out of the control room which they would have tried to dislodge us from whereas Danny and the other guy who'd now followed me came round behind them by surprise and captured them. It was actually piss easy."

"If you say so, Wattie."

Wattie took a swig of water from a bottle beside him and I noticed there was a blanket and some packets of ready to eat food there. Just beyond that as the steel side of the tank curved round I saw the end of a large, black hold-all bag positioned against the tank wall. I moved a step further forward and got a clear view of it. I presumed this was the 'overnight bag' Tres had been allowed to take with her from her flat. I had the impression that this would have been a much smaller thing, more like a shoulder bag. You could have packed enough clothes and other things in this bag for a two-week vacation, I thought. How was she able to get that past her SIS surveillance detail? Still it had been checked by them and if there had been anything suspicious they would have spotted it.

I was about to take my eyes away from the large holdall when Tres went past and sat on the edge of the tank wall between me and the bag. She still had a friendly, almost playful demeanour, her eyes shining and a warm smile on her face but when I looked at her and then looked again at the holdall, her gaze followed mine and back to my face. I immediately tensed, throat went dry, compounded by the fact that she edged even closer along the tank rim to the holdall. Wattie saw this as well, so I decided to try and lighten the atmosphere by saying: "You planning to take a month's leave after this?" gesturing to the holdall.

Before Tres could say anything, Wattie emitted a short laugh: "Women eh? Overkill every time!"

"Listen you two I had no idea of where the hell I was going or how long I'd be away for so I wanted to pack enough clothes and stuff to stay fresh. Not all of us like to live in our own sweat, thank you!" She said this in a mock, half-serious tone and again it did have a veneer of plausibility. Yet again I reminded myself that the bag had been checked by SIS. She may only have moved to get closer to the two of us. Calm down I urged myself.

"I know it was me that brought this crowd," Wattie again gestured all around himself this time, "by terrifying the security patrol. But how did they know about the meeting at the Forge?"

It was my turn to give out a short, dry laugh. "My chances of remaining a Security Service Officer are non-existent, but if they were I'd need to go on immediate MosBerBel refresher training! Two major fuck-ups. One I phoned the Shields to speak to Carl the Geek when I should have known there would been a full-blown GCHQ net over the place, which there was and they were able to trace me to a tenement block in Possil. Then, to ensure I get the dunce's cap, I saw the same bloke twice on the street in Saracen, but didn't follow the Same Face Twice in Same Place, Exit Immediately procedure." That was basic MosBerBel and by not following it, the mad car chase and capture by SIS had followed.

"I'm tired, we're all tired, Wattie. What happened on Wednesday has traumatised us all and…"

"What happened on Wednesday, boss, was nothing to do with me!" Wattie cut in sharply, "I'm not a terrorist and I don't kill women and children!"

"I didn't say you were, Wattie." I responded softly. "But the finger *is* pointing at our team, our section and there's some circumstantial evidence with that camera being diverted away from the van."

"That could have been external remote control," Wattie retorted angrily. "The Shields, Thames House, SIS, CIA; any one of a dozen fucking agencies or an al-Qaeda mole in them could have done that."

"Absolutely, Wattie, but you're never going to prove your innocence up here. Look, I'm going to be upfront with you. You, me, we've reached the end of the line. There's at least a couple of hundred cops and security people around us now. They've evacuated all the residents, and because you're ex-SAS they'll probably call on army back-up. They've given me until ten this morning to persuade you to come out or they're coming in for you. Now, unless you desire to replay the end scene from *Butch Cassidy and the Sundance Kid*, I suggest that the three of us walk out of here; at the least we can let the poor bastards that live around here back into their homes and maybe get a chance to enjoy the rest of their weekends."

"Who's 'they' that have given you until ten to get me out?" Wattie studied me intently as he asked the question.

"SIS, Wattie. I've been in their company for the last day-and-a-half. You and Tress were followed into the Square by them." Wattie raised his eyebrows. "Seriously. A Special Operations Branch outfit with military support. They were the ones that followed me to the Forge. They were trailing Qatib up to Glasgow because he was actually an SIS walk-in; yes, he was their man. This is big, Wattie, very big. Across the road there," I pointed out the south facing window, "is a small supermarket car park. There's a guy there, a cousin from the Company, who was using Qatib to capture the al-Qaeda number two, al Sharjanah, at a meeting he was going to have with him in Tunisia, and through that undermine Ali Al Hassan's claims to leadership. That's all gone now. And the CIA and SIS obviously are very keen to know what went wrong."

This was difficult because as I was saying all this to Wattie, I was constantly conscious of Tres sitting on the edge of the tank. She just sat there. I was desperate to look at her, but refrained from doing so. I was also aware of Henderson's phone vibrating once in my pocket indicating a text message had been sent, but I wanted to look at it when I wasn't the centre of their attention.

"So it's got to be the SAS man that's the mole eh?" Wattie almost snarled sarcastically. "The Special Forces man gone loco and become a mass murderer and terrorist accomplice. Typical of those fucking psychopathic bastards!" Wattie laughed bitterly to himself. Still Tres remained motionless beside me.

"Again, Wattie, nobody is saying that…"

"…Oh, but they're thinking it, man!" Wattie interrupted strongly.

"Let me finish, Wattie. Whether they're thinking it or not they need to get to the bottom of it. They need to do an investigation, as we would have done. This is way beyond MI5 or whatever's going to replace the service. It's political, it's international. And because they really do need to find out who the al-Qaeda mole is, they've no interest in a stitch-up. If you are innocent, Wattie," I looked straight at him, "they'll find that out. Otherwise you'll end up sprayed across the top of this bloody water tower!"

Did I believe that? No, not really. I had seen too many seemingly impartial investigations give way to rushed jobs because of pressure to get results from the media, politicians and society at large with the upshot that some poor innocent bastard was maligned, incarcerated or worse because they appeared an easy target, an obvious choice. And there was no guarantee that wouldn't happen to any of us, including Wattie. But we had reached the end of the line; there was nowhere else to go except death and I really wanted to avoid any further blood being spilled. So if my little speech served only to nudge Wattie to leave into an uncertain fate, then it was worth it.

Wattie stretched out his arms and yawned. "Aye I suppose you're right. This is fucking pointless." He patted his gun almost affectionately. "I'm too old for this," he said with a weary smile.

I felt a tremendous burst of relief. Wattie was giving up; he was coming out with me. As he was raising himself up he remarked, "But

I tell you now I, the two of us, were sleeping when that fucking camera was moved."

"I wasn't sleeping."

It was Tres. The two of us turned to face her. She was standing up and had a gun in her left hand, what looked to my inexpert eye to be a Beretta handgun: the holdall was now positioned between her legs. How she managed to get the gun out and move the bag without attracting either Wattie's or my attention I'll never know.

Wattie must have thought Tres was having a joke for as he stood to his full height he rebuked her saying:

"Tres, for fuck's sake, it's far too early in the morning and we're all too tired and knackered for you to be taking the piss! Let's get out of here!"

"Oh, dearest Walter, I'm not taking the piss. I repeat I wasn't sleeping; you *were*, because I made sure of that. I went to the control desk and shifted the camera for twenty minutes, enough time for the IED to be placed below the van, then redirected the camera back to covering the van, then moved back beside you pretending to be asleep until you woke up ten minutes after you were supposed to have woken me, panicking, and I reassured you it was all ok and we'd missed nothing."

The glimmer from her soft, green eyes had evaporated. She still had a slight smile on her face but her eyes were hard as she stood stock still with that gun in her hand. Then, to my utter dismay, I noticed a cord reaching from her right jean pocket down to the big holdall. Wattie was befuddled and baffled in equal measure. "Tres, what the fuck are you on about?"

Before she had time to answer, I asked her, "Tres, how did you make sure Wattie was sleeping?"

She laughed scornfully, but kept a firm grip on her gun and a close eye on both of us. "Remember the sleeping tablets, the sedatives you got for Sadeq because he was spooked about Qatib coming up? You handed them over to him at the Bothwell Service Station."

I nodded my head, "Aye?"

"Well I managed to steal four of them from you. I thought I'd need all four because of the size of him." She pointed the gun at

Wattie. "I crushed them into his coffee and he was out, snored louder than usual!" She said this almost light-heartedly, with a sly laugh at the end.

The bewilderment left Wattie as he realised Tres was not fooling around. His features turned into an angry scowl. He made a move towards her:

"You fucking terrorist loving bitch!"

But I stopped him, placing a hand in front of him, "Wattie, I think she's got explosives in that holdall; check the cord coming out of her jeans to the bag and, remember, we're on top of three-quarters of a million gallons of water so please for everybody's sake hold it!"

Wattie moved back but emitted a bitter laugh, saying:

"Ah, what a fucking dope I am!" He pointed at Tres and said: "She phones me from the bottom of the tower saying," and he adopted a mock high-pitched tone, "'even on a night like this I still act like a girlie. I've packed enough clothes to go on a month-long Caribbean cruise! Could you give me a hand?' And I ran down and took it up for her, weighed a fucking ton! Arsehole!" he spat out bitterly.

As he was talking I realised he wasn't the only one to feel buttoned up the back, though in truth I had brought some of this about. It was me who'd suggested to Henderson and SIS that Tres would be the best conduit to Wattie. And through me Tres had been escorted right through the security wall around Tannochside and delivered straight to the water tower with a bomb. No, Wattie wasn't the only dupe by far. Amazingly, I had even managed to wince at her remark about Wattie snoring louder than usual when she'd micky finned him the sleeping pills, reminding me that she deceived both of us in so many ways. Was there no end to this deception?

I tried to look behind her at the holdall. Spotting this she obliged by breaking into a hard smile and, while keeping both of us fixed with her Beretta, bent down over the holdall and with her free hand unzipped it to reveal a pink nightdress and a white bath-towel. She moved these aside to reveal two large jars of dense viscous liquids taped together with the cord stretching from the lid of the nearest jar back to her jean pocket which she now put her free hand in as that was where the detonator would be. Rising back up, she said, almost triumphantly:

"It is what you think it is, boys: fertiliser and ammonia and forty-eight ounces of TNT, oh and not forgetting sulphate powder!"

Part of me couldn't help but admire her perverse cleverness and coolness in carrying this off, which prompted to me enquire almost admiringly, "How the fuck did you manage to get that past the SIS detail?"

The hard smile was replaced by a softer but self-congratulatory one as she outlined, almost coquettishly, how she'd pulled it off. "There are advantages, sometimes but not many mind, to being a woman in these situations. If you were to go to my flat right now and look right behind the bathroom door you'd see a large holdall bag identical to this. An SIS girl called Izzy or something like that accompanied me to my bedroom while I packed clothes into *that* bag. She understood, as any female would, that I could be gone for God knows how long and so I packed as many knickers and bras and jumpers and skirts and tights as I could put in that bag. As we were leaving I lugged it to the front door and then announced to the rest of the guys and Izzy 'shit! I've left my tampons in the loo and I need a wee'. Izzy got me to the bathroom. I left the door slightly ajar and after a couple of minutes came out to the sound of the toilet flushing. I had the packet of tampons in my hand and I opened the bag again for Izzy to reassure her. When she saw the towel and the bathrobe at the top she just smiled, pointed to the tampons and said, 'you'll be glad you remembered them' and we were away and now we're here."

"You switched the holdalls in the toilet?" I merely asked for confirmation. She nodded in agreement. Again I couldn't help admiring her, no matter how wrong that appeared. She had played this so coolly and cleverly. I smiled at her and said: "Can I ask a straight question Tres and, please, could I get a straight answer?"

"Go ahead."

"Did you join al-Qaeda…?"

"…The Islamic Resistance." she interrupted me.

"Shite!" Wattie burst out probably involuntarily. I motioned him with my hand to stay quiet and stay still. I resumed:

"Did you join the Islamic Resistance before you joined MI5 or after?"

"Before." She replied curtly.

"And was it the consultant Ghazani or, to give him his real name, Jalal Asaf, who recruited you?"

For the first time Tres looked evidently surprised. She hadn't expected that connection to have been made, not yet anyway.

"Well done, Mr McIntyre, you've done your homework. Can I ask how you found out?"

"The name Syed Ghazani, occupation paediatrician, formerly worked in hospitals in the UK, alias of Jalal Asaf brother of both the late Ahmed Asaf and Amir Asaf currently a senior commander in ISIS, was flagged up when a man from Tunisia using the Ghazani legend tried to enter Belgium. The Belgian equivalent of MI5 sent an ISIR out to all friendly agencies and the Israelis responded with the information that Ghazani was really Asaf and the late brother of one deceased and one very active guerrilla activist." (I phrased that last part very carefully to avoid upsetting Tres by referring to the Asaf brothers as 'terrorists'.)

"What's an ISIR?" Wattie asked.

"An Inter-Services Information Request. It's a standardised format by which allied, or at least non-hostile intelligence agencies request and trade information with each other." I continued my explanation to Tres. "As potential suspects for assisting al-Qaeda in perpetrating the George Square bombing – and Ali al Hassan has claimed full responsibility for it – all our names were put through the grinder for any non-operational or unofficial associations with flagged terrorist suspects." I looked straight at her. "Your name and Ghazani's appears together in a medical research publication."

She laughed dryly and shook her head, but kept her gaze firmly on us. "Christ, that was ten years ago! I can barely remember it."

"It's the obscure ones that always trip you up, Tres," I remarked drily.

"When did you find this out?" Wattie asked.

"In that car park across there where the CIA guy and SIS are," I lied not wanting Tres to know I was carrying two mobiles. On cue

Henderson's phone began vibrating; the vibrations recurring for a few minutes.

"So why the hell did you come in here?" Wattie asked as if it was the most stupid act in the world, which in a way it probably was.

I looked back and forth between the two of them. "Because I mean it; I want to avoid more deaths." I studied both. Wattie was confused, angry, upset, tired and probably stressed: normal human reactions in times like these. By contrast Tres was rock solid, wide awake and resolute. I didn't recognize her as the agent I'd trained, supervised and worked with for six years on various operations. All the warmth, all the humour, even the empathy I'd known her for was gone as if it had evaporated. Had it all just been an act? Now, I could clearly discern, she was on a mission. After all, she didn't need to have come here. She'd carried out her mission doping Wattie and diverting the camera, in order to allow the IED to be placed under Sadeq's van. She could have refused my request to contact Wattie and his request in turn for her to join them. The fact that she'd done so and had carried a fully laden holdall packed with explosives all the way here dramatically told its own story. Tres was in full jihad, holy warrior, martyrdom mode. And the setting: on top of a water tower with two MI5 officers, one a section head, the other ex SAS, couldn't have been any more spectacular.

Was there any chance I could talk her out of this and extricate Wattie and me from this? Or was this just another delusion of a self-deceiving fool? Ach to hell with it, I thought! There might be some residue of that West of Scotland lassie there once was, that I could reach. I was about to embark on this when Wattie, admittedly exasperated, angry and humiliated, decided to recklessly stir things up.

"So were you shagging this Arab, terrorist doctor guy as well?"

Tres shook her head slowly, but more in sadness than in anger. "I was wondering how long it would take before that came up, I'm surprised you hadn't mentioned it earlier!" She shot me a quick glance so I tensed even more in anticipation of what she was prepared to reveal next to Wattie. Her answer, however, did come as a surprise.

"Yes, I was shagging the 'Arab, doctor guy', but I was also in love with him; I was never in love with you, Wattie."

"Oh that makes a lot of sense that does," Wattie said bitterly. "Here's a guy fights for his country against people like the Taliban and al-Qaeda, people by the way, woman, that would make you dress head to toe in a veil and deny you education, take you right back to the Dark Ages, but that means nothing compared to a guy with a silver tongue because he's a doctor that can talk you into bed then become his little terrorist girl. You're a thick, psychopathic, deluded, stupid little lassie and the first chance I get I'll kill you with my bare hands, slowly."

"Wattie, let me ask you something." She spoke to him, her right hand still in her pocket over the detonator, left hand controlling the Beretta, fixed on us. "What did you think you were actually doing in Afghanistan?"

Disdainfully, Wattie looked away from her, but replied: "Fighting terrorists and bad guys that if we didn't defeat would come and bomb our cities and kill defenceless civilians, but then, of course I didn't realise that I would end up working with a terrorist loving, cocksucking bitch like you who would do just that! Just my fucking luck!"

"Wattie, you weren't fighting terrorists. You were in a country as a Zionist Crusader imposing colonial rule on people that didn't want you. You're a tool, a tool of a corrupt, degenerate world order that, Allah willing, is going to pass away."

"If Wattie's a tool Tres, then what are you?" I asked.

"A holy warrior." she replied immediately, but firmly and calmly. "I've helped to bring about a taste of the death and destruction you bring to women and children and all innocent people daily in the lands of the Caliphate. With your Zionist allies you massacre, you starve, you torture, you enslave; all with the aim of eliminating Islam as the only barrier to Crusader Zionist world dominance."

"But," I protested calmly, "innocent woman and children were killed in George Square as they were on 9/11 and all the other bombings that have happened."

"The *Koran* teaches that innocents who die in an act of jihad will, like the just holy warrior, enter immediately into heaven and spend eternity in paradise. This is what Allah has told the prophet, praise be to Allah."

"So if I'm getting this right, if you call yourself a jihadi and blow up targets with lots of collateral damage such as civilian women and children, like a busy city centre, then that's ok because the act itself was holy and just and those killed, the 'innocents', will go straight to heaven?"

"Yes," she replied equably

"Pish!" Wattie spat out derisively, both of us ignored him.

"But where does this authority to carry out jihad come from? I mean surely anyone can decide: right I'm going to take out this target, the *Koran* says its' right and because what I'm doing is an act of jihad and has the sanction of Allah then any innocent passer-by will go to heaven. Surely you see that's open to abuse! Any looney-tunes can commit any crime and claim he had Allah's blessing to do so?"

"No, that's wrong!" Tres shook her head firmly. "Alima and Muftis have clearly pronounced on the legitimacy of this holy war to defend against the crusader Zionist attack on our people, on our divinely inspired struggle to recreate the Caliph where social justice, equality and peace will reign in contrast to this land of deceptions, inequality and injustice that prevails.

"The fatwas have been pronounced. Any attack on America or those who support the Americans in their pursuit of crusader Zionist aims is engaged in jihad and a holy war. Remember, this is asymmetrical warfare. We cannot defeat your tanks and airplanes directly in the West, but we can hit you where you should feel safe and protected. It's like for like. Your drones and aircraft take out our villages and our women and children so we attack your shopping centres. Besides the West has a rich history of causing massive destruction of enemy targets causing vast numbers of innocent civilians or 'collateral damage'. Wasn't Hamburg, Hiroshima, the bombing of North Vietnam and Cambodia, all carried out in the name of defeating fascism and communism and incurring hundreds of thousands of civilian deaths? Yet the pilots who flew those planes and the planners and generals who organised them are not regarded as terrorists or fanatics; indeed the opposite: they are awarded medals and feted as heroes and just warriors! Well it's the same from where we're standing."

As I stood there listening to her, I realised I could have been listening to Qatib during the year he spent grooming Khalid and Mohammed justifying Islamic mass terrorism. The irony was then that Qatib was playing a part, he no longer believed in jihad whereas one of the team monitoring and surveilling him, Tres, actually did and was prepared to act on it. No, Tres was a true believer, acutely convinced of the rightness of what she was doing. Not only was she a true believer, not only had she kept these committed, fanatical beliefs latent while she put herself forward for MI5 and all through the exams, recruitment, assessment and vetting stages, but she'd also kept it well hidden every day she worked with us on all the operations, the tedious hours of surveillance and of course, the times she and I had slept together: Through all of this she stayed true to her legend until the opportunity had arisen to aid the cause of jihad. Now she had connived her way up to here, where she didn't have to be (albeit inadvertently assisted in this by me). I realised no amount of talking from me was going to persuade Tres to give this up.

There were only two options. One was to take Tres by surprise and somehow get the detonator out of her pocket or for both Wattie and me to run like hell downstairs assuming she would miss one or both of us and we would get out before the large bomb in the holdall detonated, both of which were unlikely. The stair-head was about thirty feet away, but the path to it was circular as was the entire control room so with sufficient ducking and diving the two of us might make it unscathed.

I looked at Wattie who was still stewing with anger. I could read his mind as he lay against the circular wall, one hand still on his MP5. But Tres obviously saw that too. She took her right hand out of her jeans pocket which presumably contained the detonator and moved it to the other pocket and brought out a collection of large silver bullets which, palm open, she displayed. With a triumphant smile she said to Wattie:

"When you had your wee sleep earlier on before he arrived," she gestured towards me, "I took the liberty of emptying your MP5 and that wee pistol tucked in your waistband."

Reflexively Wattie took hold of the MP5 and slid open the barrel. All the cartridge slots were empty. He put the now useless submachine gun down beside him and gave her a hateful, baleful stare. Unfazed she said to him:

"It's nothing personal, Wattie, it's' war," adding rather unnecessarily I thought, "you were one of many means to the successful completion of a mission."

"Fuck you!" he responded with his middle digit in the air.

The mobile in my pocket was vibrating at increasingly short intervals alternating between text messages and calls. I was trying to think desperately of how to divert her. Could we tire her by talking to her? How long would she be able to keep the intense concentration and vigilance required for a stand-off? The sky was getting lighter outside and it must be after five now. Keep her talking until I or Wattie, once he got over his anger and bitterness, thought of a diversion or feint that could distract her sufficiently to get the Beretta off her and remove the detonator from her pocket. I also remembered that certain MI5 and SIS mobiles were fitted with a button on their keyboards, of if they were smartphones, icons on their screens which when pressed sent a 'help, assistance required' message. So now I affected to put my left hand casually into my jacket pocket and began feeling over the mobile while talking to Tres.

"Are you now a Muslim, Tres?"

"I believe in Allah and following his word as disclosed to the Prophet in the Holy *Koran*," she confirmed.

"When did you convert?" The phone was an older model with a keyboard. I presumed the help button would be just down from the screen as I tried to feel the buttons.

"I didn't convert here in Scotland. I met Syed through work. He was a warm, gorgeous, beautiful man. He was so soft, so gentle so sensitive. He was dedicated to his work and he loved the children, really felt for them. I had never seen, amongst all the nurses, and consultants I had worked with, anyone who showed such compassion and understanding for the children as he did.

"I got to know him really well in a professional capacity and then we began to see each other more socially, though it was for a long time platonic. I admired his work and also his values and the way he led his life, most of which was informed by his religion, by Islam. I was quite surprised how closely connected a Moslem's religious life is with their personal lives. Though I was born a Christian and knew it was wrong to kill and steal and so on, the church itself, which I attended less as I got older, had nothing really to say to me about my life and how I was feeling and what I should do if I had a moral dilemma.

"Syed's religion in contrast, actually guided him and gave him direction. It really helped him and gave him great comfort. I was very impressed by that and also because it seemed to help make Syed the lovely man he was."

"Did he have any family?" I had identified two buttons on the mobile phone just down from the screen and apart from the rest of the keyboard. Wattie was fumbling with the discarded MP5: I'd no idea of what was going through his head and I was careful to avoid eye-contact with him in case it alerted Tres who I kept focused on while simultaneously trying to make contact with the buttons on the phone in my pocket and trying not to make it too obvious.

"Syed had no family," she went on. "But his brothers had nephews and nieces and sisters-in-law; lots of them."

I found the other button on the mobile and pressed on it. I changed tack slightly. "I take it then that your relationship with Syed went beyond platonic?"

"Yes. I fell in love with him and he with me."

"Oh, feel the fucking love and pass me a sick bucket!" Wattie said contemptuously.

"You're actually very pathetic, Wattie, full of hatred and frustration, but with no compensating love or conviction. Your SAS might train soldiers but not men." The look he gave her was the equivalent of an incinerating laser beam.

"I say again he was the most beautiful man I've met or will meet. He doted on his nephews and nieces but was very worried about the conditions they were living in in the camps in Lebanon. He would show me videos they'd sent him. There were four young girls and three boys, the oldest no more than eleven. He'd also read out the letters he'd sent them and the ones they'd replied to. I began to feel I knew his family, those kids and his sister-in-law. I'd bake cakes and send clothes for them. Their conditions were terrible and there were whole weeks where they were living only on rice and some soup. The camps were overcrowded as well. Syed was angry that nobody in the West seemed to take the least bit of notice. He began to feel that his brothers, who as you know were active in the Palestinian movement, had some legitimate points about the West. At the least it was indifferent to his people's fate and at worst it was conniving in their degradation and oppression.

"Then came the Israeli's invasion of Lebanon in 2006. Syed's brother died in that invasion, but it wasn't just him that died then." Tres looked at Wattie who had resumed looking into the middle of the control room, a contemptuous smile on his face. "Wattie look at me!" she commanded. For the first time her face displayed anger. Wattie did as he was ordered, slowly turning to face her, but with the contempt still there.

Tres went on: "Six out of seven, I'll say that again, six out of seven of Syed's nieces and nephews died; the youngest was two. They were killed by phosphorous bombs which burns the skin off. They died in hideous, agonizing pain, utterly obscene, from bombs dropped by Zionist planes supported by the West, by the Crusaders. There were hundreds of old men, women and children killed during those raids. I saw some of the pictures taken; they were horrible. Whole piles of disfigured and burned corpses! And what was the reaction of the West? Complete silence about the massacre of the women and children, but plenty of praise for the Zionists. One civilian can be killed in a bomb attack in a Western city and there'll be pages in the newspapers about it or loads of coverage in the TV news. But what do six Palestinian weans get? Fuck all! Except, if my memory serves me right, a US State Department spokesman saying 'We regret the loss of life of civilians but these attacks are degrading the terrorist infrastructure in that part of the Middle-East'. Degrading! That's what six Palestinian weans are to Crusader Zionist forces and its media!"

"So Syed moved to Lebanon to look after the family?" I was trying to keep her talking while trying to think of a way to distract and divert her attention. I surmised Wattie was thinking of the same, though he was just sitting there full of contempt for Tres. Whether any of the two buttons I'd pressed had worked was unknown. Certainly, there was no indication of any new activity outside.

"Yes," Tres continued. "His sister-in-law had survived along with one of her nephews but he had to go as he was the only breadwinner. Going to live and work in a Palestinian refugee camp in Lebanon as a brother of a known Palestinian activist just killed by the Israelis would probably have prevented him getting back into Britain. You see he wanted to come back to Glasgow. We were in love and we were going to get married. So he decided that he would continue to use the Ghazani alias he'd been using since he was studying medicine in Egypt and pretend that he was working as a doctor in Northern Cyprus."

"And he got further radicalised out there, when he went to the camp in Lebanon?" I asked.

"We both did. I went out there. He showed me how to get there while supposedly going on a 'normal' holiday. The conditions were appalling, worse than anything I could have imagined. In the few weeks I was there I even helped out in the camp hospital. I was so proud of him and so in love with him. He'd sacrificed everything for his family. There is nothing in this life here with its obsession with materialism and comfort and the self that can prepare for what it's like out there. All those drunks and worried well people that used to clutter up the A and E when I was an emergency nurse, let them spend ten minutes at a medical compound in a Palestinian camp and see if they think they've got problems.

"I converted to Islam on my second visit to Syed in 2007. I'll always call him Syed rather than Jalal, his real name, as that's the name I knew him by and fell in love with when he was working here. If anything the conditions were even worse on that second visit. The Lebanese Government were restricting supplies into the camp. There was trouble brewing with the pro-Syrians and Zionist agents were stirring up trouble everywhere.

"When I got back here things just seemed more and more unreal to me. All the moans and gripes, the obsession with house prices, with buying the latest things, everybody trying to keep up with everybody else, the pathetic interest in plastic celebrities. I felt like screaming 'don't you know what's happening in the world around you? Don't you know how lucky you are?' And then I realised that these people were living in a false, shallow material world; that their values, if they had any, were false and corrupt. It didn't take me long to realise that not only did I want nothing more to do with those values but that people here had become manipulated through the media and the education system by the whole Zionist Crusader world order. They were the string-pullers. My new faith and Syed between them pulled me through. Islam offers the way for a fair and just society but the power-holders and elites in the Zionist Crusader countries are totally opposed to this for it threatens their power so they must sow confusion and poison about Islam and the mujahedeen who are fighting them.

"I was able to put on a face. To pretend to be plain Tres Martindale, staff nurse and talk about the soaps and celebrities and go to lassies' hen nights and talk about houses and curtains and get pissed with the rest of the girls. I honed that well over the years. Even before I worked for the resistance I had put on a face; what I would now call developing a 'legend'. I gave nothing away: about Islam, about Syed: nothing.

"And then Syed was killed. No, it was murder. His death was put down to faction fighting among the Palestinians. Nonsense! He was killed by a Lebanese militia that had infiltrated the Lebanese Army. They went to his house in the early morning and took him away. His body was found days later on waste-ground riddled with bullets and marks from the torture he'd endured."

"Why had they selected him, Tres?" I asked her.

"Because his brother Amir was rising in the ranks of al-Qaeda in Iraq, which would soon become ISIL and then ISIS. This threatened all the pro-Syrian and pro-Iranian Shia militias as well as the Christian forces in the Lebanese Army, all of which of course are just fronts or puppets of the Zionist Crusader forces. I was absolutely devastated by Syed's death."

"Did you go to his funeral?"

"Yes, outside Tripoli. I met Amir there too. I told him I was dedicating myself to the Islamic Resistance. I said I would work in the camps as a nurse or wherever my training could help them. But he said it would be better if I went back to Scotland and found an opportunity to help the Resistance there. He explained that it was getting more and more difficult to recruit resistance fighters in the West, not least because of Western intelligence service's surveillance and infiltration. What was needed was cleanskins and there could be nothing whiter-than-white than a white Scottish nurse. So, after a couple of weeks of training at a camp in Lebanon controlled by al-Qaeda or its affiliates, Amir encouraged me to go back, lie low and wait for an opportunity to become active."

"And that's why you packed in nursing, when you saw the job being advertised for the MOD?"

"I had no idea how you went about joining British intelligence. I didn't even know much about them. I did a lot of Googling and read some books about who MI5 were and what the difference was with MI6 or SIS and GCHQ. Then the chance of joining the Civil Service came up and I applied and said all the right things and passed the exams and got sent to the MOD where I thought I could do something for the Resistance there. But it was entirely clerical and humdrum; there was not a military secret or installation in sight. I thought I'd made a mistake and then the post with the somewhat mysterious description of working in assessment and collation of intelligence material came up and my heart quickened and I leapt at it and," she motioned her Beretta in the air, "well I'm here."

"Could I ask how you kept in contact with Amir over the last few years?"

"You can ask, Eddie…" She broke off. "Wattie what are you doing?" He had half-risen from his position against the wall.

"I'm needing a piss." He almost spat the words out at her.

"Make sudden movements like that without warning me and you'll never need to take another piss again in your life! Now get up slowly, that's right, and walk backwards facing me, that's right. Now turn. Use one hand to get your dick out, keep the other hand in the air where I can see it. Good. Now you can piss."

Wattie urinated at the side of the tank just in sight of Tres before the tank curved round the circle. When he'd finished he walked back round with his hands in the air; his face now a portrait of sheer hatred for Tres. He resumed sitting down next to the redundant MP5. Tres recommenced talking to me, the smell of Wattie's urine wafting in the air.

"Yes you can ask but I won't tell you. Just good tradecraft, cut outs, dead-letter boxes, brush contacts and so on. All stuff I got taught at the camp and which was reinforced through my training with you guys."

"And what else did you get training on in the camp?" I thought I could discern fatigue coming over her. If I kept her talking and honed that with Wattie's energetic anger we might get a chance to divert her attention for a second and pounce. Grey daylight now streamed through the control room windows.

Tres answered me by saying: "How to handle a gun, basic hand-to-hand combat, basic explosives training." She indicated the holdall between her legs with that cord stretching down into it. "The usual items, but the main thing was to keep a straight face. To be one of you guys, be a typical west of Scotland girl; laughing and joking, be a bit flirty, drift in and out of relationships, take a drink with the boys: just keeping up the front. Now I don't have to do that anymore. I can be me. I have done my duty and played a part in helping the Resistance. Allah has chosen me through Syed and his brother Amir and I am going to heaven to be reunited with them."

That sent a shiver of fear through me, especially the determination and conviction with which she said that. "And exactly how are you going to be reunited with them?" I asked her, though I knew the answer.

A steely but manic shine came across her green eyes as she gestured at the holdall between her legs and at the control room around her. "Do you intend to take us along with you on this journey?"

She let out a dry, bitter laugh. "Don't you see? It's a gift from Allah. I'm on top of a water tower with a former commando from the British Special Forces who's raped and pillaged an Islamic country, and a Team Leader (God that makes you sound like you work in a call centre, Eddie), a Team Leader of a Western colonial intelligence agency! Of course I'm taking you two fuckers with me!"

"You mad, deluded crazy bitch!" Wattie shouted at her. "Away and blow yourself up and do the rest of the world a favour! The only place you're going is straight to hell!"

Tres laughed again, but more manic this time. "Aw, Wattie, straight to the point, get it out, just like your lovemaking: energetic but fast. Whereas you, Eddie, well, you're nice and gentle and sensitive, but you do tend to go round the houses. I suppose it's true that a person's lovemaking reflects their personality."

I involuntarily looked over at Wattie. In spite of his circumstances and his anger, there was a look of surprise on his face. All I could think to do was shrug my shoulders in front of him and look away. She knew this was the first that we were both aware that she'd slept with each of us for she continued:

"It was part of the job I had to do. And I suppose it was symbolic. The two of you and the organisations you represent have screwed Islam so this was Islam getting back by screwing you. Mind, you weren't the worst by a long shot; you weren't the best either, but it wasn't the most unpleasant act of resistance to participate in."

"Thanks Tres, I don't know about Wattie, that's made me feel a bit better before I meet my maker," I responded. Sometimes irreverent humour is the best response in a stressful situation.

A silence descended. If Wattie and I were going to do something we'd need to do it soon, or Henderson would have to try to attempt a rescue or bring in a professional hostage negotiation team, assuming that one of the buttons on the phone had worked. But from outside there was nothing; even the helicopter seemed to have gone. My watch told me it was gone past six. I couldn't see all three of us holding out another four hours till ten when the deadline for talking expired and, no doubt an SAS unit or equivalent would come streaming in. What could we do, though? Wattie, sitting beside his useless MP5 now looked more listless than angry while Tres, although tired looking was still standing firmly over the holdall with the cord and the Beretta pointing at us. If we tried anything she could shoot at least one of us and trigger the detonator. Keep talking, I thought; it was the only hope until I thought of something. I pointed at the holdall.

"Was that a DIY job or did you get help with it?" I asked her. "You may as well tell us; after all we're going to meet our makers shortly!" I suddenly realised that I had been leaning against my left arm which had gone to sleep; my left hand was still clutched around the mobile in my jacket pocket.

"I'm actually quite chuffed with this," she replied almost breezily. "I did it on my own using a standard manual and getting locally purchased ingredients." It was as if she was talking about a recipe for a cake that she had successfully baked. "And I haven't managed to blow up half of my street in the process. Allah has been with me all the way, and Syed."

I extricated my left hand from the pocket as the blood started to reflow through the arm, but as I started to rub it with my right hand I saw that the mobile had stuck to the palm of my left hand due to the clamminess in the pocket. I tried to conceal the phone by wrapping my fingers around it, but I was too slow. "Let's see that!" Tres ordered. I held my shaking hand out to her with the phone lying on the open palm. "Throw it to me," she instructed. I did as best as I could even though my arm was still stiff.

She caught it and examined it. What she did next took both of us by surprise. She threw it in the air in front of her, aimed her Beretta at it and fired. Both of us startled. There was a bright burst of flame and a sharp explosion which reverberated around the control room with an echo while the phone was blown to pieces. As she watched the debris from the destroyed phone scatter and land around her, she said in a satisfied tone: "I do a lot of gun practice."

Christ she was good! I thought. The home-made bomb, the accuracy of her firing, the sheer effort she had put into creating, maintaining and sustaining her legend, all attested to a highly competent professional agent. Al-Qaeda had a good officer; pity we hadn't got to her before them.

After the destruction of the phone, there was a tension in the air and all three of us were completely alert. "The two of you keep your hands in front of you where I can see them," she ordered. "Anybody puts their hands back in their pockets I'll shoot you. Clear?"

We both nodded our heads in compliance. Things were about to reach a climax, I had determined and I'm sure Wattie felt the same way, though I had no means of communicating with him, that I would make an attempt, no matter how futile, at overcoming Tres before she annihilated the three of us in this tower. But before that I had one last go at reasoning with her.

"Tres this crowd you're with, this ISIS, al-Qaeda, whatever, they behead people, they stone people to death, they're barbaric, they want to put us back to the Middle-Ages! You're a strong liberated woman. These folk want to put you in a veil, never allow women an education. Jesus, Tres, they'd put women back four hundred years!"

Suddenly I heard the helicopter back: obviously it had been alerted by those on the ground by the sound of the gunshot. Tres studiously ignored the sound which seemed to be hovering closely. She shouted above the sound of the copter:

"You know nothing about the Islamic Resistance except what you've read in Western propaganda newspapers! Women wear veils to protect themselves from predatory males and to express themselves in their own space, their privacy. In the Caliphate sex crimes will be non-existent because women will be respected and if there are any the perpetrators will be severely punished. Look at young women in the West going about in virtually nothing to satisfy male lust; that will end. And as for women's education, neither the Prophet Mohammed nor the Sheikh, Osama Bin Laden, denied the rights of women and girls to education. That was the Taliban who were in error about this as the Sheikh pointed out on numerous occasions. Rather than spout Crusader Zionist propaganda, Eddie, get your fucking facts right!"

I was about to reply when a huge wave of sound hit the tower causing it to shudder and sway quite violently. The tank behind me began vibrating loudly. I stood up staggering and had to hold on to the side of the tank. I could see, through one of the small windows on the surface that the water in the tank was churning wildly. Wattie too had rose up and was clutching hold of the side wall while Tres had moved back further and sat on the edge of the tank trying to maintain her balance while keeping the holdall attached to the cord beneath her and still fixing us with her Beretta. Her face was now very alert and anxious, eyes darting trying to focus solely on the two of us while she anticipated an attack from anywhere outside the control room. I was anxiously and acutely aware she could trigger that detonator any second. I was bewildered and was expecting smoke grenades, mindful of how Wattie had stormed the tower overcoming the Dutch Marines during the NATO exercise, only those guys weren't sitting on a volatile cocktail of explosives, including forty-eight ounces of TNT. But there was no attack, although the shuddering, the swaying and the vibrating continued: but with less intensity. Eventually Wattie shouted over the din:

"It's the tank! They're draining the water; they've opened the sluice gates." And, sure enough when I looked back through the window in the tank, the water, while still churning wildly, was slightly lower than it had been.

"They must have ordered it drained when they heard the shot fired," I said, almost breathlessly. We were getting acclimatised to all the noise so the sight of the helicopter coming into view, hovering a couple of hundred yards wide of the brim on the south side of the tower like a bright shiny huge flying beetle, surprised us, the sound of its approach disguised by the cacophony caused by the tank draining.

I looked at Tres. She was on sensory overload, eyes darting between the helicopter hovering outside, watching us and every sinew alert for any other sound. She could break and pull that trigger any second now. I felt paralysed and helpless when suddenly Wattie shouted, eyes staring right in front of him beyond me at the north side:

"Fuck!"

I turned instantly to face whatever it was, as did Tres, which was the intention, for Wattie dived up from the wall and lunged at her, but the unexpected noise of the tank draining had caused her to move further away from us allowing her enough space to fire the pistol straight at him. Wattie went down like a deflated balloon; two bullets hit him square in the forehead. There was a hissing, spraying noise and a foam of Wattie's blood landed on my jacket and shirt. I felt something hitting my head and face like sharp pellets. I picked at one of these from the side of my face and realised with horror they were bits of Wattie's brain or skull. Wattie was lying, face down, blood cascading from his head onto the wooden floorboards. I looked over at Tres. She had the detonator out now in her right hand while her left hand still cocked and aimed the pistol at me: both hands were shaking.

"I'm ready!" she exclaimed, her face white as milk, eyes wide. "I'm fucking ready!" her thumb over the detonator pin, the cord taut and stretched leading into the holdall. I was aware with a terrible guilty pang, one of many to add to the list from the last few days, that if I had lunged at Tres the same time as Wattie one of us could have floored her and maybe prevented her from pressing the trigger, though even then there was no guarantee that we would have succeeded and one of us would have been shot, almost certainly fatally. But now I had to think of survival. Tres was at breaking point, repeatedly shouting: "I'm fucking ready!" And when she stopped exclaiming that she would detonate. I took one last look at her manically staring and shouting at me, hand clutched at the detonator, the helicopter buzzing outside, Wattie's lifeless body still seeping blood onto the floor, my shirt covered in his blood and bits of him embedded in my face.

I jumped up from the edge of the tank and crouched down running round the circular path towards the stair-head. The draining of the tank saved me as the vibration, swaying and whirling of the tower combined with Tres' shaky hand meant that the bullet she fired from the Beretta at me was deflected, though I could still feel it like a slight stinging sensation whizzing past me. Her second bullet missed altogether hitting the control room ceiling.

I reached the stair-head and lunged down the steps towards the first small level surface ten feet below and almost plunged into Henderson standing there, pistol in hand with three masked men, sub-machine guns in their hands, behind him. I managed to avoid him and them as I landed screaming: "She's got a fucking massive bomb in a holdall! She's going to detonate it, move!"

The three masked men looked at Henderson for a cue who studied me intensely. In those brief seconds I heard Tres, above the vibrations and the helicopter shouting once as loudly as she could:

"There is no God but Allah and Mohammed is his prophet!" Followed by an incredibly bright flash of light, far greater in intensity than that caused by the pistol firing earlier. That was followed almost instantly by a blast wave that blew Henderson, the three men and me to the floor. Everything shook around us like a plate spinning rapidly. The three masked men picked themselves up. One grabbed hold of me and slung me across his back and shoulders urging me to cling on tight; another did the same to Henderson while the third led the way down. All the lights were in darkness as the power was cut. These guys were fit, leaping down the shaking rattling staircase four-or-five steps at a time with the first leading with a powerful flashlight which illuminated the way ahead. I weighed nearly thirteen stone but the guy carrying me gave no sign of exertion as he and his colleagues bounced down the stairs leading from the control room down to the narrow passageway.

Once we reached the corridor at the bottom of the stairs and below the tank the two soldiers (for I surmised that's what they were– probably SAS) made Henderson and I stand up before leading us by the arm along the corridor behind their comrade with the powerful flashlight. The steel casing above us was crackling and rumbling, the walls beside us buckling while the floor juddered; it was like walking up a down escalator during an earthquake. Finally, we reached the curved concrete outer staircase around the central column. Once again the soldiers put us on their backs as we descended at a less rapid pace.

The staircase juddered here less than the upper one astride the tank, but even here there were cracks appearing in the concrete walls and the steel casing holding the water in the central column was making an enormous grinding, rasping noise. But what was most remarkable was the water cascading down the outside which we could see as we passed by the large windows on our descent. About two-thirds of the way down we heard an immense swishing sound as a tremendous sheet of water poured around us and lifted us forward parting me from the soldier carrying me, but at the same time forcing me against his back as the momentum of the water funnelled down the corridor, bashing and bumping all of us against the surrounding walls which we glanced off eventually depositing us at the bottom where we poured outside the column through the wooden door which was hanging off its hinges into yet more water, now about six or seven feet high and climbing rapidly. As we got driven outside, the water pulled our small group apart and we got separated from each other.

Great sheets of water were pouring out of fissures in the concrete sides of the walls of the tank where the explosion had caused the tank to rupture and buckle outwards. Most of the water cascaded directly below, but some coursed underneath the bottom of the tank and then down the central column. The water pouring down the column staircase dragged us forward onwards beyond the brim of the tank. I got a glimpse of one of the soldiers in front of me trying to make headway against the tidal wave, but ultra-fit as he was, it was futile against the sheer force of the water.

Beyond the brim of the tank a new danger lurked. Shards of concrete masonry were falling from the tank wall into the water; one piece landed right beside me and caught me on the shoulder where I felt a wave of pain. Discoloured, dirty red water streamed in front of me and I realised it was actually mainly blood coming from a gash in my head probably as a result of being bashed against the wall by the water on the final stage of the descent down the stairwell.

The water was now about twelve feet high and was moving forward swiftly taking me beyond the danger posed by the falling masonry from the sides of the tank. However, ahead lay new threats and obstacles. There were iron spikes and barbed wire across the top of the dividing wall surrounding the water tower and I was unsure whether the water was sufficiently high enough to clear it. The spikes of the fence and the wire loomed closer as the water drove me on in spasms which would slow down and speed up. I was convinced I was going to be dashed against the spikes or the wire but I couldn't even get my hands free to protect my face such was the force and momentum of the water. Just feet away from the top of the wall a sudden renewed vigour in the pressure and drive of the water forced me past the spike and barbs and across the wall, with my leg grazing against the wire, tearing my trousers off below the knee and cutting into my leg. I howled out in pain as I was funnelled swiftly over a scrap metal yard now about fifteen feet above the ground, across the back and between houses and across to a row of red pebble-dash houses where the water was coming to the roof edge.

The renewed vigour in the water was caused by the rapid erosion and collapse of the concrete wall on the south side of the tower and a large split in the tank from which the water was now emptying furiously. I was propelled against the black slated roof of the terraced houses and lay against it as the water temporarily retreated to my waist. Then to my huge surprise a hand appeared and grabbed my left wrist. It was a powerful grip and I moved further up the roof with slates tumbling off as my legs clambered across it towards a chimney stack protruding up from the roof where a man had positioned himself.

As I came nearer him and the chimney he was able to use both arms now to take hold of my waist and drag me towards him. There was one remaining chimney pot on top of the disused vent which he brushed aside. It crashed into the roof and into a bedroom below allowing the water, which was now lapping over the roof edge to pour into the house. The space created by the casting away of the chimney pot allowed me to sit beside my rescuer. I breathed deeply and tried to calm down slightly and looked beside me at whoever it was who had rescued me. It was the CIA man Herb Lange.

He had discarded the shades revealing dark brown, slightly bloodshot eyes, but even minus the shades, the stare was still deep, intense, penetrating and, above all, controlling. He had a white sweat shirt on which was both soaked through and blood-stained and his craggy lined face inspected me, his hands touching my forehead. Blood was pouring out of a number of wounds in my forehead, arms and legs, saturating my clothes. Putting one hand on my shoulders he came close to my ear and shouted: "Help is on the way!" while with his other hand pointed to the sky where a helicopter was rapidly approaching, a tow rope projecting out of its side. I later found this was a different helicopter from the one which had been hovering around the tower earlier. Lange stood up slowly on the narrow chimney ledge balancing himself with one hand on my shoulders as the rope bit by bit came towards us and the helicopter came overhead positioning itself right above us.

With his free hand he made several attempts to grab the large circular hoop at the end of the rope, once almost overreaching himself but I managed to help keep him steady by grabbing his other hand, allowing him to rebalance himself. I was pleased that I had made some contribution to the rescue. Finally he got a purchase on the hoop and brought it towards me as I felt the rotary motion of the air from the helicopter blades billowing around me swirling the water which was now only a couple of feet below us. Lange made me stand up, holding onto him and put the hoop around me like a clasp below my arms. It felt secure and locked. He motioned up to the crew and I was suddenly whisked up in a gradual circular movement towards the chopper.

Below I could see the water between the rows of terraced houses at roof height like a river about to burst its banks. I spotted a body floating down there with what looked like a balaclava mask on the face, though I couldn't be sure and if it was it would certainly be one of the SAS soldiers who had rescued me from the tower. That dreadful sight and sad thought was rapidly followed by the ridiculously prosaic memory that the girl I'd once went out with when I was a teenager had lived in that now flooded street below. That was in the innocent mid-seventies before I got Marxism, joined the Revolutionary Socialist Party and then entered into the clutches of MI5.

Those memories were snuffed out as I came in fast towards the roaring helicopter, the wind from the blades blowing at storm-force, the noise deafening. A figure with a bright orange jumpsuit and a helmet was leaning over the side of the craft and grabbed my shoulders and with seemingly effortless ease, brought me over the side and into the aircraft, quickly unfastening me from the harness and easing the hoop over me before passing me over to another helmeted colleague who settled me onto a stretcher. I watched fascinated as the first helmeted figure (who it later transpired was a woman) eased the tow rope out of the aircraft back, I presumed, towards Lange on the chimney edge.

As the second person who'd put me on the stretcher strapped me in firmly and was joined by a third who started applying bandages to my various wounds I looked out the open near side of the helicopter. I couldn't see below to the row of houses, the chimney ledge or chart the progress of Lange's rescue, but what I could see in the steely grey dawn light was horrifyingly awesome.

The copter was side on to the tower and at the same height which was a couple of hundred feet to the north with the huge gash to the tank visible and the water still pouring out. I watched with a sickening fascination as three of the thin outer columns supporting the tank buckled and collapsed into the water with an enormous splash. This caused the tank with the control room above it to tilt forward. The large antenna above the control room slid off and crashed into the water to the east of the tower. For a few seconds it seemed as if the tilted tank would balance at the new angle, the momentum of the water gushing out even more rapid now. But then it tilted even further until it could no longer be supported and, the last of the concrete masonry falling away, the control room disintegrating into pieces and the remaining outer support columns crashing over, it tumbled and fell forwards hurtling towards the terraced houses right opposite the row where Lange was.

The helicopter pilot made a sudden jerking motion, gained some height and the aircraft spun round a complete circle but much further away from the houses. To my immense relief the head of Lange with its swept dark hair and craggy features appeared at the edge to be quickly brought in and stretchered like myself. Behind him I saw the huge ruptured tank crash into the terraced houses with an incredible splash, flattening them and bringing about a huge tsunami that deluged the other houses, including the ones we had been on, as well as devastating the car park and the supermarket. Great waves of water seventy to eighty feet in height poured out of Tannochside destroying everything in its wake, sending occasional bright blue arcs of electricity leaping in the air as power circuits were overwhelmed and shorted, down the steep side of the Clyde Valley towards the town of Uddingston at the bottom of the valley where it eventually stopped (after drenching the M74 main southbound highway to England, which fortunately had been cordoned off) before subsiding and draining away. All that remained was the thick inner cylinder just protruding above the water. LN117, the Tannochside Water Tower, an iconic highly visible landmark in the post-industrial urban landscape of North Lanarkshire, was no more.

My vision was terminated abruptly by the helicopter door closing. I felt a slight jagging sensation as one of the helmeted figures was injecting a needle into my arm. I could detect a smile on the person's face from below their visor, the feeling of the aircraft ascending and moving away swiftly and then I lapsed into complete oblivion.

10: AFTERMATH "ANY MEANS NECESSARY"

At roughly the same time as the events in Tannochside were unfolding, an equally dramatic episode was unravelling, two thousand miles away in the barren emptiness of the Western Libyan Desert. Some eighty miles to the south-west of the capital Tripoli and about forty miles from the nearest town of any size, Sabratah, lay an abandoned airfield built originally by the Italian air-force during the 1930s. It had been commandeered by the British RAF after the allies had expelled Axis forces during the Second World War and abandoned by Colonel Gaddafi's air force in favour of more modern bases closer to the capital since the 60s. The crumbling, rotten white grey and brown collection of buildings which had once served as barracks, offices and hangars had been brought back to life over the past two months. Though a casual observer would not have noticed much difference from outside, this was deliberate as the new purposes of the base had to be concealed.

Behind the crumbling facades, a Libyan Islamist group affiliated to al-Qaeda called the Libyan Shield whose local operational division was known as the Western Shield was in control of the area. Western Shields's commander was a close ally of Al Sharjanah, the overall al-Qaeda number two. Back in March, Al Sharjanah had requested the Western Shield's commander to identify a number of sites, in the end six otherwise empty and abandoned sites in a region covering over two-hundred miles in the midst of the Western Desert that could be requisitioned and converted quickly to serve as a meeting place. As with the other five sites identified, the abandoned airbase received a coat of paint inside, was cleaned up, some basic furniture and provisions including access to water and a generator supplied, all to make it habitable for at least a one-off meeting lasting no more than a few hours at most.

The purpose was to provide the insalubrious venue for a meeting of senior commanders of the various regional insurgent movements which had sprung up since the 'Arab Spring' of 2011, who were posing a serious threat to established regimes in the Middle East, North Africa and the Arabian Peninsula. This meeting had been planned for some time and was intended to be the forum by which Ali al Hassan could stake a claim to overall leadership of al-Qaeda and provide it with a unified command structure.

When the George Square bombing occurred, the regional commanders were effusive in their praise of al Hassan; among them Amir Asaf, second-in-command of ISIS. This was the first successful attack and 'spectacular' on a Western target involving mass causalities by al-Qaeda in years: and was supported by the ISIS commander who was closest to al-Qaeda and was agitating for ISIS to affiliate once more to the group they'd arisen from. As a result al Hassan's stock rose. Things got even better when al Hassan revealed in his video delivered to al Jazeera and thence the world's media that there was an al-Qaeda mole in MI5. The announcement of a mole was a political and psychological master-stroke which reinforced the regional commanders' support, admiration and even respect for al Hassan.

Security precautions for the meeting were elaborate. The first day mooted for the meeting was Wednesday then it was postponed to Thursday, then Friday before finally agreeing on the early Saturday morning. Out of the six possible desert sites chosen to host the meeting, the one finally decided upon would be selected at random by Al Sharjanah and communicated to his boss al Hassan only ninety minutes before the meeting was to start. Once al Hassan had been informed and approved of the location, Islamic Shield couriers would be speedily dispatched to a series of safe houses located in tents, barracks and other sites where the regional commanders were waiting and brought quickly to the abandoned airfield. In this way it would be impossible for the Americans or anyone else to know in advance where the meeting was to be held or have sufficient time to prepare an attack on it.

The regional commanders, all veterans of living on the run and having a price on their head, had their own ratlines which brought them to the Libyan Desert. ISIS reps led by Amir Asaf came via Lebanon and then through the porous Egyptian border into Libya.

Yemeni and Somali reps came through the Red Sea and the Sudanese Desert to get there while the West African and Nigerian Boko Haram reps used old Saharan smugglers' caravan routes to reach their initial safe house rendezvous. All were escorted by the couriers to the former airstrip.

It was intended to start the meeting at 7am local time which was an hour ahead of Glasgow and just at the time when Tres detonated her holdall bomb and destroyed LN117 and Tannochside. But the meeting was held up as Al Sharjanah was delayed much to al Hassan's and the various reps' concerns; the longer the meeting took place and they were all in one place, the more exposed they all were. Hassan was keen to show a united front between him and Al Sharjanah and silence speculation about any tension or friction between them.

After thirty minutes a messenger arrived from Al Sharjanah's quarters to say that he had severe stomach pains and was unsure whether he would be able to travel to the meeting, but to go ahead without him. Frustrated and angry at Al Sharjanah's no-show, but aware that time and security were of the essence and not wanting to incur any irritation on the part of the commanders that would get in the way of the virtually guaranteed confirmation of his position as chair of the unified command, Hassan went ahead with the meeting. Wearing his customary white robes and headdress, a beaming smile on his face and accompanied by an aide, Hassan walked into a long, windowless interior room furnished only with three bare wooden tables and chairs arranged in a U-shape. Air conditioning in the otherwise stifling room was supplied by an overhead rotating fan powered by a generator as were the ceiling strip lights. As al Hassan entered the room, applause broke out from the assembled representatives who were already seated and who were now relieved that the waiting was over and the meeting at last about to commence.

As al Hassan made his way to the middle table where he would be seated and open the proceedings he acknowledged or shook hands with the reps, all of whom he knew. There were nine in total, each accompanied by up to three aides; all of them either the senior military man in their group or the number two or the actual leader. Six of them, from Mali, Nigeria, Libya, Yemen, Somalia and

Iraq/Syria had direct control of territory and substantial numbers of men and material. Three of them, from Saudi Arabia, Algeria and Egypt, were not in such a strong position, but would benefit immensely from a unified command which would considerably boost their own campaigns.

Hassan sat down at the middle table. In front of them by prior agreement, a lone cameraman from an al-Qaeda allied Arab TV news outlet, shot footage of the group. While he waited out the few minutes they had agreed to allow for the camera to scan the room, Hassan took stock. He was still annoyed at the absence of Al Sharjanah and fervently hoped that he would still be able to attend even if only for a few minutes for the sake of the show of unity. In spite of this he was immensely satisfied that this meeting was actually happening, that he had managed to get all these groups together round a table in one place and he was on the cusp of leading a unified al-Qaeda and officially become the successor to the legendary Sheikh: Osama Bin Laden. He looked over and saw the gaunt, weathered features of the Palestinian military commander and Deputy Leader of ISIS, Amir Asaf, huddled in conversation with three of his aides. ISIS was by far the most powerful of the regional groups and Asaf the representative he most had to garner allegiance and support from.

What Hassan wasn't aware of was that he owed his imminent, uncontested accession to the leadership of al-Qaeda in large part to Asaf. It was Asaf's recruitment and grooming of Tres Martindale that allowed the 'spectacular' in Glasgow to go ahead. That, together with the revelation of the MI5 mole, had completely disarmed any residual resistance to Hassan's accession. Asaf returned Hassan's glance with a slight bow of the head. An aide standing next to Hassan tapped him on the shoulder: the allotted five minutes for the cameraman were up. Hassan rapped the table with his knuckles. The cameraman switched off his camera, bowed to the group and left the room.

Hassan spoke for five minutes thanking the representatives for attending and the risks they had put themselves through, but Allah was with them and this meeting was the start of the new phase against the Crusader-Zionist forces. He went on to speak about the devastating blow delivered to the heart of the Western front in Scotland and then the lights in the room went out.

From three-thousand feet above the former airstrip, a US Predator UAV or Drone which had been flown from a base in Sicily and was controlled from a Special Operations Centre in Florida, fired two explosives-packed Hellfire missiles in sequence, which slammed into the buildings below. After the lights went out, an intense burst of sound effectively shattered the eardrums and most of the bone structure of the people inside. This was followed by rapid asphyxiation as oxygen was completely sucked out of the blast area, then an immense sheet of flame causing the bodies to combust and take fire. Finally, the blast blew the bodies apart spiralling limbs, heads and other body parts around until they became entangled in the rubble as the debris from the explosion settled. All of this took place in seconds. Everyone in the surrounding buildings were also killed outright, even the cameraman whose footage was destroyed.

Nine senior commanders of powerful militant Islamic groups had been annihilated, as had the head of al-Qaeda, Ali al Hassan The attempt to create a unified command structure had been stifled at birth and the new leadership of a powerful, formidable al-Qaeda had been decapitated. Only Al Sharjanah survived as he had failed to attend the meeting.

*

My recovery from the events at Tannochside was slow: three months to be precise. There was the physical recovery from the numerous wounds and gashes I had endured on that horrific exit from the tower. I had suffered a serious wound to my forehead when I'd been bashed against the inner wall of the middle support column of the tower by the force of the water on the last part of my exit down the curved staircase. My shoulder had also been injured and almost dislocated when the lump of concrete masonry had fallen from the side of the tank. But the most serious injury was to my leg when the spikes from the top of the surrounding wall railings and barbed wire had caught against my leg and cut a deep tear along it. There was concern I would contract tetanus or even gangrene, but good medical care and attention prevented this.

Immediately after I'd lost consciousness in the helicopter I'd been flown to hospital in Glasgow, ironically it was one of the hospitals that Tres Martindale had once worked in as an emergency nurse. My wounds were cleaned and bandaged; stitches placed in the head wound – which a CT scan showed was only superficial – a sling put across my shoulder, my leg encased in plaster and plenty of painkillers and antibiotics. For the first two weeks I was kept in a room in the hospital guarded by CTC, though fortunately I wasn't visited by Hammy Anderson. Throughout the two weeks, when the medics permitted, I was interviewed in the room by people from a range of agencies including CTC and SIS. The questioning was firm and probing but not too heavy.

After the fortnight I was transferred to a hospital in Ayrshire where I convalesced further and my wounds healed rapidly, though the scars would last for a while and I would be left with a permanent limp from the leg wound. There was further questioning from CTC and SIS, which was more intensive and almost borderline aggressive, but nothing that was really too daunting. After what I'd been through, there was a lot I could cope with; externally that is: inside my head was swimming.

I was at the hospital for just over three weeks until I was discharged and then I realised why I was sent to an Ayrshire hospital. Upon release I was transported by armed CTC just up the road to Troon, the joint MI5/SIS safe house which posed as a farm, but also served as a detention-cum-interrogation centre when required. There was further questioning at Troon, but only two sessions of this crossed over into outright hostile interrogation and, at both of these three sharp-suited officials from the Cabinet Office, Foreign Office and JTAC were present. They questioned me sharply on the background to Grand Minaret, individual members of my team and how they had been selected and how I had managed them both before and during the operation.

Predictably most time was spent on Tres with the inevitable benefit of hindsight line of questioning that I should have picked up indications, signs and clues before the bombing. The fact that I'd been having a sexual relationship with Tres was gone over in depth:

the propriety of that relationship was considered alongside whether it had clouded my ability to manage and assess her objectively.

In the end, in spite of effectively frowning on the relationship as 'ill-advised' (which they always did on such occasions when the relationship had come to attention for some reason) they concluded it had had no bearing on the outcome. The plain fact was there were no indications, signs and clues to be had: Tres Martindale was the perfect cleanskin who had stuck rigorously to her legend. Nobody would have caught the link to Ghazani before Amir Asaf, in retrospect foolishly, attempted to reactivate the Ghazani alias. And then it was only the diligence of Vincent in Registry that unearthed the medical journal research article which brought the house down on Tres. I thought I dealt with these sessions well and fully rebuffed any insinuations of incompetence or negligence and I was borne out in that confidence because, after the second session, there was no more hostile questioning and further sessions focused exclusively on fact finding and what we called topping or tailing or just brushing up odd ends here and there. Certainly the interviewers were friendlier, the gaps between sessions became longer and I was able to spend most of my time relaxing, walking along the nearby coastline or reading.

One day I was taken into the town of Troon to a dainty tea and cake shop whose clientele were mainly elderly ladies. It was here that I met my daughter Louise for the first time in a year. She had been very worried about me after George Square, and though reassured by London that I was alive, wasn't allowed to communicate with me until now. She looked well and was enjoying her second year at university in London where she was in a relationship with a law student which was working out fine. I listened intently to her and asked what I thought were appropriate and not too crass or insensitive questions. I was genuinely interested in everything that was going on in her life as any father would: I loved her and was immensely proud of her. But then it ran out of steam, as it always did, because I had nothing to give her. The curse of the secret world was that we couldn't confide even in our family; legends and covers had to be maintained: the strain that placed on relations was often too much to bear with the results that we, agents and officers, ended up in relationships with each other, thus further insulating us from ordinary people.

My relation with my daughter was no exception. Here was me her father, at the centre of what happened at George Square and the almost biblical deluge that swamped Tannochside, and all I could reply to her inevitable questions about them was bland platitudes about how terrible it was and some agents had lost their lives. To her question about how I came by the nasty bruise on my forehead and why I was walking with a limp and had it anything to do with the bombing, I replied that I had fallen down some stairs in a badly lit tenement on the south side of Glasgow during a routine surveillance operation. She bent forward and almost whispered in my ear:

"I know you can't tell me much, but did you ever work with or meet *that* Tres Martindale?" "Twice in training sessions," I confidently lied, "but she was in a different team from me so I never really got to see or know her."

She would have learned more in ten minutes on the internet than from her own father. I could sense her frustration and our conversation dawdled to a desultory and unsatisfying end after an hour. I didn't ask her about her mother, who I hadn't seen in five years and she didn't volunteer any information about her.

We walked to the train station and I spent a couple of minutes with her on the platform waiting for the Glasgow train. I said that I would try and visit her over the Christmas period, enquired if she had enough money (she had) and cautioned her to take care before the train slid into the station and I gave her a peck on the cheek, watched her to her seat and waved her goodbye as the train pulled away. On the way back to the 'farm' I could have wept. I wanted to hug her, to hold her, to confide in her, to get to know her, but this huge gap was there and always had been right from her early childhood. I resolved that when I left the secret world I would seriously try to spend some time with her and try and make up for all the lost time and the lies and the evasiveness; if she would let me.

At the end of the first month in Troon, I was told by an officer from Human Resources that I was being discharged from the service, on full pension, with a clean record, a 'good' reference and I would get assistance with finding employment in areas such as defence contracting or security consultancy. I knew this last was bullshit. The ex-intelligence officers' community was a small and incestuous one and word would get around fast of my connection with the disastrous Grand Minaret operation and, even worse, I'd had direct line management of the spy, traitor and terrorist accomplice Martindale. No security consultancy or defence contractor would want anyone associated with George Square or Tres on their books, no matter how deep cover it was. I was going to struggle out there. The HR officer also told me that I would be at Troon for a further month for 'final recuperation' and then I would be on garden leave until the beginning of November, a few months hence.

So I spent the rest of my time at Troon relaxing as best I could and going for long walks alone on the seashore. There was a bench which afforded a magnificent view out on the Firth of Clyde and I would sit there for long periods contemplating and reflecting on all that had gone on, my thinking only interrupted by the occasional roar of an overhead jet as planes landed or took off from the nearby Prestwick Airport.

Invariably, my first thoughts on these occasions, was on the sheer scale of the devastation and loss of life. Aside from the eighty-two people who had died at George Square, including of course Sadeq, Khaled and Mohammed in the van and my agent Tony Boyd, not forgetting the hundreds injured, another twenty-four lost their lives at Tannochside, all of them security personnel. Among them were the three SAS soldiers who had helped me escape from the tower and one of whom I was sure was the body I had seen in the water between the terraced houses as I was waiting on the chimney ledge to be rescued by the helicopter. Henderson, from the SIS Special Operations Branch had also perished at Tannochside as had the tousled-haired chap, although pram lady, I was assured, had survived. I never did find out the fate of my ex-interrogator army guy seconded to SIS whose lightning punch had floored me at Bridgeton Railway Station.

My questions as to what happened to my rescuer, Herb Lange from the CIA, after he was winched into the helicopter after me was met with silence or outright denials on every occasion I raised it. Eventually one of my questioners, in an informal moment over coffee after one fairly relaxed interview session and just at the end of all the question sessions, informed me discreetly that the subject of a CIA presence at Tannochside was strictly 'taboo' as was any mention of CIA involvement with anything to do with George Square. This was 'deniable' I was told and that deniability stretched all the way to St Andrews House (the seat of the Scottish Government), Downing Street and the White House.

"It never happened, Eddie, so forget it and give yourself an easy life," my questioner strongly advised.

"So there was a ghost on the chimney ledge with me and that ghost directed the rescue helicopter in and that ghost strapped me into the winch rope that lifted me up and I must have been hallucinating when I saw him getting dragged into the copter after me, eh?"

He just shrugged and merely repeated: "The CIA was never involved in any aspect of this. You must have been confused: you were quite badly injured after all!" I let it go for now but determined to find out more when I got the opportunity after I'd left the service.

In spite of the devastation wreaked at Tannochside and the loss of the security personnel there, the remarkable fact was that no civilians had died. All the residents had been evacuated in time. The Scottish and UK Governments pledged to fund new homes and create a new township with shops to replace the supermarket that had been destroyed. As for the water tower, it was never replaced. It was of its time when it was built in the 1950s and new technology meant a smaller replacement could be constructed elsewhere. Where the water tower had been, a park was built complete with a memorial garden.

George Square, or rather the western end where the bombing had occurred, became a virtual shrine. The buildings which had been so badly damaged were demolished and a memorial built. The Square itself was rebuilt and redesigned and the statues which had been wrecked replaced anew, but although Glasgow, with its indomitable spirit, picked itself up and recovered from the atrocity that had been wreaked upon it, the Square never again became the hub and centre of Glasgow life it had been for generations. It took me nearly two years before I could go near it and when I did I was reduced to tears, helplessness and a strong sense of guilt. One good thing, though, the mini-riot between white and Asian youths that broke out on the night of the bombing wasn't repeated and Glasgow did not become a hotbed of racist activity.

Apart from the identified bombers, Khaled and Mohammed, Qatib was revealed as the groomer/recruiter and Sadeq as the driver. Thus two informers for different agencies of British intelligence, SIS and MI5 respectively, who, in the case of Sadeq, had provided over twenty years of valuable service, were vilified as terrorist associates. I decided that when I got out I would try to give a true account of Sadeq's role.

The main villain of the piece, though, as far as the press were concerned, was Tres Martindale. The calamity of an al-Qaeda mole within British intelligence could conveniently be reduced to part gothic horror, part Mills and Boon in the persona of Tres. It was a neat concise story: girl falls in love with exotic foreign doctor who seduces her and sweeps her off her feet. Said doctor's family is killed; he goes abroad to be the breadwinner, gets killed in turn. She is heartbroken, bereft, grief-stricken, which turns to bitter anger and then hatred of the West, her fragile state of mind further twisted and manipulated by al-Qaeda 'terrorist ringmasters'. She became the 'Glasgow Black Widow'; the embodiment of a love-struck, besotted woman whose love is transferred into bitterness and the pursuit of a single-minded evil culminating in George Square and the 'Siege of the Tannochside Water Tower'. It was a perfect tabloid story and they ran with it big time. For British Intelligence, the Scottish Government and Whitehall it was neat and black and white: shorn of all complexities. There was no network of terrorist moles still to be uncovered. It was all down to one woman and her love-turned to hate. In spite of what she'd done I felt for Tres' family as they were hounded and left hanging out to dry by officialdom and pursued by a vociferous media and angry public.

Within intelligence circles it was reluctantly conceded that Tres Martindale had been a 'near-perfect cleanskin' and that enhanced vetting or EPV procedures would have to be tightened still further. So, for instance, when her recurrent holidays in Cyprus were examined, rather than just take the word of one friend who said she met her there and accept that as corroboration, in future at least several witnesses would be interviewed as well as people such as bar staff and taxi drivers to verify that she actually spent most of her time where she'd claimed she was. But, as usual, this was just catching up.

In the Middle-East and among supporters of Islamic militancy and al-Qaeda Tres became a sort of hero: the West of Scotland woman who understood and embraced the cause of jihad and became a holy warrior. When a Scottish tabloid managed to procure a picture of her in her nurse's uniform from a couple of years' back, it became a virtual icon in the souks and bazaars of the Middle East, especially among young militant Islamic women, some of whom regarded her as a hero and for young Islamic men for whom she became the nearest equivalent of a pin-up (though for this reason hard-line Islamists frowned on her picture being circulated).

Whether hated or looked up to, Tres Martindale was on her way to being a celebrity with publishers vying to buy rights on several books on her and talk of a TV series or even a movie about her. One thing was sure: the Tres Martindale story would run for some time.

By contrast, there was little written or mentioned about Wattie Craig. Partly, this was due to a certain shame that everyone, including me, had, at least initially, jumped to the conclusion that he was the al-Qaeda mole because of his SAS and Afghan background. He was awarded a posthumous George Cross for his services and a private memorial service was conducted in his honour. But that was it: Tres Martindale was the only MI5 officer ever publicly mentioned in relation to the 'Glasgow events'.

Three out of five members of an MI5 section team had been killed on an active operation; a sixty percent kill rate that was the highest ever recorded in the service. Another reason why the Team Leader, i.e. me, as with anyone even remotely connected with Grand Minaret was regarded as 'damaged goods', both within and without the intelligence world. In addition, although I was never able to find out the exact figure a whole swathe of the SIS Special Operations Branch team assigned to watch Qatib, had also perished, including of course the target of their surveillance. Grand Minaret stood out as the first ever British Intelligence operation where the number of officers killed was equal to if not greater than the agents and informers they were handling.

Danny McKay who aside from myself, was the one surviving member of the Team, was assigned to work under Stu Hutchinson who, rightfully, emerged unscathed from Grand Minaret as he had nothing to do with it. But this only lasted a few months as Stu and Danny never got on. Danny requested to be reassigned to CTC, but they didn't want him: too involved in Grand Minaret. He ended up in CID, but that only lasted a year and now he runs a hardware store with his brother-in-law, still happily married and happy to be free of the secret world.

I was pleased, however, that partly through my efforts the people on the side-lines of this whole affair were safe. My reckless telephone call to Carl the Geek had led SIS to trace me to Possil. It had also resulted in Carl being hauled in and suspended from the service. On the verge of being dismissed I defended him vigorously and he was reinstated although with a warning on his record. I also spoke highly of Vincent and his role in uncovering the Tres/Ghazani link. As with Carl, they wanted to throw the book at him for conveying unauthorised information to me who was technically still AWOL at the time and even a potential suspect as an al-Qaeda agent. I was able, however, to point out forcefully that if Vincent hadn't, at my request, worked on establishing any connections between members of my team and terrorist suspects and as a consequence alerted me about Tres and I, in turn hadn't texted Henderson and by extension the whole intelligence community to zone in on Tres, she might never have been uncovered. I could have gone ahead up to the control room and Tres could have detonated her bomb and Wattie or even myself, would have been the suspect. Vincent still earned a mild rebuke but was also praised and retired with honours a few years later.

All the people involved in the ratlines were safe as well. Andy is still driving cabs and Shaban is still forging passports and providing disguises. As for Amber…well she's still working 'on the game' but safe as you could ever be in that 'profession' and still occupies a great deal of my thoughts.

Contrary to every expectation MI5 survived the aftermath of Grand Minaret and Tres. An official inquiry concluded that she had been a 'lone wolf' and couldn't have been predicted. Recommendations were made, as already mentioned, that vetting procedures be tightened and greater co-operation made with the Police and NCA around anti-terrorism, but the Service as a whole was to retain its lead role in counter-intelligence. After several months being all over MI5, SIS was ejected and told to restrict itself to foreign intelligence gathering. A whole layer of MI5 middle managers were promoted and replaced all the former senior directors and managers who had been suspended or had resigned in the wake of George Square. Within a year Stu Hutchinson had replaced Colin Mulrooney as Scottish chief of MI5: the Service was still intact, though I was to have no further role in it.

Al-Qaeda suffered badly after the attack in Libya. After being on a high for forty-eight hours at scoring a 'spectacular' in a Western city in Glasgow, supporters were disillusioned and hopes dashed with the elimination of a whole echelon of the top regional group commanders. Al-Qaeda's 'brand' never recovered after. Though some Islamic groups still used the name or paid homage to it, the attempt to create a unified command structure working to a coherent, agreed strategy with a franchise model for terrorist cells in the West was abandoned as too risky. Though the various regional groups still continued to pose a threat to the Arab regimes and individuals in the West still plotted to plan attacks on their own initiative, the threat of a combined, co-ordinated al-Qaeda evaporated after the demise of al Hassan. In that sense, in spite of the suffering, the misery and the carnage caused, George Square and even Tannochside were partly atoned for by the attack in the Libyan Desert.

And there it would have remained with Tres as the main traitor who let al Hassan and Al Sharjanah almost realise al-Qaeda's aim of committing their first major attack on a Western city in years in order to be assured to take control of a newly unified al-Qaeda. That ambition was of course then shattered by the American drone attack on the Libyan compound.

So the official version of events went. But of all the many aspects to the case, there were two big outstanding questions which nobody seemed too interested in pursuing. The first was: who assisted Tres in placing the IED under the van? According to her own testimony, she had micky finned Wattie and then diverted the camera. So who actually placed the device outside? As the questioning of me wound down and became more relaxed I asked my 'interviewers' that question and the logical follow-up: was there a current investigation going on into finding out who this was and how far had it got? Yes, they responded, there were inquiries ongoing, but the likelihood was that Al Sharjanah had sent someone up on a 'one-off' job to assist Tres, but that individual had probably departed immediately once they'd placed the device and had gone into the labyrinth of Arab and Middle-Eastern networks in London or was abroad and would be difficult to apprehend.

Some of that gelled with me, as, despite all the now well-known flaws in Grand Minaret, the shared intelligence community consensus was that the team planning the Glasgow bombings were the only active al-Qaeda cell in Scotland, let alone Glasgow. So the notion of a one-off guy imported for that specific job and then fleeing the scene wasn't unrealistic. But the casual and almost fatalistic response to catching him and perhaps finding out vital information as to how Tres communicated with him, and by extension Al Sharjanah, was disquieting.

My next big question was about Al Sharjanah himself. By all accounts he was solely entrusted with selecting one out of six possible venues to hold the meeting with al Hassan and the regional commanders. When he had selected the specific location, the commanders and al Hassan had only ninety minutes to get to it. To me it seemed clear: if Al Sharjanah was the only person who decided on and knew the exact venue and the Americans were then able to destroy it and all those inside with precision, then surely it must have been Al Sharjanah who had divulged the location with all the implications that entailed?

This question, which I obviously thought was of immense importance, also seemed to me to be dealt with lightly. At first the interviewers agreed I had a point here, but came back the next time with an article in a restricted circulation US journal widely seen as 'close to the American intelligence community'. This article, citing 'highly placed but un-attributable sources at the Pentagon and CIA', asserted that between them the Israeli service MOSSAD and the CIA had recruited several moles amongst the couriers escorting the commanders to the disused airbase. When Al Sharjanah made his decision as to which venue was to host the meeting, one of these couriers, so the article alleged, was able to inform their CIA handler (how and by what means in the middle of the desert in the close company of men who were highly suspicious and alert to any unusual or dubious activity of those around them, was never explained in the article) and from there on the drone attack was mobilised.

As for Al Sharjanah, the official line was after al Hassan he was now the most wanted al-Qaeda fugitive and had gone to ground with a price on his head. Alternatively, some sources claimed that he had actually made a recovery from his stomach illness and was entering the airbase to belatedly attend the meeting when the drone attacked and he was either killed during it, or managed to flee into the desert. Either way, the article concluded, he had been rendered ineffective and was no longer the 'clear and present danger' he and al Hassan had been. I got the clear impression from my interviewers that this article, speculative though it was, was regarded as the 'official' line in Washington and London: Al Sharjanah was either dead or a fleeing, impotent fugitive who posed no further threat. It *was* plausible. But, as with Tres' assistant with the IED, I got the clear impression that there was no great urge or enthusiasm to investigate further or explore alternative options. It was neatly wrapped up. For myself, I had been at the centre of so much deception that neat solutions no longer cut it with me, if they ever had.

My last four weeks in Troon I was left virtually alone. All the questioning ended and I saw no more of my interviewers. There were only the Troon housekeepers, who I kept a polite but respectful distance from – and they me – and a final visit from HR to conclude my pension and other outstanding arrangements. Apart from that I had the place to myself during August which was a typical Scottish summer month combining beautiful sunny days with squally rainstorms or dreich, dull cloudy weather. I slept fitfully as I would awake suddenly with my head racing with a dozen thoughts and vivid images swarming through my mind. A service medic suggested sedatives, but I resolutely refused these. I kept busy by reading, watching TV and going for long walks along the shore, irrespective of the weather, culminating with sitting on the bench for long hours, gathering my thoughts as I gazed over the Firth, with only the occasional dog-walker passing-by as itinerant company.

One Thursday afternoon I sat exhausted on the bench. There was only just over one more week to go at Troon before I would go back home to Glasgow. I had hardly slept the night before. Images of Sadeq, Tony Boyd, Wattie, the boys Khaled and Mohammed, the dead SAS soldier floating in the flooded Tannochside street, bodies in George Square, Tres, then back to Sadeq kept flitting by in a loop, over and over again. These images were interspersed with the continuous background sense of guilt at escorting that van into the Square combined with self-deceiving and beguiling myself into letting Tres be escorted straight to the water tower in an effort to bring Wattie in. Not forgetting my 'relationship' with Tres.

All of it: Grand Minaret, Tres, Qatib and his role as an SIS mole and all the unanswered questions, was based on layers of deception which, now I was no longer at the frenzied centre of it, I could contemplate at leisure. What I found was not peace or ease of mind but profound discomfort and revulsion at my own utter naivety and self-deception that was beginning to spiral into depression. I had been in dark places but had been too busy, too intent on survival to take notice. Now the memories of those dark places were becoming all-consuming. I felt lonely, uneasy and above all guilty. Sitting there on the bench, alone, with not even a dog-walker around, I was about to put my head in my hands, relapsing into despair.

A cough from behind brought me out of my deep self-misery. I turned round. A man of medium height, wearing deep, dark shades, a light jacket, white shirt and jeans was standing there; a bottle of whiskey and two glasses in his hand. It was Herb Lange, with the same craggy, unsmiling deep-lined face.

"Mind if I sit with you?" he asked. I was astounded: Lange was the last person I expected to see. I gestured to him to sit beside me.

When he'd sat down he placed the glasses between us and opened the bottle. "Scotch?"

"Normally in the afternoon, no, but this is exceptional," I replied. I actually detested whiskey, but again these were exceptional circumstances.

He took this as a yes and poured two generous measures. I took the glass he offered. "Slainte." He used the traditional Scots Gaelic for cheers and clinked his glass against mine. "Slainte," I responded.

He gave me a long appraising look which this time didn't unnerve me, probably because the last time I had seen him, he had saved my life. Finally, he turned away and looked out to sea. "You look tired," he said.

"I'm feeling very tired. I've had a lot of thinking to do and a lot of time to do it in. By the way," I said almost flippantly, "thanks, the rooftop, Tannochside, you rescued me, thanks!"

Still looking out to sea he raised his left hand in a gesture of dismissal, saying "Aw that's the pilot and the people in the helicopter you gotta thank for that."

"Yeah, but I wouldn't have got to the helicopter without you." He stayed silent. I continued: "I didn't believe in ghosts until now. Always a sceptic and a rationalist me. When I asked my interviewers at the hospitals I was in and here about the CIA man Herb Lange I was told there was no such person and certainly no CIA man at Tannochside! So I've become converted to the supernatural. Are you an apparition sitting on this bench beside me drinking this whiskey with me?"

He turned to face me. "No ghost, just good old-fashioned deniability. Deniability, not sex or money is what makes the world go round."

"And deception."

"Deception is the offspring of deniability."

I smiled at that and drank my whiskey. It tasted bitter and felt like a flame singeing my throat as I swallowed, but then miraculously became milder and left a pleasant after-taste. I could feel a congenial glow pervade my body, loosening and relaxing me. Maybe this would cure my aversion to whiskey.

Lange refilled my glass and his and asked: "Why are you tired, Mr Macintyre?"

I took several minutes to answer. Finally, I said: "Because I feel deceived. And I feel very, very guilty because I was deceived. My deception led to a lot of innocent people losing their lives."

"You were at the centre of a web that you didn't even know you were in. You've got nothing to blame yourself for. Ok you got screwed by Martindale, but we all get screwed. But, if you pardon the expression, you could never have seen her coming. She was good, very good, for all the wrong reasons. Her deception was honed by anger and love.

"I've lived with deceit and deniability too, nearly all my adult life for a cause I do believe in which is freedom and liberty and democracy. What was Martindale fighting, screwing, spying and dying for? A twisted religious utopia because she thought she'd found salvation through the love of a doctor."

"The guy's nephews and nieces had been killed in Lebanon: by all accounts they didn't die nicely or easily," I reminded him.

"Look at that kid down there," Lange pointed to a mother and child, no older than three or four following in his mother's footsteps along the beach. "Would that kid's death atone for those kids' deaths?"

"No, but wouldn't it be better if there were no kids dying needlessly at all?"

"Ok say there's a full-blooded al-Qaeda terrorist walking along that beach carrying a suitcase full of explosives or whatever. And suppose he was on his way to blow up a nearby bar or restaurant full of hundreds of innocent people and you had to stop him. So you fired a gun and the bullets hit him, but one of them ricocheted and hit the kid seriously injuring him or even killing him. You didn't intend it: it was collateral. Are you on the same level as the al-Qaeda terrorist? No. Why? Because you didn't *intend* to injure or kill the kid! Those fuckers do and that makes all the difference.

"Martindale's lover loses his nephews and nieces to Israeli bombers trying to get terrorists because they're operating right from the heart of a civilian camp. What does Martindale do in revenge? Participate in a mass destruction of a town centre. That's not revenge or atonement: that's psychotic mass murder masquerading as redemption: there's no equality there."

He turned away and gazed into the horizon, savouring the alcohol. "It's a beautiful country you got here. I've got some furlough and I thought I'd spend a few days with a friend and look you up, see how you were doing."

"Make sure you get to the Highlands, especially the western Highlands, they're spectacular," I said as if we'd only been talking about taking in the scenery.

He turned to face me again: "So what's eating at you? You didn't spot Martindale? You thought you were in control and it all got taken away from you? What else?"

"There's unanswered questions that I can't get out of my head."

"Such as?"

"Well for a start, who placed the IED in the van while Tres doped Wattie Craig and diverted the camera? The service people say it was a one-off sent up to assist her by Al Sharjanah, but I don't know."

"You still refer to her by her Christian name." He looked straight at me and I could feel my face going slightly red before replying:

"I worked with her for five years. I slept with her. It's difficult to take the human being out of it!"

Was I protesting too much? But Lange didn't come back on it. Instead he looked back at the beach and took me by surprise by saying:

"Apart from Qatib, Al Sharjanah had no contacts or capacity to send up to Scotland. Between you and your colleagues in London, SIS and us, we were all over al-Qaeda in the UK."

I stayed silent, digesting what Lange had just said to me. After a few minutes he asked: "So what's the other unanswered questions?"

"Just one more really. The role of Al Sharjanah on the night of the attack on the Libyan airbase. Only he selected the venue with just ninety minutes for the regional commanders to get to it; not even al Hassan knew where it was going to be held until Sharjanah had picked it. Yet the Americans got to it. Again, the service and your guys are pinning the blame on some of the couriers, but I'm not too sure."

"There were nine couriers escorting nine guys to the meeting. One of them could have been a MOSSAD or CIA asset. Besides, one scenario has Al Sharjanah killed as he arrives at the base just as the attack is underway."

"But there's no proof of that," I countered.

"There's no proof of anything. It's all supposition and speculation. But Mr Macintyre, if we suppose that Al Sharjanah *did* supply us with the precise location of the meeting, it would logically follow that he is an informer for us, and that would have some pretty serious implications."

We were now looking straight at each other. I drained the remains of my second glass of whiskey, some seagulls were squawking in the air above us, before saying:

"It would also mean that, including Qatib, Western intelligence agencies had two senior al-Qaeda informers on their books and yet a mass bomb attack in Glasgow went ahead."

He poured a third glass of whiskey for both of us. I was feeling lightheaded and disinhibited. "What you suggesting, Mr Macintyre? That we let the Glasgow bombing go ahead."

"I don't know what I'm suggesting, Mr Lange. There's questions that keep swirling about my head, that won't go away, that disturb me. I suppose, to use that terrible term, I'm looking for closure, I don't know." I looked away and shook my head.

"Closure eh," he gave out a short laugh. "We all want closure, but few of us ever get it." He glanced at his watch. "I've got just another hour here. I had intended to come and see how you were. That was pretty hairy stuff back there at the tower and on that roof. It was good to have come out of that and help get you out of it. It's not every time it ends like that. So I thought, he's a good guy, a good spy, a good record, who just happens to have been in charge of an operation that's right in the middle of so many other operations going on. Go and see him, check he's ok and then continue on your Scottish sojourn.

"And what do I see? A guy that's wracked in pain, full of guilt and desperate for answers to questions. A guy who's lost three agents, a long-term Joe and saw his town get blown up in an operation that he thought he was he was in charge of and was meant to prevent that happening. That's a shit deal. I think you deserve to know some answers, but there's a price for those answers."

I shrugged: "What's that?"

"You might not get your closure, which is really peace of mind, because you might not like the answers."

"I'd like to take that risk."

"That's only the first part. The other more important part is that what I tell you here on this bench has to stay with you and no one else. Mr Macintyre everything I'm about to tell you on this is deniable. And if you were to go about telling people some or all of it or speak to some reporter we – your side, my side – would traduce you as a burnt out, bitter ex MI5 agent thrown out for utter incompetence and peddling crazy conspiracy theories. And that's just the start. Because I would take it very badly and, after a suitable time had elapsed, I would come and find you and suicide you. I wouldn't want to do that, seriously, but I could and would."

He was looking at me very closely. I had absolutely no doubt that he would carry out his threat. He went on: "If you agree to those terms then I'll continue."

Why not? I thought. What would I do with whatever he was about to tell me? He was right: there was nothing easier to ridicule or discredit as a fantasist than a disgruntled, bitter ex-agent with a sordid past. And I certainly had no intentions of drawing attention to myself when I was in civvy-street, especially after George Square and Tannochside. And, nothing haunted a 'retired' agent more than the thought of someone from a hostile service he or she had crossed in some operation seeking revenge when you hadn't the full protection of your agency. This was much worse as Lange was CIA and as such from Britain's most important ally, free to wander the streets in pursuit of me with, no doubt, tenacity and ruthlessness and, once he'd found me, 'suicide' me with some ingenuity. No, there would be enough shit to deal with out there without looking out for shadows and those shades and that craggy face.

"Deal." I clinked my glass against his.

"Deal." He agreed.

"I've been hunting al-Qaeda since 9/11," he began. "For me it's personal and professional at the same time. I've personally taken out five of the bastards and seen the whites of their eyes before pressing the trigger. I'm not a psychopath or a sadist, Mr Macintyre, but I got immense satisfaction from that." He took a deep swig of his whiskey before resuming:

"You've been in this game long enough to know that, contrary to what the public think and the press suggests, we've actually had great success against al-Qaeda. Ok, things might not have worked out as expected in Afghanistan and Iraq, but we've confined them to the Middle East and North Africa, we've degraded them, taken out operative after operative, rolled up their franchise networks and their infrastructure. Before Glasgow, there has been no significant or successful al-Qaeda attack on Western soil since 2007 with the exception of the ISIS attack on Paris. Every attempt in the name of al Qaeda since then has been radicalised locals working on their own initiative, but with no backing or direct support. And, because we've upped our game in terms of agent recruitment from the Islamic community and more sophisticated use of informers, we've managed to stop any of those attacks too. Result: al-Qaeda has had nothing in the West for years.

"Then we got Bin Laden in 2011, in which I'm extremely proud to say I played a part. The Sheikh was dead, but and again you'll know this, his power and influence had long diminished: more symbol than chieftain, but that didn't lessen the satisfaction of taking him out.

"For a while things were quiet. The focus was on the Arab Spring and the mass street protests which promised so much in bringing down dictators like Gaddafi and Assad, but they quickly turned sour and we watched carefully as the radicals gained in strength and groups like ISIS emerged. But as long as they stuck to the Arab lands we could contain them and occasionally bomb them.

"Then we noticed al Hassan rising to prominence. He cut a dash with the media and was quite a performer, a good orator. I marked him down as someone to watch as he started gaining support. The Agency, and America, has two primary objectives in relation to al-Qaeda. One: prevent them from grouping together and forming a unified command. Two: prevent the re-emergence and formation of any networks in the West that could deliver another 9/11. Our instructions were clear: to use *any means necessary* to achieve those objectives which, repeat, were to prevent, disrupt and destroy any attempts to create a unified command and develop networks in the West." He stopped and faced me again.

"We're at war with al-Qaeda, Mr Macintyre. It might not feel that way here in the West most of the time and that's because we wage war covertly and overtly, in such a way that allows the Western public to go about their business peacefully. But war brings with it demands and sacrifices. Covert war demands secrecy and deception and that sometimes has to incur big sacrifices."

As I listened and watched him carefully I wondered at the strange mixture of world weariness, cynicism and idealism in him. At times he came across as a jaded spook, who'd seen and done everything and had lost sight of any ulterior, positive motive for intelligence work. At other times he sounded like an eager freshman spouting the virtues of liberty and democracy as the reason why Western spies do what they do. And, all the while, there was that undercurrent of utter ruthlessness and control epitomised by that infamous aphorism he'd just quoted: '*use any means necessary*' in pursuit of what he would regard as legitimate objectives, including deception and lies. I listened further as he continued.

"Ali al Hassan was pitching for the unified command and using this other rising star on the block, Al Sharjanah, to set up the networks in Western Europe. The quiet period after Bin Laden's death was over and these two became my primary targets. Because the networks directly threatened the West, including ultimately the USA, Sharjanah was my priority.

"I watched and studied him intently for two years as best I could. I picked up that the word on the Arab street was that al Hassan and Al Sharjanah detested each other. Sharjanah was older and had actually took part in real fighting and setting up terrorist networks. He despised al Hassan who'd never fired a gun in anger or run agents and who'd came from nowhere bullshitting about his links to the Sheikh. Meanwhile Hassan regarded Sharjanah as a clever but rough peasant. But Hassan needed Sharjanah's street cred among the fighters while, for his part, Sharjanah needed Hassan's organisational skills, media savvy and gift of the gab. Because they needed each other they worked together, but there was little love lost between them.

"But as time went on Hassan began to treat Sharjanah more and more with contempt which really enraged him. Eventually Sharjanah realised that at the first opportunity Hassan would dump him, because he saw him, rightly, as a threat. And that would be after Sharjanah had delivered the networks in the West and the spectacular which would give Hassan the credibility to gain control of the unified command. In other words Sharjanah would do all the dirty work to get Hassan the leadership and then Hassan would get rid of him.

"Sharjanah put out feelers against Hassan among the fighters. But while some of them were a bit cynical about Hassan and respected Sharjanah as a fighter, they wanted a new Bin Laden that they could unify under. Sharjanah just didn't cut it as the successor to the Sheikh while Hassan looked and sounded the part. Sharjanah looked condemned to be the man who helped Hassan to get the crown and was then abandoned or worse by his boss. He was stuck and frustrated.

"And that's where we moved in. It would take hours to tell how you we did this, but over a period of eighteen months, we managed to get to Al Sharjanah, work on his frustrations, his bitterness and growing resentment at al Hassan, the resentment turning to anger and then honing that anger."

"How did you manage that?" I asked.

"It wasn't easy, Mr Macintyre. But unlike most al-Qaeda people, including the regional commanders, even to a certain extent al Hassan himself, Al Sharjanah, despite his coarseness, hadn't cut himself off from the non al-Qaeda world. He still mixed with people in that outside world who he trusted and listened to and, occasionally, took advice from. One of these people became a go-between from us to him. It was a dance; a long involved dance where we had to reach a point where Al Sharjanah could convince himself that any action he took that, shall we say hindered al Hassan, was just that: an action against al Hassan not the resistance or al Qaeda or jihad.

"And if that act of hindering meant sabotaging al Hassan's hopes of a spectacular in the West through divulging information to us, then we had to get him to rationalise that working with us was only a short-term manoeuvre; a one-off. After all: hadn't almost all the original al-Qaeda founders and commanders, including Bin Laden, taken American funds and arms in the fight against the Godless communists in Afghanistan? At some future point a new Islamic caliphate might actually ally itself with the US, very unlikely though that might seem just now, but in politics nothing is impossible. Anyhow the point was we had to get Al Sharjanah into a position where his anger and bitterness at al Hassan overtook his revulsion at working with us. That took some time, but through the go-between, we got there."

"You got Al Sharjanah to blow his own networks and ops?" I asked incredulous.

"It was Barcelona, two years ago, the start; the first time Al Sharjanah sabotaged an attempted attack by an al-Qaeda cell. Great gains were being made by the Islamic Resistance in Libya, Mali, Yemen, Nigeria, Syria and Iraq where the real armed struggle to establish the true caliphate was. By sabotaging Barcelona he would not be impeding the armed struggle and would set back Hassan who needed a spectacular to further his aim of achieving control of a unified al-Qaeda command which he would head up. So Barcelona was busted.

"And having done that once and seen how it set back the cause of al Hassan, it was relatively easy to persuade him, after a gap of a few months, to do it again. That was Arhaus in Denmark. Having done it twice he was in deep, not least to us.

"Then came Qatib who Sharjanah delegated grooming and recruitment of cells to in a series of European cities and God was good to us because Qatib promptly walked into the Brits' Rome Embassy and delivered himself unto SIS who duly came to us…"

"And you let Al Sharjanah know?" I interrupted.

"Of course and it was perfect. Qatib could blow the operations through working with SIS and the finger would eventually be pointed at him not Al Sharjanah. Qatib was a gift."

"I am assuming you didn't let SIS know about your, eh, connection to Al Sharjanah?"

Lange's answer and stare at me was direct. "No. Al Sharjanah's role as an American asset was a highly classified US Eyes Only program, known only to a few even back home. Besides, with Qatib doing all the sabotaging oblivious to the fact his boss was too, we could let Al Sharjanah take a back seat.

"And so it went on for another year. Dortmund, fucked. Cracow, blown. Genoa, rolled up. Lyon, fucked again. Al Sharjanah appears to vent his frustration at Qatib and lets a few trusted lieutenants know that he's beginning to suspect Qatib, which of course is true, but not the whole truth. Meanwhile Hassan is being driven mad by the lack of, shall we say success in the Western cities and he's getting even more dismissive and contemptuous of Al Sharjanah. By this stage I reckoned that we could sabotage one more operation in a Western city and then SIS would stand down Qatib who they would let stay in London under protection. Qatib's defection and his role as an informer would then have been 'leaked' – no doubt to SIS's fury, but hey fuck, there's a bigger picture here – and Al Sharjanah would have his fall guy, the apparent explanation for all the blown operations.

"And then there was Glasgow; and one almighty fucking headache! You know how it begins too well, Mr Macintyre. Your informer lets you know that a radical preacher's brought in a contact, 'a man of action' (I read your transcripts and your reports) who's stirring up the youngbloods at the mosque until he eventually manages to start grooming and recruiting two of them. All of this was, of course, given to both SIS and us and Al Sharjanah by Qatib. Through your informer and you, of course, MI5 are on top of it. It's the same routine as in the all the other European cities. We don't have to intervene and no-one's aware of our presence. Glasgow seemed to be going the same way and SIS and we would have kept a watching brief but let things roll until you moved in. You would never have known we were there.

"But then things took a strange twist. Last August Sharjanah, through the usual intermediary, let us know that Amir Asaf, a senior commander in ISIS in Iraq and Syria, had asked him to come and see him in ISIS occupied Iraq. At that meeting Asaf told Sharjanah a 'great secret'; a secret that he'd had to keep to himself because it was so precious but which would be of inestimable value to the resistance, to al-Qaeda. Naturally Sharjanah wanted to know what this was. Asaf let him know that he was aware that a cell was being formed in Scotland, in the city of Glasgow. He knew this because there was an informer that was assisting the cell. This informer was divulging details to British Intelligence of who the recruiter was, the grooming and the radicalisation that was going on.

"How did Asaf know this? Because, there was a mole in British Intelligence and that mole was in Glasgow. This mole was the great secret and their identity was known only to Asaf and even though Sharjanah made several attempts to get him to reveal a name or even some background on the mole, Asaf was adamant: only he would know who this person was and that was how it was to be.

"The identity was irrelevant, Asaf insisted; the point was that with a mole on the inside they were a step ahead of MI5. Not only would the mole provide them with intelligence on what MI5 knew and what they were about to do, they could pre-empt that and catch MI5 off-guard by using the mole to ensure that this time, the cell succeeded and there was a spectacular in a Western city.

"But Asaf followed with an implicit threat. Only Asaf knew who the mole was. There was a cut-out employed at the Iraqi Embassy in London who passed communications between the mole and Asaf, but the cut-out didn't know either who the mole was or what the contents of the communications were. The Embassy official sent the communications back and forth by diplomatic pouch from London to Baghdad and vice versa. In Baghdad an ISIS agent in the Foreign Ministry circulated the encrypted messages out to Asaf and received messages from him to send back to London, again without knowing the contents or who the mole was. Now Asaf was passing on the fact that there was a mole to Sharjanah. This mole had never been used in an active capacity before. This was the first opportunity as it was the first time that the part of MI5 the mole worked in had encountered and was watching over a real live terrorist cell in the making.

"Now that Al Sharjanah knew this he was compelled to assist the mole and thereby indirectly aid the cell to finalise their mission and carry out the attack. But, if the mole was blown and arrested, Asaf would have to consider that carefully."

"Basically Asaf's warning Sharjanah: anything happens to this mole and I'm blaming you!" I butted in.

"Precisely," Lange concurred. "So the two of them agreed to watch this unfold and move when the time was judged right. Of course, through Qatib and SIS, we knew all about what was developing in Glasgow."

I shook my head. "This must have been the most spied on terrorist and counter-terrorism set-up in history," I reflected. "There's the terrorist cell in progress which we're onto thanks to our informer. Unknown to us, SIS are running Qatib who's master-minding the progress of the cell. SIS are working with you and keeping you informed of what's going on, but they and Qatib don't know that you've got Al Sharjanah working with you. And then in the background is the MI5 mole which only Asaf and Sharjanah know about, and then you, but you don't tell SIS or us." I looked straight at him.

"No, we had a problem there. Act on the mole and Sharjanah's blown, so we couldn't tell you or SIS."

"But don't take action on the mole and chances are Glasgow gets hit," I threw back.

Lange concurred. "Yeah, we had a serious dilemma there. So things develop, your guys go to Pakistan and get trained and come back and are now ready to act. All of this we know. Then it's March and Qatib sets the recruits the targets in Glasgow. It's going to be a mass attack: two busy railroad terminals in the morning commuter hour planned for a date in April. In the meantime Sharjanah has persuaded Asaf that he should take over communication with the mole and actually run the mole. His argument is that a much faster and more efficient communication route is needed. The dependency on the Iraqi Embassy official and the diplomatic pouch is too slow for a fast moving operation like this. Al Sharjanah tells Asaf that he has an Iraqi student based in Glasgow, one of his sleeper networks. This guy takes over the dead letter boxes and other hiding places around the city where the mole has been leaving information and picking up messages and instructions from Asaf, only whereas the Embassy guy was picking up the mole's product at most on a fortnightly basis, the student living locally can do this virtually on a daily basis. The student then passes on the product to Sharjanah.

"Asaf is ok with this because he knows that neither Sharjanah, nor his cut-out know the identity of the mole. And, if it goes wrong and the mole's blown, suspicion immediately settles on Sharjanah. Of course the Iraqi student is ours: a CIA asset we were able to provide with a plausible legend fast. Therefore, we were now running the mole, but, crucially we *still didn't know* the identity.

"We'd originally come up with a plan that would allow Qatib to survive, suspicion to be deflected from Al Sharjanah and the Glasgow operation to be plausibly aborted. We knew from SIS that Qatib wanted out desperately and his SIS handlers, the Special Operations Branch, had promised him Glasgow would be the last operation he had to go on. Qatib, therefore, was coming to an end.

"We arranged, through the intermediary, for Al Sharjanah to summon Qatib to a meeting in Tunis. Remember this was *before* Asaf encouraged Hassan to hold the meeting with the commanders. SIS and Qatib immediately thought this meeting was called by Al Sharjanah to emphasise to Qatib that Glasgow better succeed or he'd be called to account. That meeting was arranged in March for the day in April, as it turned out, that the reconnaissance was planned for, a week before the bombings. We led SIS to believe an anti-terrorist Navy SEALS commando unit stationed with the US Sixth Fleet off the coast of Tunisia would ambush the meeting and capture Al Sharjanah.

"The reality was Al Sharjanah would be in the vicinity of the meeting when the SEALs attacked but would 'escape' in time while Qatib would be 'killed' trying to flee: again the reality was we would exfiltrate Qatib to SIS who would provide him with a new ID and, after a decent interval, let him settle in London. We'd take all the political shit and diplomatic fallout from the attack on Tunisian soil. We'd also explain the absence of a body re Qatib to his incineration in the total destruction and firepower the SEALs would have unleashed on the venue where they were supposed to have met while apologising to SIS for having missed Al Sharjanah and allowing him to escape – though letting the world, particularly al Hassan and Asaf, know that he had been the intended target. Qatib would have been fingered as the mole allowing the Glasgow operation to be rolled up. Result: Qatib is identified as a mole but is safe, has a new identity and is looked after by us. Al Sharjanah's reputation and stock is enhanced in al-Qaeda and we could get to work finding out who the mole was in a way that wouldn't implicate Al Sharjanah. Neat eh?"

"But it didn't work out that way!" I said.

"No because during the intervening period, as the Glasgow cell is progressing, Asaf and Hassan have got closer. He encourages Hassan, now that a spectacular is on the way - effectively it's in the post - that this is the time to call a meeting of the regional commanders, to get that unified command structure. Asaf will support that and with the most powerful group, ISIS supporting it, the other main groups in the resistance will attend.

"Hassan is ecstatic, but Asaf makes it clear that Sharjanah has to deliver. The meeting must take place two-to-three days after the spectacular, which Sharjanah has let him know is due for mid-April. If there's no spectacular, then there's no meeting: simple. Hassan calls the meeting, Asaf supports it and Libya is chosen as the location to host it with Sharjanah left in charge of liaising with the Libyan al- Qaeda affiliate, Islamic Shield and providing the security arrangements.

"Nine regional commanders affiliated to al-Qaeda will be in one place. Nine uber-terrorist commanders in one site, conditional on the spectacular happening. That's an opportunity that doesn't come around every day. Remember, we want to stop the Western terrorist networks happening but we also want to prevent the unified command. In this case one was dependent on the other."

"So one was sacrificed to another in a British city!" I said angry at where I thought this was going: Glasgow had been the diversion to get those commanders to one location and allowing the Americans via Sharjanah, to set them up for a devastating attack.

"You're running ahead, Mr Macintyre. Let me outline what we were trying to do. We have the opportunity to take out nine senior al-Qaeda commanders all meeting in the one place; we would never get that chance again. We also have an active terrorist cell about to launch an attack. But what do we do? Tell SIS that there's a mole in MI5 in Glasgow. Then you guys are taken off the operation, the mole's either alerted or arrested, the operation's blown, suspicion falls on Al Sharjanah and no meeting. We couldn't go in there and cut down two guys on our own! Apart from the fall-out, it would also raise suspicion and the meeting wouldn't go ahead.

"No, we had to be clever about this, Mr Macintyre. How could we minimize the damage from the cell, but still allow it to operate in some way, so that a result could be claimed by al Hassan that would allow the meeting to go ahead with Asaf's support?"

A breeze blew in form the sea whipping small speckles of sand over me which I gently brushed aside. What did Lange mean by 'minimize the damage from the cell'? Three simultaneous intelligence operations that were meant in whole or in part to prevent a mass terror attack on this one particular Western city, Glasgow, namely ours at MI5, SIS and CIA had, for at least one of those services turned into a damage limitation operation for a wider purpose. I listened intently as he poured two more measures from the nearly depleted whiskey bottle. We were on four glasses each, but I felt very alert and sober now.

"So we had to come up with an alternative plan after we'd aborted the supposed attempt to capture Sharjanah and exfiltrate Qatib that would ensure the meeting would go ahead. And for that to happen, an attack of some description would have to happen in Glasgow. So a second plan was devised." Lange looked at me, those shades locked on me. "Working with Al Sharjanah, we agreed to bring the attack forward by a week, accepting there would be collateral damage, but minimize it."

"Jesus Christ!" I shouted out. "'Collateral damage'; that was George Square, fuck, you let them blow up George Square for Christ's sake!" I put my head in my hands. I felt Lange's hand on my arm.

"You're not listening: I said we would have to accept there would be collateral damage but attempt to minimize it."

I shot back at him: "George Square was *minimal* was it? Eighty-two civilians killed! Fuck, I'd love to know what your idea of maximum is!"

He almost whispered his reply to me: "We didn't *intend* to blow up George Square."

I was confused. "You didn't intend! But it happened!"

He looked back out at the sea. Another plane was taking off from Prestwick Airport, its engines straining to lift the aircraft into the air. As the noise from the plane started to recede, Lange went on.

"Plan B was to capitalise on the reconnaissance day, the Wednesday. Al Sharjanah instructed Qatib to get up to Glasgow on that day and accompany the guys on that reconnaissance. We knew your informer's van was to be used to transport them into the city. That van was to be crucial. Qatib going up to Glasgow spooked your informer. At his request, you brought the surveillance forward on his van. The mole informed Al Sharjanah, in reality of course us, via a dead letter box picked up by the Iraqi student of the shift arrangements for the MI5 team, your team. Through this we knew the mole was on the two-person watch detail covering midnight-to-six am on the Wednesday morning.

"The next communication from the student asked the mole to divert the surveillance camera for twenty minutes from 5.20 to 5.40 am which would allow sufficient time for an IED device to be placed underneath the van."

"You placed an IED under the van! Ah Jesus!" I shook my head.

"Please *listen*!" he urged.

"Remarkably, we never did find out the identity of the mole until the water tower, the same time as you did. We could not risk arousing the mole's suspicions and there was no legitimate reason why the CIA would want specific details of MI5 agents engaged on a domestic anti-terrorist operation. Al Sharjanah never knew either. Until the end, only Asaf and the mole knew who the mole was.

"The mole responded via the student that they would arrange for the camera to be diverted. We got one of our guys to place the IED at the arranged time. It was hairy because we didn't know how the mole, on a two-person watch, even houring (our people do it as well) was going to ensure the camera was moved. That was left to the mole's improvisation. Using the sedatives on Craig was clever. Anyway, we got the device placed successfully. We reckoned that the van would be checked before the reconnaissance started, but there would be no point in checking it again as it was being watched by you guys. The mole was vital, therefore, in getting the explosive to the van, creating a false sense of security.

"IED successfully installed, the plan went ahead. Qatib came up, tailed by SIS (unknown to you) and your own people of course. Qatib meets your informer, they then pick up the guys and travel into the city. What was supposed to happen was the guys did their dummy runs at the railroad stations while Qatib and the informer travelled back to the safe house. Qatib had been told by the cut-out he normally received instructions from in London to retrieve a message with new instructions placed in a dead letter box in a park not far from the safe house. Qatib would have left the safe house and, following directions previously given to him by the cut-out would have located the dead letter box in the park and got the message.

"We knew that you and SIS would have been intrigued by these developments but wouldn't have intervened, but just kept watch; after all you didn't know about the IED. The message Qatib would have picked up in the park, allegedly coming direct from Al Sharjanah, would have informed him of a change of target. The attack was being brought forward to the following weekend, to the early hours of Friday morning and was to target the moral degeneracy of the West. How? Each bomber was to walk through the throngs of people milling about and leaving clubs in the Sauchiehall Street pedestrian area about 2.30am and detonate their bombs; one coming from the western end of the street, the other from the eastern end. A couple of thousand people gather in that street in the early morning hours of the weekend after going to nightclubs a lot of them hanging about, going into fast food outlets, and the casualties would have been numerous.

"Qatib was told to convene a meeting of the bombers that afternoon. He was to inform them that a new reconnaissance was required and that they were to do a dummy run on Sauchiehall Street in the early hours of the next morning, Thursday morning. The instructions were quite precise: using the same van that had taken them on the afternoon reconnaissance, they were to make their way to the corner of Blythswood Street and Sauchiehall Street to arrive there at exactly 2.25am. This corner marks the start of the pedestrian precinct section of Sauchiehall Street. They were to sit there for three minutes and then get out at 2.28 and do the dummy runs. Only they wouldn't have.

"Because, at 2.26 am, the IED under the van would have exploded, killing the two guys, your informer and anyone else around. Qatib wasn't intended to have been killed as the original plan was, after he'd delivered the instructions at the afternoon meeting he would go back to London, but as we know he didn't make that meeting. Our assumption was that up to about twenty-to-twenty-five people in the area at the time, would also have been killed or injured on that mid-week morning; a fraction of the number that would been there at the weekend or if they'd attacked the original targets at the railroad stations during the commuter hour. It would have been regarded as an acceptable level of collateral damage. If we were very fortunate, there might be no casualties at all, excepting the bombers and the informer. But it would have been enough for the Libyan meeting to go ahead as al-Qaeda under Hassan had shown it had the ability to attack in the West again. And with that meeting underway, courtesy of Al Sharjanah who would tell us which of the six possible sites for the meeting he had actually chosen, we could program an explosive laden drone to attack the site of the meeting and take out the commanders; which we did."

"So, the bomb under the informer's van went off accidently?"

There was a silence and he looked away from me. Eventually he said to me: "You might find this the hardest part to take."

After a long pause, I urged him: "Go on please, let's get it finished."

"Our profession, Mr Macintyre, leads us to do lots of good work, most of it unseen and unheard. Occasionally however, and regrettably, we have fuck-ups – sometimes we have cluster-fucks. And from those fuck-ups we concoct conspiracy theories to deflect attention away from the fuck-up and those in turn lead to further fuck-ups and so on.

"What I am trying to tell you, Mr Macintyre, is that the bombing of your home city wasn't a result of the IED going off prematurely or by accident. It was as a result of a mistake. There was a miscommunication. Whoever set the timer in the Technical Services Division in the Agency and sent it to us had either been misinformed or themselves mistakenly set the timer on the IED to detonate twelve hours earlier than intended."

"*Twelve hours earlier!*" I repeated.

He sighed. "Yes, twelve hours earlier. The whole secret of this operation comes down to this: we had intended the IED to explode at 2.26am and kill the occupants of the van and a maximum of twenty-to-twenty-five people in the street and considerable damage to a bank the van would have been parked outside of and other nearby property. Instead, due to a genuine miscommunication, the timer on the IED was mistakenly set for 2.26pm, twelve hours earlier."

"Twelve hours earlier!" I repeated.

I remember vividly the early Wednesday afternoon buzz and anticipation as recce Wednesday was underway. Sadeq's van was coming into the Square, I was in the hired office near the station, the banks of CCTV monitors on the station in front of me, then the thunderous sound of the explosion and the compressed blast from the shockwave. I looked up at the time on one of the monitor screens: it read 2.26pm.

2.26 pm when it should have gone off at 2.26am, killed the bombers and Sadeq and taken out perhaps up to twenty-five innocents. As it was, eighty-two were killed in the Square and scores injured. Mass carnage in the Square or carnage lite at Sauchiehall Street: all down to a mistake in instructing someone what time to prime the detonator for.

"So George Square was a timing mistake due to a communication error?"

"Yep, regrettably it happens a lot more than we intend."

"But you got your 'contrived spectacular' and the meeting went ahead and you got your targets."

"Yes we got the 'spectacular', though on a larger scale than we intended. We took out nine commanders and al Hassan and killed off the unified command. And, as Al Sharjanah is out the loop, all attempts at setting up Western franchise al-Qaeda terror networks have ceased. The two major objectives of US and allied states' policy in relation to al-Qaeda (which is also incidentally your own country's objectives as well) achieved. Job done: for now."

"And eighty-two innocents massacred on the square along with scores injured!"

"That wasn't intentional."

"Up to twenty-five could have been later, 'an acceptable level of collateral.'"

"It's a war: innocents do get hurt. Think of Hiroshima, Hamburg or Dresden in the Second World War. Tens of thousands of innocents slaughtered by the Allies, but we didn't start it and our cause was just against evil and oppression as has been justified as you live in free, democratic societies."

"And use any means necessary to achieve that?"

"Any means necessary. The timer mistake was a fuck-up. But I have no regrets in saying to you that if the night-time option to minimise the collateral wasn't possible, I would have gone ahead with the Square, in spite of the numbers. We have probably saved tens of thousands because of this."

"And Al Sharjanah?"

Lange smiled as he stood up. "In hiding, biding his time. He's got three options. Stay dead, come over to us and he can have a nice easy life; no doubt there are pages in the *Koran* that'll justify him in what's he doing. His second option is to resurface and try and take over from al Hassan and start all over again. In which case, we're back at war with too much dirt on each other for either of us to reveal the extent of our previous dealings. Or, option three, he can push al-Qaeda towards the West; though that seems unlikely at present, it's not impossible."

He offered me his hand which I accepted, a firm handshake. "And we got the mole, even if she did decide to exit in grand style."

Looking down at me he continued to smile. "Enjoy your retirement, Mr Macintyre. Don't go stirring up old memories. What I've told you is everything, which of course is completely and utterly deniable. I do hope you've got your personal closure now. But if you do decide to tell anyone some or all of this, I will kill you."

And with that he turned his back and walked, slightly unsteadily along the sandy path towards the farm. I had absolutely no doubt that he would carry out his threat.

I sat on the bench for a further hour. He'd left the whiskey bottle and there were some dregs in it, but I didn't take any more. Instead I looked over the shore as the evening light began to fade and a wind started to whip up, deep in contemplation. So, after all the machinations, after all the deceptions, and all the deceptions within deceptions, it had come down to a mistake in the timer due to poor communications – a fuck-up, though Lange had left me in no uncertainty that he would have gone ahead with the IED deliberately targeted at the Square if he had to because they had to use *any means necessary*.

I went back to the farm and stayed there a further week. My time with Lange and his revelations, despite their implications, seemed to have been cathartic. I slept better, ate better, felt better and went for long walks. After the week I went home and spent the remaining two months at my west end Glasgow flat sleeping late, reading widely, taking in a lot of movies, walking a lot and dining out. I kept myself occupied with an eye on my little savings and the last two months' salary coming in. I was conscious. though, that even with a reasonable pension, I was going to have to cut back and I had no idea what I was going to do next: I had been in the secret world since I was seventeen and I had absolutely no idea or confidence as to what I could turn my hand to out there. As September gave way to October, my final month on gardening leave before my 'early retirement' at the start of November, I began to feel more anxious about the future.

Then October brought a very pleasant and unexpected surprise. Decades earlier, way back in the 1950s, an uncle and aunt had immigrated to Canada. They'd come over occasionally to see my parents and being childless, doted on me. Anyway, both had passed away a couple of years ago and my uncle had died a reasonably wealthy man having built up a farm supply business and hundreds of acres of farmland in Nova Scotia. The upshot was I'd been left money in his will which amounted to £90,000, a tidy sum which, on top of my pension from the Service, would keep the creditors from the door and keep me afloat for a while without having to worry too much about how I was going to make a living.

In late October, a week before I was officially due to leave the Service, I received my last ever letter from MI5 asking me to attend an 'exit interview' at an address in the city centre. It was in a rented office in the Merchant City with an anodyne young bureaucrat from Thames House who thanked me fulsomely for my work on behalf of

Queen and country, safeguarding democracy, civil liberties and the British way of life. After that encomium, in a less praiseworthy tone I was reminded that any future writings (books, articles) even if only private musings just intended to be shown to families or friends, and a summary of anything I proposed to say or respond to if I was ever intending to go on TV or radio broadcasts or any internet activity, which might have a bearing on my work with MI5, must be submitted in advance to the Service. I was also reminded that I had signed the Official Secrets Act in perpetuity and must never disclose anything relating to my work. The meeting lasted thirty minutes and I left with a letter summarising what the bureaucrat had just told me.

And that was it. Forty years' service over and no formal farewell, no leaving party. Well I suppose after three members of your team have been killed (one of whom was an al-Qaeda informer) and inadvertently letting off a bomb which devastated Glasgow city centre, it was the best you could expect. Certainly better than being dead, in jail, hiding in exile or in open public disgrace. Late in November I looked up Danny Mackay, apart from myself, the only surviving member of my team. He was still with CID at that time, though barely hanging on in there. We went for a liquid lunch which turned into an all-day session until closing time which I thoroughly enjoyed and found quite therapeutic, but which I took days to recover from the hangover. I resolved to keep in contact with Danny.

Before Christmas I spent a couple of days with Louise in London, staying in a nearby hotel in case it was a disaster. But it was ok, much better than Troon and augured well for our future relationship. Now she knew I had left the service it felt we could talk more freely, though obviously nothing tangible about the past, which would be an obstacle for us. I even got on with the law student boyfriend who she'd moved in with, even though as with all fathers, I thought she could do better. I felt better after seeing Louise this time: there was something there to build on.

Then it was Christmas and New Year and I felt in two parts. It had been a momentous, traumatic year, but I did feel closure, whatever that was, particularly after Lange's revelations with all their sordid, seedy deceptions within deceptions and brutal realpolitik. I had been told everything and not all intelligence officers, active or retired (if you every really get to 'retire' from the secret world) get to see the wider picture of what they've been involved in and why. I had seen that wider picture in all its murky, duplicitous and horrendous detail. And I had made my peace with it because in spite of all the deception and the loss of life my team and I, with the obvious exception of Tres Martindale, had also been innocents in this. We hadn't even been the 'B' team; we were the also-ran 'C' team manipulated and running to everyone else's agenda: *at the centre of a web we didn't know we were in* as Lange had put it so eloquently. With that knowledge I had closure, even though the knowledge that we innocently and inadvertently escorted that fucking bomb into George Square will haunt me for the rest of my days.

As I passed through the festive season, content as best I could be in one part of myself, my other part was suffused in loneliness. I was on my own, cut loose from the secret world which had been where all my friendships and acquaintances had been. I felt lonely and I felt that gap acutely and Christmas and New Year just accentuated it. There was one individual I could not get out of my head. Was I just going to fantasise about her, wallow in self-misery and mope over what might have been and do nothing because of fear of rejection?

So in the first week of January, the comedown week after the festive holidays, I phoned Amber. I still remembered her number. She was in the first time I called. It was great to hear her voice again, that husky, sexy voice, and I hastened to reassure her that I wasn't calling on my kind of 'business' and just wanted to meet up for a coffee and a quick chat. Whether she believed me or not, I don't know, but she did agree to meet me.

Was this madness? She was an active sex worker on the game and, seemingly, content with that as well as an occasional paid informant for MI5, not forgetting she had been one of my former ratline contacts. The morality was not the issue. Jesus after all that had gone on leading up to George Square in the name of democracy and I suppose Western Christian values, accusing Amber of immorality was rich. Others would say she was being exploited, but unless it was all show and allowing for all the constant risks she faced in her profession, she appeared to be in control of her life. My concerns were more selfish. Assuming for a moment, she reciprocated my feelings for her, which was completely unknown and that she was fine with the twenty years' age difference between us, could I have a relationship with a woman who was having paid sex with other men virtually every night? Could I try to persuade her to come off the game through showing her love, affection and care? Or was that just naïve romanticism? Certainly I didn't think Amber was the kind of woman who would buy into the knight on a white charger routine, there to rescue her from being a fallen woman.

Bugger it! I thought. You'll never know unless you try. Which is why I ended up at five in the evening in the massive, crowded frenetic, buzzing concourse of Glasgow Central Station, outside a newsagents', waiting anxiously for Amber. Dozens of other people were waiting beside me as this was one of the standard places on the concourse to meet people. As I stood there looking at the busy crowds hurrying to and fro (I had chosen five simply to accommodate what I thought Amber's working arrangements would require; a lunch date was out I assumed because she would be sleeping), I couldn't help but reflect on a Mohammed type figure walking through the station, oblivious to everyone, and pulling his ripcord and transforming this everyday scene into absolute carnage, destroying lives and hopes and dreams. But I had to banish all thoughts of that aside now and focus on this.

She was late; a woman's prerogative. Five minutes went by and my mobile pinged. I had her number in my new civilian mobile phone address book. There was a text from her which read:

Sorry held up. On way, be there in five.

And I waited another fifteen and she came through the crowd. My heart leapt. She looked stunning; that curly jet black hair, the dark skin, the large hazel eyes, I was mesmerised by her as she approached. Her appearance was complimented by a black skirt just above her knees, a white blouse and a black jacket; she looked no different from any of the other well-dressed young female office workers. As she came near, her face broke into a beautiful smile.

"Gary Carson, how are you?" (I was still using the agent pseudonym she only knew me by; if there was going to be any mileage with this relationship, I would revert to Eddie Macintyre with her as soon as possible, but now was too soon). She rose up and pecked me on the cheeks.

"I'm fine, Amber," I replied. "You look lovely."

"Aye, you're looking well yourself. Where did you get that?" She was pointing at the slight scar on my head where the stiches had been when I'd bashed my head on the way down from the water tower. "Bumped my head in the house. Anyway fancy a coffee?"

"A coffee!" she exclaimed incredulously. "I've not seen you for months and that's the best you can do for a lady?"

"Ok, there's a beautiful Italian restaurant on Hope Street which I couldn't recommend highly enough."

"An Italian restaurant!" Her hazel eyes lit up like big white saucers. "Now that's more like it, Mr Carson."

She took my arm in hers and we walked across the concourse out into the bustling street with its busy taxi rank, cars and buses coming and going and newspaper venders. We walked round the corner into Hope Street to the restaurant. She noticed my limp. "God, you've been in the wars, Gary!"

"It's fine, Amber, I'm ok. Just a wee accident. I'm feeling good, don't you worry."

We reached the entrance to the restaurant which was down a flight of steps in the basement. As I opened the door for her to enter I looked up at the drone-free, early-evening darkening, Glasgow winter sky and felt more hopeful, alive and invigorated than for many years.

Maybe, I thought to myself, just maybe this was finally the end of the deception road.

THE END

Printed in Great Britain
by Amazon